# The Dragons Forty Year Hitch

By

David G Rosser

**UPSO**

The Dragons Forty Year Hitch © Copyright 2002 by David G Rosser

Cover Illustration © Copyright 2002 by Bonnie Phillips

All rights reserved. No part of this work may be reproduced or stored in an information retrieval system (other than for purposes of review) without prior written permission by the copyright holder.

A catalogue record of this book is available from the British Library

First Published: August 2002

ISBN: 1-84375-005-8

To order additional copies of this book please visit::
http://www.upso.co.uk/davidrosser.htm

Published by: UPSO
5 Stirling Road, Castleham Business Park,
St Leonards-on-Sea, East Sussex TN38 9NW UK
Tel: 01424 853349  Fax: 01424 854084
Email: info@upso.co.uk   Web: http://www.upso.co.uk

Dedicated to the memory of

David G. Rosser

# The Dragons Forty Year Hitch

# Introduction

## "A Forty Years' Hitch" - Europe to Asia

It began more than forty years ago. They were the less sophisticated days of caravanning and camping, but well advanced from the itinerant and traditional Romany travellers' image with which caravans were generally associated. Yet, those early post war days were to my mind the happiest of our long and cherished saga of roaming the highways and the byways of our own native land, and all except three of the countries of Europe. With hindsight and the advantages of modern caravanning, now an industry and an established way of life, were I to be asked if the present day sophistications and the luxuries of electrical hook-ups, running water, hot and cold, and ablution amenities generally, as well as thermostatically controlled heating, have erased the joys of those early days the answer would be an emphatic NO.

In fact we who took to the road in the late forties and early fifties, prompted I have no doubt in a great many instances by wartime service experiences abroad, must feel a tinge of sadness for the present day caravanners who will never be able to experience the "pioneering" spirit and the days of the rough and ready weekend forages and the early Centre Rallies which enabled us to forge powerful and lasting friendships. In the same way we "oldies" regret that we did not sample the even more challenging exploits of the between the wars caravanners whose numbers countrywide could be calculated then in the hundreds.

Indeed, the growth of caravanning, both as an industry and a leisure pursuit, has been tremendous during the post war period. As things settled down to a normality the Caravan Club, as the organising body for the rapidly growing numbers who were relishing the weekend breaks, and longer periods during holidays in caravanning, realised the vast potential and got to work to provide the amenities and the authority and representation which these people of the countryside would require. Much of this work in the early days was accomplished through voluntary efforts and very largely through the assistance of the very keen officials of the Centres which had been established to promote and encourage a caravanning fraternity which, before the war, had had to rely on very basic amenities.

From the pre-war hundreds the build up in membership of the Caravan Club was rapid. By 1950 it had grown to 6,462. Thereafter increased membership snowballed. By 1952 it had reached 8,181 and two years later it had peaked 10,750. By this time it was obvious to all that the pursuit was firmly established and reaching out for undreamed of expectations. With a keen and increasingly appreciative and rapidly growing army of customers to cater for the industry set about its task to produce caravans which improved in sophistication and comfort year by year. As with the motorcar industry so the caravan builders increased in numbers, and their increasingly attractive products naturally served to attract more people, and especially the younger families, to the greater freedom of caravanning. And with the changes came an astonishing growth in the structure and membership of the Caravan Club. By 1983 it was almost on a par with the motorists' associations on a capita basis of owners. The mid-fifties membership of 13,000 had reached 251,069 by 1983 and had topped the 280,000 mark by 1988. Since then it has continued to grow and prosper. At the time of publication the membership has passed the 284,000 mark.

To what can this rapid acceleration of growth be attributed? In the main, I assume, discovery of the facilities and vast differences abroad from those in the United Kingdom was the biggest single factor. The autobahns of Germany and the French and Italian AutoRoute's coupled with the networks of camping and caravan sites which had been a long established feature of continental holidays and leisure pursuits was a new venture for the average British caravanner. In addition, of course, there was the sun, and generally better weather for the open air than was the case in Britain. Another factor in the beginning was the strong wish of so many who had served in the armed forces during the war to return to those countries across the Channel in which they had seen active service, and while memories were still fresh. They were the vanguard of the very many thousands who now make the cross channel journeys with caravans and camping equipment an annual event.

It was with the growth of this cross channel activity that the Caravan Club set up its own Foreign Touring service in 1967, a landmark in caravanning history which has made it possible for caravanners to travel far and wide and to the innermost recesses of foreign countries to which, without this service, it would be practically impossible to go. The whole of Europe, and even beyond, can now rightly be claimed as the caravanners' oyster, as I hope to prove in the chapters ahead.

The remarkable developments of the past forty years or more during which change and progress have accounted for a great deal, are more significant perhaps for the older caravanners in that they have served to accentuate memories, and the reminiscences, which mean so much more as the years roll by.

When it was suggested to me that I should put pen to paper to record some of those fond reminiscences and to present an insight into the pleasures and events which have occurred over many scores of thousands of miles of towing and travelling there was no hesitation. Why should we, my wife and other companions of those often hectic and demanding journeys with our homes constantly - well mostly - attached, not share our pleasures and experiences, and perhaps tempt others to indulge? So it has come about.

This forty years' itch in roaming through Europe into Asia is a factual record of a great many, but not all, of those uninhibited travels, and if it stirs the minds and intentions of readers to participate in the future, albeit in cosseted forms with the ever increasing modifications of 'vans and services and abounding highway attractions, something will have been achieved.

We became known as the Red Dragon people, a title derived from our earliest practice of proclaiming our Welsh national identity on our caravans. As was customary in the early post war years British cars being taken abroad were required to display the international GB sign. The same was frequently applied to the vehicles on tow. Being Welsh, however, and from a strong nationalistic sense, we decided also to adorn our caravans with the symbol of Wales, the RED DRAGON.

These were about the same dimensions as the international signs and had been painstakingly prepared by my wife Myfanwy, -Van for short - from a template which was to be used for each new caravan, and also to provide our companions with an unmistakable identification. The Dragons Rampant were magnificent! They declared the presence of the Welsh as well as British, and over the years among the caravan fraternity we became known as "the Dragon people". They more than once proved their usefulness too when it happened that we became separated from our companions. The symbols frequently overcame language problems and pointing to the Dragons on the 'van usually was enough to bring a response which guided us in the right direction to bring us together again.

The basis on which this book is written are the daily diaries painstakingly kept by Myfanwy during our days of travel. The detail is so precise and full that reference to them immediately calls to mind any particular journey or happening. Without the help and stimulus of these precious contributions it would not have been possible to complete the book, or indeed have an incentive for doing so. I must also credit the support of friends who have shared with us so much of what is written here, particularly Len and Eileen Davies, and Margaret and William Pierce Rowlands who had been our constant companions en route from our chance meeting in Hungary, on the shore of Lake Balaton, in 1966. It is fitting that mention is made of Eileen, wife of a childhood friend Len Davies, who played a major part at the very beginning in this saga of wanderlust. She died tragically, a victim of the Paris air disaster in March, 1974, and her loss was greatly felt by us all. As Myfanwy still contends, however, her spirit continues to accompany us on our caravan travels to this very day. Tragically, too, Margaret died in 1991, since when Myfanwy and I have carried on alone, but all the time making new friends en route and consolidating old friendships. So, read on and savour!

# Chapter One

# How Sir Frank Sowed the Seed

Our first interest in the "open air" was aroused in 1951. By this time I had been a Lobby Correspondent at Westminster for more than four years. Part of my duties in that capacity was to keep an eye on the activities of Ministers and their Opposition "shadows", and especially Members of Parliament who had a special interest for my paper, the "Western Mail". What they were involved in and where they went, and for what reasons, was very much a part of that duty. And that included holidays. Where they went and for how long was deemed to be of local public interest. In most cases the elected Members were very cooperative. After all, rightly or wrongly, it kept their names and activities in the forefront of the public eye. But there were in some instances a reticence to reveal holiday arrangements because these were regarded as personal and family matters which did not involve a Member's accountability to his or her constituents. Fair enough!

So it happened in the run up to the Easter holiday that I chanced to meet Sir Frank Soskice, then the MP for Neepsend, but more importantly from the news angle the Attorney General. It was the Thursday when the House of Commons adjourned for Good Friday and the ten days' Easter recess that we met in a virtually deserted Library Corridor and, as much as anything, wanting to have a brief chat but with nothing special in mind since Sir Frank was not one of my particular clutch of local MPs, I asked where he would be spending the Easter holiday. Always the kindly and gentle character that he was, particularly in his association with The Lobby, he surprised me with his retort. "Got to be off in a few minutes, picking up the bikes with Susan and off to France". He must have read the amazement in my eyes because with a smile he volunteered the explanation which at first I found difficult to believe and was to change our whole family way of holidays in the future.

Shortly after leaving Westminster it appears Sir Frank and Lady Susan would assume an incognito, put on their oldest serviceable clothes and entrain with their bikes and knapsacks for one of the channel ports. Crossing over as ordinary pedestrian passengers they would mount up and cycle off on a week's tour without any pre-arranged itinerary. It was his further explanation which was the greatest surprise. "Where do you stay overnight?" I enquired. "Aha" he replied with a grin. "In the tent. Anywhere it is possible to pitch it, even on the roadside in the country".

What tent? "Oh, we have a bivouac into which the two of us can squeeze. It's great. We've been doing this for a couple of years now and wouldn't change it for anything" he added.

Here was the Attorney General of the United Kingdom on a cycling tour in France with his wife, incognito and bivouacking; free as the air and claiming they would not change it for anything! For the whole period of that almost vagrant stolen week the high Office of State was virtually deserted, and the two of them enjoyed a care-free escape. My first thought was, "This is a good human interest story". That was quickly disposed of however. "I don't want you to write this in detail. Just mention if you like that Susan (Lady Soskice) and I are off to France for a few days and leave it like that will you?" he asked. "It would spoil it completely for us here and anywhere we might wish to go if you did spill the beans" he added seriously.

So far as the gossip story was concerned I just "left it like that". But it got me to thinking. That evening Myfanwy and I kept referring to the tenting part of the story. We had three children aged one to eleven years. As a political correspondent our holidays were governed by the parliamentary sessions, and the childrens' schooling, of course. This meant a couple of weeks during the summer holidays either with respective parents or relations, or a week's guesthouse stay at one of the seaside resorts. This was a kind of regimentation which the Soskices' camping break made all the more unattractive as we thought ahead to the holidays. Neither of us had experienced life under canvass, but the idea grew.

It was nearly three years later, however, when the possibility of a camping holiday abroad was raised again, that we discussed it with our friends Len and Eileen, who also had a two year old child. We found them quite enthusiastic and the whole thing snowballed. They had already taken their small daughter abroad for a short motoring holiday to friends and had experienced no problems.

Within a matter of months we were on the lookout for a tent, urged on by the exciting thoughts of a cross channel sortie in the sun and free of the irks and demands of, by now, our typical type of family holiday. The search for a tent capable of encompassing the two families numbering eight, including four children was on! But that is another story.

It was another year before we were actually able to take to the roads on the other side of the Channel and face up to what had appeared to be to us at the outset the rigours of driving on the "wrong" side of the road. But since 1954 it has been almost an annual event.

For many years thereafter during which Frank and I retained a close personal friendship (a few years after his revelation which led to our thoughts turning to camping and ultimately caravanning he was to become one of my clutch of Welsh MPs as the Member for Newport) that 1951 Maundy Thursday chat in the Library Corridor of the House of Commons was a frequent topic of conversation between us.

# Chapter Two

# The Search is on!

It was our friends, Len and Eileen, who came up with the promise from a friend of the loan of a tent. It should be remembered that in those early post war days such leisure equipment was virtually unobtainable in the shops. But shortly after the new year of 1954, now knowing that we were able to set our hands on a tent, we set about planning the first big adventure. It became infectious as we started planning a route, and the children joined in with an enthusiasm that matched anything the grown-ups had to offer. Nearly every weekend we met to discuss plans which changed as regularly almost as the days of the week. Fresh motoring maps were sought and alternative routes to the sun and sea along the Mediterranean were discussed, approved, changed, renewed or reinstated. In those weeks of paper planning and preparation I think we got to know the prospective continental routes better than any English, Welsh and Scottish roads which led to the established holiday areas. Of course, there were much fewer starting points on the French side then because of the scarcity of car ferries. But, on reflection, those weeks and months of preparing for life's newest adventure were the happiest moments... and so inexpensive! Every weekend almost was a new holiday, savoured to the full as grown ups and children wondered what actually lay in store for us and all this was going on simply on the promise that we would have a tent. We never for a minute doubted that there would be a tent, and one which would accommodate us all. We did not at any time give a moment's thought to the conveyances. We each had cars which we were certain would be up to the demanding task of conveying two families, and a tent, across France and to the shores of the glorious Mediterranean. Breakdowns and the possible stresses of long daily "hops" in unaccustomed heat? Poof, nothing to worry about. Insurances and spare parts? These were matters yet to come and be faced in the experiences of years ahead. The vitally important thing at that time was to agree where we would be heading for... and of course, The Tent.

Then came the day we had all been waiting for. The owner of the tent, to whom I shall always be grateful but whose name has escaped me over many years past, announced it was ready to be collected. It was suggested that we should turn up in both cars. That should have alerted us, but we were oblivious to everything except that all the weeks' planning could now be completed. The Tent had been the missing piece in a fast and furious jigsaw; and now it was ready to be put in its place.

What faced us when we arrived for the pick-up was a mound of dirty grey canvass alongside a number of bags containing such things as guy ropes, pegs and other necessary equipment, and a centre tent pole which in itself looked and felt to be half a ton in weight. With a cheerful "Well, here it is, all ready for you to put up", its owner proudly pointed to what had been for many weeks the object of our minds. For a fleeting moment both of us were nonplussed. The first thing that came to my mind was: Where do we get another vehicle to carry The Tent? It seemed to me at first sight that a third car, even if we could get one of our wives to drive it, would be totally unsuited for such a load. Perhaps a fifteen hundredweight van, similar to those which were fairly easily obtainable in those days as Army surplus, would be a better proposition. But the thought was dismissed almost as quickly as it had been conjured up. What was I thinking of? Surely a tent was a tent, and all our plans had been built around one. But then, not around what was before us. I must confess that in the recesses of my mind, and although I had never questioned him, or had any reason for doing so, I suspected Len too, as I had, had formed the impression of a lovely bungalow type tent similar to the ones used as Officers' and S.N.C.Os' quarters during wartime service; ones with more than one compartment, standing erect and with a canopy to act as a sun shade. All further thoughts were banished as the cheerful owner asked "Who's taking which then?" This, it became immediately apparent, was the reference to the ton weight pole in two parts, the mound of unruly canvass (dirty white) and the other baggage's of equipment. I could see immediately there was going to be a problem. Both cars were of the saloon type, but neither had what seemed an absolute requirement in the circumstances - a roof rack. What had seemed at the beginning to be a plain and simple task of collecting an ordinary tent - well, perhaps not an ordinary tent, bearing in mind it was the nub of all those weeks and months of planning -had now developed into a major problem requiring the most careful and considerate (bearing in mind we did not want to upset the donor's feelings) handling to reach the right solution.

"Tell you what" said Len, always quick off the mark, especially on this occasion when, I strongly suspected, he did not want to be saddled with a ton weight two-part tent pole, "I'll take the equipment and we'll try and get the canvass into your car." I wasn't quite sure. It didn't look all that clean to me, and that dirty-white might rub off on the back seat. More than that, it might also spoil the roof lining since the volume of canvass manhandled into the back would be bound to take up every available inch of space. I didn't want to appear to the owner to be ungrateful. After all he had produced a tent, albeit not one of the type I had been thinking of. But one had to be reasonable; the car was only a couple of years old and in reasonably good appearance.

My hesitancy, I think, prodded the donor into a sort of take it or leave it attitude. "I can't help you now because we are about to go out" he said with a kind of finality. "Why not take the canvass now and pick up the pole later on?" Because I thought he was about to add that if we thought we could not handle it we'd better leave it - and bang would go all that planning and holiday in the sun etc - I agreed.

Only then did we ask what sort of tent it was. "It's a Bell Tent" he said tersely. "Army surplus". There was no point in, or opportunity of, examining the contraption then. "It'll take both your families" we were advised. Inwardly I thought that with a pole, two-part, such as we had to contend with it should be big enough to house the cars as well! We got the canvass and equipment finally sorted out with the promise that we would be back as soon as possible to collect the pole(s) as soon as one of us could get a roof rack.

That weekend discussions on routes and ancillary matters were out. The only topic was the Bell tent, represented at that time by a mound of dirty-white canvass and some bags of equipment. We could not erect it in either of our gardens as we had planned because we were still short of the pole(s). Furthermore, it seemed too large and unmanageable. We would have to wait until the vital component, namely the ton weight two part pole(s), was available. I had already arranged for a roof rack, and so had Len. So the following weekend, weather permitting, was to be the day when all would be revealed. We planned to take ourselves, and the Bell Tent, to Burnham Beeches, some ten miles away, and Common land, where the edifice would be erected in all its glory and the apportionment of space per family could be settled. But, until then, the theory could be worked on. The children were each given their respective responsibilities and duties, and once more the excitement of camping in the sun pervaded.

A couple of evenings later we collected the two half-poles, one to each roof rack.

## Chapter Three

## The Tent goes up!

As I recollect it the eagerly awaited weekend arrived with the promise of fine weather and excitement had been honed to the sharpest point. It had been agreed that both cars would carry half each of the pole and an equal proportion of the canvass and equipment, thereby leaving a reasonable amount of room inside for passengers.

The meeting point was a lay-by on the A40 towards Beaconsfield where the first arrival would await the arrival of the other. The children had great fun pretending we were off to Egypt. Actually they were right in a sense because Egypt was the name of a tiny hamlet on the fringe of Burnham Beeches which we passed through to our destination. The meeting took place alright, but it should have occurred to all of us then that here was something to which we had given little or no thought when the actual holiday took place. No one had considered the possibility that en route during the real holiday it could happen that we might be separated with one half of the tent going in one direction and the other half going in another direction! Sum total of the equation in that event - no tent at all! Still, that was at this stage an eventuality which did not enter our minds. We were too much engrossed in seeing what was to be our place of refuge in far off places at the end of each day's travel.

By mid-morning we had reached our destination and the unloading was quickly under way ... well as quickly as could be reasonably expected with none of the adults certain how to best unravel the mound of canvass and the children, having only been delegated their responsibilities in theory, not quite sure which was which corner (being a Bell tent, of course, there were no corners!).

Eventually, the outline of the bell took shape as the canvass was laid out and the equipment, that is the tent pegs and the guy ropes, spread out around the base. The two part pole was unified but it was extremely difficult to manhandle in one piece through the slit entrance of the canvass. So it was halved again, and David, the eldest of the children, was instructed to creep through the entrance and drag the top half of the pole with him. There was a steel tip protruding from the top of the pole and once this was safely manoeuvred into a cavity which we had found in the apex of the bell shape it was reasonable to expect that that part of the tent would easily be raised from the ground. An elementary supposition! But as it turned out not as simple as the theory would have us believe. In the first place it was as dark and dingy inside that mound of canvass as the Black Hole of Calcutta. Secondly, David was not strong enough to manoeuvre the pole into its required position. Thirdly, it was almost impossible to make him hear the instructions and encouragements which were being hurled at him from a group of agitated adults and which included by this time a number of interested, and no doubt amused, onlookers. Finally, by dint of pushing from the outside and some patient coaxing, contact was made between the steel tip and the cavity.

I cannot recall which wife - or it may have been both - crawled in to attempt to raise the half pole to its upright position but after some heavy shoving and panting, success. At last our tent was taking shape, even though it was only about five feet high in the centre. This was where the theoretical training given to the children and our wives really paid off. Each one had seized his or her guy rope which by this time had been threaded through the steel rings around the canvass circumference and on commands were pulling, or easing off, to keep the centre half pole erect. The next problem, however, was how to get the lower half of the pole into place which would give the tent its ten to twelve feet height. Exhausted in mind and body we called a halt. It was lunch anyway, and half the tent was up. The all too brief respite was not the enjoyable picnic we had expected. I'm afraid some tempers had become frayed, which was only natural in these unnatural circumstances, and the sandwiches, even though they were laid out on the camping tables (another procurement in readiness for the holiday) as attractively as the wives could possibly make them, had lost their taste. In our Welsh colloquialism we were really and truly "fed up". Yet, strangely enough, so far as I was aware, nobody had attempted any comparison in what was taking place with any similar situation that might arise sur-le-Continent. Just as well I suppose, otherwise I would not be chronicling here the events over the next forty years. Back to the grind, Len and I decided that between us we might be able to lift the first half-pole high enough to enable some of the others to put the second part into the connecting place. It was hopeless. It would have needed a crane and tackle to lift that mound of canvass which was reticently taking the shape of a tent and to give it its right perspective. The whole situation was rapidly deteriorating into a labour's love lost. Then, it was suggested that if the top half-pole was placed on the ground and the lower half-pole inserted the outside helpers could pull it up to its full height. Some of the new onlookers, fascinated by the operation which by this time had taken up half the morning and ruined a perfectly good picnic, readily joined in. It was success at last! There it stood, erect even if a bit shaky, a monument to our ingenuity and exhaustive labours. I cannot say that our first impressions were even a little exhilarating.

The dirty grey appearance which had infused some disappointment when we had first seen the canvass seemed even more depressing as we gazed at it for the first time as a Bell Tent, fully operational. Army surplus, we had been told. But surplus to army requirements for how long? I'll swear that tent had seen service in the two wars past if not in the Boer War! However, it was ours on loan, and the only way we were going to embark on that smashing holiday in the sun.

It looked large enough in circumference to have housed a full platoon so there would be little difficulty in sorting out the accommodation for our two families of eight. We busied ourselves with various accoutrements like pegging down and unrolling the ground sheet which had come with the canvass. But we never got as far as the business of allocating who would sleep where. Out of the woods, descending on us like the wolf on the fold, came the Warden. What's this? A tent in the glade in Burnham Beeches! Strictly against the bye-laws… an offence to good taste and the pleasures of the public who came to enjoy the beauty and serenity of these historical wooded acres. And so on, and on. Of course the dirty-grey edifice did not help matters, I suppose. There was a threatening authoritarianism in his glare and command as he insisted "this tent has to be taken down and removed instantly". And us not having had the opportunity of testing its aura or capacity after so much hard work! He stood there, immovable and without any compassion or sympathy, whilst we moved crestfallen from peg to peg until finally the whole structure collapsed like a deflated barrage balloon.

All we had profited from this excursion was the knowledge that it was a tent and that it could be put up. We retained the memory of the operation but we never attempted to repeat it before we took the fateful step again en route for the Med and the sun.

# Chapter 4

# The Big Adventure

The holiday date was fixed without much trouble. Because of my parliamentary obligations I had to defer the starting date to the beginning of the House of Commons summer recess, always at the end of July or beginning of August. But this suited everyone because it did not interfere with school for the children. It also suited our friends who usually took their holidays in August. Looking back to those days when the arrangements for channel crossings and such things were so casual I am amazed at the big difference from present day demands.

There was no such thing as booking months in advance as is required nowadays if a firm booking has to be assured; very little of the paper work which Channel crossings and reservations of both shipping space and camping/caravanning sites necessitate now. In those early pre-E.E.C. days, however, with customs requirements stricter in relation to vehicle imports and exports, it was essential that one carried a Green Card (issued free by most insurance companies). Otherwise the rules demanded that one paid a third party insurance premium for the car at each frontier. All that was required of the prudent motorist was that the car was given a pre-holiday check up and that some necessary spare parts were carried. I remember that one of the advices given on this particular holiday, and for others for some years, was to carry some tins of petrol and engine oil. The general impression in Britain in those days was that the Continentals were unable to provide the same garage facilities as at home and that "foreign oil" especially was of a much lower grade. Of course this was not so, at least I never experienced such a situation. Granted things generally were not as good as in this country, but France, Belgium and Holland, the countries most visited by British tourists, were still recovering from the ravages of war, and the economies and road conditions were still showing the impacts.

Preparations for the fortnight's holiday included the stocking up of enough food supplies. This was the responsibility of the wives, it being considered then that the foreign food would not be suitable to either the adult or children's' palates; apart from which the cost of food abroad was very much higher. A list of supplies and motoring and other requirements was drawn up and added to each week as the departure date drew nearer. In this particular instance our reservations had been made for a crossing to Dieppe. Our departure port was Newhaven. After final checks on the Friday evening we set out, and not without some trepidation. The main problem, once again, had been the apportionment of the load carrying. We each took the half- pole and as much of the canvass appurtenances and equipment as could be carried on the roof rack and, in my case, a kind of sea chest which another friend had loaned me and which he assured me would be rainproof. It occupied about two thirds of the roof rack and there were times when I felt it was top heavy and liable on cornering to topple us over. But at least it gave enough room for the confounded half-pole to be safely wedged in alongside. Can you imagine this sort of thing happening today? It might be regarded as slightly reminiscent of those Prairie Schooners which helped to win the Wild West! And I must admit that during that first part of our adventurous journey, from Uxbridge to Newhaven, I felt something of a pioneering spirit myself. Nonetheless, we were all in high spirit.

The next surprise, and consternation, came at the loading aboard the ferry. None of your roll on roll off facilities. There were only a few vehicles at the dockside when we arrived, surprisingly intact after a trouble free run. I must confess I had given no thought to the manner in which we would get aboard so when I saw this huge rope net, something like a fishing trawl dangling from a ship's boom, and being lowered to the quayside, the penny dropped; and I had my first misgivings. The net was spread out and one of the vehicles ahead of us was driven on to it. It was parcelled up then raised slowly to deck height and pulled aboard. Eventually it was our turn and everyone, together with their personal belongings, vacated the vehicle and stood a safe distance away. I got increasingly worried about the roof rack and the chest and the half-pole as the net tightened around the car and it began its precarious journey upwards, swaying gently at first and then developing a kind of pendulum effect which it seemed the handlers were having trouble to correct. What if it crashed to the ground, and with all that weight in and on it? What if the net slipped and the car took on a more acute list?

These and other depressing thoughts raced through my mind as the upward lift progressed agonisingly slowly. Bang goes the holiday before it has really started! We stood there with bated breath, and the children turned away. They couldn't bear to see it happen if happen it did. One slip and all their dreams would be dashed. I knew exactly what was going through their minds because it was going through mine and my wife's as well. But the process went off without a hitch and we all felt a great relief; that is until Len's car was pushed on to the net which had made its safe return to the quayside. Then it was heart in mouth again for the next fifteen minutes! With the first real hurdle safely negotiated everyone felt tolerably pleased. Now for foreign shores and the wide open roads where we would have to drive on "the wrong side". Some more tentative worries, but the spirit was working up well. The first major step had been successfully taken. Now it was Dieppe, here we come.

# Chapter 5

# The Long Trail Begins

My recollection of the long night, and if anyone had any sleep, or for how long, is too hazy to be certain. One thing however is still clear. The journey across the Channel - it took about four and a half hours I believe - was greatly enjoyed. We were favoured by a calm sea and the early sun shining on tranquil water coupled with the excitement and expectation of what lay ahead served to build up an acute sense of adventure, not only among the children but also us adults. As the ferry slowly nosed its way to the berth and the raised voices of the dockers and crew mingled with the crescendo of screeching gulls we gazed enthralled, hardly able to contain the growing urge to be on the road again, yet a little apprehensive I suppose that driving on the French roads meant driving on the "wrong" side. So far as Len and I were concerned there remained one major hurdle. As the vehicles had been loaded in Newhaven so they would have to be unloaded. Our concern was the more acute, I suppose, due to the cacophony of strange voices and the hubbub of foreign tongues. Talk about the Tower of Babel! I wondered whether the operation would be as successful to the background of this excitable (or so it seemed at the time) conglomeration of voices and movements as it had been on the other side of the channel. There we stood on the quayside, watching anxiously as the booms swung out from the deck with vehicles wrapped in voluminous nets swaying away from the side of the vessel and miraculously depositing them with hardly a bump. On reflection it seems strange that in those early days we did not give a thought to a drive-on/drive off system which would be operational within a couple of years. Sufficient unto the day thereof, I suppose. Neither did it occur to me and my family then that this was the beginning of a way of life and leisure which was to be repeated without a single omission, where Myfanwy and I were concerned, for more than forty years and during which we would travel more than 150,000 miles throughout the length and breadth of Europe and into Asia.

A speedy check of the cars and their contents, a re-positioning of passengers and equipment, and we were off on our great adventure. The itinerary for each day had been carefully worked out during the many weeks' preparations for the holidays. Routes had been outlined on maps. Everything was in order. Why should anything go wrong? Why, indeed! But it happened, as it has ever since.

The first thing which became very apparent to us was the lack of directional signs. Finding our way from the port to the open road was the first ordeal. We had routed ourselves to Rouen, and from there, by-passing Paris, it was to be on to Versailles. Our first overnight halt was scheduled for Sens where we would erect the tent, take things easy in the cool of the late afternoon, enjoy an open-air meal and then to bed. That's what the plan had been. But, at this very early stage we were to discover that theories hardly ever became the practicalities.

The roads to Versailles were littered with false trails and place names which seemed to have no resemblance to those marked on our map routes. Another off putting factor was that distances were marked in kilometres. Without the aid of instant conversion gadgets we had to work out the mileages on paper. Before long I was being reminded more and more frequently that we (collectively) were on holiday not undergoing a course on mathematics. I can admit that I was never all that good at maths in school but those early trips did more for my mathematical prowess than the classroom. The mental equation of multiplying the kilometres by five and dividing by eight became almost second nature and the request from driver to passengers for distances covered in miles rather than kilometres almost dried up. I do recall though that the two older children, David and Nigel, could be kept relatively occupied and away from any sense of boredom by a timely demand that they worked out how far to go in miles before we reached the next point of call.

With Versailles and its beautiful roads and wooded areas safely negotiated without mishap or any trouble, except for those irritating problems of what we called the false trails, that is signposts which pointed to anywhere but the places we had marked on the route, and which caused us to backtrack many times, we were well on the way to Sens. It was remarkable how light was the traffic on those French main roads, and how we all enjoyed the practice, which almost became a custom, of acknowledging other vehicles with GB plates with flashing lights and the tooting of horns. This was great fun. Possibly the forerunner of the "I spy" exercises in which young and older occupants of cars on long journeys indulged to keep boredom and irritations at bay.

It was on this first leg of our first continental camping holiday that I learned the most important lesson of such holidays, and later I was to find it even more applicable as we graduated from tenting to caravanning. One should never seek to travel too far and too late in a day. I suppose we had been carried away by the excitement and attraction of being in a strange land and experiencing entirely different surroundings and situations, and paid too little attention to the divergences of the" false trails" during the journey, but the fact was that even before we reached our "staging post" of Sens all of us were in the most frustrating stages of exhaustion. Could we face up to the added frustrations of putting up the tent into which we would then have to crawl? Not likely! So our first night under canvass had to be a pleasure delayed.

More appealing to all was the prospect of a cosy abode for the night under the protection of a roof and the warmth of beds and blankets. It was almost dusk when we came across what appeared to us to be a farmhouse but which turned out to be a kind of Pension with a few chambres available for the tired travellers. My French was sufficient to ensure us two chambres and there was no argument as to who should sleep where. That first resting place for both families was truly a haven in need and everyone slept soundly. Nobody gave a thought to that mass of canvass and the two half-ton poles which, having been placed in the most strategic position for a comparatively easy and quick removal from the roof racks, had been completely ignored.

What sticks out in our minds now about that first stage of the holiday was the morning after. Unlike the British way where such a halt would have been on a bed and breakfast basis there we were. and the children particularly, getting ready for the second stage of our journey without any offer of breakfast. What about that prospect of dashing out of the tent in the freshness of a sunny morning for a summary ablution and breathing in the pure morning air, heavy with the aroma of crispy fried bacon and a couple of eggs? It's what our camping holiday was supposed to represent. Then, after a magnificent repast, and totally refreshed, we would be off to new adventures....

But here we were, sans petite dejeuner and no movement from the kitchen to suggest any would be forthcoming. Then it happened; the most wonderful thing that has remained in our minds to this day. Madam emerged from the house with a copious jug of coffee, au lait, the milk fresh from the milking barn. It was an aroma the like of which I had never experienced before, nor since. Bearing down on us with a smile which was fully a half-metre wide she poured the glorious liquid into bowls which must have held more than a pint each and then produced a plate of hot croissants and confiture. It was the childrens' first taste of French hospitality, and it has remained with all of us clearly and enjoyably.

## Chapter 6

## Memories Are Best Left

Refreshed and eager to be on the go again we were soon on our way to Dijon and thence Avignon where, according to our itinerary we would encamp for the second night of our journey. But, of course, we failed to maintain our schedule. We had been travelling for hours through much of France's wine country and the acres upon acres of vineyards were a constant fascination to everybody. There were even uncalled for, but persistently demanding, halts for the calls of nature. I had never known such frequency; and propriety also required, of course, that one disappeared behind the most convenient hedgerow. Never had any one band of persons communed so much or so regularly with nature as we did on that stretch of the journey.

Getting a bit fed-up with these demanding stops, particularly from the children, I recall following them on one occasion. I went through the same opening but could see no one. I walked down the serried ranks of the shoulder high vines then caught sight of them twenty or thirty yards into the field. They were quietly and painstakingly picking the, to them, best bunches of grapes. They had never seen so many grapes, and certainly not so easily accessible. What they did not realise was that these were not the same type grapes that were sold in the fruiterers' for the table. But curiosity and temptation I suppose got the better of them.... but not for much longer!

Gripping a couple of bunches they raced back to the car intent on enjoying the fruits of their labour as we drove along. Hardly had we got under way when there was a shout to stop from the rear, and a mad scramble to get out when I was able to pull into the side. The bunches of pea sized grapes were covered with minute spiders and ants and all sorts of creepy crawlies. In addition the few grapes that had been swallowed were not, I was assured, nice to eat or "like our grapes".

It was a good half-hour before we were able to assure our back seat passengers that all the offending insects - and every single grape - had been cleared out. It had necessitated virtually completely unpacking and repacking the whole of the back, something which did nothing to placate my roused feelings at having been delayed and further upsetting our schedule. But it did not stop there. For hours afterwards there were complaints from behind that some of the blighters were still with us. "Oh Mam, I've been bitten again" or "There's something tickling inside" were among the plaintive calls. After a few stops which failed to reveal any of the causes of the complaints these appeals fell on deaf years so far as the driver was concerned, but the innumerable halts had had a disastrous effect on the itinerary.

Dijon we did not see. I cannot recollect any other time having visited this historic town, but I know we did not make its encounter on this journey. Where we went wrong again I do not know but well into the afternoon, and when we were thinking about choosing a camp site and hauling down those two formidable half poles still as tightly secured as they had been when we left Uxbridge, there appeared ominously and unpredicted above us a massive rain bearing cloud. How far we were from Avignon we could not tell but the patter of raindrops drove from my mind any question of putting up the Bell tent. A hurried consultation with the Davies's and the decision was reached. It would be another night under a roof, and the sooner we found one the better.

This did not please the children one bit. Under a roof in France was no different to them than under a roof in Uxbridge. Rebellion was in the air! "Oh Dad, why can't we put the tent up?" was the enquiry which sounded more like an ultimatum than a genuine request for information. Ah! Were memories so short that it had already been forgotten what happened when we first, and last, put up that confounded peripatetic edifice of first world war - or before - vintage? And that had been when the weather was fine! Here we were, (well in fact we didn't know exactly where we were) facing a likely deluge and being urged to grapple again with a volume of almost unmanageable canvass hanging from two half-poles seemingly weighing nearly half a tonne provided we could get them together. It could hardly bear envisaging, and Len and I, Van and Eileen, were unanimous. The answer was a definite NO.

An hour later we had made contact with one of those most blessed of all French institutions, a Pension. It was a repetition of the previous night except perhaps we felt even more composed and relaxed in the warmth of our Chambres whilst the rain teemed down. Furthermore, and with the youngsters having got over their resentment, and, overcome with tiredness from a hard day's travel tucked up securely, there was the charming atmosphere of a nearby bistro to console the adults.

It was for the wives their first experience of the traditional French "local" and their introduction to the aperitif. "Cora" was something tasted for the first time, and it became a password with us on the journey, and was sampled again as the holiday spirit was being exploited to the full. When we returned to our Pension we really felt we were at last coming face to face with the merits of a continental holiday of the kind we had envisaged over the past weeks and months since the idea had been fostered. And it didn't seem to matter quite so much when we turned in that it was still raining outside and that the morrow could mean a wet start. Come the dawn, and to our delight we left our overnight lodging in bright sunlight, early and refreshed by an overnight sleep of the just and an early morning cafe au lait served in a mug which more closely resembled a miniature chamber pot and which was a source of great fun and giggles among the children. Within an hour or so we were in sight of Avignon joining the children in a sing song. "Sur le Pont, D'Avignon". We were approaching the river with its spanned bridge but pointed out that this was not THE bridge in the song. We were on course again, everything seemed to be going well and the Midi sun shone beautifully overhead. This was the life! That phrase was conjured up in Avignon and it has been a stock family comment ever since.

It was around here that I suggested that I might be allowed to divert our itinerary to revisit some of the places where I had served along the Mediterranean coast when seconded to the American Air Force during the war. They were not so far away, and I reckoned my wife and family at least would be interested. Besides they were among the most beautiful seaside resorts and fishing villages along the coast. Which is how we came to turn up at Cassis, La Ciotat and Bandol - hardly to be noticed on the maps in those days. Of course, attractive as they were they were not what I remembered them to have been. And I do not think the rest of the party were so enamoured of them that they considered the deviation all that worth while.

At this point I learned my first lesson about never going back. These were not the places as I recalled from those wartime days and experiences. Things were absolutely different. The same thing happened on our next continental holiday the following year when as the final leg of our return journey through the Ardennes we agreed to visit the Normandy coast and the invasion beaches. Yes, they were still there, but not those places I had left, and so clearly retained in my mind. Things had changed, and with them the characters and surroundings. So I would say that if you value memories hang on to them and never seek to retrace your steps. But to revert: It was as a result of the break in the schedule that we were much later than expected on our way to the next overnight stop. We had thought we might make Cannes, some fifty or more miles away along the coast, and that we would arrive in plenty of time to find a suitable camping site since this was to be our resting place for a couple of days. For a variety of reasons, however, dusk had arrived before us. We found a site alright, but it was pretty full. We were invited to find a place for the tent and left to our own devices it seemed. Eventually we found one by virtually groping around in near darkness for a space between small bivouacs and larger tents. Then the real ordeal commenced. All the practice and instruction of Burnham Beeches were to be put to a severe test in these circumstances. The poles were removed from the racks and placed easily to hand. Then the canvass and the appurtenances and equipment laid out with each one attending to his or her respective chore. "Wow, I've trodden on something" was the first intimation anyone had that our chosen site might have been a pasture for animals very recently. "And me too" came another cry from the gathering darkness. What had we landed ourselves in? Another couple of squelches from right and left and Len and I and Van and Eileen were frantic. Everything had to stop immediately. Len skirted the laid down canvass and promptly skidded on his backside. He was the most temperate of men, and usually held young people in the greatest respect. But groping in the semi-darkness with some unknown quantity underfoot, and hearing it being endorsed from all sides as one after another of us trod another squelcher, was not conducive to parlour-room behaviour. I exploded as my feet slid from under me and my hand found a soft and sticky substance. Where it came from, and who had the gumption to go for it, I do not know but suddenly the gloom was pierced by a shaft of light from a torch. And there it was…. That which we had all feared was not what it seemed. The one space available for our tent happened to be under some fig trees and we had been treading on very ripe and over ripe figs and the effects had been similar to what we had thought had happened. Small wonder we were able to find one space large enough for our Bell tent in a site which was almost overcrowded! Had we arrived earlier we would have noticed the conditions and doubtless moved on. After that experience, and having got the tent erected over the ground sheet which protected us from most of the trodden ripe figs, it might be thought we would be entitled to a trouble free first night under canvass. The drill had been that each person would rest with feet towards the pole. There being no camp lights it was difficult by only the dimming light of the torch to carry out this operation, bearing in mind that the Rossers were two in number more than the Davies's. I should have explained also that there was only one "door" to the tent, a flap in the wall. Obviously this would be a much favoured position if one was to get some fresh air during the night.

I had noted the fact and kept it in mind as the small airbeds for the children and larger collapsible beds for the adults were being moved into place. But Len beat me to it. When I returned from ablutions and reached into the darkness of the tent, where I had intended laying down my tired head was already occupied. So be it, and I thought this was something I would have to bear in mind for the remainder of the holiday. But tired as I was I just couldn't get to sleep. The inside of that Bell tent which we had carried for the best part of a thousand miles I think was no better than that historical Black Hole of Calcutta. It was so hot, and black, and not a breath of air. Suddenly there was a silent cry from somewhere in the depths. "Dad?" It was David "What's the matter?" I whispered. "My Lilo is going down. It's flat" came the whispered answer. What could I do? I didn't have a pump to blow it up again. In any case they were made of plastic and the heat must have caused a seam to open. "Try and sleep" I answered. "It'll be morning soon". Poor chap, I was sorry, but there was nothing I could do short of awakening everyone. But that was not long delayed. A few minutes later there was a little squeak to my right. "Mam, there's something in my sleeping bag". It was Marilyn, our young daughter. "I think it's ants". That was it. Enough! It was a case of one up all up.... except Len who had his head half way out of the door and oblivious to everything. But this couldn't last for long and suddenly there was movement. Van wriggled herself through the door, waking Len in the process, and both went outside to make a cup of tea on the primus.

This, then, was our first night in that infamous Bell Tent and without doubt the most torturing experience in all our camping. Afterwards we made our way to San Remo where we had already arranged to stay with friends of the Davies's, and the holiday really took off. But, as for the BELL TENT, that remained firmly emplaced on the respective roof racks until our return home.

Such an experience, it might be thought, would have completely disillusioned one from further camping. But no, it was only the start. It was the beginning and end of the Bell Tent episode, but the yearning for continental holidays had in no way been diminished.

# Chapter 7

# The Night the Clock Struck!

The shattering experience of the Bell tent episode did have a disquieting effect upon us for a while because thoughts of our next holiday abroad were left unspoken until early in the Spring of 1956. Frankly, I didn't have the courage to broach the subject of another tenting experiment, certainly not with a borrowed one. Still, the memories of those better days in the sun during our first forage were difficult to dispel. We had been bitten and the bug would not go away.

Strangely enough when 'Van and I opened the subject we found our friends more than ready to join another two-family trip abroad, only this time with a difference. It would have to be a touring holiday, moving or staying as the spirit moved us or the facilities dictated. Instead of camping sites we would have to rely on the French Pension, the German Gasthof and the Swiss Albergo. We were confident enough that the problems of language presented little difficulties.

The form of the holiday and the approximate date having been settled it was back to the planning routine. It must be admitted that at the beginning the decision to tour instead of to camp had brought a measure of relief all round. In the first place we realised, what we had not done when we had planned the Bell tent holiday, that there would not have to be a division of equipment, and that should we lose one another en-route there was no danger of either party being in difficulties about overnight arrangements as had been the case when the tent poles and equipment had been shared between two cars previously.

This was a new challenge and we accepted it with relish - not that there was a lot to prepare in the way of documentation. Compared with our experiences to come in the years ahead, and with hindsight, those were the halcyon days. One got to Dover with no difficulty, crossed over to one of the French ports and provided the passports were in order one had the feeling that the typical French "D'accord" comment of the official at the port of entry was a genuine welcome to their country, and to the continent generally.

We were loaded up by late afternoon on 31st July and set off to catch the midnight ferry out of Dover. According to our record "we entered Germany at Aachen on Saturday 1st August at 2.30". It was here we experienced the first of the frontier changes which brought pleasure and a little reward to the motoring tourists. Some of the largest multi-national companies, and particularly the petroleum and oil companies, as well as the newly appearing Super stores on the continent, often showered the entering vehicles with gifts such as maps, free tokens, perfumes and even the traditional food titbits of the country in question. There were also invaluable guides and advices for one's stay in the country and, very important to the travellers, conversion tables for weights, measures and distances. Here again was a little touch which made the visitor feel he or she was welcomed to the particular country. What a pity so much of this has vanished over the past thirty years!

The visit to Aachen was brief because we had planned to make for Cologne in time to look around for a friendly Gasthof. As it happened we got to, or had no need to go further than Limburg. This to us, as we viewed it from the commanding hill over which the Autobahn took us, was a fascinating and typically German rural town. It was the general consensus that here was where we would rest for the first night of our three weeks' holiday. And how right we were in our decision. From that introduction to Germany and it's general hospitality and customs was created a lasting opinion which has brought us back year after year, and which has in that time created and sustained many friendships. It was particularly good for the children too.

It was very late afternoon when we enquired at the Hotel Gasthaus Priester whether they could accommodate us. We were made extremely welcome and language proved no barrier. In no time we were being introduced to some of the "locals" in the German equivalent of an English bar, and again according to the diary, "we had a lovely dinner in the evening". Thanks to the travellers' guide we had been given on the frontier at Aachen which showed the D. Mark then was 11.76 to the Pound we were able to calculate our first night's stay cost us £2.15 for four, including food.

Our next objective was to be Karlsruhe. The Autobahn roads in those days, whilst in parts still showing the effects of their wartime use, were an exciting means of fast travel, and something which had yet to make an appearance in Britain. The traffic load was comparatively small and one was able to cover long distances reasonably quickly, and much more safely than nowadays. There were a few stops en route to look at some of the small towns and country communities off the motorway but we reached Karlsruhe by early evening.

We had anticipated no problems after our experience at Limburg, but Karlsruhe was an entirely different situation. The big industrial city had few of the type of guest houses we were looking for. There are some things one experiences in a lifetime which, for whatever reason, sticks in the mind. Our night at Karlsruhe was one of those. Because we could not find a place where both families would be under the same roof 'Van and I, and our children, had to take two rooms on the top floor of the Hotel Zumzinburgh in the outskirts of Durlach. There could be no complaint about the state of the rooms nor the cleanliness. After an evening meal of pork schnitzel, grun salat and pomfrites, we all took a stroll, it being a lovely evening. Tired out we retired for what I expected would be a good night's rest. But I had not bargained with the Town Clock!

Just across the road from our hotel was the Rathaus and perched on its tower was a large and very impressive clock. I paid little attention when it chimed ten o'clock just after we had got into bed. It was a little annoying when it struck the quarter and then the half hour, but we expected it would be silenced from eleven o'clock until the morning. Not a bit of it! As the sound of the traffic died away the chimes seemed to take on a more deliberate and crashing noise, and adding to the annoyance was the reverberation in the bedroom. By the time the twelve strokes of midnight had struck the bedroom floor felt as though we had been on a trampoline or lying on a mound of jelly, and thereafter, through to dawn, we were just laying there waiting for the next hour to sound.

The Davies's had fared better and were refreshed and breakfasted, ready for the next stage of our journey, when we met up in the square. Where to next? The reminder was "Towards Munich". It was 7.45 am and after an uneventful journey we arrived at Munich shortly after 1 pm. After the experience of Karlsruhe we thought it prudent not to seek a night's stop in Munich itself. After an enjoyable lunch and a few gift purchases we set off for an alternative rest-over place somewhere in the Bavarian countryside. That is how we managed to find what had been Hitler's favourite mountain retreat, and so soon after the Allies had purged it of much of its infamous Nazis connection that it had not yet become a much sought out tourist attraction.

Berchtesgaden then was one of the most beautiful sights we had seen on our journey, and the view from the small village up towards the actual Hitler retreat was breathtaking. One of our greatest regrets has been that we did not at that time take advantage of the occasion to visit what was left of the Retreat. My recollection however, reinforced by Van's diary, is that, although we had found the villagers most amicable, and friendly even, no one had volunteered to show us the way there. In retrospect it could have been that they were still suffering pangs of guilt by association with the Fuhrer.

The stop over was for one night only and the record suggests that it wouldn't have taken much to stay longer. We were fortunate enough to have secured a room with a balcony which overlooked the hillside track leading up to the Retreat and the view that morning as we gazed across the couple of miles which separated us from the place where we later learned Hitler's wedding to Eva Braun had taken place, or at least the reception had been held, was so outstandingly beautiful that it will forever remain vivid in our minds.

Our sojourn at the Hotel Wittlesbach had been comfortable and the food left nothing to be desired. By this time we were all well into the type of food served up in Germany with the inevitable Stewing schnitzel and salad being the favourite. The journey from Munich had been uneventful and our arrival at Berchtesgaden at around eight o'clock had meant a leisurely and most enjoyable trip, crowned by the delightful panoramic views of the mountains. "It was lovely, and we will have to visit this place again one day" my wife wrote. Unfortunately that has not been possible. There have been so many other attractions and interests to be indulged in during our continental trips since then. But perhaps it is still not too late, only I wonder whether the next time will give us the same feeling and excitement as happened on our first visit.

Our ultimate objective on the outward leg was to be Venice, and it was towards the Tyrol and the Italian frontier that we set out on a glorious Monday morning around 10.30pm. It is remarkable how, after all these years, and by reference to the diaries which 'Van had the wisdom to keep whilst we were on the move with events fresh in mind, things come back to mind so clearly as I put them on paper. Before we were to reach Venice there were so many things that we were to encounter for the first time.

## Chapter 8

## En Route to Venice

If Berchtesgaden had been the heavenly experience then, as we proceeded higher and higher and into the Tyrol, we felt we were consorting with Paradise. We had seen nothing quite like this before. Not only was the weather perfect, as I am reminded again by the diary, but the scenery was superb and sustained.

With both cars behaving impeccably we rode on contentedly. This was the life, indeed! The only problem was that time was passing too quickly. Whilst we were eager to get to Venice there was so much to see and enjoy that our shaky timetable went by the board. We had not yet experienced the challenge of mountain passes which we knew from our holiday preliminaries we would have to face and surmount before reaching the land of sun and beaches which epitomised Italy in our minds. Sufficient for us as we made our leisurely way was the mind boggling mountain scenery and the bracing air. Regular stops to take in all around us ate into our schedule, but eventually we succumbed to the wonderfully picturesque Tyrolean village of Zell am Zee. We were so captivated with its charm that we drove round and round the fountain in the centre of the pave square just as though we were intoxicated. Possibly we were, but only by the mountain air and the sheer enchantment of all that was around us. There was nothing like this to be seen at home. We had travelled a great many miles but up to then each mile had been a step nearer to the experiences of a lifetime, and we were now relishing to the full the scenes and atmosphere which had been offered to us through the various brochures during those planning sessions several months before.

Within a very short drive from Zell am Zee and we were up in the clouds. The change from the warmth of the lower reaches to the top of the Grossglochner was both sudden and extreme. The climb up the Pass had been nerve wracking for someone who had not had the experience of such steep gradients requiring a continual change of gears, nor the S-bends which brought one to the brink of an awesome drop of many thousands metres into an enticing valley below. Understandably drivers and passengers made the journey to the top in silence, but once the summit had been reached the reactions were of relief and astonishment. We were into a snow field and for the best part of half an hour we be sported ourselves with real snowballs.

Eileen had been advised somewhere that it was dangerous to leave any journey over mountain passes later than three o'clock and since it was already well past mid-afternoon we decided that discretion should be the better part of valour and made our way down to Heiligenblut. It had been an exhilarating journey, and obviously there was more to come, so that when we reached the valley, and Lienz, it was prudent to call it a day.

Here again we were fortunate enough to find a good bread and breakfast guest house. We had been somewhat perplexed earlier in the mountains to see that most of the Gasthofs had the appearance of rather pricey hotels. Then we had noticed many of the beautiful Tyrolean houses en-route displayed notices "Zimmer Frei". It was outside one of these that we pulled up at the entrance to Lienz and enquired for directions to a Pension or Gasthof. We were fortunate that the lady could understand some English but mainly through signs and an invitation to come inside we were able to deduce that there were rooms available, and that the "Zimmer Frei" was equivalent to the British Bed and Breakfast notice. Thereafter we had no problems about finding a place for the night on our journeys and not once did we ever have the misfortune of a bad and inconsiderate patron at a Zimmer Frei.

The stay at Lienz was just overnight and the following morning our journey took us to Cortina d'Ampezzo. Here again we were captivated with the little town which shortly before had played host to the Olympic Winter Games. A visit to the Stadium was a must and the children stood (and fell) on the ice in the particular rink on which some of the games were contested. The two girls were each allowed to purchase Italian dolls which they prized very much over the years. On our way out of the town for the direct route to Venice we stopped to have a better view of the great Ski Jump erected especially for the Olympic games. There is something else which happened during that brief stop. We were approached by a gentleman who professed to be from a nearby spectacle factory. We knew there was one because the local guide made a special point of it.

We hadn't encountered one of these individuals before (but we were to again in the weeks ahead) and fell easy prey to his blandishments. He convinced us that he was doing us a favour as tourists in his country by offering us pairs of sun glasses, which were the local product, at a price well below the retail price. He had a few pairs which he had secured as one of the perks of an employee and we were welcome to them at the same price paid by him. They were retro-something or other and very special. We fell for it, bought a pair each for the adults and went off into the sun. A few days later we found they were just ordinary cheap glasses which we could have purchased anywhere in Italy for half the price we had paid. It didn't hurt the pocket a lot but it dented the pride, being caught by the first Spiv we had encountered on holiday. We learned the lesson however!

It was virtually down hill all the way from Cortina via Belluno and Mestre to Venice and we arrived early enough to find a pleasant hotel outside Mestre which was then nothing like the industrially polluted area it has become. We decided we would make a day of it in Venice the following day, but under pressure from the children the arrangement had to be changed. But that makes for another story.

The author and his son, Nigel,
posing in front of the Olympic ski jump at Cortina d'Ampezzo, 1956.

# Chapter 9

# Lagoons and Gondolas

It is worth recounting how it happened that we chose the particular hotel in Mestre. Before leaving for the holiday I had mentioned to my old friend Alban Ford, in London, that we were off to the Continent for our holiday. It was to be a touring holiday, but we had not made any bookings. At this point he offered me his assistance, which turned out to be considerable.

Alban was the Public and Press Relations Officer for British Electric Traction Company, at that time one of the biggest of British multiple companies, and which had among its diverse interests at least one of the British tour operating companies, Blue Cars. Within a few days I received from the company's chairman, who was also a close personal friend, a letter addressed "to whom it may concern" and a list of hotels with who Blue Cars were connected on Continental tours. Also included was a list of the hotels. The idea was that should we be at any particular spot in which one of these hotels was situated we should at least expect some kind of preferential treatment by presenting the letter.

One of the hotels was at Mestre. However it seemed to me to be a rather imposing building, and I had not given any thought to my appearance as I strode into a rather impressive lobby and up to the reception desk. Was there any room for one or two nights? "No" was the curt reply. They were full up. And no wonder, for there I was, in khaki shorts and open neck shirt, reminiscent of my Service days, and not looking anything like the type of person who would frequent that particular class of hotel.

Could I see the manager please? I asked politely, delving into my pocket for the "to whom it may concern" letter. With a hesitant look the receptionist held out for the letter and disappeared. A few minutes later I was being ushered into the inner sanctum where, ignoring my appearance I thought, a smiling manager advanced with a proffered hand. Of course there would be room for my family ... and yes, for our friends too as I explained the situation. They were kindness personified after this, and although we had to meet the charge which was more than we had budgeted for - less a very generous 15% - we enjoyed the brief stay. Later I discovered that there was a very close liaison between the hotels on my list and the B.C. company, and indeed most of the British tour operators who were held in the highest esteem across the Continent. That letter was a magic key, and it was to prove invaluable on at least one other occasion.

The trip from Cortina in the heat of August had obviously been more demanding on 'Van than any of us had imagined and for the first time during the holiday we all had some reason to worry. She had become depressed and complained about severe headaches and a listlessness which was not like her. First of all we thought it might have been something she had eaten, but we had all eaten the same food together, and no one else had suffered. She had to take to her bed shortly after arriving at the hotel, but insisted that I should take the children into Venice so as not to cause any disappointment. We had all looked forward so much to seeing the City on water and, if possible, to ride on the fabulous gondolas.

For me it took a lot of the gloss off the introduction to Venice in having to leave her behind but I determined that if a night's rest saw no improvement a doctor would have to be consulted the next day. I must admit that when I explained to Nigel and Marilyn that it would be only the three of us taking an evening trip into Venice they demurred and suggested we should put it off until Mam was well enough to accompany us, hopefully the following day.

Eventually, and on the advice of Eileen, who was a State Registered Nurse, it was thought better to have a doctor look at her immediately. So we were faced with the first real problem encountered on the holiday. Not so much emphasis was placed on medical insurance in those early days as is done nowadays, and the reciprocal arrangements under the State Health Scheme must have been unknown to us because we had no cover. It was down to paying whatever the charge would be for a doctor's consultation. Of course we were worried. We were not over blessed with money, and the holiday had been carefully budgeted. But even if it meant using up most of our resources and cutting the holiday short it was obviously necessary to call in the doctor immediately. That instance was a lesson which we learned and took to heart because, ever since, ample provision against any illness has been the prime consideration in any Continental holiday. However, here again as with other changes in planning and preparation for modern day holidays abroad, much more is available through insurances and EEC medical reciprocal arrangements.

It is remiss of us that we did not record the name of the hotel, but the events of the evening are still very clear and I recall with gratification how helpful the manager and staff were when I explained my wife's illness and that we required a doctor. There was no hesitation. A telephone call straight away and we were assured that a doctor friend of the manager would be with us soon. I remember hearing the manager use the word "pronto" when the doctor rang back almost immediately to confirm the call and thought he was requesting an immediate attendance. That's jolly good, I thought to myself. But later I realised that had not been so. The word is used to acknowledge a telephone call. Still, within a very short while 'Van was being examined and the outcome was somewhat reassuring. The diagnosis was a middle ear problem. Apparently the unaccustomed height during our passage over the Grossglochner had created a pressure which resulted in middle ear. And from that day to this she is prone to the occasional attack under certain circumstances, an occurrence which brings back very often our first of many subsequent visits to Venice.

The doubts and uncertainties about 'Van's illness having been removed we proceeded with our plan for a quick trip on the train into Venice station, accompanied by Len and Karen, but with Eileen remaining for company with 'Van. It was a memorable though short train journey. It was darkening even as we boarded the local train in Mestre, and within minutes it seemed we were coursing over water which held a myriad of fairy lights reflected from the street lamps and the lights of the shops, houses and many hotels. Added to this pulsating vision were the bobbing lights of various crafts and in particular the large water busses and speedy water taxis. Venice at night for the uninitiated and first time observer is a sight which cannot fail to move even the most blasé. If the same local railway line is still operating I would suggest that nothing can beat this for a first sighting... but it must be at night.

The railway station of Venice was in itself a sight to behold with its gleaming white facade and pillared structures, and those rolling steps which took the traveller down to the walkway along the Grand Canal. Suddenly, as we were taking in the magic of a hustling waterborne cacophony of sounds, the slap of water, the whine of outboard motors for small private boats and the more resonant sound of the water busses with their propellers cutting into the water, and the thud of wooden hulls on water, there was the most awesome crack of thunder. Only then did I realise that the sharpness of what was happening around us was being accentuated by an impending father-and-mother of storms. The lights seemed the brighter because the heavens were black and heavy with rain clouds.

We did not see a single Gondola on that first visit, and no wonder! The locals had obviously read the signs and the small crafts had disappeared to wherever small crafts are taken when storms of this kind descend upon Venice. Not in more than thirty years during which 'Van and I have paid our annual visit to Venice have I experienced such an electrical storm as beset us in 1956.

Len and I rushed our children back under cover of the station and fortunately found the Mestre train ready to leave just as the heavens opened. For the best part of an hour the rain, thunder and lightning gave a terrifying concerto and it was good to arrive back because both our wives had been considerably upset by the thunder and the thoughts that we were out in such weather. As sightseers we were disappointed in not having had the opportunity of walking through the quaint lanes and waterside walkways of the City, and especially that the children particularly had not seen a single Gondola. But that was to come very soon.

The following day dawned bright and sunny, and the excitement was still high as we gathered for breakfast. It was during this that I suffered a particularly agonising ten minutes thanks to Len's deviousness and penchant to play what I described at the time as a cruel joke. Whilst sitting at the table I had apparently dropped my wallet from my back pocket. It had been noticed by the Davies's on the floor behind my chair and on some pretext or other Len had come behind me and picked it up. Pressing us to be off - the hotel had provided us with a guide and we were to be taken on a comprehensive tour of the islands of Murano and Burano which were the centres of the Venetian glass industry - I was casually reminded that we would have to pay off the guide before we returned, and did I have enough on me? A touch of the back pocket showed it was empty. "Thanks, Len", said I. "Shan't be a few minutes. I must have left it in our room".

A full search of the bedroom showed no results. There was no wallet. I was frantic because all our cash and cheques were in it, as well as some introductions I had been given by a friend in London who had some useful contacts on the Continent. Without that wallet I was lost! Perhaps I had left it at the reception the previous night on our return from Venice? Perhaps... this... that... It was awful. Everything went through my mind as I raced downstairs to the reception. 'Van and the children were standing by, as ignorant of what had actually happened as I was. At the reception desk my fears were realised. No, there was no indication that anyone had picked up and returned my wallet. At that moment I think I was reduced to the greatest despair in my life. I retraced my steps to the breakfast table and was about to confess my loss and the sudden end of the holiday when Len grinned and produced the wallet. I was about to thank him when he explained he had seen it drop and picked it up during breakfast. I could have killed him! I had been through hell for about ten minutes, and he had enjoyed the joke.

The day which started off so abysmally for me turned out to be one of our most enjoyable. With the aid of our guide Andre, who turned out to be a local student and able to speak excellent English, we saw most of the city and the islands. The diary notes: "We spent a wonderful day, wouldn't have missed it for anything. Took films and bought souvenirs, also went to the glass factory where we bought a beautiful Venetian mirror and liqueur decanter and glasses as well as a coffee set". A constant reminder of that great day is the Venetian mirror which has so elegantly graced the lounges of our successive homes since and which today still has pride of place. But it nearly did not!

At the factory where we had been persuaded - not unwillingly I should add - the cost had been itemised to include packing and freight by sea to our home in Ruislip, Middlesex. The whole lot was to be less than £40, quite a bit of money then but a good and safe investment. Furthermore it was to be packed and shipped within a month. The mirror is made up of dozens of exquisitely shaped Murano glass and consequently had to be carefully packaged and itemised to be properly put together again.

Four months after we had returned home we were still waiting for the mirror to be delivered and we thought we might have had a recurrence of our sun glasses spiv. Through my contacts at the House of Commons I had the matter taken up with the Italian Embassy in London since there had been no response to my letters to the factory. In fact I gathered it had been put before the highest authority at the Embassy. Within a few days I received a frantic cable from Murano acknowledging that the crate containing the mirror had been despatched weeks previously and had been passed by Customs. It was. I later understood, gathering dust in the carrier's warehouse in South East London whence it was delivered with great ceremony and abject apology to our home. But at an added cost. In addition to the £40 paid at the factory another £30 was demanded for storage, insurance, and whatever, and it had to be paid because the carrier's terms were cash on delivery. However it had arrived which perhaps again proves the adage that it's not what you know but who you know that matters. Anyway the mirror still adorns the lounge wall and is a daily reminder of that first visit to Venice.

We had reached our outward objective and the following morning we set off for Ferrara, land of the peaches. After an uneventful journey we found a splendid overnight resting place at the Grand Hotel, with the intention of starting early the next morning for Pisa and its famous leaning tower.

# Chapter 10

# The Leaning Tower First Time

According to our notes the overnight stay in Ferrara was quite uneventful, except for one thing. We had been fascinated as we approached the ancient town with the tremendous plantations of peach trees and fruit orchards which lined both sides of the approach roads. Unlike the temptations which had faced some of us during our earlier holiday through France where the open vineyards invited closer inspection with the inevitable outcome - remember the insect infested grapes which the children described as "not like the ones we get in the green grocers"? The Italian orchards were more enclosed. Unlike the countryside at home, however, there were few hedgerows and this permitted a much better and greater view of the various fruit trees. But it was the heavily laden peach trees which attracted the greatest attention and after being safely ensconced in The Grand and enjoyed a light evening meal we all made our way back to the outskirts of the town where we had seen the peaches. We had to buy some of those luscious fruits.

Although the evening was well advanced it was surprising to see so many workers in the groves, not so much picking the fruit but mainly, we gathered, preparing the work and the areas of work for the following morning. Our presence attracted some attention and in a very short while we were surmounting much of the language difficulties, mainly through the children who were able to make our intention clearer and much quicker than we adults. In no time we were having the riper peaches thrust upon us and there was much merriment. It was obvious, and the fact has been borne upon us many times during our subsequent visits to Italy, that there is a greater rapport between children and the Italian adults than between the grown-ups. The Italian attitude generally to the BAMBINI is warm and endearing and a much to be admired quality.

The author and his wife, Myfanwy, visit the Tower of Pisa.

It was a most enjoyable experience and we arrived back at the hotel not only laden with some of the best tasting peaches I have ever had but full of praise for the generosity and warmth of feeling which these ordinary people of Ferrara had shown towards perfect strangers to their land. Apart from some slight inconveniences during the night resulting from an overindulgence of the fruit everyone had a good night's sleep and by seven o'clock we were all in the foyer ready and eager to set off for Pisa. There was no breakfast only some orange juice. What with the fruit and some bread we were proposing to buy en-route we considered a picnic meal would be ideal. It was 7.10 am (and with 2,001 miles on the clock so our diary informs me) when we left The Grand Hotel with Pisa our main destination.

With both cars and their passengers behaving perfectly, and apart from a brief stop for a roadside meal, the first leg of the journey as far as Florence went without a hitch. The only occasional discomfort was the blazing sun and a temperature up in the eighties but by 11.45 we were entering Italy's centre of art and culture. It was so hot, however, and surprisingly to us the long and wide streets being so sparsely populated, that we did not tarry long. By courtesy of the maps and advices on what to see which had been presented to us at the Austria-Italian frontier we lost no time in locating the famous Arcade along the Arno River. It was a slight disappointment I recall because in the first place the river itself was barely a trickle and secondly the bridge across was practically deserted at the time. It being the wrong time of the day, of course, with people observing the age old practice of The Siesta few shops were open for browsing or purchases.

For the grown ups the objects of fine art, the monuments and the tradition of Florence were something which should not be passed by. For the younger members of the families however there was no attraction. So were decided to move on with the promise that the next time we came we would do full justice to the City and its offerings. It was another twenty years before 'Van and I were to redeem that promise.

And so, onto Pisa. Every one of us to the youngest knew about the Leaning Tower of Pisa and so as we made for it there was a lot of speculation about what we would find. Apart from the general information leaflets which had been handed to us we had nothing to inform us about its history. This, again, was something we learned for future visits. It is absolutely necessary to read up in advance or, better still, bring with one well informed literature on items such as the Leaning Tower of Pisa which was once one of the wonders of the world. It makes life so much more interesting and easier where younger members of the family are concerned to be able to answer the interminable questions directed at one. I'm afraid I was as ill-informed as anyone as to why the Tower was not like other edifices, straight up and not leaning to one side.

One other redeeming feature of the journey to Pisa apart from the constant questioning from the back seat was the knowledge that we were proceeding in the direction of the sea. And in the heat of the day and the confines of the car the thought of cool sea breezes was very sustaining. I had no idea how far from the sea Pisa was. According to our map it couldn't be more than a few miles. In fact from that point of view, Pisa was a disappointment. We arrive just after five o'clock and immediately aimed for the Tower which was well within our sights as we approached the town. It was fantastic. At first our approach was from a side where the lean did not seem so pronounced. But as were drove nearer the building gave the impression it was about to slide to the ground. We have been back since and more than once but the building has never given us such an impression as on this occasion. Neither was it so touristified as we found it to be on subsequent visits. Regrettably, we were not able, or not permitted, to climb inside the Tower and the outcome was that the major attraction of this part of the journey did not match our expectations. A few souvenirs as a reminder of the occasion and we made for the coast road which runs along the Ligurian Sea towards Genoa.

Sight of the glistening sea changed all our spirits. The cool breeze swept away the disappointment of Pisa and there was general agreement that we should look for a place on the coast. For the time being at least we had had enough of inland travelling. But in one respect our problems of the day were far from overcome. Where could one find a suitable guest house or hotel in high season at any of the seaside resorts of which there was a plethora along the coast even then? The answer was the same from Livorno on until we reached the small resort of Marina di Massa. In vain I had searched for a hotel which was included in my list. It appeared Blue Cars was either unknown or had not yet reached these parts of Italy. Eventually, as we were about to give up any idea of a good bed and breakfast and face an uncomfortable night in the cars, the Hotel Milano offered us two rooms each with double beds and, as was the custom along that part of the coast, enough for two large families. So, when in Marina do as the Marinans do! We took the rooms and sorted out the sleeping arrangements later.

To be able to breathe some salt air and have a sea breeze fan the face was a delightful bonus after three days driving inland. We did what all the other holidaymakers were doing, promenading along the sea front and planning a splendid evening meal now that we knew where our weary heads would be resting. What a wonderful feeling it was that evening!

It was during our meal that we decided we would proceed further along the coast and if possible as far as San Remo where we had spent some days with friends after the fiasco of the Bell tent. It would be about a day's journey, and with this in mind we determined to be up and about early the following morning. Indeed, by 7.30 am all was ready. We said our farewells to our very kindly hosts at the Hotel Milano and looked forward to a pleasant trip with the sea likely to be visible on our left throughout the journey. It turned out to be a mishmash of events. This was before the large scale road improvements had been started and the Coast Road turned out to be a nightmare with a continuous stream of traffic, the biggest volume by far being Italian. It didn't take us long to find out that Italian drivers seemed to have only one ambition, namely to squeeze the top speed out of a car and to sustain it for as long as possible. It was the foot on the accelerator and a hand on the horn!

There seemed to be more bends and blind corners between Marina di Massa and Genoa than the mountain pass over the Grossglochner, and each one seemed to produce an Italian driver hell-bent on self destruction. The fact that we avoided any serious mishaps was perhaps due more from the divine protection which those drivers seemed to enjoy than our own cautious attitude and the nervousness which increased by the mile... or shouldn't it be kilometre? In truth, however, though we were forced to think at times that all Italian drivers were crazy and a menace to other users of the road they were on the whole extremely skilful, and particularly in making it appear that the other fellow was to blame.

We managed to avoid any trouble until after a brief stop for lunch at a kerbside cafe near Finale Ligure. The respite calmed the nerves and with a short lull in the traffic, no doubt due to Siesta, we felt more assured as we were approaching another resort, Allasio. Up to now driving on the right hand side had caused us little or no problems, and this was not the cause of the first accident which befell us on the holiday. It happened as we were emerging from the one-street town. A local railway line crossed the street and as we approached the signals went up to stop. There were quite a number of cars coming from both directions and Len had taken the lead. He applied his brakes but they had only a minimal effect on the car and it came into contact with a vehicle coming from the other direction. It wasn't a serious mishap, but any accident in those days involving a foreign car inevitably gave rise to considerable agitation. In this case it was no one's fault, simply that Len's car had not responded to the brakes.

After much argument and agreement not to call the polizia (perhaps the other victim couldn't stand a police investigation) Len's car was driven to the nearest garage on the way to Laguelia. There it was found that the brake seal had gone, rendering the brakes almost useless. And small wonder with the amount of braking we had been forced to do on the Coast Road!

The hold-up cost us a valuable hour and a quarter, and the nearest place we would have to stay the night was Laguelia. That was how we never reached San Remo where we had thought we might have continued the holiday we spent there the previous year. The accident proved to be the most fortuitous for us. We had never heard of Laguelia. But it turned out to be a smashing holiday. It was only a small fishing village, and we nearly did not stop there because of the smell. As we entered it off the main road we drove almost on to the beach. The road was narrow and I thought the smell was from the gutter, a kind of open drainage. But this was not it. What we were smelling was the fishermen's nets and equipment and the small fires on which freshly caught shrimps and lobsters were cooked on the beach.

In any case, even if the smells had been caused by open drains, the time was getting on and we had to find a place for the night. There was no great difficulty. We were directed to a Pension run by the "Punchenellos" and they gave us such a warm welcome, and offered us their best accommodation, that the static holiday began the moment we went through their door into a spotlessly clean apartment. Their English was as good as our Italian but this presented no difficulty. I can even confess that it was through the Punchenellos that I came to eat spaghetti! I would not touch it before, but the way they made it, and offered it at every main meal, meant I had to eat or go without. Eventually I took a helping, largely because I couldn't tell them I disliked the stuff, and from then on my dislike was resolved.

Laguelia had none of the ballyhoo of the Mediterranean coast resorts in those days. It possessed a fine sandy beach which cost nothing for the holidaymaker, not like San Remo and the other more sophisticated resorts where one had to pay a toll to get on to the Bagni, and a further charge for a deckchair. In Laguelia all was free. In the evenings the only entertainment was an open air dance floor alongside the cafe. Charlie, who owned both, had spent some time in England and we found him to be the soul of generosity. Towards the end of the week we spent at Laguelia we found we were running short of cash. There was no local bank. A quick word with Charlie, with whom we had become friendly through our hosts, produced all the cash we thought we would need for the rest of our return through Italy, and this against the presentation of Len's and my cheques drawn on a London bank.

It was with much regret that we took ourselves away from Laguelia, and it was with even greater regret that I have to confess now that we have not returned to what was for us a simple but lovely fishing village, but what has "developed" into yet another holiday spot typical of that part of Italy. Because of the overstay the first leg of our holiday would have to be a rush back to Calais. But not direct. The pull of Paris was to draw us slightly off the straight line.

# The Dragons Forty Year Hitch

Pulled over for speeding again?!

# Chapter 11

# Grand St. Bernard and the Dogs

It was a bold decision to take but we planned to return via Switzerland and, whilst we were without any such encumbrances as tenting equipment or caravans, to negotiate as many mountain passes as we could. Our route was to take in some of the most beautiful areas of the Swiss Alps and travelling light as we were this trip gave us opportunities for sightseeing such as we were never able again to undertake during our caravanning holidays.

We backtracked down the Coast Road for some forty miles and took the road to Torino. This had some interest for us since most of the Italian cafe proprietors and ice cream sellers in our native South Wales when we were young seemed to hail from this area. Who knew, perhaps we might meet up with some of the Rabiotti, or Rossi, or Allegri, or Fulgoni families?

Despite a casual search for any of the above names during a brief stop for a meal it seems we were not successful so off we went in search of the best approach for the Grand St. Bernard, still some considerable distance away. At a quaint little town of Pont St Martin we were fortunate to find a small Albergo typical of the Tyrolean flavour we had all fallen in love with. There was not much to offer in the way of entertainment, but who should want for entertainment when the surroundings were so beautiful and the walks so appealing, and safe for the younger members of the party? It was also our first overnight change from the seaside.

Had it not been for the reminder that it would be folly to attempt to negotiate the mountain passes so late in the day, it then being very late afternoon, we might have pressed on. Instead we decided to remain and make for Aosta the following morning. From Pont St. Martin it was steady climbing from one plateau to another, and Aosta was reached without any problems - except that I recall I almost ran out of petrol and the compelling need to fill up before reaching the more severe climbs prevented me the full enjoyment of our surroundings.

Aosta was a larger place than we had imagined, and was the "last stop" before attempting the 2473 metres climb over this majestic mountain. I was able to fill-up, as did Len, in the town where we were assured the pass was quite clear and should present no problem. But we were again advised to make our descent the other side before the early afternoon mist came down. The climb to the top, due to the S bends, seemed to be more difficult than that of the Grossglochner which stands some hundred metres higher at 2576 metres, but there was much more of interest than the scenery when we reached it.

At the Monastery on the peak was a kennel for the famous Great St Bernard dogs. They were, we were assured, truly working dogs and took part in many mountain rescues. The children were enthralled, as were the rest of us; but the moment suffered a setback when one of the children taking a photograph of the dogs being fed by one of the Monks was approached and asked not to do so. When we enquired why not we were told there was a charge, and to the best of my recollection this was 10 Swiss francs. I believe at the current rate of exchange this was more than three English pounds which I personally considered to be extortionate. An explanation for the high charge was two fold. Firstly it was to dissuade a form of commercialism where it was contended some people took photographs for commercial use only, and secondly that any money received was used entirely towards the upkeep and maintenance of the dogs. Even so, it was a high price to expect from children who could not possibly be involved in commercial activities.

As a result of this and other items of interest which made us forget the passing time it was considered too late to attempt the descent. And as a reminder of the possible danger heavy clouds began to form. There was nothing for it but to stay put, and that night was another to be added to experiences never to be forgotten. We were able to secure rooms in the Hospice which we were told had walls five feet thick. Cold as it was outside it was lovely and snug within, and after a much appreciated meal it was early to bed for an early rising.

The summit of the Grand St. Bernard can be either magnificent in the early morning sun or it can be dank and dismal if the winds have not swept away the clouds and mist. I'm afraid for us the expectation of another magnificent scene was dashed. We saw only mist and light drizzling rain as we emerged, but we were assured again that this would give way to better weather as we descended. And so it turned out to be. By the time we had reached the outskirts of Geneva we were panting in the heat.

We would have liked to stay and have a wider study of this beautiful city on the lake but the holiday was drawing quickly to its close and an hour or so in the car park alongside the southern end of the lake and a coffee and drinks in the cafe whilst we watched the magnificent fountain in the centre of the lake shooting its spouts high into the air was all we could afford before setting off for Chalons Sur Saone and Beanie. The only distinction in this area in my mind was that Beanie was a rich wine producing area. But regrettably we would not have much opportunity of sampling the native brew!

From here on the main signposts kept reminding us that we were on the road to Paris and that in itself was both a special attraction and a spur to our efforts. With luck we might be able to squeeze a night or two in the Capital. Neither 'Van nor Len and Eileen had been to Paris and all were keen to do so this time. I had been stationed there for some months during the war and had got to know my way about pretty well. This would be my first revisit and I was as anxious as anyone to get there. So it had to be virtually a non-stop, all out, drive. Vitteaux, Tonnerre and St. Florentin which were places I had thought we might stop, all flew past but when we reached Sens we had to call a halt. We pulled up in the pave town square in search of a public convenience but discovered a wonderfully French bistro where we were made welcome by Msr le Patron in such a fantastic manner that all thought of Paris was almost banished. It was conviviality personified as he and a band of jolly "locals" insisted we joined them. I do not know what they were celebrating - except I did know it wasn't Bastille Day or the end of the war - but the atmosphere was infectious and so far as I can recollect it did not cost us a sou! But it did cost us a lot of our precious time.

Thence to Fontainebleau and the Forest of Versailles, which is where we suffered our first setback.

Perhaps it was the Sens affair which had put any thought of refuelling out of his mind, but just as we entered the Forest with about twenty miles to go, Len's car came to a grinding halt. He was out of petrol and the Forest of Versailles then was the last place where that should happen. There was only one thing for it. Out came the towrope and we towed the Davies's for the best part of ten miles to the nearest petrol station. This, added to the problem which had been exercising us, namely where in Paris or the outskirts would we find a place for a night or two at the price we could by now afford?

Out came the "Whom it may concern" list and there was one in particular which struck me as a distinct possibility. The Hotel de la Republic, bang in the middle of the Place de la Republic. And, lucky again, I knew I could find my way there. We arrived in one piece, or two pieces actually, but it was getting rather late. At the reception desk I was told the manager was not there... but fortunately he had newly returned from England and would be back presently. We should wait. But with tired children it was difficult and I finally persuaded the clerk that on the basis of the letter I had - and there were rooms - it would only be routine for the manager to agree. Perhaps a little reluctantly she consented and we were quickly installed.

Not long afterwards a telephone call to our room notified me of the manager's arrival, and he would like to see me. I'm sure there was no intention to raise doubts in my mind but I imagined I was being summoned to be told we had to get out. A few minutes later all worries were dispelled. Not only was he an agent of Blue Cars in Paris but we recognised one another as having had dinner together in London with Alban, God bless his memory for he died a couple of years later from a heart attack whilst out duck shooting on The Fens. Of course we could all stay, and for as long as we liked. It could be bed and breakfast or full board.

With relief all round we had a hot drink and retired. It was much too late for a meal anyway. Only when I got back to our room did I confess to 'Van my real worry. We had very little money left, barely enough in fact to pay our hotel bill, even at a preferential tourist rate. Certainly there was no possibility of seeing Paris! We were miserable at the thought of having to tell our friends our predicament and even in an attempt to keep down expenses we, 'Van the children and I, left the hotel before breakfast to have a coffee and croissant at a nearby cafe because it was cheaper.

Imagine our surprise on returning to the hotel to find the Davies's sitting down to a bacon and egg breakfast in the visitors' lounge along with a party of English tourists newly arrived. They had been invited to breakfast and so had we, but we couldn't be found. Naturally! We had been in the cafe. All turned out well, however. I went to see Peter, the manager, and explained the situation. Without hesitation I was asked how much I needed. What was pressed into my hand in Francs was almost equivalent to what we had taken out with us at the beginning of the holiday, and when I proffered an IOU - I had no cheques left - he was profoundly hurt. We were able to enjoy our further two days in Paris without worries, and the money was repaid when Peter came over to London a few weeks later and I took him to the House of Commons for lunch.

There is one matter of which I am still constantly reminded by Len regarding the Hotel de la Republic. The second morning of our stay - being flush again - I rang down and in my reasonable French asked that breakfast be served for us in our room. "D'accord" I was assured, and we waited and waited and waited, but no breakfast. After a while when my patience was about exhausted there was a knock at the door. "Entre" I commanded sternly. Another knock. "Come in" I bellowed. And in came Len. "What, not up yet"? He asked rather smarmily. On being told we were still waiting for our breakfast he doubled up laughing and suggested I should get Karin to do the ordering. Apparently she had telephoned down and asked in English and within a few minutes the breakfast had arrived. That was enough. We marched out and downstairs where we breakfasted in English style, but I have never lived it down.

There was, however, another incident at the hotel which would have ensured, were it required, that Hotel de la Republic remains always in our minds. After the breakfast Nigel and Marilyn went ahead of 'Van and I back to our room. Instead of using the staircase they went into the lift. We had been advised not to use it as it had been out of order and was liable to a further breakdown. And, of course, this was bound to happen. It was only a small contraption, somewhat antediluvian as hotel lifts go, with room for two persons and perhaps two pieces of luggage.

In between the second and third floors it crunched to a halt. They could not be seen but the children started shouting for help. Marilyn in particular was greatly distressed and finally an engineer had to be lowered down the shaft to free the lift and raise it to the third floor where the children were released.

My comeback at Len has always been his practice when abroad and unable to order his meal or drink in the native tongue to shout at the waiter. Like most Britishers he thinks that the louder he shouts the better the chance of waiters understanding him. Admittedly you don't hear it quite so much nowadays, but that is only because most Continental waiters and shopkeepers have learned English whilst we seem content to continue on our lazy and inconsiderate way.

For the remainder of this holiday all went well and the journey back home proved uneventful. During the winter months it was the occasion for many reminiscences and served to whet even more the appetite for further holidays abroad.

# Chapter 12

# "Abbot and Sitges"

Having covered a considerable amount of ground during our tenting and touring holidays the idea of taking a peek at what lay beyond the Pyrenees was being urged early in 1957. It was a temptation to go under canvass again but the experience with the old Bell tent still rankled somewhat. Anyway, the decision was eased when we were told of a scheme whereby we could book our holiday at a Spanish resort through a connection in near-by Harrow. One of the attractions of this scheme was that the holiday could be paid for in England and spending money, that is Spanish pesetas, could be included at the current rate of exchange. Which is how we became acquainted with Abbot.

Whether that was his real family name I cannot tell but when subsequently we met him on location, as it were, it was the only nomenclature to which he responded. It was "Abbot" whenever he was needed in the kitchen or at the reception desk and the shrill demand from his wife Maria had an electric effect. He was here, there and everywhere, and never a more obliging person one could ever wish to meet.

There was some family connection with Harrow and when we enquired about the arrangements and system we were surprised with the simplicity of it. We made a booking for the Pension Maria in Sitges on the Costa del Sol, paid in English money for the period booked, and then added whatever one thought was needed for the holiday as spending money. This could be paid over a period of weeks or months and as such was eminently suitable for those who preferred this holiday club method with the knowledge that there was already a firm booking.

So Sitges it was to be for our 1957 holiday in Spain. Little was known about the place at that time, but a ten days' stay at the Villa Maria, which is what Abbot preferred it to be called, was quite cheap. Much of the Spanish coastline then was undeveloped, and since it was under the rigid dictatorship administration of General Franco and the strict Civil Guard stewardship the tourist industry had yet to take off. The Civil Guards, police officers with the back to front shiny hats something like a Napoleon titfer or a Gilbert and Sullivan character from the Pirates of Penzance, had a great deal of authority we were told and it could be serious for the individual who was apprehended for some offence - like women wearing underdressed swimsuits such as the Bikini, or a breach of the peace such as shouting or misbehaving in some trivial manner or other.

It was surprising I suppose that in view of these stories one heard we decided to go ahead with the holiday. Indeed, on this basis it was surprising that anyone went to Spain. In fact much of it was a gross exaggeration, but it was noticeable that the Civil Guards were given a lot of respect generally. Perhaps other British tourists had been given the same build-up that we had. Still, the lure of the sun, blue sea and long sandy beaches, and the fact that we were law abiding citizens both at home and abroad, was an inducement stronger than the cautions.

Without the appurtenances of camping it was a much simpler operation to get prepared for ten days in Sitges and a two weeks' there and back journey in the two cars. Both Len and I had changed our cars and were confident the trip would be without mechanical troubles. Helped by our earlier experiences of virtually the same journey through France we arrived at the Pyrenean town of Perpignan, just before the border crossing, tired but unscathed. It was already early evening and the shadows were gathering fast. Should we or should we not cross over and commence the run down towards Barcelona and Sitges? It would be new territory for us and in our tiredness possibly we might lose our way. I well remember there was a discussion over a snack meal and drinks and the consensus was that having come so near to the promised land of sun and sand we should press on to start the holiday early the following day. Then it was that consternation struck!

We checked all our documents, such as passports, and the Green

Cards and bail bonds for the car insurances to minimise any hold-up in going through. Search as I might, and we had all the children at it as well, there was no trace of the Green Card. I knew I had it before we left home... and after a futile search I then knew I had left it behind. Nothing for it then but to try and explain the mistake should the frontier guards insist on their presentation. Snatching at straws we considered the possibility that it being late in the day the guards wouldn't even bother to examine our documents. After all we were British! But what if they demanded the missing documents? The alternative could be to purchase a short term car insurance; but we had very little in the way of Spanish currency having availed ourselves of the Abbot scheme. Back flooded the old fears which still existed in the mind as we approached the various frontiers in those days. Were we going to be turned back after having come so far? We decided to chance it and planned a subterfuge which could work if the queues crossing the frontier were heavy or the guards were not too particular with tourists. Len would be immediately in front of me and having shown his documents he would slip his Green Card to me. We hoped that the guards' scrutiny would not be too close.

At this point the crossing required the driver of the car to leave the car and present all the documents for his passengers at the Entry office. The officials would conduct a scrutiny and if all was well a form would be issued which one would have to keep and surrender on leaving Spain at whichever exit point. My heart dropped to my boots as we filed into the little office and I saw the armed Civil Guards supervising the clearances. But it was too late to turn back. This would only call attention to myself and my situation. Len, deliberately pompous - his best "We are British, you know" attitude (and being British then really meant something I suppose) - handed over his documents then raised some confusion in speaking Welsh. Naturally no-one understood what was being said but I got the message which signalled that I should take the Green Card from him as he turned to speak to me. I answered in Welsh which brought some bemused comment from the official processing the documents. We had been correct in assuming that the scrutiny would not be so strict at that late hour, and with such animation as crowds of locals were crossing back from their work along the frontier area.

I grasped the Card and slipped it into my documents. There was a cursory glance. I received my entry form and a couple of minutes later, rather weak kneed, I followed Len's car across the border. A brief stop for a hot drink and we were ready for the descent into Gerona and then Sitges which we knew we could not reach until the early hours of the morning.

After the trauma of the crossing it might be expected that all would be alright. But our problems had only just begun. I realised as we were moving off that the car had no lights. Something had happened during the climb up towards Perpignan which had put the car's lighting system out of commission. This was the last straw. The Davies's were pulling away into the darkness and I hooted to him to stop. This was, to say the least, a serious quandary. One could not remain in the area adjacent to the border in case we were questioned again. In any case no-one among us could speak Spanish. It was agreed to proceed and that Len would take the lead with headlights on and keep an eye on his mirror to be certain that I was close behind. We had not bargained on the state of the route which was as bad as any of the other passes we had negotiated in daylight during our previous Continental holidays. Occasionally Len's car drew away from the car's length I had urged we should keep between us. It meant I would have to spurt into the sheer blackness to restore the distance. All I could see ahead was the little red spot which was Len's rear light, and I had to keep my eye, and 'Van's too, on that as we negotiated the countless bends. It was a nightmare! The rear light had a mesmerising effect. After the first hour I was drained and seemed to respond automatically to the bobbing spot whilst I was able to keep it in sight.

It was at least two hours before we reached any sign of civilisation which was Gerona. The street lights were dim but we passed through without incident, and on towards Barcelona. Utterly exhausted I pulled over to the side as we were proceeding down a deserted Avenue di General Franco. I had had enough. I didn't care how many Civil Guards pounced on us I had to have some sleep. Len noticed I had stopped and he came back. We were outside one of the city's big hotels and what the night clerk must have thought I couldn't care less. We needed at least two rooms for both families. And two rooms we got. It was near to two am and I must have been a frightening sight having driven well over a hundred miles in the most mind boggling conditions.

After a few hours sleep and without breakfast we made our way to Sitges which was no more than thirty miles away. But I am convinced that had I attempted that further journey we might all have ended up in a crashed vehicle. I had reached the last stage of endurance and never will that crazy journey be forgotten.

Sitges turned out to be a small and pleasant sandy beach with an assortment of houses bearing a marked Moorish flavour and a couple of streets with small shops and the inevitable "sippers". These were a kind of off-licence premises or bodegas which offered the customer a variety of wines drawn from the wood. The small barrels arrayed around the premises each had a tap and before making a purchase it was customary to sip the content. Hence the name "The Sippers". They made a valuable contribution to the social life of the little town for it was along this parade that a nightly ritual took place. With the evening meal at the hotels and pensions being rather late, as is the custom in Spain, visitors would promenade the "Avenue di Sippers" , as it became known to us, drop in for a taster or two, meet and make new friends, and return to their meals suitably fortified at little extra cost.

That was the Sitges we first knew. It had little or no resemblance to the resort of today, or even of the Sitges we visited again in 1964 when we popped in to see Abbot and the Villa Maria. There is a rather doleful tale to be told about that last visit because, had things worked out for us we might have hit the jackpot. It was about this time that the development of the Costa del Sol and Costa Brava took off with astonishing rapidity. The Germans were moving in and buying up every available acre of land alongside the coast and converting it into what has become the most overdeveloped leisure and holiday coastline in Europe. Abbot had a friend who was the owner of a prime plot of land between the Villa Maria and the beach. He wanted to sell, and agreed to a sum equivalent to £2,000. We could have raised the money without too much trouble, but back in London after the holiday I encountered the greatest frustration. Chancellor of the Exchequer L.J. Callaghan, the new Labour government's economic aficionado, had just frozen the transfer of sterling and there was no way we could get the money out of England to make the purchase. It was galling, and the nearest I had ever come to making a financial killing because with our option exhausted the property was bought by a German speculator and resold afterwards for close on to a million pounds.

The remainder of our Sitges stay, which turned out to be the last of our purely motoring holidays on the Continent proved most enjoyable and particularly our visit to Barcelona and our first bullfight. As part of the holiday Abbot arranged for his guests a weekly coach trip into Barcelona with tickets for the bullfight. This would cost so much a head but would be optional. He hadn't considered however the astuteness of our Len who had enquired the possibility of hiring a small 'bus with driver. It transpired that this could be done at less than half the cost of the Abbot trip, but it required at least fourteen people to make the trip viable. As a further inducement to this private enterprise venture we were promised a crate of Coco Colas at a much reduced price. Abbot charged ten pesetas a bottle of Coco Colas at the Villa but the price on the 'bus would be five pesetas. Furthermore, the bullfight tickets through Abbot were Tourist and our driver could get the Sol e Sombre (sun and shade) tickets favoured by the locals for a lot cheaper. Len's package was by far cheaper and we had no difficulty in wooing the extra five passengers required from the Abbot contingent. It turned out to be a great day, but there were moments when we regretted the switch, especially when our happy go lucky driver insisted on negotiating some vicious mountain bends between Sitges and Barcelona at suicidal speeds and in full song! We never discovered if Abbot ever found out why his coach load was at least five short, or if this entrepreneurial exercise was attempted afterwards by a highly satisfied 'bus driver.

The final episode of our stay in Sitges was getting the car's lighting system working again. A local garage which looked more like a Fred Karno outfit compared with the more sophisticated English counterpart agreed to have the repairs done well before we were due to leave. On the penultimate day I went to collect the car and found there had been a complete rewiring job done under the dashboard. I was shown the work and feared for the cost. Imagine my surprise when I got a bill for just over £1. The lights worked satisfactorily for several months but suddenly the same thing happened. At my local garage some surprise was expressed that the wiring did not conform to the standard wiring. I explained the reason and was then told it had been completely unnecessary. The only trouble was that the dip switch for the headlights had stuck and required only to be released with a screw driver, an operation that could be done in two minutes! Provided, of course, one had the knowledge. Still, the holiday had been one well spent, and it provided us with many happy memories and not a few hair raising experiences which it has been a pleasure now to share with others.

## Chapter 13

## A New Challenge Beckons

With the disastrous first attempt at camping now a thing of the past it didn't take long in the autumn months of 1957 to prepare for the new challenge. The prospect of another sojourn across the Channel excited us all, but the first requirement was a replacement for that iniquitous tent.

Obviously the appeal for continental camping holidays was on the upsurge because 1957 saw a major drive by the leisure orientated companies to attract interest in a large range of tenting and outdoor pursuits. The post-war boom got under way with a flourish and one company in particular, the Headquarters and General Supply, in East London, advertised a new and classy type of bungalow family tent with sleeping and dining accommodation separate and a protective fly sheet and sun canopy to boot! Compared with what the Bell Tent had to offer this promised almost sheer luxury.

So, back to the drawing board in a series of evening and weekend sessions between our two families. I well recall a Saturday afternoon summons from the Davies's to tea at their house in the spring of 1958. There was nothing extraordinary about the invitation. We frequently went to each other's houses (we lived less than five miles away) for a reciprocal cuppa and a chat. But that Saturday did turn out to be unusual.

We were shepherded out to the back lawn and there, in all it's splendour and looking extremely inviting, was the HQ and G bungalow tent in a colourful brown and gold. They had "slipped into London" and purchased the very latest in tents and equipment only that morning and obviously had erected it without much trouble and assistance. We were looking at something which would open new vistas, and from that very moment Van and I were completely resold on camping.

Needless to say were did not delay our purchase. By the following weekend the Davies's were across at our house surveying the Rossers' efforts in setting up the second HQ and G bungalow tent, complete with made – to - measure ground sheet and canvass walls to separate the rear of the tent into two bedrooms, and a "dining area" under shelter in case of rain.

In addition there were such extras as a canvass washbasin on a tripod, an easy to assemble gas ring with two burners and, a "must" for anyone travelling in warmer climes, a cooler which was a kind of chalk-substance box that had to be regularly fed with water on the outside. Nothing like the later gas and electric refrigerators but effective enough in keeping food cool.

Thus equipped we were now ready to plan our second camping holiday abroad. But even in that short time since the Bell Tent episode remarkable changes had been taking place in opening up the continental countries to the eager to travel British. Notably, and without doubt the biggest development in cross channel touring, was the introduction of the roll-on roll-off cross channel ferries. No more anxious moments as cars and the rapidly increasing numbers of touring caravans descending on Dover were able to drive on instead of being hoisted aboard.

In those days it was very much a do it yourself operation. Not only had one to work out the dates and the length of time to be spent abroad but many other calculations had to be considered. For instance how far was one to travel and what were likely to be the best routes; and since the trip would most likely involve crossing more than one or two frontiers what would be the requirements to be satisfied at the crossing points in addition to the passports. For example the various regulations regarding insurances and driving rules. There was the all important matter of currencies which required the fullest consideration if one was to have the best return for one's conversions. Then there was the need to establish the availability of petrol and oil and the comparative costs. In the earlier periods British motorists going abroad were very much concerned that the continental countries which had suffered so greatly from the ravages of the war were unable to give the petrol pump and garage repairs facilities they were accustomed to at home. To some extent in the lesser populated and visited areas as one travelled towards and beyond the Maritime Alps this might have been so but our own experiences did not substantiate the stories of shortages and of motorists and campers left stranded. However, and as a general precaution, many holidaymakers travelling by car used to carry up to five gallon jerry cans for spare fuel.

I suppose all this added to the excitement of advance planning, and was the situation until The Caravan Club established its Foreign Touring Service in 1967. With the advent of the Club's increasingly sophisticated service much of the hassle was removed, but for us old stagers it also took away a great deal of the preliminary excitement and pleasures of detailed planning. Camping and caravanning abroad thereafter became a piece of cake with the only real essential being the cash availability. Some critics today, and there are still many who regale in the old way (sorry if my petticoat is showing!), feel that the present organisations, whose objectives are no problems and made to measure arrangements, including full itineraries and where to stop and for how long, have taken much of the excitement, the sense of adventure, and even glamour, out of the preparations for those two three or four weeks out of one's own country.

Strengthened in our resolve to make the forthcoming and second camping holiday abroad a more enjoyable affair by the acquisition of the bungalow tent we held a series of pre-holiday planning sessions and eventually decided on a most ambitious circuitous tour of France, Switzerland, and Germany, beginning and ending at Calais. What did it matter that we could not work out the mileage! There were two vehicles, two tents and four adults and, this time, three children. David, our eldest child had decided to opt out of this "camping lark". We were not happy about it, but we realised it was an inevitable occurrence and accepted his decision.

The Willaby caravan outfit
about to board the Airolo train en-route to Italy, 1958.

## Chapter 14

## Paris in the Bungalow

As Spring of 1958 lengthened, giving the prospect of better camping weather, we were tempted more than once to try out our new bungalow tents with the occasional weekend, but it never got further than the thought. This was largely because we had not graduated to membership of any organisation dealing with camping at that time, and our knowledge of the English camping scene was scarce, if not non-existent. So we had to bide our time, and as each month passed the urge to be off to the sun and the better weather, and to sample whatever excitements lay ahead of us, got stronger. I cannot say, though, that our preparations underwent the amount of chopping and changing that the previous expedition had required. We had acquired a new confidence I suppose. With the backing of that Bell tent baptism and the knowledge of what to expect of route schedules and map reading we had developed a more philosophical attitude. The only thing that mattered was to cross the Channel, point the cars in the direction roughly to where we had planned, arrive there safely and enjoy the holiday.

After a final check up and a little more re-stocking (I remember one item which had been omitted, namely a supply of candles and a carton of matches, had to be purchased as an essential requirement) we set off on Friday tea time to catch the midnight ferry at Dover. There were at least two reasons why we continually made it the midnight ferry. One was it was not possible to leave for the holiday before the teatime of our Friday departures which meant we arrived in Dover usually only about two or three hours before sailing, and there was no desire to hang about once we were on the docks. The other was that fewer people and parties seemed anxious to sail on the midnight ferry for whatever reasons and this usually meant there was more room aboard. In those early days the price factor did not matter so much, but later, and as holidays abroad became more popular and the ferry fleets increased, the midnight and early morning crossings were cheaper and became more sought after. Consequently, and it is today and has been for many years past, early bookings with the respective ferry companies are very necessary.

One thing which springs to mind about this particular holiday with the bungalow tent was the publicity given to a new camping scheme being offered by a French camping and leisure organisation. This invited campers to sample the excellent facilities and attractions of new sites in conjunction with French chateaux. It had a taste of the medieval history of that country and the prospect of relaxing in and around the surroundings of famous historical buildings was very attractive. We determined that part of our holiday would be spent in the rural areas. And so it happened that we headed for Beauvais and on to Chartres.

But the magnet that was Paris was irresistible, and we found our first overnight halt was in a Champs d'Elysees site. It was a souring experience. Not only was the site filthy and completely disorganized, but the rain came down in torrents. It did not help any that Marilyn was taken ill and that there was no doctor within call. Fortunately it turned out not to be serious and did not affect our progress. I have to say that in those days the quality of French camping sites was not good. They were considered by many early campers as lacking in hygiene and the necessary basic facilities. It was such a far cry from what is generally the standard in French sites of today.

It was on to Chartres the following day, fortunately, the diary informs us, in weather which was warm and sunny. It was here that we had our first experience of a chateau site and very acceptable it turned out to be. Not only were we sited on a beautifully green and level stretch of ground on the perimeter of the Chateau, whose name unfortunately I have forgotten, but we were allowed, no encouraged, to visit the building itself and enjoy its superb furnishings. Furthermore we were allowed the use of the outbuildings and especially conveniences which were completely out of style and character with the Chateau itself in that they were specially installed with modernised flush sanitation. All these made our stay for a few nights all the more enjoyable and with the added "luxury" of our new bungalow tent it gave us an encouragement of what real camping life could be. Why hadn't we done this before we asked ourselves. It was healthy, inexpensive for a family, reasonably secure and one was not tied down to staying any longer than one felt was enough. *This really was the life!*

What added as much to the pleasures was the ease with which we were able to erect the bungalow tent and also to take in down. The tubular alloy structure was both light and strong and the partitions separating the two sleeping quarters and also the dining area meant there was adequate privacy and seclusion. Not like that other monstrosity where it was a case of all feet towards the centre and stale air unless one could find headroom near the tiny flap door.

With the exception of the downpour in Paris the weather had remained ideal as we made our way across to the western side with brief stops at Le Mans, Tours, and then to Angouleme. It was here after what seems to have been an uneventful journey that we were advised to visit a little seaside resort of Royan, at the mouth of the Gironde River. It had suffered badly during the war we gathered but was now being redeveloped with a magnificent promenade. We reached it during mid-morning and found it to be a delightful spot, everything that we had been told it would be, except for one little, but very important matter; we could not find a camp site that pleased us.

With our sights now turned to the leg for home we reached La Rochelle by late afternoon and immediately drove into the first camping site we came across. It was a big mistake; but then we were novitiates to the pursuit! Everything looked alright. There was a grassy level with a slow running stream bordering the field. It was very attractive and we thought this would be the place to stay for a couple of nights to allow us to visit some of the places associated with names which were still familiar to us from wartime, and especially the U Boat campaign. But that stream was to cause us a great deal of inconvenience. The sun had barely set and we were preparing our evening meal, when hordes of nasty biting mosquitoes rose from the almost still waters and we became their targets and their meal. I've never seen anything like that cloud of mosquitoes, nor seen such havoc as their bites caused to us. No one escaped... except those wiser ones who had pitched their tents across the other side. No wonder we had the entire stretch of that river bank to ourselves!

Outside or inside the tents into which we had been driven for refuge even whilst the meals were being cooked it made no difference. The invasion was complete and the whole night was a shambles. Come the dawn and we were striking camp, itching and scratching, with bites and lumps visible wherever one looked. The mere mention of La Rochelle brings back the horror of that night and the reminder that we said as we were paying our dues on leaving... "never again to this place". And we haven't.

It was some days later that we arrived at le Monte St. Michel. Practically unspoiled in the immediate post-war period it was a delight to the eye as we approached it along the road from Rennes. By this time we were into the last week of the holiday, and we had agreed that the last few days would be a leisurely journey through Normandy with its still vivid memories of the Second Front invasion. Mont St. Michel had a splendid camp site overlooking the beach and the causeway, along which at the ebb tide one could walk out to what the guidebook at that time referred to as "the isolated majesty of Mont Saint Michel".

There were no problems. We were welcomed into a sloping campsite which had ample space and few tents. Whilst I was satisfying the attendant at the office the others went in search of a pitch where the two bungalow tents could be erected near each other. By the time I got to it Len had already marked out his pitch, and would you believe it! It was the only level piece of ground. What was to happen, however, was no more than just retribution as I viewed it at the time, but often since we have had many a laugh over it. There was no warning that it would rain during the night but just past midnight the deluge happened.

The bungalow tent proved its worth that night. We were snug as a bug in a rug and waterproof, but about an hour later I was awakened by a rustling noise. From outside came Len's voice punctuated by raindrops. "Can you give a hand?" he whispered. Through the open flap was pushed a drenched capped head which glistened like a reflecting icicle in the light of his torch. "I've got trouble" he went on. "Rain's come in. Our beds are soaking".

Pulling an anorak over my pyjamas I scrambled out into the rain and dashed for the other tent which had looked so much neater than ours when it had been erected. Whilst we were on a slight slope theirs had been ship-shape and Bristol fashion. But now it appeared to be truly afloat. The three lilo beds really were on water, and the clothes soaked. Eileen and Karin were totally miserable, as they had every right to be, and to make matters worse (or perhaps less worse in the circumstances) there was only one small torchlight to see what was happening. With wellies and macs on they were taken into our tent whilst Len and I tried to mop up. What a job, and utterly useless to attempt. The rain continued to pour in under the side flaps, and with no slope to allow it to drain away it was getting deeper and deeper within the tent.

A small channel which had been dug around it as a pre-requisite to setting up a tent, (as every experienced camper would know) had become a small moat. It was the overflow from this which had caused most of the trouble.

Anyway, it was obvious that the Davies's and the Rossers would not be able to share the one serviceable tent for the night, and unthinkable that one lot should be stuck in a car and the other within the relative comfort of our tent. Being the only one able to converse in French, and also more or less dry, I went to the camp office to explain the problem and to seek some alternative shelter for Eileen, Karin and Len. Since it was the early hours of the morning, and although the rain had by now practically ceased, it was a thankless reception I received after waking up the attendant.

Explaining as best as I could, and inviting him to come and survey the situation himself, he came up with a suggestion which, despite the plight of my friends, I found terribly amusing. There were a few wooden structures nearby into which they might care to go until the morning when he would look again at the situation. When he showed them to me I almost burst out laughing. They were just like a coop used for battery chickens. But they were dry and clean. Finally we got the Davies's over and by going in feet first, so small was the aperture, we got them installed.

Little sleep was to be had for anyone that night and come the dawn it was all hands to the pumps to dry out tent and clothing. Just one of the joys of camping, I suppose (when it happens to some one else not to you!), but it meant an extra day's stay at Mont St. Michel of which we made the fullest use. I believe the island then was more vulnerable to the tides than today because of changes to the causeway. Our notes refer to the beautiful buildings which are a masterpiece of Norman architecture between the eleventh and fifteenth centuries, and which justifies the claim that the place is a marvel of the western world.

There was only one street on the island but this contained many restaurants and hotels as well as the attractions provided by numerous souvenir shops, but the outstanding feature, so far as I can recollect, was the sight of an advancing tide creeping over golden sands at an amazing speed until the walkway from the mainland was completely obliterated and which turned Mont St. Michel once more into an island with its unique Abbey and Church which stand out boldly on the horizon when one looks out from the mainland. Nowadays it becomes an island only at high tides and it is during the equinox periods that these are the most impressive. They then reveal a rise and fall of almost fifty feet which constitutes the greatest tidal fluctuation in Europe.

Further wartime memories were invoked on the last leg of the return journey to Calais, for instance at St.Lo, where my R.A.F. unit was almost cut off from the Cherbourg peninsula by the German counter offensive against the Americans, and again at Bayeux where we were able to view the famous Norman tapestry recording William the conqueror's 1066 conquest of Britain. It was at a little village of Cussy a few miles from Bayeux that we were "contained" for a while during the 1944 advance, but there was no clue as to it's whereabouts this time. Until, that is, I chanced to meet a Priest at the Abbey who addressed us in English and offered us any assistance.

By an amazing co-incidence it happened that he had been evacuated to London in 1940 and had spent some time at St. Paul's Cathedral where he had been a part time organist. He promised to make enquires about Cussy and returned shortly afterwards to tell us that the village was no more. But its situation had been some twenty kilometres away. On its site, and including the little orchard where we had spent a couple of hectic days, was now one of the largest of the Allies' war cemeteries. A last look at the beaches at Arromanches, with its German Tiger tank still embedded on the hillside as I had vividly remembered it, but now a wartime memorial, and the ruins of the famous Mulbury floating harbour still visible, we bade farewell and made for Calais. It had been a wonderful holiday, packed with pleasures and traumas, enjoyable and memorable. The bungalow tents, notwithstanding one or two blips, had proved their worth and restored confidence in the joys and advantages of camping holidays. The question then was: What are we to do about 1959?

The family's first visit to the Eiffel Tower.

# Chapter 15

# Caravanning Comes to Mind

After the successful under-canvass holiday of 1959 there seemed to be no reason why 1960 abroad should not be on similar lines. The usual winter and spring preparations followed the now well established pattern of planning the routes, agreeing on provisional dates and looking around to see if there were better ways by which we could extract the maximum enjoyment from the minimum expenditure. It was noticeable that costs all round were escalating, and especially in respect of the channel crossings and insurances which we had agreed would have to be taken out as a precaution against any untoward occurrences. This was in reality the first time that we considered seriously the need to be covered by insurances beyond that of the Green Card for the vehicles.

This holiday was to be much the same as our previous ones in that France, Switzerland and Germany were to be the main venues. What no one realized, however, was that there would be a significant change in one's camping outlook for the future before the holiday was to end.

Again we traversed the same route from Calais to the German border at Aachen and according to the diary it was an uneventful beginning. This time, however, we stopped over for one night at the Municipal Camping site which proved to be an ideal jumping off spot for the Autobahn which would take us to Limburg. We had determined to return to this town which had given us such a wonderful experience of German hospitality four years earlier. Below the massive arched bridge which carried the autobahn across the valley and the river Lahn, which flows into the confluence of Koblenz, we found an ideal camping site. It was just a few hundred yards from the Gasthaus Priester where we had stayed in 1956, and it was an ideal location. Since those days it has developed into a large and very popular Camping platz not only as an overnight stay but also as a base for a lengthy holiday with many large towns and cities well within its compass for day by day visits by private car or public transport - not excluding the river.

Koblenz, which opens the door to the Mosel valley and the rare delights of big vessel cruises on the river as far as Luxembourg, and as such is an outstanding attraction to tourists, is within easy distance of Limburg nowadays, though in our earliest camping days the nomadic urge to move on to the next watering place offered us no encouragement to use the place as much as it should have been.

It was this urge to get about and see as many places as humanly possible within our limited holiday period which made camping the ideal means for us - that and the relative cheapness of the travel. The bungalow tents continued to please us immensely with the ease with which they could be erected, and their compactness which enabled us to get the tents and most of the equipment, including the light alloy tubular framework, on to the roof racks. This meant the boots of the car had more room for the food boxes, an important consideration as in those days one brought as much food as it was possible to carry.

This did not mean that as campers we only ate on site, or picnicked en route. In fact, almost from the very first, there was a rule among us that wherever possible we would have at least one meal a day in a restaurant or cafe so that we could sample en route the different kinds of foods, and especially the local wine. But, by and large, the real enjoyment was to have our meals prepared by the wives and, weather permitting, to partake in the fresh air. And this was not a question of money saving!

West Munich seemed to have the only campsite off the autobahn, some twenty kilometres from the City. This appealed to us, and it was here that we pitched tents for a couple of days, enabling us to motor in and visit Munich, the capital of Bavaria, without undue haste. They were enjoyable from both weather and tripping points of view, and we appreciated the camaraderie which is always found whenever campers get together in foreign fields (and at home too). It was from here that we set out for Basle.

But something went wrong. Somewhere along the road from Memmingen towards the Lake Konstanz, also known as the Bodensee if you approach from the Arlberg Pass, the two cars became parted. It hadn't happened before, and this time we had the good fortune that each of us was self sufficient. Neither of us was dependent on anything the other had, not like the sharing days of the old Bell Tent when to be parted meant that neither family had a tent. According to the notes 'Van and I, Nigel and Marilyn, agreed there was nothing else one could do but proceed to Basle in the hope that we would pick up the trail again and join forces. This was one time when it would have been useful to have had the Dragon symbols on our cars at least so that one could have asked if another car carrying the Dragon had been seen. We must have been very naive in those days! Basle as a three frontier town was the hub of traffic entering and leaving France, Switzerland and Germany in constant streams; and we had thought we might meet up with the Davies's without an arranged rendezvous!

It seemed futile to search out a campsite in such a busy and complicated set-up so we did the only sensible thing. We knew roughly which route we were going to take before we had lost one another, and that the chances of meeting up again were better if we continued along that route which was to take us to Bern. The answer, therefore, was to look for a hotel for the night and set out the next day. We had no problem in finding one suitable to us on a main thoroughfare into Basle, and it had parking space for the car on the opposite side of the road a little way up alongside the canal. For the rest of the day we went sightseeing, and spent a couple of hours at the Zoo which we all enjoyed. Towards the end of an exhausting day we crossed the bridge into Rheinfelden where we had a snack at the Hotel Krone. But throughout it all we were worried and wondering what had happened to our friends.

The odds on bumping into one another must have been astronomical but the odds very nearly did mature. Arriving back at our hotel I chanced to go over to the car for a final check up and there, on the windscreen, was a short note: "Failed to find you. Have gone on. Keep lookout. Eileen". It had been there from the morning, shortly after we had booked into the hotel. Obviously they had taken the same route behind us, whereas we had thought they were ahead of us.

The following morning it was early up for a start without breakfast, and off on what I considered would be the best route for Bern. Here again whimsy fate took a hand. Less than an hour out of Basle, and as we were approaching a cross roads, 'Van spotted it. Eileen standing at the roadside was waving a teapot, or coffee pot, or something. She had seen us coming. They had pulled up at that spot for a roadside breakfast having, as we had, spent the night at a Gasthof. It was amazing that their break was on a crossroads which could have taken either of us further away from the other. But we were together again, and normal conditions were resumed.

Bern we shall remember for the rest of our days. It was here that the vital change in our camping habits was formulated. After several days of warm sunny weather, and daily excursions into Bern from our campsite some three or four miles out of town, we had to pack up for the journey home. There had been a slight downpour during the night which prevented us from striking tent immediately after an early breakfast. This was one of the drawbacks of tenting. It was not advisable to pack up until the canvass was dry and therefore there were occasions when departure times had to be extended due to the drying out process. On this particular morning I remember a cycle race was due to pass the campsite before 9 am. Nigel had asked to be allowed to wait for this. He wanted to take some photographs. But it would mean upsetting the schedule, and I was not keen on this.

However, whilst we were waiting for the drying, and he had gone to the road hopeful that the race would pass before the tent had been dismantled, we noticed a small caravan a few yards away. It had arrived the previous evening and we had not been particularly interested. But as I was sitting on my campstool patiently waiting for the drying the door opened and the occupants stepped out. Obviously they had breakfasted because the man started jacking up the four corner steadies. It was simple. No frustration. A few twists of the jack handle and they were pulling out of the camp. Five minutes was all it took, and there was I after nearly two hours' wait still not able to pack up the still damp canvass. That settled it. "That's for us next time" I said to 'Van. She agreed a caravan had its advantages but even then loyalties to the bungalow tent prevented her conceding totally.

I called the Davies's attention to what I had observed and received a cautious agreement. But that was enough. Strangely, and for the remainder of the journey home, there appears to have been no other occasion when we were unable to pack up our tents within an hour or so of dismantling but I was determined to give the caravan idea another airing when we returned home. And that was the beginning of an era which was to take us throughout the whole of Europe and into Asia, and during which caravanning developed into what it has become, the biggest of the holiday and leisure industries.

Were I to be asked which of the two phases have been the best I would say that both have a prominent place in my make-up, but moving into a caravan from the tent was a graduation process which we have never regretted. Both, in their own way, have a special attraction and a spirit of comradeship and fellowship which is not to be found in the type of organised packaged holidays available nowadays.

## Chapter 16

## The Vagabond

All the camping equipment had been stored away and still the thoughts of caravanning were only thoughts, and the subject of occasional mention between Van and myself without any real idea of possessing a caravan. Except for that fleeting glimpse of what one had to offer as seen in the camping site in Berne a few weeks earlier we had no conception of what caravanning would be like.

We were greatly attracted to a newspaper advertisement of the "Modern Caravan Exhibition" in Olympia a few weeks ahead and decided this had to be the first step towards deciding whether to adopt this new fangled (at that time) concept of family holidaying. Looking back now to that first of many, many, more such exhibitions gives one an astonishing realisation of the fantastic advances that have been made in an industry which surely must rank as one of the most progressive and farsighted leisure concepts throughout Europe. It must also surely be accepted as the biggest aid to travelling abroad, to and from, but particularly from, Britain to the rest of the Continent.

But back to the decision to visit the exhibition for a closer study of what caravanning offered and what it would require. We kept the visit to ourselves, preferring not to commit ourselves at this stage to our friends. Van and I can recall vividly still that momentous occasion which was to change our lives. The first impression was that there were so few people there that caravanning was anything but a public pursuit; that it was something only certain sections - perhaps the more affluent - of the community indulged in. How wrong I was to be proved! As were entered the hall we caught sight of what appeared to be a small box-like contraption. It turned out to be a ten-foot 'van which Willerby claimed could accommodate a family of four. Neither of us believed it. But again how wrong can one be!

We moved on through the few ranks of caravans of different sizes and seemingly exaggerated claims, examining almost each one with increasing interest and marvelling at the prospect of being able to cover large distances in comfort and without the bugbear of unloading and setting up camp at least once a day at the end of a day's travel. We were virtually "sold" on the idea of transferring allegiance from tenting long before we had completed the tour of the exhibition. But there were some qualms too. For instance we had never towed anything with our cars, and whilst we thought we might manage towing in Britain what about pulling a caravan on the "wrong side" of the roads abroad! Against this, however, was the thought that at least we, as a family that is, would be able to sleep above the ground in proper beds, or bunks for the children, and, even more important, there were the ablutions in modest comfort which tenting could not offer, and reasonable cooking facilities… and above all one need have no worries whether it was raining or not. It would be a case of up with the steadies (or jacks, as they were then called) and off to go!

After a full tour of the exhibition we found ourselves back at the entrance and the little Willerby. Perhaps, as much as anything, the name and the claim that it could accommodate four, because we had three children and the smallest then could be squeezed in, was the deciding factor. The Vagabond became our first caravan, and it doesn't matter how many we have since had (the present one is the tenth) or likely to have in the future not one will take its place in our hearts.

There was one other feature which endeared The Vagabond to us. It had "running" water! This was a water tank over the collapsible sink which had a tap. It held about two gallons of water and was detachable to be refilled. The gravity system was the only one on view as we recall and it proved the major selling point for us. What a contrast to the highly sophisticated present day features which provide almost without exception home from home comforts and modern labour saving and least exertion utilities!

But for most of us older caravanners those were the days! The decision having been made it was then a question of when would we be able to collect. Those were the days of made to purchase and not, as now, mass production awaiting buyers. Having placed our deposit we were then told we could collect our Vagabond "before Christmas", and it meant a journey to Hull. Apart from the actual caravan outings since the acquisition that journey from London to Hull, overnight so that we would be at the factory first thing in the morning, was perhaps the most exciting journey we as a family have made. It is something which present day new caravanners cannot experience since collections from factories are no longer encouraged. Now it is delivery from the dealers or the show rooms.

Our reception at the factory gates was warm and gratifying. It was personal service at it's best and the couple of hours during which we were shown how to hook-up, how to distribute weight when loading, how to effect minor repairs and adjustments could be a lesson to modern day practices. We left without any idea that it was our money the Company was after! There was a lot more caring in those days. It was, after all, an industry in the process of growing up. And as we left, having been virtually seen off with hand waves and cheers, we all felt that now we belonged. We were caravanners in our own right! An hour or so later we pulled into a lay-by where we had our first meal prepared in a caravan. It was sumptuous... and I was proud that I had been able to master the intricacies of turning on the gas bottle on the plain unencumbered tow bar which provided Myfanwy with the heat to boil a kettle. No more tea or coffee from the vacuum flask. Some five or six hours later we arrived back in Ruislip where we lived, a tired but happy family having covered the first two hundred miles towing which set us off on countless thousands of miles during the following thirty years. What enjoyment, what experiences, what memories!

# Chapter 17

# The Bambino: We Join the Rallie

Remembering how our friends had put one over on us when we were procuring our bungalow tents (the time they casually invited us to tea on a Saturday afternoon only to display their new tent which they had purchased "secretly") Myfanwy and I decided to do the same with our new purchase. Up until then the Davies's had no idea we had bought a 'van. The quid pro quo having been achieved there was nothing more to be done but wait to see what our friends would come up with. And they did in a week. Our expected summons arrived and we found they had purchased a Sprite Alpine, slightly larger than the Vagabond.

We had begun our new venture, something which has remained with Myfanwy and I up to this day, and, we hoped for many years to come. It was not without some perturbation on Len's and my part as I recollect. Although I had driven all the way from Hull and had found it not too demanding, nonetheless pulling a ton weight behind what had yet to be proved to be sufficiently powerful vehicles, was bit worrying. And neither of us, nor our spouses, had given any thought to the complexities of reversing should anything go wrong in the towing. And even more worrying was towing abroad. We had managed our sorties on the continent, and driving on the wrong side of the road, but this would be something different. But, at least, and something to be thankful for, we did not have to undergo any driving tests with these caravans!

The possession of these first caravans immediately added zest and expectations for the forthcoming holiday. It had to be abroad. That was the purpose of buying the caravans. We would be able to tackle our routes and overnight, or longer, stops without the cares of weather. The sight of the caravanners in that Berne camping site six months ago just lifting the steadies and off to go had fired me with a new enthusiasm which had been transferred to Len. All that would be required now was practice in towing. And, of course, deciding where we would head for during the summer holiday.

Practising towing became a regular weekend fixture. It was mainly down the byways, and reversing improved but, it must be confessed, was never really mastered in those first months. More than once it had been necessary to unhitched the caravan and manhandle it when we had to turn around and return on narrow country roads. Where we were fortunate, I suppose, was that in those early days one saw very few caravans on the roads. Later, however, and especially when the Caravan Club centres organised their country-wide weekend rallies, these became the centre-piece of our weekly social activities. Such rallies, then in a much more intimate and informal atmosphere than nowadays, did more than anything to create and sustain the special camaraderie which brought like minded people in all walks of life together, and established the base for the most progressive post-war industry in Britain.

Our first trip abroad with the caravans as I recall caused us less hassle in the route preparations than any of the previous exploits. Which is where we made the first mistakes. Without the towed weight it had been possible to overcome the most difficult of terrains and climbs. We were to discover, however, that caravan holiday preparation on the Continent required even more detailed planning. We had set our sights on a trip through France, then into Switzerland and Italy, a very ambitious trip for first time caravanners. Too ambitious as it proved to be.

Without, at that time, any of the sophisticated routing by the motoring associations and the Caravan Club, and warnings about passes (except what the motoring maps showed) we encountered our first setback between Lausanne and Geneva. Neither of us - or at least one of us, which meant the other could not proceed - was able to negotiate a particularly steep climb. It meant a change of plans. Instead of proceeding to Geneva we rerouted to Berne. But it taught us that in future we would have to pay regard to terrain. Otherwise the holiday went off superbly well. We returned full of confidence. Not even the episode at Boulogne had caused us more than a passing hiatus. What happened there was that on arriving on the ferry around mid-night on the outward journey we were all so tired that we decided to rest on the quayside. No one questioned this and in no time we were all fast asleep. Came the dawn, and we were aware something was happening outside. The noise came from the hustle and bustle of the fish market! We had only parked our caravans slap in the middle of what was the area reserved for fish stalls, whilst a few yards away the fishing boats were unloading their catches! Ignoring our presence the diligent fishmongers had set about erecting their stalls and had we not been awakened then we would have found ourselves fenced in and having to stay there until the market finished.

It was strange perhaps that Berne should be one of the places visited on our first trip as caravanners since less than nine months earlier it had been here than we conceived the possibility of becoming such. And equally ironic that this was where I was "caught" by what at that time was a current spate of confidence tricksters. A very plausible individual offered to sell a 15ct gold Parker pen for a quarter of the market price. I fell for it and only on my return home did I find it was worthless rubbish which wouldn't even hold the ink. Len was also offered a "gold watch" on similar terms, but turned it down. Later I discovered this confidence trick was being practised throughout the Continent, supposedly by ex-service prisoners of war, and they undoubtedly reaped a great harvest from unsuspecting dupes like myself. Well, there's always a first time!

Nineteen sixty one saw the Vagabond and Alpine, and we having proved ourselves as fairly competent towers, taken on an even more ambitious tour. The winter and spring months following the 1960 baptism having been spent planning a visit through Germany, along routes with which we were fairly conversant by now, and across the Dolomites (passes and climbs having been properly appraised) into Italy, we all felt that this would be the holiday to upstage all holidays. And so it turned out. Having safely negotiated all obstacles, and using the tunnels wherever possible, we fond ourselves in Udine, a part of Italy we had never been to before. The spirit of adventure was coursing through all our veins, and the fine and sunny weather urged us on until we reached the outskirts of Trieste, the Free Zone, and at that time the centre piece of many thrilling stories of international intrigue and espionage. It was the neutral zone through which one travelled to

Yugoslavia, a country which had suddenly become a magnet to us. The snag was we had no visas for Yugoslavia, but the attraction was becoming irresistible.

It was then that we came across a delightful seaside place called Sustiana. Its entire ambience exuded an old world charm the like of which we had not encountered anywhere through our now much travelled visits to the Continent. We were lucky enough to find a small camp site on the side of the deep water port, with towering rocks shadowing the site and in the lee of which we were extremely lucky enough one night to hear a concert given by the world famous Vienna Boys choir. It was a most moving experience, especially since it took place in the light of candles supplemented by a bright moonlight over the Adriatic. Can one ever forget such happenings as these, and to such backgrounds can we ever question the worthwhile pursuit of our caravanning holidays?

A few days afterwards, after some careful probing in the cafes and inns which abound in Trieste, we were assured that there would be no problems if we drove over an unmanned part of the frontier with Yugoslavia into Kope, another small fishing village a few miles away. And we were further told that the restaurant on the beach was the place to get the best food. At that time when the political life of Yugoslavia was extremely turbulent it seemed a big challenge to risk entry without a visa, but go we did. And it was an unforgettable experience. We found the restaurant on the beach, and although no one spoke English we managed. We were hailed with gusto and after a complimentary glass of wine and minerals for the children we were set down at a table under a massive vine, looking on to a white sand beach with a cooling soft breeze which made the entire situation idyllic. There were course after course, and the seafood was sumptuous, among it one of the biggest fishes we had ever seen, laid out on a massive tray. The wines were superb, and Len and I enjoyed our pipes in regal ostentation. We had no care what it would cost. And we had no Yugoslav currency anyway; but after paying in Italian Lire we counted the cost at no more than the equivalent of less than £3.00 for the seven of us!

The few days we remained in Sustiana were among the most enjoyable of any we have ever spent since, and it was not many years later that we returned... but only to find that commercialism had reared its ugly head and the Sustiana we first saw is no more.

And it was then that we discovered another treasure in camping sites along the Italian Adriatic, the German administered N.S.U. holiday camp reserved for employees of the giant motor company but which we were allowed a one night stay as possibly the first British caravanners to the site. Len, however, felt it was too regimented... we had to surrender our passports and the camp was fenced, "Like a POW camp" was his verdict. For us, however, it became almost an annual attraction in the years to come.

There was only one other incident, on the way back, that really calls to mind the journey home. The little Vagabond was behaving excellently. It was all that we had wanted of it, but regrettably it was to be its last trip with us. I was to blame, but it could not have been avoided. We were travelling fast, but not excessively so, down the main highway to Udine when I noticed a railway crossing less than fifty yards away and suddenly the red light came on. I judged that with the caravan behind me I might not be able to stop in time so I put down my foot and the car leapt like a wild thing towards and over the slight bank in the road across which the railway lines were laid. For about ten yards we literally flew over the rails with the lightweight Vagabond in the air. It came to ground with a screech for its brakes had been activated somehow. For a few seconds I was afraid there would be a knife-jack. Car and van survived, but the strain had been too great for the little Vagabond. I noticed the difference in performance straight away and although it we got back safely we felt we could no longer keep it. A few months later it had gone, and in its place was The Bambino. There is much to be said about this great little caravan which began its days in the factory in Cardiff, but which having served us well for a couple of seasons eventually found a new home in New Zealand.

For that period in the early sixties The Bambino was perhaps the most self contained and idyllic caravan in its price range. It's towing capacity was superb, its interior design in the incoming lightwood veneer gave it a much more spacious appearance but, above all, and so far as we were concerned, it's biggest selling point as a 12 foot four berth tourer was the novel pull-down bed. This was a full double bed complete with mattress which "disappeared" into the offside of the caravan into what seemed to be a recess but which, when the bed was tucked away, gave the appearance of a sideboard. The duplicity was completed when one placed a few light ornaments or a vase of flowers on the shelf which made up the "recess". The two bunk beds as extras were erected across the rear part of the 'van. Myfanwy and I have often thought that this idea could have been further implemented by manufacturers because apart from the convenience of having a ready made bed tucked out of sight it allowed the occupants more space during the day and less hassle at bed time.

With our newest acquisition the holiday ahead seemed set fair, and again Italy was to be the choice. But the decision was taken to break in the new 'van by taking advantage of the Caravan Club weekend centre rallies as new members of the club. These were among the most delightful, and instructive, periods of early caravanning but with the passage of years, and the inevitable changes which the years imposed, I regret we bowed out, unable to take the new order of things.

# Chapter 18

# And the Rats Came Too!

For ten glorious days of sunshine and warm blue seas when we spent more time in the water than out of it, or so it seemed, we lounged our days away in what, undoubtedly at that time, was the finest of the Venice-Jesolo camping sites. The boys however had to return three days before the rest of us and we saw them off with much waving and tears from Myfanwy and Marilyn, and under stern orders to use care on their return journey. It was a great relief to us all to learn a few days later by telephone in Switzerland that the journey had been uneventful.

It was 4.30 pm on Saturday 31st August when two glistening outfits nosed out of N.S.U. (after a refreshing last dip) and set off for home. Why a Saturday? We had been advised by other campers that this would allow us a better journey on the first leg since no heavy vehicles were permitted on the main routes on Sundays. This is a rule we have observed ever since. The trip meter registered 1,187 miles. After an overnight stay in the forecourt of a garage (permission was readily granted) we set our sights for Milan. Then came the rains again. It deluged all the way to the Italian-Swiss border at Chiasso having travelled 238 miles.

The plan was to reach Lake Zug by early evening, and possibly a climb over the Gothard. But wiser counsels prevailed and instead we took the train through the tunnel from Airolo at 4.50 pm, mileage was 1,504. Emerging from the tunnel was like entering another world. It's a constant source of amazement how these Alpine ranges change the weather patterns, but in this occasion we entrained in heavy rain and emerged into brilliant sunshine and warmth. Taking the Zurich route the diary recalls: "Taking the route to Zurich we arrived safely at Brunnen, a small but well organised site on the shore of Lake Zug. In the evening we went to the local hotel where the English speaking proprietor put through a call to home. We were delighted to hear the voices of both David and Nigel. It was as if they were in the same room. They told us they had enjoyed the journey back to Ruislip and the 26 Swiss Francs we were charged for the call was worth every penny. "Celebrated with a lovely dinner at the hotel - soup, chicken, chips, cauliflower, coffee, and wine of the country. Went to bed happy. It rained heavily overnight... but who cares!"

Monday 2nd September: "Woke to lovely sunshine glistening on the water. Shopped in Brunnen before starting our journey. Glan bought lovely walking stick... and the coffee and cream cakes were beautiful. Mileage 1,539 and heading for Zurich through glorious countryside."

It was 4.30 pm when we arrived at Zurich and booked into Camping Seebrucht. We took the bus ride to the town which we found to be very exclusive and very expensive. The following morning in excellent weather we set off for Rheinfelden on the Swiss-German border and during the drive experienced one nerve wracking moment. The Davies's had gone ahead and I took the wrong turning which led us steadily up a mountain road which gradually turned into a track. There was no room to turn and no alternative but to reverse some couple of hundred yards to the roadway. It was all out - but the driver - and gradually the outfit was eased back nervously because of the terrifying drop on the nearside. I must have aged twenty years in as many minutes, but finally we made our way back and eventually caught up with the others about 30 kilometres from Rheinfelden.

This was such an occurrence we desperately had tried to avoid. Losing one another with a whole country as our backyard could mean a spoiled holiday and a solo journey. It had happened once before when we were camping, and strangely enough it was then in the Basle area. That time we had put up at a hotel and spent some time in Rheinfelden before fortuitously on the following day meeting one another again. This time we decided to lunch at Rheinfelden, at the same Hotel Krone, which recalled memories of our earlier escapade.

"Stopped at 4.50 pm at restplatz Freiburg and decided to look for camping site along the autobahn" the diary states. "Now this is the part that Glan wrote: 'Myfanwy took over for the first time on this journey. Did good time -50/58mph! Speed hog! Drove for 80 miles without break.'"

"Glan took over at 6.30 pm near Rattstadt - 35/40 mph. Hedgehog!"

Made Karlsrhue and stayed overnight at our old camping site. Mileage 1,771.

"Wednesday 4th September: A lovely morning. Hoping to make Essen today. Our roadside lunch interrupted by police who said we should not have stopped there, but they let us stay until lunch over. At 3 pm we are on our way again, mileage 1,914, but Len has changed our minds about Essen and now we are on our way to Duisburg. Raining again and we are all miserable and fed up after long journey and no site. Arrived at Mulheim Ruhr. Were permitted to stay overnight in Hotel Ruhr Stresan on promising to take dinner there. (This type of overnight stay has since been a feature of our holiday treks). Dinner was usual filling German meal and quite good but Eileen couldn't eat hers and went to Caravan for a sleep. The journey has been too trying perhaps."

It was 12.30 pm and 2,093 miles on the clock when eventually we started our next leg to Rotterdam, and this was a journey I shall always remember for en route we were passing Arnhem. We were especially anxious to visit the war cemetery of the British Airborne Division at Oosterbek. It brought back acutely memories of a day in September 1944 in a field at Nijmegen when the skies overhead were filled with planes and gliders, preparatory to the big drop on Arnhem, and we in an R.A.F. unit had no idea what was happening. We found the war graves in the beautifully kept cemetery, read the register and signed it, walked along the lines of the fallen and, the diary states, "The very tranquillity, beauty and peace of the place brought tears to my eyes, and a silent prayer that our boys would not see such a war".

We went on to Amsterdam which we reached at 6.55 pm and found a site. Despite another and persistent rainfall we went out for dinner. On our return we found the caravans surrounded by water. During the night we were awakened by great activity outside... and were we thankful that we were caravanning and not camping! Several poor campers were bailing water from their tents and some were frightened because of an invasion of rats which presumably had been driven from their holes by flood waters. It was the most disturbed night of our holiday and we decided never again to visit that site.

For some reason which escapes me now the diary recalls that there arose some friction between Len and I on our arrival at Amsterdam, but after the rats episode it was mentioned that Myfanwy and I would be celebrating our Silver Wedding anniversary in a few days. Matters were soon resolved between Len and I (there had never been any strain before and has not been since either) and we thought this was the occasion for presents. Myfanwy bought me a pipe and pouch, I bought her a silver ring and Eileen gave us a pair of silver picture frames with mine and Len's pictures in it. A nice touch of diplomacy! We enjoyed a cup of tea together and set off for Rotterdam via Den Hague. There were 2,234 miles on the clock when we arrived at Rotterdam at 7.15 pm and since this was to be our last holiday evening we decided to celebrate. It was dinner and cabaret at the Rutetck Restaurant and a wholesome night's sleep. The last lap to Ostende, some 130 miles away, was uneventful except that by arrangement we and the Davies's had parted near Antwerp because they wanted to divert and visit their old friends, the Clemputts, in Sas van Ghent. It was 7.05 pm when we arrived at Ostende and the boat was due to sail at 8.45 pm. But by sailing time no sign of the Davies's. The diary takes up the story again: "I can see Glan waving frantically and speaking to the Captain. Len and Eileen and Karin have just appeared. They are last on. They had to reverse on, much to the amusement of the passengers."

The rest is plain sailing. After a perfect crossing and home by 4.45 am Sunday, we calculated the round trip had been 2,478 miles, and the general verdict was that the 1963 holiday had contributed to our pleasures and experiences in a way that a holiday in any other form could not have done.

The "house" proud Myfanwy outside her second home at Camping Union Lido (formerly N.S.U.), Jesolo, Italy.

1954 and the beloved bell tent!
Preparing to go through the Airolo tunnel by train.

## Chapter 19

## Three Dragons Set Out

Before the spring of 1964 had given way to early summer the outline of the holiday for this year had been well set. And it was going to be a holiday with a difference because we had almost persuaded another friend and Centre member to join us. The one thought which was slowing down preparations was whether with three outfits, the third of which had not been abroad before, it might be too difficult to keep together; would the responsibility for whoever was to be the leader to keep the "train" together be too onerous and therefore mar the holiday for one and all.

It was finally agreed that we proceed with the idea. Our friends, Vernon and Jose, and their two daughters, were experienced caravanners and proved very keen to have a go. Weekends became the period for planning and preparation, and Vernon proved invaluable. Not only was he an engineer but he was also an expert with gasses, and any problems with the calor and propane gas equipment would have special attention... not that we had up to now experienced any such problems.

The contingent having been agreed, the next thing was where were to go. Vernon and Jose had heard a great deal about our earlier trips and having seen our snaps of the holidays their appetites had been thoroughly roused. It was not to be Italy again. This time we would attempt the French Mediterranean coast, using quite different routes. And the first big change was to be the cross-channel ferry.

We had heard about the Zeebrugge crossing and that it offered a part-cruise beginning to the holiday - that is the crossing itself was a daytime one of about five and a half hours compared with the Dover-Calais and Dover-Ostende crossings of an hour and a half. We had been further advised, according to the diary, that the Belgian port also offered an excellent setting off-point for Brussels and the south of France, and an alternative easy route into Holland should we be so minded. It was therefore decided that the holiday would start on Friday 14th August and preparations began in earnest.

Contingency plans were drawn up in the event of one member of the party losing touch. It was thought the rule should be that before leaving an overnight stay there would be full consultation among the three drivers as to the destination for the day and the route to be taken. In the event of anyone losing touch there would be an end of day rendezvous. It was all a question of planning. Of course, what we could not safeguard against were any breakdowns and the inability of contacting the others should this happen. But we considered the safeguards sufficient in so far as they went, as it so proved.

Friday 14th August dawned bright and promising. We, that is the Davies's and ourselves, had agreed to meet Vernon, Jose and family at the Dover terminal, so we made a leisurely trip from Uxbridge. At Orpington we stopped off for lunch at The Black Prince where we spent an enjoyable couple of hours in the company of Peter Glaze, then a well known television figure and children's celebrity. These one-off and unexpected encounters from time to time always helped to make a holiday. By 4.55 pm we had reached Dover, a little bit disappointed because we had not been able to make the much vaunted daylight crossing. The cross channel expeditions in those days were so different, and less reliable. However, resigned to a six hours wait we spent the time indulging in the customary visit into Dover for our Dover Sole and chips, and were joined by Vernon and Jose in the middle of our meal, they having found a note I had left on the car explaining where we would be.

It was 4.00 am when we docked and by 5.00 am we had arrived in Sluis, the small frontier town, where we found a convenient car park in which to rest for a few hours. Our first visit to Holland and a two hours shopping expedition was full of surprises. Then it was off to Brussels... and to the first spot of bother. We were in the lead and en-route for Marche and Luxembourg when the front brake of the car seized up with smoke belching from the underside. A short roadside stop was sufficient to correct the trouble but a few miles further and Len's shock absorber packed up. Fortunately we were close to Camping Morene where repairs were effected and the "convoy" relaxed for a 10 hours sleep. There were 280 miles on the clock, and we wondered whether, on only our second day, this was to be a bad augury.

The stay cost us 45 Belgian francs apiece and in another 65 miles we had reached Luxembourg. A cryptic entry in the diary: "Lost Len. Hope he catches up. Vernon OK." Obviously we were in one piece again pretty soon because Myfanwy records "Stayed on Belgium douanne between 11.30 am and 12.45 pm for lunch of soup, chicken, chips, tomatoes and Welsh cakes. Now off to Thionville and journey through France making for Basle".

By 7.30 pm the Rossers had reached Basle with 570 miles registered, but no sign of the other two! It appeared they had gone into Camping Belmonte on the outskirts of the city but finding we had not booked in they pressed on through the city. A few miles out on the road to Lucerne we had stopped for petrol and this is where they caught up with us. Reunited again - and it seemed our arrangements were working out alright - we found another camping site within a few miles and a well deserved night's rest.

Monday 17th August: "Another lovely day. We hope to do the Gothard Pass today, but first to Lucerne", it is recorded. But bad luck struck again. The spring on Len's caravan splayed and not even Vernon's expertise could put matters right. It became a limping journey to Altdorf with all thoughts of doing the Gothard now banished. At Altdorf by late afternoon we found this to be a charming Tyrolean town in the William Tell country, but equally important was Mr. R Geser's Carrosserie, for he sympathised with us and agreed to make the repair straightaway. Things were looking up again! It was obvious now that it would have to be another rail journey through the Gothard Tunnel and not over the top, but at least the morrow would have us in Italy, and the trip down to the Mediterranean. We did not know at this stage that we were facing another major change in our planning! After a wonderful dinner, typical of the district which meant pork schnitzel and chips following a cream soup, and a fascinating tour around the town which oozed William Tell from every pore, including his commanding statue, we enjoyed a good night's sleep which put us ready for the next day's travel.

Tuesday 18th August: "Woke at 6.15 am to the sound of a train and cow bells... What wonderful scenery with mist and snow over the mountains" the diary reveals. With the trip meter at 660 miles we began the journey to the rail terminal at Goshenen which was reached at 9 am with 20 minutes to wait for the flat bottom carriages which carried us through the tunnel to Airiolo. "Clouds are low and it is raining, the first rain we have had. Arrived Airiolo 9.30 am on way to Bellinzona and still blinding rain" the diary states. At this stage came the change in plans. Vernon and Jo and the children (as did the rest of us) had been expecting the proverbial Italian sun but as we approached the frontier at Chiasso it was still pouring. Now we had 753 miles on the clock, and local predictions of electrical storms ahead. The way ahead was to Genoa where we would take a "right hand turn" for the French coast. Instead we decided to make a "left hand turn" when we reached Genoa and take the Italian Riviera. So much for months of planning! But that, surely, is the beauty of caravanning. The option to change one's mind at any point and not be tied down to any rigid plan make's this type of holiday almost unique and especially attractive.

We had heard about a place called Marina di Massa on the Italian Riviera where there was supposedly lashings of room for caravanning and camping on sandy beaches. It seemed to be the answer to our search for sunny skies and warm blue waters. So the decision was made. Left turn at Genoa to La Spezia and beyond.

It was eight o'clock when we reached Genoa having come through one of the worst electrical storms ever experienced and with 892 miles showing. But there was much worse to come! "Went through Genoa... don't like the town, too big" the diary reminds us... Then, after a lapse, the story is taken up again... "We have had a ghastly experience", Myfanwy writes. "Looking for a camping site... it was very stormy and the clouds were black and forbidding... we turned at a camping sign to go up a rising road, but it led up a mountain... it was nearly dark when we started climbing, Vernon in the rear... it was nerve wracking with dozens of hairpin bends and sheer drops... when we reached the top there was nothing there... we couldn't go any further, and didn't know how to get back".

Whilst we were on top where there was no more than a 20 yards plateau which did not allow room for more than one caravan to be unhitched and turned, the way back was blocked by the other two caravans perched precariously on the mountain track of no more than ten or twelve feet wide. To make matters worse it was a stygian blackness and only the car headlights gave us any help to solve our problem. We managed to unhitch and manhandle our 'van to allow Len to move on to the plateau and do likewise. Vernon was magnificent in such a situation. He took over and marshalled the whole procedure; but there was no way we could get his outfit to the top. Finally, with everyone out helping, he decided to reverse his outfit all the way back, yard at a time, steering largely by directions from front and rear and helped by the headlights of the two cars at the top and always mindful of the drops on one side or other.

It must have been two to three hundreds yards to the widening of the road, and there is no record of how long it took, but to me this was the most magnificent piece of reversing I have ever witnessed and it fully deserved the cheers we all gave when the manoeuvre was completed. We were all exhausted and glad to get away. A couple of miles along the road to La Spezia we found a petrol station and were allowed to park for the night.

By lunchtime the next day we had found the camp site about which we had heard such glowing reports. It turned out to be one of our biggest disappointments ever. Sure, there was sand and dunes and more sand, but it was higgledy-piggledy, and with hardly a square metre of flat ground. There were tents alongside the dunes, on the dunes and even under the dunes. Had we been able to get a caravan on the site, I doubt whether we would have been able to get in and out without treading on bodies. It was a shambles. After our previous night's experience it was almost enough to call it a day and turnabout. But, as I have already said, one of the attractions of caravanning is the ability to change the programme to suit any occasion, and this was one such occasion. After a brief lunch the maps were out and the answer staring us in the face was: VENICE (N.S.U.).

By using the autostrada we estimated arrival at N.S.U. by late afternoon the following day. A quick fillip with the reading at 1,023 miles and then, hopefully, the last stage of our outward journey, saw everyone in better spirits. That evening was one of the more pleasant occasions for we had reached the outskirts of Padova and on enquiring at a peach farm whether there was a camping site nearby were invited by the Patron to stay on the farm. It was a massive stretch with, as far as we could see, peach and other fruit trees fully laden. The air was sweet with the smell of peaches, and all around us as we put the jacks down on concrete which had been the floors of wartime Nissan huts were the fruit pickers. The scene resembled the Kent hop-picking, and it was obvious that there were families with many children who did this work at their harvest time. They were fascinated with our caravans as were we with them. They did not intrude on us but watched from a distance and smiled as we went about our own chores. Clearly they had not seen anything like this before.

As night closed in after we had eaten we brought out our chairs and sat chatting and called on the still inquisitive observers to come in and see the caravans. Some did this, and brought with them a few peaches for which we were very grateful. It was like something out of an old wild west show with the covered wagons pulled up in a semi-circle for the night. I haven't enjoyed anything better ever; and this surely is another example of the difference and joys of caravanning. Everything was so serene and the night passed in deep sleep.

Come the dawn and the pickers were up long before us and at their work. We, and especially the children, were invited to hop on the horse drawn carts down the lines of trees from which the fruit - not quite ripe - was being picked, and each time they came across the ripen fruit they tossed them into a separate crate. By the time we were returning to the Patron's packing station the crates of ripe peaches were nearly full. With the consent of the Patron these kind people insisted that each of us accepted several trays of peaches... as the diary states "They stocked us up with peaches and pears, enough to last us for weeks. In exchange we gave them sweets and biscuits."

The last stretch of the journey was uneventful. I think we had had enough incidents on the way to last us, and we rolled into N.S.U. at midday, having travelled 1,246 miles in seven days.

After ten glorious days of sunning and bathing and the odd evening out with dinners at Fernando's, then a tin roofed diner but which developed over the years into a salubrious and popular restaurant with each table having the personal attention of my friend Fernando, Saturday, August 29th, saw the three caravans rolling out en route for home. Mileage was 1,298. We had decided the return should be via the Dolomites, a new route for us, and the scenery was superb, as was the weather. On our way to Cortina we were saddened at the sight of the

Italian village and district where 2,000 people had been killed only the previous February when a dam had burst and flooded the area.

Two days later, having safely traversed the Dolomites we pulled into Innsbruck where Vernon and Jose decided to leave the convoy because they wished to visit Munich. We and the Davies's went on to the Black Forest and spent several happy days before setting off for Aachen where we were due to meet up with Vernon and Jose. Our arrivals coincided within hours (mileage 2,172) when we heard they had suffered a smashed windscreen on the autobahn with almost serious consequence. After an overnight stay we reached Ostende (for we had been able to change our return crossing) in time for a late afternoon boat. Safely home early morning, tired but content, the Three Dragons had covered 2,450 miles in what had turned out to be a most enjoyable holiday of many gratifying experiences. It was then, I think, that Myfanwy and I decided that from now on, and God willing, hotel or packaged holidays were no more for us.

# Chapter 20

# Our First International

During the Centre's social events of the winter and early spring we had heard a great deal about the International Rallies which were then gaining in popularity. These were a gathering of the Clans as it were among caravanners in most of the European countries and accounts of the most recent, at Ruhpolding near the Austrian-Germany border, interested us greatly. When, therefore, we made enquiries as to the next such rally we discovered one was to be held at the invitation of the Dutch organisation in the coming August. That settled our holiday plans for 1965.

The event was to be at a small coastal town of Wassenaar near to Scheveningen. This was new territory for us but seemed fairly easily accessible. So it was out for Italy and curtailed travelling for this year - or so we thought. Again it was just the two caravans, the Rossers and the Davies's.

On Friday, 30th July, we set out for Dover and the crossing again to Ostende, and the diary gives an interesting recollection after so many years of the pattern we followed in those days. "Arrived Ostende 9.30 pm, parked 'vans in car park and went in search of a meal in the rain. I (Myfanwy) had mussels in wine with chips, Glan and Len sole and chips, Eileen shrimps on lettuce. The two girls had chips with Mayonnaise. Retired at 11 o'clock."

By 6.00 am Saturday we were on our way and it is recorded that we crossed into Holland at precisely eight o'clock. To everyone's surprise the frontier was unmanned and the town of Sluis seemed still to be undisturbed. But there was a large empty car park in which we stayed for breakfast (bacon and eggs and fried bread cooked in the 'van) and afterwards did some shopping. Flushing (or Vlessingen) was to be our next halt for lunch but this required a small ferry crossing at Breskens. "A bit rough... it rocked the 'vans like a cradle'" it was observed.

"Here Goes!"... is the next cryptic entry. It referred to a small Dutch town on our way to Bergen op Zoom. What delightful names, and what fun and pleasure we had trying to pronounce them. At Bergen op Zoom we found a lovely camping site and settled down quickly. Our spirits were high because the weather had improved and it promised a long sunny period. We dressed up for dinner. Even in these early days we had decided that when travelling we would try during each overnight halt to have at least one meal out. After scouring the town we decided on a very attractive and clean looking hotel for dinner. Strangely enough it was named "De Draak" which we later were told meant The Dragon. "A fabulous meal of crab cocktail, pate, veal schnitzel and the ever present chips, followed by fresh strawberries and cream, ices and coffee" it is written. So, you see, we lived well on these early safaris as I have come to regard them.

Sunday morning, 1st August: "We plan today to do the whole journey to Wassenaar so we can enter the rally a day early" the diary states. Mileage on leaving Bergen op Zoom was 200. Our fine weather hopes appeared to have been dashed, however, because the rain came down so heavily we had to pull up at a tiny village. I do not know why but it seemed to us that the weather in this part of Holland is so changeable one cannot be certain from one hour to the next; but it is recorded that by 2.30 pm we reached Wassener. What greeted us was a shambles of mainly tents and a few caravans dotted around a field. It was not only a disappointment, but also a shock and according to the diary "We were all of the same mind - to pack up and go." What we had not realised, however, was that we had arrived three days too soon. The rally was not due to open until the Tuesday, and even as we were cogitating our next move campers were packing up and away.

True to typical Dutch organisation and method by the next day all the lines had been pegged out by the marshals and we were allowed to stay on what was to be the British line. The Dutch are a warm hearted and kindly people and I still believe that only in this method of touring a country and meeting the people on their own doorsteps, as it were, can one really appreciate the character of the people. We learned more about the Hollanders during these couple of weeks than ever before. It was at this particular rally that we were befriended by the Koops, a lovely family from Amsterdam, and that friendship endured until fairly recently when time took its toll.

The diary takes over again: "Monday, 2nd August. The sun is shining this morning and we intend exploring. Even now the camp is getting to look more like a rally with the official opening tomorrow. I imagine the bulk of the caravans will have arrived by tonight. Our little section is all in order and looks quite nice. There are five or six British 'vans in our two rows. A lovely touch this morning was a floral float sponsored by the Shell Company in the shape of a sabot with blue and yellow colours and five pretty Dutch girls in national dress going from 'van to 'van wishing everyone a good rally and a happy time. They presented the women each with a bunch of Freesias and the men with dusters and ball point pens".

Hospitality is a very important feature of these functions and inviting your hosts into your van for, in the English and Welsh way, a cup of tea and cake, is a recognised part of the proceedings. But we also like to be provided with the tipple of the country and with this in mind we stocked up on the eve of the opening with some spirits, wines and (in those days very important, too) cigars. Before retiring for the night Myfanwy and Eileen had prepared our awnings for the next day's encounters, and very nice they looked too. But, off we go again! "It's started to rain" I am reminded, "but that didn't prevent us going down to the Sheep Shed for dinner". For those who might have attended this rally they may recall that "sheep shed". It was a converted barn which the organisers had laid out as a dining place. Among the trees and beautifully decorated, it was festooned with old lamps and antlers, cart wheels and stuffed birds.

"The food was excellent and reasonably cheap with the choice of veal schnitzel, chicken and beefsteak. The chips here are the best I have ever tasted during all our travels" Myfanwy records. The wine was a Schwartz Katz (Black Cat). One thing in particular which enthralled all the British contingent at the opening was the Festival of Bells and the carillon accompanied by a wonderfully painted "Fair Organ". And it is also recorded that there were many visitors to our awnings who sampled

English tea and Welsh cakes with approval. Among the customary exchange of presents on these occasions the ladies received boxes of Dutch chocolates and the Len and I were handed a sabot each which one of our visitors gallantly took off on the spot. These are still much cherished reminders of the long ago.

It was during the rally that we were told some of our North London Centre had arranged a "post rally meet" at Ingolstadt near Munich. So early on August 7th we left Wassenaar and a jolly four days' rallying en route for another round of holiday spirits. The impression at that time as recorded is "This rallying is not at all bad; great fun and comradeship". With the mileage at 389 and our designated rendezvous with the four or five 'vans taking part in the post-rally being Ingolstadt we set off for Frankfurt, but within an hour we and the Davies's got separated. I had been leading and stopped several times along the autobahn, but no sign of our friends. We reached Wurzburg alone and stayed the night, having done a further 320 miles.

Sunday morning was sunny and hot as we started off for Ingolstadt and we decided to cut across country rather than take the new autobahn. Just as well we did because as we were approaching Ansbach who should turn up ahead of us but the Davies's . They had been delayed by a procession of festival floats through this country town, it being a beer and brandy Fest in that week, and fortuitously we were reunited. But not for long! They apparently turned into the procession and went on to the festival marquee and had a whale of a time whereas we, unaware of this, pressed on towards our destination which we had hoped to make by late afternoon. For the second time in consecutive days we became separated. But the rule we had adopted worked out alright because shortly after tea and at the designated camp site in Ingolstadt we were joined.

What a sequel to Wassenaar this turned out to be. Ingolstadt is a centre of Bavarian brewing and it did not take long for the local brewery to extend an "official invitation" to visit their premises. Furthermore the whole Stadt joined in and within a day we had become virtually British ambassadors to the area. A conducted tour of the lager brewing was the first highlight of our stay; and it wasn't only the smell of the hops which raised the spirits and mussed the heads. For British palates the frequent quaffing from Steinjugs of that potent product was perhaps too much, and the visit was a staggering success! The only sobering effect was on our return to the camp. We saw the Barradell's arrive. Cedric was the centre secretary and a close friend. Unknown to him, his wife Cynthia and their two daughters, Carol and Collette, their water container which they carried in their 'van (an aqua roll of about 15 gallons) had leaked and when they opened the door the water gushed out like a river. It was all hands to the pumps to dry out soaked carpets. But we managed.

A coach tour to Munich on the following day saw our first such visit to the City where among the more interesting sights we saw the famous clock in the square and were fascinated at the sight of traditional figures emerging from the tower when the clock struck representing various sections of the populace. It was in commemoration of the Great Plague. "Had an awful lunch" we are reminded. So much for Munich!

The real highlight of our stay in Ingolstadt was without doubt what turned out to be an official reception and dinner in the Rathaus, graced by the Burgermeister and town officials. Just one word to describe it; magnificent! It is recorded: "The Burgermeister was a jolly and affable man. Eileen and I sat beside him. Before the evening was out we were singing English and Welsh songs for him. Eileen was 'well away'. I kissed the Burgermeister after dancing with him a Blue Danube waltz and he gave me the Ingolstadt pennant which he signed, also to Eileen. Cedric and Cynthia joined us. We had a merry do and got back to camp very gay and happy". The diary makes no reference to myself or Len, but I assume we also had had a good and merry time. It was almost a sad departure when the rally came to an end, but not before most of us had made a memorable trip down the Danube passing through a magnificent gorge, and on disembarking being taken into an old monastery restaurant for a snack of raspberry gateau and fresh cream.

Yet another incident is recalled. On our way home we stopped at the medieval walled town of Rottenburg. During a brief shopping expedition we were served at a shop by an assistant who was obviously American and in conversation it transpired she was the sister of actor Clark Gable. I explained to her that I had met her brother when in 1942 he had flown into Bodney in Norfolk as an American Air Force officer on a PR exercise and I was then attached with an R.A.F. unit on secondment to the American Army Air Force. We spent quite a while chatting, and Myfanwy came away with the purchase of an original etching of Rottenburg.

Monday 16th August: Mileage 1,037. Left Rottenburg with

intention of making for the Harz Mountains and possibly a glimpse across the Iron Curtain. Got as far as Hildesheim, about 220 miles away when we lost the Davies's in a traffic queue. He got over the lights and I failed. What I did not know was that beyond the lights the roads merged and I did not know which one to take. We ended up on top of a steep mountain overlooking Hildesheim wondering where the Davies's had got to. It was too late to follow up so we stayed the night.

The intention earlier had been to visit Hamelin, of Pied Piper fame, and it was there we made for. Bingo! Just after 9 o'clock, as we found the only camp along the river outside the town and drove in, there they were at their breakfast. Together again. We were somewhat disappointed with Hamelin. Perhaps we had expected too much based on the fable, but even in those days it was so heavily commercialised. The following day Eileen (who had served as a nursing officer in the area during the war) expressed a wish to retrace steps of her wartime sojourn and we agreed to part and hopefully meet again in Venlo, Holland. Arrived there late afternoon after a casual journey and surprisingly were followed in by the Davies's shortly afterwards. There couldn't have been many steps to retrace! And it reinforced my dictum of wartime experiences... never go back, it's not the same!

Masstricht was a delightful tourist centre and we thought of staying a day or two, not being due to catch the boat for another three days. But it was not to be. A telephone call home had elicited for the Davies's the news that Sooty, their dog, was not well. So this became the parting of the ways. They went direct to Ostende and we made for Antwerp, Ghent and Brugge which we reached in heavy rain again. Mileage was 1,734 when we pulled in at a delightful Camping Solarium for overnight. It was Saturday 21st when we reached Heist and had a chance meeting with two couples of very disenchanted British campers on their first visit to the Continent. Their first impressions of Belgium on arrival at Ostende were greatly disappointing and they felt like turning back. We had some time and suggested they followed us to Sluis on the Dutch border where they might change their minds. This was also a lucky break for us. "We found a lovely site behind the town, and it's the nicest and most quiet site we have had yet" Myfanwy writes. It was the local policeman and his family who ran the site for the local council and we made a firm and lasting friendship with the Family Ultee which has endured to this day. The site has long since grown to become De

Meirdoon under different management. Sufficient to say we stayed there for the two remaining nights. During this time we discovered many charming places along the coast including Cadzand, then almost unknown to other than local holidaymakers.

Monday 23rd August: Arrived Ostende but failed to get earlier crossing so sailed on the Belgium ferry Fabiola at 5.45 pm, but not before witnessing the ferocity of Belgium police in dealing with a demonstration. They used a water cannon which was very strange to us, but effectively dispersed the crowds. The crossing was uneventful and by 2.00 am Tuesday we had arrived home at Four Winds, Uxbridge, having travelled 1,965 miles safely.

## Chapter 21

## Crossing the Iron Curtain

The Wassenaar International Rally had left its mark upon us. It had fired us with the urge and the will to sample the added and different attractions which these events offered; the facility and the opportunity to meet people of our own ilk from other countries and nationalities on an equal basis. That is why, when we heard that the 1966 International Rally was to be held in Hungary, there was no question in all our minds that we should be there. But there were to be many problems before I was permitted to attend.

This, of course, was the year when the Russians were imposing their will on the Soviet satellites, of which Hungary was one, and when forces opposing the might and oppression of the Stalinist regime were being subjected to a tyrannous military rule. The previous year the tanks had rolled in and savagely crushed a Hungarian uprising and we were eventually to see the marks and effects of this not only on buildings but in the people themselves.

However, when we learned that the Caravan Club was to organise the British participation at the Rally and that we would be supplied with routes and itineraries with the goodwill of the Hungarian government in allowing visas everything seemed set. The Rally was to open in the second week of August, and we were allowing ourselves a minimum of a week to get there. All the facilities would be extended by the Hungarian Embassy before the end of June, that is to say visas would be granted to those who would be attending the rally. There were not many from Britain. The deadline was around mid-June for processing the visas and I, along with others, applied. Passports were handed in and within a couple of weeks Myfanwy's visa and that of daughter Marilyn were granted. My application however was rejected.

I should have realised why immediately. I had been turned down because my passport described me as a journalist. Furthermore, I was a political journalist based on the Lobby of the House of Commons at Westminster. Before appealing against the rejection I made extensive enquiries of my friends among both Ministers and MPs, and contacts in several other Embassies, pulling a string here and a wire there because if I were not permitted entry then my wife and daughter would not go; and I so desperately wanted to be there. Not until a week before we were due to set off did I get the all clear and consequently, on 4th August 1966, the Rossers and the Davies's set out for Dover and ultimately Lake Balaton, the largest inland sea in Europe. It was another adventure during which we were to encounter so many different things which were to make it a very memorable journey indeed.

The diary records, as you might expect by now, that after a trouble free tow to Dover "we had a wonderful meal of Dover sole and chips" before embarking on the smallest ferry we had travelled on up to that time, the Josephine Charlotte of the Belge Maritime. We docked at Ostende at 1.30 am and, I am reminded again, "on our way to Brussels and Aachen on a very romantic run along a moon drenched autobahn for 102 miles, pulled in at 4.30 am exhausted and glad to put our heads down". Unfortunately we had mistakenly parked on a tramway loop line in the centre of Louvain and barely had we closed our eyes than the clang clang of trams woke us in a panic and we had to resume our journey, hoping for a quiet lay-by out of town. On reflection I wonder what would have happened with a similar occurrence these days. Probably, and at least, we would have been shouted at perhaps been handed a summons. But things were so different then, and people were more forbearing, especially for visitors to their country. They were lovely times!

It was two days later that we approached the tiny village of St Florian en route for Vienna, and it was totally new ground for us. There was no camping platz, but the Gasthof St Moritz looked so typically Tyrolean and the Patron so kind to invite us to stay the night alongside, that there was simply no alternative but to remain overnight. And what a night!

We chanced to coincide with the stag night of a forest verderer, and all his friends from miles around - about thirty of them - had taken over the Gasthof for the evening. We had had the usual schnitzel and kartoffle meal and Len and I were paying when we missed our two ladies. They had been "hi-jacked" and when we found them they were the only two females in the stag night do, joining in the merriment with abandon and having the time of their lives. We two were taboo and had to make our own entertainment. The result was that Len, two hours later, was banished from their caravan and found refuge in the driver's seat of the car. It must have been a couple of hours later, in the middle of the night when all around us was peaceful again, that we heard a loud shout. Rushing out I found Len in a right state. He had been fast asleep, but unfortunately had left the window down. A friendly cow, possibly attracted by the snoring which had been the cause of Len's banishment, had sought to give him a gentle bovine kiss.

Peace was soon restored, however, and the banishment lifted so he was quickly returned to the bosom of his family. I must confess that had it happened to me I would not have taken it as laconically as my friend. Vienna was reached the following day, August 7th, and with 925 miles on the clock, after a hot day's travel, and an hour in the camp swimming pool did us all a power of good. The highlight of the one day stay in the Austrian capital included, naturally, a tour of the Schonbrunn Palace, one of the most wondrous sights of any holiday yet, but I must confess we all thought the place, and the City generally could have done with a lick of paint. This "lick of paint" feeling remained with us throughout the visit and to be truthful it has been sustained through the many other times since that we have visited Vienna. Maybe it is due for a general facelift any year now.

Monday 8th August. This is a memorable day, and the diary recalls the tenseness felt by all of us as we approached the Austrian-Hungarian border. In particular I think the thought of entering a Communist State for the first time, and probably fired by the many stories we had read and heard about State dictatorships, gave rise to a general uneasiness. It may be laughable today but the idea that we might not be allowed back again was not one in an isolated mind. And our first encounter with the military style police immediately we trod on Hungarian ground did little to dispel some of those early thoughts and fears. On arrival at the border - the time was 4.40 pm and the mileage from home 994 miles -

we were told we should be staying overnight at a rest camp. En route to this we were suddenly directed into a kind of lay-by and told to produce our passports and declare any items which were not permitted to be carried into the country. What is still very fresh in my mind was the intrusion into the caravans and the spot searches conducted by armed police/soldiers. They went through our caravan without uttering a word, just pointing at cupboards and compartments which they wanted opened for the search. It was completely out of character with the European way and in a way was frightening, particularly for the women and the children.

Cedric Barradell and the Davies's underwent the same experience, as did our old friends from Wassenaar, the Koops, who by a strange co-incidence we had met on the border. They, too, were heading for the Rally. It was during this inquisition and search (we had not been subjected to anything like this on the border itself) that second thoughts arose about proceeding further. And it did not make things any easier when, the incident having attracted a crowd of what appeared to be itinerant gypsies, these people crowded around our little convoy, even entering our caravan and touching things and expressing amazement I suppose at the luxury of it all. Myfanwy gave some of the children a few sweets, but it only exacerbated the situation because in no time we were up against a rising clamour from the obviously poor "travellers", and our escorts, for that is what they were supposed to be, did nothing to quell the crowd. We were glad to move off and for the rest of the night we were ensconced in a very poor class type of camping site. With the incident now over it was decided that we should all press on to Balaton as early as possible the following day.

We awoke to heavy rain, but the rest of the journey to Balaton was uneventful except, as the diary relates, "It was wonderful seeing all the children running out of their houses waving to all the caravans as we passed through the villages, and all the horses have very long legs". Tuesday 9th August, a hot sunny day augured well for the Rally activities over the next few days and the girls who had been surveying the camp and its nationalities reported back that everything was "super". This became a memorable day for another occurrence because it is recorded that I came across another Welsh caravanning family of which earlier we had no knowledge. I had been organising a dinner at the Balaton Restaurant, complete with traditional gypsy music I had been assured," when Glan met people from North Wales with their two daughters" it states. "When we were fully settled Glan said something about nice smells and went towards the Rowlands' caravan. The daughter was cooking and Glan wanted to know what she was cooking. It is nice to meet other Welsh people, being that we are so far from home". That entry has become historic, for from that chance encounter emerged a friendship that has endured for more than twenty five years, a period during which, and without a single trace of acrimony, we have travelled the highways and by-ways of Europe and into Asia with our two Red Dragon emblazoned caravans totting up nearly eighty thousand miles. And God willing there are many more thousands left in the locker!

Buda-Pest was a must on our itinerary of places to visit and a coach trip to this ancient and historical City in which vestiges of the Austro-Hungarian empire are still much in evidence, although the worse for wear and lack of care, was early on. It was here that I bumped into Fyfe Robertson, then a notable television figure, who was making a news documentary about the aftermath of the anti-Soviet uprising a year earlier with a BBC team. We had known each other in London for some years, being in the same profession and I, at that time, was also a political contributor to the BBC with my own Welsh commentary and chat show programmes. In cautious undertones he warned me about the "listening ears" and the prying eyes around us and then with his pronounced and high pitched Scottish accent turned to the cameras and continued his assessment of a Budapest returning to normal. But his warning was heeded because a couple of days later the evidence turned up. That is another story.

The sightseeing trip was excellent, very impressive were the churches and cultural edifices. The Church of St. Mathew in Trinity Square and the Holy Trinity Memorial was followed by the Church of St. Stephen, then across the bridge which divides the two parts of the capital to the Parliament House. One reflection in the diary worth special note, however, is "We were shocked at the poor state of the shops, and the people who seem to look frightened, and the police who all carried guns. The shops are half empty... couldn't buy any gifts, too expensive."

That evening from camp we crossed Lake Balaton to Siofok where the hosts had arranged a superb water ballet and fireworks display... one of the best we have seen. The trip across was in a surprisingly large ship and very comfortable, but obviously more for the tourists even though at that time Hungary saw very few foreign tourists. It was near midnight when we returned and the only incident recalled about that trip was that Marilyn and the girls failed to make the last boat back... at least we failed to find them. But when we got to the 'vans they were there, having caught the penultimate crossing.

It was on the following day that I had occasion to recall Fyfe Robertson's warning. I had been swimming and was taking the sun on the beach when two young men sat beside me and quickly engaged me in conversation. Their English was quite good and soon the talk had switched from Balaton and how we were enjoying our first visit to Hungary to what I thought of the Hungarian government and its policies; whether I had any views on certain aspects of the ruling Communist party and, later particularly revealing, whether I was attending the rally on holiday. Warning bells rang and I stated emphatically I was on holiday with my family and had no interest in any political events in that country. They suggested they, too, were on holiday and would be only too happy to help and make my stay a pleasant one... but they didn't say how. During that day and the following day, wherever I went, into the water or strolling about, I was aware they were close to hand. In the diary Myfanwy writes "Glan tells me two people have been asking him questions because somehow they know he is a British journalist. He is very suspicious about them."

Confirmation of my suspicions came on Sunday 14th August because it is then that the diary states "Glan still thinks the Hungarian people who seemed to be making a point of talking to him are suspicious persons to do with the government..." and then refers to a meeting I had with another young man. I was paddling in the Lake, and with no sign of the other two, when I was approached by a lad of about eighteen or twenty years who casually remarked, again in very good English, "be careful sir. You are being questioned by Communist agents." He suggested we walked along the beach and he told me that he was anti-Communist and had watched the two agents approach me and keep me company for two days. He further explained his hatred of The Party was because of what they had done to his family. His father had owned a boatyard (presumably on the Lake) which had been in the family for many years and immediately after the war and on taking power in Hungary the Communists had confiscated it. He was very bitter because now he was just a labourer in what had been his family's business. But, if his story was true, and I had no reason to disbelieve, what had the agents wanted with me, and how did they know I was someone involved in any way with politics? I don't suppose I shall ever know, but it has taxed my mind considerably over the years and especially because of the stories which I have heard from the inside during my working life at Westminster.

# Chapter 22

# We Encounter the Borer

The return journey from Balaton had to be by a different route which took us through Yugoslavia, in blazing sun with heat haze shimmering for as far as the eye could see almost we set off at 8.30 am on 15th August. Within two and a half hours making good progress we suddenly found the Davies's were not with us. We still had a good distance to go before reaching the border so decided to pull in and wait. The wait dragged on for more than half an hour and suddenly we saw a British Ace caravan approaching. They stopped - as is and always has been usual with the caravanners' code - and we enquired whether they had spotted the Davies's. "We saw the caravan with the Dragon pulled in at the side of the road some distance back" we were told. At least the Dragon had again proved its worth! The pull-up it seemed had been no more than a required halt. Nothing seemed to have been wrong and the Davies's had waved them on. With this assurance we set off again this time with Zagreb as our destination which had been agreed before we left camp.

We made it by 5.30 pm only to find there were several rest sites and most already filled with caravans returning from the Rally. But where were the Davies's? Again our many enquiries elicited that the Dragon caravan had suffered a breakdown just after crossing the border - engine trouble we were told. I drove back in the car and eventually found them proceeding very slowly towards Zagreb. What had happened was that whilst crossing a railway line an iron projection had ripped a small hole in his petrol tank on the Singer Gazelle. But how was it that he was now making way? "Eileen had a brilliant idea" he explained. "She took the tin foil from a jar of coffee and stuck it over the hole with some selotape after we had saved as much of the leaking petrol as we could". Every appliance and container which could be got under the tank to hold the draining petrol had been used, even their water containers. When I stuck my head inside the car it was stinking with petrol fumes. The salvaged petrol, a very precious commodity then and procurable only against coupons, filled the rear floor... and some even in the caravan. Furthermore, it appeared that in order not to put too much strain on the tinfoil plug they were pouring only a small quantity of petrol into the car and were able to do only about 10 miles in between refills. Poor Len, Eileen and Karin, were in a most dejected state, and no wonder. After a dreary and also hazardous journey with petrol slopping around in the rear, and with the two girls in my car, we reached camp utterly exhausted.

First priority the following day was to check and assess the possibility of continuing with the Davies petrol tank in such a hazardous condition. But there was no option. Nowhere around the overnight site was there a garage to undertake repair work. So we carried on as gently as possible and eventually made Rijeka. Road conditions were not all that good (no motorway in those days) and to make matters worse it began raining heavily as we clambered steadily across the mountains. We had left camp at 10.15 am and the diary records "At the moment, 3.15 pm, we are still climbing in thick mist or cloud and we have another 40 miles before we settle down... Arrived at Baccar... terrific wind, just like the Mistral". In fact we had arrived simultaneously with The Borer, a terrifying wind which blew about this time of the year.

We managed to make a small camping site at the neck of a small valley and were advised to peg down everything. Caravans had been known to take off in powerful bursts of the wind and we were both fortunate to find places alongside a tree to which we tied our caravans with the aid of tow ropes. The locals thought it would blow itself out in a day or two, but however long it took we would be tied down to this place. Any attempt to continue our journey towards Trieste would have been extreme folly. The diary recalls that we spent a very fitful night. "Its terrifying while it lasts" wrote Myfanwy. "We are sheltering from the main force of the wind by some trees, but the tents have already been blown away. I know we won't sleep much tonight. It's the most terrible experience of wind I have ever had".

Come the dawn, however, and still the wind persisted, if anything it was worse. Braving the element for a brief stroll towards the seashore we were rewarded with a sight never before witnessed. The Borer was lifting some of the waves clear of the sea and sweeping them into a desiccated pattern just like confetti. "We are in a small bay with high cliffs all around us and it is surprising how the fir trees are still standing. What a test for the caravan, and it is as well that the car and 'van are still hitched", it is observed. Otherwise the comment is that this could be a very pleasant place in fine weather.

With astonishing suddenness the force died - not completely but enough to persuade us to get away. The locals predicted it would be back and we did not want to experience another such night. By early afternoon we were on our way in sunshine but then ill-luck struck again. Just 20 kilometres from Kozina Len ran out of petrol, not a drop left in any of the many containers. We took him into Kozina and with pooled coupons managed enough fuel to see him across the border into Trieste. He insisted hitch-hiking back and an hour and 20 minutes later we saw them coming along. Only 17 kilometres now from Trieste, but the Davies's were still out of grace with Lady Luck because barely had we restarted than the tinfoil plug gave way. Too much juice in the tank Eileen thought. This was the last straw! We had to get that tank repaired, but how and by whom?

What followed was for me a most astonishing example of make do and mend. A few kilometres back we had passed a kind of transport cafe and garage. Len and I went back to see if any repair work could be undertaken. We found a couple of chaps in a tin shed doing some welding work. Could they help us? Sure, they could. But it would take a couple of hours. Why not stay the night while the job was being done? Having towed the car back and then manoeuvred both caravans alongside the cafe car park we went to see what was being done to Len's car. We found it on a makeshift ramp with both men underneath with an airline. The place was stinking with petrol fumes. Without attempting to remove the tank they were using the airline to blow the tank free of fumes. We tried to protest because by this time the penny had dropped and we realised they intended welding the fracture. We both had visions of the vehicle being blown clear of the ramp and the men with it. It was the most stupid thing I had ever seen. Quite apart from the probability of a fatal accident how were we going to get two caravans back home with only one car! Whether they understood what our gesticulations meant I do not know. They didn't understand a word of English but they had understood the rustle of notes when we had negotiated a price for the job with them, and they were determined at any cost to get that money.

The two families had reconnoitred the cafe and arranged for two evening meals. While this was going on we two were going through purgatory. Having satisfied themselves that the tank was clear one of them seized the blowtorch which he thrust towards the hole in the tank. We had retired to what we thought to be a safe distance. Nothing undue happened. Then the other "mechanic" approached under the car with the welding equipment. Within a few minutes it was done. Water was splashed everywhere underneath the vehicle and it was rolled off the ramp and pushed towards a barrel which contained some petrol. An injection of fuel and a quick examination under the car whilst we still kept our distance satisfied the workers that the job was done. As we approached there were broad smiles, and no doubt complimentary comments, as they extended a handshake... or was it to take the money? Of one thing I am certain. Nowhere else would this have happened and never have I experienced such a breathtaking and intrepid, or plain daft, attitude as was shown by those two men. I can also state that that repair job lasted the duration of Len's ownership of the Gazelle which was to my knowledge another four years.

It was just after eight o'clock the following morning, and after we had had a splendid night and meal at the Transport cafe that we began our journey to the border. Just after leaving Trieste there was another memorable incident. I had overshot a stop sign on a slight gradient and suddenly a motorcycle policeman stepped into the road and flagged me down. Despite my protestations that I had not been at fault and he not being able to quite understand what I was saying, as equally I could not quite understand what he was saying in Italian, he produced his pocketbook and started to write out a fine for 5,000 Lire. At that time his partner arrived. He could understand some English and I tried to explain that back home in London I was a Magistrate and would be dealing more kindly with a foreign tourist in this situation. There were a few hurried words in Italian and with a beaming smile and profuse apologies his partner crossed out the 5,000 Lire and substituted 1,000. Furthermore, they both mounted their machines and showed us the road to catch up with the others, which we did within the statutory speed limit. Within a short while we had reached Sustiana and were in a much more contented frame of mind as we settled in for a few days respite.

Despite several days of mixed weather, hot and sunny and wet and stormy, we enjoyed three days of complete rest in and out of the water and on 22nd August the time had come to set for home again. It was here that we parted company with the Davies's by agreement. They wanted to take a different route via the Gothard whereas we had plumped for the Simplon, a Pass we had not done before. We agreed to meet in Sluis in Holland in a few days' time, all being well.

Lake Garda was to be our first overnight stop and we reached it by 6.30 pm. Marilyn remembered this was where our friends the Barradell's (whom we had not seen since leaving Balaton) spent a great deal of their annual holidays, at Camping Belvedere. There was no problem finding it, but we were greatly surprised to find that the Barradell's were there as well. It is an uncanny feature of caravanning holidays on the continent how one meets up with friends and acquaintances at most unexpected times and places. We agreed to stay over the following day and this gave us the first sight of beautiful Desenzano where the orange trees lining the streets were full of fruit which we forbade the children to pick despite the great temptation. A visit to the local market was an absolute, and a first class dinner at a lakeside restaurant that evening crowned a very enjoyable, if brief, stay.

Another memorable occasion on the return journey was our visit to Kandersteg. "We changed to the mountain train which took the car, caravan and the three of us from Brig to Kandersteg. We have never experienced anything like it, Myfanwy wrote: "All passengers had to leave their cars and sit in proper compartments and we travelled for 40 minutes up the mountain. The view was awe-inspiring... fantastic... We arrived in this Swiss mountain town for climbers at 6.30 pm to the background of brilliant snow and the sound of cowbells. The cable cars start from just a few yards from where we have parked our Caravan. The only blot is that my middle-ear trouble has started up again. I feel sick and giddy. Glan has found a lovely restaurant not far away. I shall make the effort tonight to dine out with him and Mally..."

Regrettably the evening was not a complete success, but I did manage to blow an Alpenhorn, one of these terrific Swiss mountain horns which sound like a steamer in distress if one can manage to get a note out of it. After another day with heady feelings due to the altitude we set off for Berne and Basle, enjoying every minute of a journey through Alpine scenery which moved the soul and pulsated the blood. Myfanwy wrote "It is like turning over the leaves of a fairytale book". It was on this journey that I became the victim of a tummy bug on the German side of the Swiss frontier at Basle and this necessitated an unscheduled halt before reaching Freiburg at a small camp not mentioned in our camping and caravanning camp sites book. It was the Fischerinsel, complete with swimming pool. We thought at that time it should be one of the highly recommended sites in this region. Completely recovered after a good night's rest we set ourselves a 230 miles target for Limburg which we reached at 7.10 pm, less than the average daily trek but enough in the circumstances. Lo and behold! At 8.10 pm who should turn up alongside us but the Davies's. The diary says "They had missed us. It's nice to be together again". It is only 190 kilometres from Limburg to Aachen where, by midday, the ladies were out shopping again, and where, for lunch, we sampled for the first time the traditional German Haxen - a kind of exaggerated pig's trotter. We liked it so much we always eat it now whenever we are in Germany.

Saturday 27th August: It was here that we parted with the Davies's for the second and final time on this holiday. We went on to Sluis and they made directly for the Oostende Ferry. Rediscovering this quaint and charming part of the Low Country, and especially between Cadzand and Breskens, was a delightful conclusion to the holiday, enhanced again by another chance meeting with our friends the Barradell's who had remembered our recommendation to the Sluis campsite and had turned up out of the blue the evening before our departure for Oostende and home. For the rest it was just as usual. An enjoyable crossing and arriving in Uxbridge safely and quite exhilarated after a holiday trek of 2,604 miles.

## Chapter 23

## 'Twas on the Isle of Capri....

During the winter months and long before the snowdrops and the daffodils had added their beauty to the Four Winds lawns the preparations for what we considered to be the most ambitious yet of our caravanning holidays were virtually completed. Rome, and Naples, the often read about enchantment of the islands of Capri and Ischia, and the fascinating narratives of Pompei and Herculean and vestiges of the Roman Empire, had acted like magnets in our forward planning. It had to be Italy again, only this time it would have a more cultural content.

As a family we had never been to Rome. And Florence had often been talked about but had yet to be reached. For some reason the Appenine Mountains had registered in my mind as a too formidable obstacle to be tackled and overcome. Hannibal had done it with his elephants, but for the Rossers, traversing the west to east route with a 2 litre car towing a fourteen foot caravan - oh yes, we had acquired a new Fairholme, our third new caravan since those heady days of the Willerby - was a prodigious and very challenging feat. We had heard stories of high temperatures and rough roads which had been very off-putting. Then, during the few months after our return from our previous holiday, there had been encouraging reports about the new Appenine Autostrada with magnificent road bridges and easy to negotiate bends which greatly facilitated the journey to Rome.

So this is what it would be all about for the 1967 holiday. This time our constant friends the Davies's had decided to opt out on a continental holiday, but the gap was quickly filled by other friends, and caravanning enthusiasts of longer standing than us. The Barradell's, Cedric, Cynthia and the two daughters, Carol and Collette, would be accompanying us.

The pre-holiday planning had set the furthermost destination as Naples. The dates of the holiday would be for the whole of August and into the first part of September. And now the diary takes over: "We are setting out for Dover, and a new type channel crossing to Calais, at 2.45 pm on 3rd August, and it is a beautiful day" Myfanwy wrote. We were due to meet our friends at Dover in time to catch the 10.30 pm ferry. "It's a thrill for us going on a different boat" it is recalled. It was 7.30 pm when the two families joined up in the port and what followed was the now traditional (for us) supper of Dover sole and chips. "It is a mild and lovely night made all the more so by the sound of the seagulls" the diary records. By 9.30 pm we were boarding the new ferry and, she wrote, "The interior of this boat is fabulous. Len would have loved it. It is surprising that there are not many on board, and it is very comfortable... It is a fairly rough crossing, but very enjoyable... Arriving Calais one o'clock... All the caravans stayed the night on the quayside... After early morning cup of tea we began our journey at 6.45 am... a lovely morning and every one is happy and very excited. This crossing is bound to be very popular in the future."

Friday, 4th August, we made our way via St Omer and Bethune hoping to reach Rheims well before the lunch break. A misdirection owing to poor signposting cost us time and excess mileage approaching St. Quentin but by 2.30 pm we were pulling in at our appointed campsite near the centre of Rheims, not far from the Cathedral. So far, so good, but we had still to come what was to be one of our most memorable social-cultural experiences of holidays abroad. Thanks to the good offices of Cedric who was in the wine wholesale and distribution business in U.K. we had all been invited to a reception at the Moet et Chandon cellars in Rheims. By 3.15 pm, we are reminded by the diary, we were on our way afoot (there was no way we were going to be inhibited in this long awaited experience by having to contain the appreciation of the commodity with frequent sips because we would be driving!).

"We were all treated like VIP's... It was a fabulous experience", the diarised recollections bring back the occurrence just as if it were yesterday. "We saw how the bottles were fermented from first stage to the last corking. There were 31 million bottle of Champagne in the seventeen miles of corridors underground and they ranged from half bottles to Magnums and Jereboams, and even special bottles and containers of exceptional historical significance. We were offered rugs to place around our shoulders because of the cold in the cellars, and of very special interest we were shown the Napoleon barrel! It was all so tremendous and we owe a lot to our special guide. He was German - I forget his name - and a friend of the founder Moet family".

The diary goes on: "It was fascinating to see how the fungus grew on the cellar walls just like balls of dirty cotton wool and we were told that there were huge spiders lurking in the fungus, luckily I did not see any otherwise I would have been away! Finally we were shown a huge cellar in its natural state, but with red plush curtains around the damp walls. There was a massive bar, and heaps of chairs and tables around with unlit candles on the tables. This was the cellar that Maurice Chevalier had hired for a special Champagne party to which he had invited a thousand guests, and we were told they had consumed 5,000 bottles of Champagne.

"Philip Lovell, a very nice boy from England who is studying wines here, showed us around the cellars and we were entertained right royally in the room where Kosygin and Khrushchev, the Russian leaders, were entertained on their State visit to France."

According to the writing we were each presented with a commemorative gift and it is recorded that we demolished two bottles of Champagne between the adults before being taken into a beautiful garden resplendent with multi-coloured flowers. The consensus of opinion was two-fold... either "It was magnificent" or "It was marvellous". Personally, I cannot remember either being asked for or volunteering a view or opinion but there are some sharper recollections than others about the visit thanks to the diary which goes on "On our way back we went into a lovely hotel Auberge du Bois Joli and had a lovely five course meal of hors d'oeuvres, fish, chicken a la Rheims made in a gorgeous wine sauce, and stacks of chips.... Then we made our way back to camp tired but satisfied." Thus ended the first and very satisfactory day of what promised even then to be a pleasant and rewarding holiday.

Switzerland was to be our next port of call and en route we had planned to stop in Pontarlier. However the effects of the night before were rather retarding on our best efforts yet we covered 106 miles before pulling up for a snack lunch and a petrol fill-up. Here the diary observes "It's been surprising how many British cars and 'vans we have seen compared with previous years, yet the traffic on the whole is very light". This second day ended in a fashion which would have been difficult to contemplate in any other type of holiday. "We found a nice little pub near our campsite which reminded us very much of Wurzburg and it had a Juke Box in the corner. We danced to its music with the locals and it was great fun. We strolled back to our 'vans and got to bed at 10.45 pm".

It was boiled eggs and toast for breakfast, the following day being a Sunday. The weather was beautifully sunny and warm and in no time we were on our way to Lausanne. The border was crossed at 9.25 am and we had an expectancy of coffee and cakes on the side of the Lake (Le Marne). But our plans received a severe set back. "Glan wants a garage" is the simple statement which presaged a chapter of happenings that was to have a marked effect on our planning. "We've developed an awful noise in the engine, we shall have to get to a garage soon to have it seen to... hoping its not as bad as it sounds... Stopped in a garage and we have called for the Swiss R.A.C.".

The outcome was a search for a Rootes' garage. Our car then was a Singer Gazelle and only the local Rootes agent would be likely to have the required part which had to be changed. The 'vans were unhitched and, fortunately, were able to be towed by Cedric to a nearby site on the lakeside. We had to be prepared for a longish stay! A visit to the garage the following morning revealed that we had stopped just in time. Another few miles, according to the mechanic, and the gear box would have fallen out causing a nasty accident. Fortunately also the repair could be effected without using new parts and the car would be ready the next day at a cost of about £50. This would make a considerable dent in the holiday money so we decided to make use for the first time of the Red Pennant facility which we had luckily taken out for the holiday. A telephone call to London assured us that the money would be telegraphed to the nearest Post Office by midday following, and so it was.

By 11.30 am on Tuesday 8th August the car was returned, repaired and running sweetly again, and the bill settled we set off for the Mont Blanc road tunnel with the intention of a lunchtime stop in Italy. With

Geneva receding and the snow capped Mount Blanc getting ever closer it was 3.30 pm before we came in sight of the tunnel entrance. It had been a stiff climb and the car nearly boiled a few times but this was as nothing compared with the glorious scenery of the glacier, snow and mountain peaks glistening in the sunshine. Although since then we have negotiated most of the Alpine passes and travelled through many road and rail tunnels this remains in our minds as the most wonderful experience, fascinated as we were with the feat of construction. Seven miles long and travelling at 50 kilometres per hour was the most exhilarating experience and in less than twenty minutes we had emerged into the brilliant sunshine of Italy. There was still some way to go to the foot of the mountain and we thought we might reach a camping site long before it became dark. Progress, however, was slow, and we had forgotten that watches had to be put forward one hour to Italian time. We also were obliged to stop at a customs halt where we were able to purchase petrol coupons and autostrada toll tickets which would take us to Rome and as far as Naples. Carrying on to 7.30 pm was as much as our tired bodies would allow us and 209 miles after leaving Lausanne we eventually pulled into a lay-by on the approach to the Milano autostrada. "Had a good steak and kidney meal and turned in early to be ready for an early morning start" it is written.

We found we had only a short distance to go to Verres and start of the autostrada when we began our journey at 6.30 am on 9th August. This was to be another memorable day... in fact it turned out a record making day. According to the diary "we have 489 miles to do today, all autostrada, to get to Rome. With a bit of luck we should get there this evening although we have never done so many miles in a day before". No thought had been given at this time in the cool of the early morning to the sweltering heat which lay ahead. But we had all agreed that Rome was a possibility that day and that we should go for it. And go for it we did!

"Stopped for breakfast at 10 o'clock for one hour, very hot but beautiful, and we have already done 127 miles" it is recorded. It is further stated that having restarted the journey thoughts were turning to an overnight stay and reaching Rome receding, the heat being so intense and affecting the cars' performances. By mid afternoon the shimmering reflection from the road was affecting our driving so badly that our earlier determination to make Rome our bust was sadly wilting and the temptation to stop for a brew-up in the 'vans thrust aside anything but an enforced halt for petrol. When we saw a Pavesi in sight I turned in, and Cedric needed no further encouragement. Marilyn and the two other girls raced to the shade of the services station and in the blink of an eye they - and the rest of us also - were furiously licking ice cream cornets. It was pure bliss and a salvation! But less than half an hour later with body temperatures subsided the urge to press on returned. There were 172 miles to go and we calculated we might make it by 7.30 pm providing we did not succumb to any further temptations. We had already covered 290 miles according to the diary and it was still 90 degrees in the shade!

"Stopped for petrol at 4.45 pm but cannot eat. It's too hot. All we do is drink and eat fruit. Cynthia has just found the water hose the attendant was using and played it over our faces... gorgeous!" the diary states. From here on it was hell for leather and Rome before dark, and the twilight which precedes a dark Italian night had set in when, bang on 7.30 pm we arrived at Camp Monte Attenne in an area surrounded by Pine trees. This was high above the city of Rome and the twinkling lights below presented a fairyland picture. It was still hot, but what the heck we had made it! The longest ever one day journey and in the most trying conditions. We'd travelled over five hundred miles with tyres sticking to melting tar and bodies oozing perpetual perspiration. It was more of a test of endurance than a holiday journey, but in retrospect it was worth every minute of the discomfort. We have regaled ourselves many times over on that feat, but the last word on it shall be that in the diary; "We were terribly tired and hot. Before we put the steadies down we dived for the shop for a lager and lemon, and the children their cokes. It was heaven. After a good wash and putting the 'vans tidy we dressed up and went out to dinner. It was great fun even though we were dreadfully tired... back and in bed by 11.30 pm..."

# Chapter 24

# Rome and Thereafter

The prospect of an exciting day visiting so many of the things and places we had read up during the winter months urged us to an early start after a night's fitful sleep. Not even the fatigue of a five hundred miles tow could lull us into a sound sleep with the oppressive heat of the night causing everyone to toss and turn. However, the dawn brought a little relief it seems because a gentle breeze swept through the open windows of the 'van and by 8.45 am, after a breakfast of cereals, fresh rolls and jam, we were on our way to the Vatican City, and hopeful of having a glimpse of the Pope and other dignitaries. By the time we reached St. Peter's square the temperature had soared to 98 degrees and the search was on for the nearest cafe and some cool drinks.

Many thousands of others must have had the same intentions as us because by the time we returned to the Square it was almost impossible to move easily. Nonetheless for the first comers that we were the Square was a wonderful sight, and the heaving mass was a veritable Tower of Babel with all kinds of languages, recognisable and unrecognisable, heard from all sides. The diary recalls that we went inside the Church, one of many, and were reminded immediately that the ladies and girls had to have arms and heads covered. "It was magnificent, and we walked and walked, even down to the Catacombs where tombs of past Popes were shown to us" it is recorded.

"The Church of St. Peter is such a beautiful church with dozens of chapels inside, and the painted ceiling of Michael Angelo is a sight to behold and truly magnificent. It has made yesterday's effort so much worth while", she wrote. The entries also recall our taking a lift to the first part of the Church dome and then climbing "it seems like hundreds of steps up a narrow spiral staircase until we came out among the statues of the Apostles. From here we have had a wonderful view of all Rome and its Seven Hills. It is fantastic"... I cannot think of any other adjectives which could have done justice to that first downward glimpse of the birthplace of the Catholic Church and its myriad of adherents paying a pilgrims' homage to the Holy Father. It was truly a moving and soul lifting experience which we would not have missed for anything.

The visit to the Forum and treading the paths trodden by the Caesars two thousands years earlier was another exciting event when the mind was let loose to imagine what it must have been like in those days of Roman Empire glories. But perhaps the most gripping visit of the day was to the Coliseum where we were fortunate to recruit the services of a good English speaking guide who seemed to want to impress us as much with his command of the language and his knowledge of the subject as being paid. It is on occasions like this that the mind runs riot. I know mine did. The arena where the Gladiators fought for the "privilege" of the Emperor's thumbs up and the right to live and fight again, came alive again, and from the cages which housed the lions and other wild beasts one could look out into the arena where the Christians huddled, awaiting their fate and jeered and spat upon from the terraces by crazed audiences demanding that the "sport" begin. It seemed all so real somehow, especially as our guide pointed our certain aspects of the tour. It was a totally weary party of seven that made its way back to the parked cars towards the end of a day during which the heat had been at an almost unbearable 98 degrees in the shade. But the diary sums up what all of us had felt that day: "It has been truly wonderful... would not have missed this visit to Rome for anything in the world".

Friday 11th August: "Another scorching day. Back in Rome and more sightseeing. It's unbearably hot but we have just had a lunch of egg and bacon sandwich and lashings of cold milk and ice cold lemonade. We have to see the Catacombs of St. Priscilla today". She was the daughter of one of the Roman Senators of the first century. The diary records that among the paintings we saw were the Madonna and Child, and Moses striking the rock to open the Red Sea for the children of Israel. Truly wonderful and somehow different from many of the other religious paintings we had seen. There was also the painting of the three young men, Shadrach, Messnach and Abendigo, in the burning fire. The diary recalls: "We were shown tombs of a very early age that have yet to be explored. The caves were deep down in the earth and very dark and narrow. There were alters covered with white cloths where the nuns prayed; it was so cool and peaceful, and such a shock as we came up to ground level and into the heat of a hot sun again".

Saturday, the 12th August was parting day. The Barradell's wished to stay in Rome for another day and we agreed to meet in a day or two either in Naples or Sorrento. Sounds simple, just as though we were speaking of a school playground or a small village instead of hundreds of square miles of territory. But there was never any question in our minds that we would not be meeting up again in a few days.

We took the autostrada and among the more significant landmarks we passed was the Monastery of Cassino, the Montecassino of world war two remembrances. It looked so peaceful and commanding perched as it was on the summit of the hill which was the scene of some of the bitterest fighting of that war, and enduring no doubt to the memories of the Polish troops which suffered the greatest losses of that assault. But for us it was only a name that has figured so prominently during the war years and the immediate aftermath.

It seems from the diary that there was no problem in finding a site around Naples, and it was only 200 metres from the sea thankfully. "It's sweltering, never felt it so hot" it is recorded, "It's even hotter than Rome!" But with the awning up and giving us a welcome protective shade it seems as though the holiday, lazing away the hours, is just starting. No crowds, no pushing and jostling through crowded streets, just sea and sand and tranquillity. Not the sort of situation one could expect with a package or hotel holiday; this expresses more the attractions and enjoyment of caravanning than anything".

The site we had discovered was at Pozzuoli, on the outskirts of Naples, and it turned out to be one of the best. The journey from Rome and the efforts of putting the awning up and getting things ship-shape had reduced us all to a state of complete exhaustion. Reliving that time as written in the diary I can thoroughly enjoy again the respite which followed. "After we had finished putting our things together tidily, table and chairs under the awning, Glan absolutely flopped on the settee in the 'van and went fast asleep. After a while Mally and I decided to find the beach, which we could not yet see though we could hear the sea. Everybody in the camp wore swim costumes, it was so sweltering hot. We were absolutely fascinated by the way we had to go to the beach. It reminded us of the film "Inn of sixth happiness" because we had to walk through a path of tall reeds to a little stream only a couple of minutes away and then cross a very wide river by a narrow two-foot wooden bridge which moved as one walked across, and with the occasional lizard. It was wonderful to watch the big fish jumping out of the fresh water with their silvery bodies glistening in the sun. As the bridge took us to the end of the tall reeds the sea lay before us, beautifully clear with white topped rollers crashing on to the sandy beach. We walked down a long narrow path of wooden boards which took us almost to the water's edge, obviously to help bathers because otherwise the sand was too hot for the feet. What we had reached was a large private beach of beautiful white sand which was part of the camp's facilities. The crowning moment" the diary goes on "was when Mally and I went to test the water. It was like going into a warm bubble bath. The waves were ideal for surfing and we enjoyed it immensely. After a little sunbathing we decided to go back and fetch Glan. He was delighted with the way to go to the beach and I watched his face when he trod the boards and then ran into the water. He was just like a schoolboy!"

For this simply related episode I have to thank Myfanwy very much. It has brought back such enjoyable memories as I write and relive these excerpts in life of which our caravanning abounds. And if it gives the reader the urge to fulfil similar experiences then the diary and it's recounting will have been worth the efforts.

That evening, as we relaxed in a cool breeze from the sea, thoroughly refreshed, we strolled down to the camp cafe-restaurant and joined others of so many nationalities - but we were the only British - indulging in a pastime of cold drinks served on little tables and listening to the sound of music from guitars played by four young lads. A few couples tried valiantly to dance on a patio floor and it was great fun and very pleasant. What a lovely end to a most enjoyable day.

An example of how changeable and suddenly the weather can be in this part of Italy was clearly demonstrated when we were awakened the following morning at 6 o'clock by heavy rain, thunder and fierce lightning, but it had the welcoming effect of clearing the air and sweeping away the energy-consuming heat... at least for a few hours. We decided this should be the occasion to visit Pompei and a trip up Vesuvius, but the latter had to be postponed due to the amount of time spent in the ruins of Pompei.

The totally unexpected is what adds to the interest and enjoyment of this type of holiday and it happened that as we were taking a light lunch at the foot of Vesuvius we were approached by a peddler offering a variety of wares, including some beautiful cameos and necklaces made from the lava of Vesuvius's last eruption. Suddenly his faced beamed and he told us he was Tony whom we had met plying his same trade on the beach at San Remo about eight years before. We had found him very fair and made a few purchases. He was no more than fourteen then but we made friends with him and he had recognised us. It was a fantastic reunion and he could not do enough for us. His fortunes had changed considerably. He was no longer the beach boy peddler but now was head of the business in the Pompei area employing many. His home, which turned out to be a beautiful villa, was ours during our stay, he insisted. As for purchases of trinkets and cards there was no question of payment. In fact when I told him in answer to his query that I had paid 2,000 lire for the brochure I held in my hand he called over one of his sellers and insisted he returned my money immediately. We had a wonderful spell with him and received good advice how best to spend the couple of days we had planned to stay. He remembered clearly our friends the Davies's who were with us at San Remo, and a couple of days later he took us to his home to meet his family.

After a hectic day and a return drive through the picturesque coast drive of Sorrento and Amalfi we returned to camp with yet another surprise awaiting us. Yes, there they were pulled up alongside the empty space next to our 'van... the Barradell's! Neither of us had knowledge of this particular site when we parted in Rome but they, as we had done, had spotted the camp sign and it being late... it was almost dark when we returned from our day out.... had decided to pull in and resume their search for us the following day. It was sheer luck, but we were all together again.

# Chapter 25

# Vesuvius and its Safety Valve

After the shock of finding the Barradell's next to us again it did not take long to plan the day's activities. There was barely the trace of any cloud, and the sun shone with such clarity and promised warmth out of the clear azure blue sky, that we could hardly wait to set out for another day's adventure. Myfanwy, Marilyn and I were glad that our intended visit to Vesuvius the previous day had had to be postponed due to the extended Pompei stay for now we had the opportunity of making the trip as two families. Neither of the families had been up to the famous volcano but we had all read about it. Even so, when eventually we made the summit it was an extremely thrilling experience and more awesome than we had expected.

On our return journey from Pompei the previous day we had encountered some terrific traffic jams and were fearful of a repetition. We had taken the coast road because we had been advised that Sorrento, Amalfi and Portafino had to be seen for their beauty to be realised. Sorrento was already well known to us. Who doesn't know of it from the famous Italian song. Come back to Sorrento is indeed an invitation we would willingly accept, and indeed intend so to do one day in the near future. There may be one proviso though; it took us what seemed like hours to join the coast road on the descent from the little cafe where we had stopped for a Cappuccino, overlooking the bay, and another bumper to tail journey along the narrow cliff road above Amalfi. The views were magnificent but the tardiness of the journey was such that not a single photograph was possible. Twilight gave way to darkness with a swiftness which is common to this part of Italy and prevented use of the cameras. It took more than one and a half hours to cover seven miles. And to cap it all the mother and father of storms struck with weird suddenness. It brought some of the heaviest rain we had seen, and the streak lightning and cracks of thunder, just above our heads it seemed, were extremely frightening.

But that had been the day before. Now we were raring to tackle Vesuvius and the portents were favourable. The first part of the journey up the mountain towards the crater was a tremendous thrill even though that side of it was practically bare of vegetation. We were travelling over roads that still bore the traces of the lava of the 1944 eruption. When we reached the car park at the chairlift station the scene had been set for a trip to the summit and a never to be forgotten experience. The sun's warmth had virtually evaporated and the women and girls had to wear their cardigans and anoraks as a protection against the cold. The chairlift carried two passengers per chair and by the halfway stage we were in cloud that fortunately cleared before we reached the summit. It was the sight of the actual crater, however, that surpassed everything else. We were fortunate to have Old Rossi - the veteran with the ginger beard and known to countless visitors to the top as Barbarossi we were told. Before us lay a crater we were told was a mile in circumference. Below us the "cover" of molten, but subdued at that time, lava just about sixty metres down. Occasional burps and rumbles and wreaths of smoke were a constant reminder of the horrific consequences of another eruption and the fantastic power contained within the molten heart oft his particular volcano. Yet those guides who took viewers to points of best vantage, and with their multi-lingual patter explained the pros and cons of vulcanology as applied to Vesuvius, reduced the visit, or tried with commendable success, to one of a fearless interest. I was greatly impressed.

I suppose the ritual still goes on, but what pleased the girls and the women most was the surreptitious "gift" of volcanic stones, quartz and crystal souvenirs of an unforgettable visit, which they were told had been gathered from the rim of the crater. They treasured them like gems from the Amazon. With the assurance that Vesuvius was not ready for many years again to blow its top we decided to make the downward journey to the cars by way of a zigzag path across a veritable dustbowl. Apart from presenting walkers with a serious fall should one's footing slip this particular descent played havoc with footwear. By the time we had reached the bottom some of us had practically gone through our soles. It also gave us the sensation of moving from one hot zone at the crater through a cold zone and again into another type of heat at the foot of the chairlift; and one astonishing recollection was the bushes of Mimosa we passed towards the foot of the mountain with an overpowering scent. Very strange!

An unexpected event when we reached the bottom was meeting our friend Tony. I believe one of his sellers must have seen us driving up and told him. Anyway he was there waiting for us and insisted on all of us returning to his villa to meet Maria, his wife, and Anna, their child. Their hospitality was superb and as we were leaving Cedric and I each had a bottle of Vodka pressed into our hands. "To drink and remember at Christmas", said Tony with a show of sincere emotion.

This was something which I cannot believe could happen except during a holiday of this kind. It is a scene which can be and is constantly thrown up during the travels of caravanners, and is what makes holidays of this kind so special. It is the way to make friends, and to find out how people in other parts live, and to enjoy a freedom which other types of travel cannot provide.

This visit to Vesuvius, however, was not to be our last contact with the volcano. The following day had been earmarked for a trip to Naples and the two families used it for the occasion to cross over to the Isle of Capri. The crossing, in a hydrofoil over very choppy seas, was in itself an experience but the disappointment was that the state of the sea prevented us from visiting the famous Blue Grotto. The only other aspect of this trip registered in the diaries is the extreme commercialisation of the Island and especially the tour to the Gracie Fields residence. It was very disappointing.

The next day was to provide us with another exciting and second episode of our contact with the volcano. We had heard a great deal about a small village some ten to fifteen miles from Vesuvius which supposedly was the safety valve for the volcano. The Barradell's were not so keen to follow this up but, fortunately, we had chanced to meet another Welsh family at Pozzuoli who wanted to see this fabulous place. They were Gwyneth and Ieuan Butler from Treorchy, and their son Melville. Both of them were school teachers and this meeting led to a friendship which has survived to today, sustained each Christmas and holiday with the exchange of greetings. If they should come across this reference we hope it will revive many happy memories of that day and also of the occasions we met afterwards on the crossroads of Europe for they, like us, were avid travellers.

The journey to Solfatara was uneventful but awareness of the place was established long before we actually reached the village through the distinct and overpowering smell of sulphur. It was fortunate for us that we should encounter a local who was also "English speaking" and obviously very proud of his locale. On enquiring the whereabouts of this famous safety valve he immediately offered to guide us. We had reached a spot about the size of a football pitch devoid of any sort of vegetation. We could see, smell, and feel the features of this strange place as we approached the edge. Picking up a largish stone our new found guide and friend hurled it into the middle of the area which perhaps could best be described as an overdone pie crust. It landed on what I thought was a hard baked soil and immediately there was a deep and resonant echo from below, one which seemed to set up a tremor underfoot. The echo, we were told, was because there's a kind of vacuum between the surface and the liquid of molten lava many metres below.

At the same time we detected wraiths of smoke belching from several areas of the pitch and could hear the plop, plop, of some form of gooey liquid and the occasional belch, all of which increased the sulphurous odour. All this, I must confess, gave the impression of some overfed gargantuan breaking wind.

The resonance and strength of the echo from below we understood was an important factor in assessing the activity of Vesuvius and was constantly monitored. The flow of molten soil or lava was fed into Solfatara through a kind of tunnel that had thrust itself out from the side of the volcano, emerging in this strange area. Whilst the pitch remained quietly active it eased the pressures building up inside Vesuvius, but when a constant burst of activity turned the pitch into a heaving and frightening mass, as had happened in 1944 when Vesuvius erupted with horrific results, this was the signal that something terrible was about to take place some ten miles away.

That is how it was explained to us. Whether any poetic licence had been introduced into the explanations and gesticulations I was not able to judge. Sufficient to say, however, that it was a mesmerising half hour which none of us would have missed. I was to pay another visit to Solfatara some years ahead when another unusual experience was to unfold, but what we learned and warmed to that afternoon could never be surpassed. I clearly recall our friend, gesticulating between the "pitch", as I dubbed it, and the outline of the towering volcano, and emphasising that Solfatara had first erupted 17,000 years ago. "If Solfatara did not "boooble"... bubble he meant... it would cause Vesuvius to go into eruption" he explained solemnly, and throwing his hands heavenwards.

Whilst these explanations were being offered the heat from the pitch, right up to the edge, was increasing. Steam from a crack towards the centre increased in pressure and I thought we were due for a local eruption there and then. We actually walked on the edge of the crater and were invited to poke a finger into the ground. Some of us did and were nearly scalded by the escaping steam. It was becoming too hot to stand and the smell of the sulphur was becoming obnoxious. The time had come to retire but before we did, and with a last burst of gesticulation, our friend proudly declared that Vallerie Friedleander used to cook eggs and spaghetti on the hot sulphur. You know, I never did find out who Vallerie Friedleander was, or why she/he had cause to use Vesuvius's watchdog - another name bestowed upon the "pitch" - to fry eggs and spaghetti.

This was the last of our very enjoyable sojourn in the hospitable and volatile area of Naples for the following day we struck camp early and were on our way to Venice (Cavalino) via Florence. The diary says "It's been very, very, hot travelling; approaching Uscita 22 (Florence) and a very pretty camp near the Autostrada. We shall have tea and an early night". So we did. Had a wonderful night and awoke refreshed and ready for the trek ahead. Goodbye Florence, City of Art and Culture, we shall be back someday.

# Chapter 26

# The Saga and Scandinavia

Whilst the enjoyments and memories of the 1967 holiday were still fresh in mind, stimulated by frequent "refreshers" of the many photograph sessions during the mid-winter months, our intentions for 1968 were focussed on the very attractive proposals for the F.I.C.C. rally in Sweden. We had never been across the North Sea but were tempted to take the crossing from Tilbury to Gothenburg and then motor to Norrkoping, venue for the rally.

It had been two years since the Davies's had joined us on a continental holiday but they readily agreed to our suggestion for a two part trip which would take us first to Sweden and then down to Italy via Germany and Austria. It would be one of our most ambitious undertakings, and with the difference that this time we would be just the four of us. The children were growing up and were opting out of holidays with mum and dad!

Preparations for the extended tour went well into the spring and reservations for the International Rally - and possibly a three days trip into the Arctic Circle - having been made we suddenly encountered the first problem. Len and Eileen were not keen on the sea crossing. So we agreed that they should make the journey across land, from Calais, through Holland and North Germany, Denmark and up to Norrkoping, whilst we travelled from Tilbury on the two nights' ferry crossing. For 'Van and I this accentuated the thrill of the journey as was subsequently proved. The vessel was the "SAGA", already well established, and for us, with its luxurious decor and appointment, it was the nearest we had been to a cruise, and the first holiday we were having together since 1938. Our first evening aboard, the diary recalls, was very pleasantly spent between the dining room, with its extremely attractive Smorgasbord and selection of fine dishes in Scandinavian style, the postprandial hour in the lounge savouring a selection of drinks, and the promenade deck. The weather was glorious and the sea like the proverbial millpond. Had we been able to arrange the conditions ourselves they could not have been better. The first-felt excitement having subdued we retired to our cabin for an excellent night's sleep. Nothing disturbed us until a quarter to seven when a shaft of sunlight through the porthole woke me. Not all the tea in China could have prevented me bouncing out of bed and up the companion way to savour the glory of a sun drenched early day with the ship barely off an even keel and the salty smell of the sea breeze tingling the nostrils. As I write now I can sense again that tremendous experience.

After an enjoyable breakfast we did all the things cruise passengers would do; we lounged in easy chairs on the top deck, played deck quoits, and surprisingly, but which showed the calmness of the sea, we were able to play table tennis in the lee of the top deck structure. Later we even sampled the Casino roulette wheel (with some small measure of success). And so the day passed quickly, too quickly, and another night of undisturbed sleep ended with a discreet tap on the cabin door at 5.30 am. We had docked, but we had not finished with the surprises. For as we were preparing to go on deck the tannoy called for Mr. and Mrs. Rosser to go to the Information Office.

We were disturbed at first, imagining a call from home and perhaps bad news. But when we reached the Information Office there, awaiting us with an outstretched hand and a broad smile, was the Immigration Officer informing us that he would conduct us to the immigration office and there would be no need for the formalities about passports. We would be shown straight through. Naturally we were somewhat perturbed at this V.I.P. treatment and I enquired why when we were being directed through the raised barrier. "Ah, we have our ways and means of finding out who is on board" was the answer, accompanied by what I assumed was a Scandinavian wink. "Have a lovely time on your visit to our country". How can I remember all this? Easy. It's all in the diary, word for word.

So is the very embarrassing incident at the same time. Having been escorted to our car and caravan on deck with several deck hands alongside to ensure we would be the first off the vessel, the engine just would not start. The battery was flat. I had inadvertently left the car radio on when we boarded. So there we were, central figures in a V.I.P. operation, privileged to be first off board, suffering the ignominy of deckhands having to unhitch the caravan and giving us a bump start which was not being successful. Eventually the car was pushed to the sloping gangway where, fortunately, it fired. But the caravan had to be manhandled on to terra firma and re-hitched. If anyone reading this can recall such an incident at Gothenburg on 1st August 1968 we now apologise for the delay caused in the general disembarkation and can only offer as an explanation for the extraordinary event that the ship's Purser had mistaken the "J.P." on my passport (and the fact that it had been issued through the House of Commons Transport Office facility) for M.P. and construed I was a visiting Member of Parliament incognito. But for a while it added a distinctly pleasurable flavour to the holiday's experiences.

The journey to Norrkoping was uneventful and Len and Eileen were awaiting our arrival. Unfortunately our other friends, Percy and Margaret Rowlands whom we had first met at the Hungary International Rally, had not been able to make the journey, though we did collect their rally plaque for them. What can one say about this exceptional Rally hosted by the Swedes and to some extent the Finns except that here again was something quite different and immensely enjoyable. A highlight of the occasion was our meetings with the Laplanders, the most friendly and jovial of people who delighted everyone with their exuberant displays of Lap customs and culture. We came away with some of their picturesque headgear and the knowledge that if the women wore it with the tassel hanging to either side this indicated they were single and eligible. If worn to the front it was a "hands off" signal because the wearer would be a married. The Laps also carried away the honour this time of having one of their contingent elected Rally Queen. The five days we spent at Norrkoping were among the most enjoyable of any period during all the years of holidays... and amazingly enough I find that although so far north I had to receive treatment for sunburn after the second day!

En route for Italy the journey through Denmark is recalled for the three days' stopover in Copenhagen and the visit to The Tivoli, which in 'Van's words, after spending a couple of hours there during the evening, is "the most stupendously fabulous place I have ever been to in my life. I was awestruck by the beauty of the millions of coloured lights decorating every building, especially the replica of the Taj Mahal." Fortuitously we had been advised to delay our visit until dark, which enhanced the beauty of the place and also enabled us to track down the world famed Langaline, the Mermaid. This was a beautiful lifelike figure but the position of the statue wasn't impressive in the least. There may be a reason why it is cast away in isolation on the water lapped rock outside what appeared to be a working port, and most difficult to trace, but I am quite unaware of it.

Two other events of our three day stay in Copenhagen were the visit to the "Coq D'Or" which served us the most elegant and finest meals we have ever had abroad, and the morning spent in Deyerhaven which houses the famous herd of deer. We paid 25 Kroner each to ride in a magnificent horse-drawn Landau around the estate. 'Van writes: "Our coachman was a dear. He took his time to show us everything of interest, even to the horses being shod, and then explained to us that the carriage in which we had been riding was in fact an old Royal Coach. No wonder I felt like royalty".

It was with regret that we left early morning of the 8th August to resume our trek to Italy, and having to leave our friends the Davies's behind. They had decided to forego the Italy journey to spend some more time in Denmark and then Holland before returning home. We however, decided to fulfil our plans and made for Hanover via the crossing at Puttgarden. Alone again we travelled 310 miles before finding a lovely Gasthof out in the Harz mountain country where we were invited to pull our car and caravan behind the house and partake of our dinner in the Gaststatte. It's wonderful what a good meal and a bottle of wine can do at the end of a long journey, and the fact that we hardly understood our German hosts nor that they could understand English in no way affected our mutual enjoyment. This, again, is the real enjoyment of caravanning abroad.

Friday, 9th August 1968, is a black day in the annals of British aviation. That was the day an airliner Munich bound from London crashed with a heavy toll of life on the Munich autobahn. It is also a day we shall never forget for we had just switched on the radio to a local

American forces station when we heard of the crash and appeals for local assistance. Because of this we decided to put up for the night on the forecourt of a garage a few miles from Ingolstadt. Come 6.30 am the following morning we were on the road again.

Suddenly we were in a traffic jam of massive proportions as autobahn traffic for Munich was being diverted through hop fields and along cart tracks to avoid the scene of disaster. According to the diary the weather was terrible, rain and mist, as we neared Ingolstadt. It took half an hour to do a few miles with vehicles bumper to bumper diverted around the town and a detour of 14 miles to avoid encroaching on the scene of the crash. In fact we were just able to distinguish the charred wreckage and the cranes, and it gave us the shivers to think that 49 British bodies were burnt on that spot.

Our destination was Salzburg, which we reached by late afternoon and were able to find a place at "Sam" camping site which had suffered badly from a day and a half's deluge of rain. Here again we experienced another chance encounter out of the blue, none other than my colleague in the House of Commons Lobby, Bob Scott, of the Yorkshire Post, and his wife Irene. Together we decided to make for the N.S.U. Camping, Venice, which we assured them would be the highlight of their holiday. At least we were certain to be out of the rain! And so it happened that two caravans were again en route, with the first overnight stop at Lienz, then over the Dolomites, through the new Felbertauern tunnel and on to Cavallino and sun, sand and blue water. But the tragedy of the air crash remained with us throughout the holiday.

By the evening of August 12th we had settled in at Camping N.S.U. and for twelve glorious days we lounged around taking the fullest advantage of sun and sea. It was the Scott's first visit and they and the children thoroughly enjoying themselves was a bonus. The stay there was memorable for another friendship made, and if they read this reference I am sure it will recall many happy memories for them too. I refer to David Chaplin and Gerald Brookes, two schoolteacher friends who were ensconced in their Sprite caravan behind us when we arrived and who, in the true spirit of caravanners, had immediately come to our assistance in setting up our caravans and awnings on our arrival. Sadly, in the meanwhile, we have lost our good friend and my colleague Bob who died so tragically and unexpectedly in the prime of life, but Irene and the children, Helen and Julian, will without doubt also remember that special stay in Cavallino.

A feature of the newly made friendship was that the two chaps had a massive household type 'fridge in their awning and its capacity was such that they were able to, and did, take all our liquid refreshments and keep them ice cold. It was a life saver! I was astonished that they were able to transport such a massive piece of equipment around with them but they assured us that wherever they went abroad the 'fridge went with them. That association made at N.S.U. has been sustained throughout the twenty three years since then and wherever they may be in any part of the world - and they still do travel extensively - we are kept informed, and so are the Scotts.

August 24th was a sun-drenched morning and also the day we had to leave. The Scotts had decided to stay on but our schedule would not allow us. The return journey according to the diary was practically uneventful, except that is for two happenings. The first was our attempt to cross the Arlberg Pass from St. Antoine to Bregenz. All went well to start with and the car was just holding its own. Suddenly I was aware of another British outfit attempting to overtake us as we were approaching a bend on an acutely steep stretch. It was obviously underpowered and presented an extremely dangerous situation. I braked and came to a stop. The other outfit just managed to pass as a coach came round the bend. Had I not braked the chances are that a collision was unavoidable on a road which barely allowed a single overtaking. But having braked we couldn't get any further traction. Some climbers lent a hand and we were able to ease the outfit back slowly to a narrow lay-by and allow upward traffic to pass. It was a hair raising experience and only by unhitching the car were we able to turnaround and make the journey back to St Antoine and Imst and take an alternative route.

The second event of note was our "dropping in" on the Walter family at Bad Durkheim. We had met them at Camping N.S.U. where they extended an open invitation to call on them at any time. Since we were within a few miles of the Bad this would be as good a time as ever. We received a tremendous welcome but the feature of the visit was the Cossack type barbecue to which we were treated by Karl Heinz and Jenny Walter, herself of Cossack upbringing. Never had there been, nor I guess will there be again, such a wonderful repast. The Walters had collected all the dead vines possible from nearby vineyards which made a marvellous hot bed and across this on half a dozen Cossack cavalry swords were barbecued an assortment of meats. The verdict: Absolutely fantastic! The meats, impregnated with the aroma and the taste of the vines, were really out of this world!

Since then we have met again, the last time being in North Wales in 1990 when the Familie Walter paid their first visit to the U.K. and we were able to repay some of the debt we owed for that wonderful couple of days we spent in Bad Durkheim. And so ended yet another pleasurable and educational Continental trek.

## Chapter 27

## And the Snow Came Too

Preparations for the following holiday were routine affairs by now. And so it was to be Italy, 1969, and the sun and the blue sea, and lots of cappuccino, ice cream and so many other things associated with that country. But it turned out to be yet another unusual experience as will be explained later.

Again the venue was to be Camping N.S.U. and with the Davies's we set out from Uxbridge on a Wednesday, 6th August for our reserved crossing by ferry to Zeebrugge. En route, and of some interest perhaps in these days, we stopped for a meal of gammon steaks, chips and peas for which we paid six shillings, and had we arrived at this particular cafe a few minutes later it transpires we would have had to pay an excess of sixpence each, since the surcharge was imposed after 11 pm. It is recorded that the meal was excellent and very filling. I wonder how much one would have to pay nowadays for a similar meal?

After a beautiful and calm crossing we were greeted at Zeebrugge with the sight which caused a flutter of the heart. Our dreamboat of the Sweden crossing had just berthed and there in all her glory was the "SAGA". What lovely memories it recalled through Holland, as far as Roermond and the German frontier, and down the autobahn network into Austria with a stopover at another of our favourite places, Limburg, we reached Kufstein three days later. The trip meter registered 385 miles and we decided to bide a while in what was a pleasant but very plain camping platz alongside the river. What we wanted was a few days' rest;

but we did not have them. They turned out to be extremely active days of sightseeing which usually ended in a visit to one of the traditional Bier Kellars in the old town where we mingled in and enjoyed local festivities. These are what make our holidays abroad such exciting and enjoyable affairs. On the last night when we arrived back at camp near to midnight we could not find the keys of our caravan anywhere. Len and I raced back to the Bier Kellar and retrieved them. They had been found on the floor and handed in. That instantly removed the thoughts that without access to our own caravan it might have necessitated a four in a bed situation.

Two days later we were looking for a campsite in Tolmezzo, well over the Italian border. What we did find was a partly constructed restaurant offering fresh river trout... and sufficient room at the rear for two caravans. It was just the job! In no time we had made a deal with the portly proprietor. It was four trout suppers, desert and coffee for four, and a place for the night, all for less than 8,000 lire. And as a bonus Len and I were told we could have as souvenirs four terrazzo tiles from the unfinished building. As I write these few lines now I am aware that outside my window are the four tiles, safely preserved after twenty five years!

The fortnight's stay in N.S.U. was virtually a carbon copy of previous holidays with a large measure of annual reunions. But the diaries do reveal that this year the weather was not so kind. There were many more storms and much more rain than we had hitherto experienced. It was a harbinger of what was to come that one night the hailstones were so heavy that caravan roofs were badly dented, and the damage generally was something they had not experienced in that part of Italy. In fact it was interesting that during one of our latest sojourns at the camp we found, among a list of photographs in their thirty years' museum record, pictures of that exceptional storm as worthy of record.

The return journey was to be via Switzerland. In those days there was no talk about tolls on roads for tourist traffic and the country enjoyed more of the advantages people like us brought to the economy. Since they have introduced the special tax for caravans using their major roads we have not been to Switzerland, and there are a great many in our circle who likewise have given the country a pass. It is a great shame because Switzerland is one of the most fascinatingly beautiful countries on the

Continent of Europe, but regrettably being priced out of reach of many thousands' caravanners.

We crossed from Italy into Switzerland by way of the Resia Pass with St. Moritz our objective for the night. But as we neared the top of the pass we realised there was a dramatic change in the weather. They'd had snow on the mountain tops already, and it was still August. The late evening temperature fell to freezing and we managed only 18 kilometres on the Swiss side before giving up any thought of making St. Moritz. Fortunately we came across a small camping site, already partly snowbound and here, thankfully, we were permitted to stay the night. The diary shows that "the snow we have had has transformed this delightful little site into a fairyland. It is situated on the side of the mountain and we have had to cross a narrow bridge over a ravine to get to it. Both Eileen and I have middle ear trouble and our heads are bursting. Its bitterly cold and pretty dark... maybe more snow! The lights from the mountain reflecting in the snow is a sight I shall never forget. It reminds me of a glorious picture I once saw in a picture gallery".

It is of moments like this that the diaries are proving their real worth. They bring back forgotten moments of joy and recall, as on this particular occasion, instances which otherwise would have passed into the oblivion of time. How thankful we who now read them are for the restoration of those treasured memories and the ability to relive those precious experiences. Once again in our minds we relive that evening when we ventured down to a little village some half a kilometre away to partake of a meal at the Sports Hotel and to share an evening with many climbers who had also been obliged to seek the refuge in most unusual weather conditions for this time of year. The Swiss proprietor spoke perfect English, a fact he explained as having been a chef at the Park Lane Hotel London. We exchanged reminiscences since I knew that Hotel very well. Possibly he had prepared one or some of the several meals I had enjoyed at that establishment during my years at the House of Commons. In any case it made for a special attention and we are reminded that a "lovely soup was followed by a delightfully spit-roasted chicken with white cauliflower, chips and salad, then fresh fruit salad and cream with coffee to follow".

We were also told that the St. Julier Pass which we were to go over on the following day was covered with snow 15 inches deep. The snow was three months early and had taken everyone by surprise. And we were surprised further by the site owner's claim that he had taught Prince Charles to ski at this particular spot. The route to St. Moritz probed just negotiable and we arrived there early afternoon. That one afternoon and evening we spent at St. Moritz was, I believe, one of the coldest we had ever experienced. Not even gas fires at maximum could dispel the chill and there was no objection when it was suggested that, beautiful as were the surroundings, we should move on and to lower pastures come the morn!

Thereafter it was through Chur, on to Lichtenstein and thence Lake Constance, with the sun once again on our backs. According to the record there were no more unusual events; but we have been very lucky during the passage through Germany in that every night we were able to find a Gasthof where an evening meal for the four of us was accompanied by an "invitation" to put up our caravans alongside for the night. This is setting a new pattern for future holidays abroad!

August 31st, a Sunday, and, after an overnight stay in Sluis on the Dutch-Belgium border, we have decided to take an earlier boat from Zeebrugge to Dover. On arrival back in Uxbridge and checking the milometer we find we have covered 3,568 miles. And each mile has strengthened our resolve to make our next holiday abroad an even more venturesome one, and caused us to think why we had left caravanning so late in life.

## Chapter 28

## We Make a Hurried Return

Wednesday, 22nd July, was the beginning of our holiday 1970 and what an extraordinary one this was to turn out. In the first place 'Van and I were to be on our own, and because of this had decided the programme should be more flexible than hitherto. We had made little or no planning, except to decide that once more we should spend some time at Union Lido, still affectionately regarded by us as N.S.U. Camping, Venice. When we were to get there, and how long to stay, were to be decisions of the moment. Which perhaps was just as well as things turned out. Anyway, we had made the usual ferry reservations from Dover to Zeebrugge and our arrival at port of embarkation was in perfect weather which augured well for the five hours crossing. But this was to be a crossing with a difference.

We had on a previous crossing made friends with Captain Dawson, Commodore of the Townsend Thoresen Line who were the ferry operators in those days, and were delighted to find our vessel was the Enterprise Five under his command. Shortly after casting off we heard our names called over the tannoy and the request that we attend the Captain on the bridge. It was indeed, Captain Dawson and he immediately offered us the full facilities of his own cabin. What a pleasure it was to be able to put one's head down and sleep for a few hours of the crossing and to be awakened by the steward with a pot of hot tea and toast. THIS was the ultimate in V.I.P. treatment for which we are ever grateful to our old friend.

It was a grand start to the holiday, especially to view from the bridge the docking and then to be permitted to use the private lift which took us down to the car deck. Our heads were still swimming as we made for Brussels, our first brief stop, and then on to Luxembourg. Having docked at 4.30 am and with the advantage of a beautifully sunny and warm morning, we had reached Namur by 7.10 am and breakfasted at a lay-by. It was a leisurely drive from there to Luxembourg, reached before midday, and had no difficulty in finding a small but pleasant site. The outfit had covered 287 miles. We left our Camping Grunewald at 7.00 am the following morning after a good sleep overnight and set out for Strasbourg and then Basle, which we reached at 4.15 pm. It was to be an overnight halt in Switzerland and after a four countries' journey we were heading for Luzern.

At this particular point I was mentioning to 'Van that the area looked very familiar and that it would be great if we should come across the Croix Blanche Gasthof where, a few years earlier with Marilyn and Nigel, we had spent the night forever etched in all our minds for the "raspberries and cream" episode. 'Van will confess to a weakness for cream and on this particular occasion we had been offered with our evening meal a large bowl of freshly picked raspberries and the largest bowl of fresh cream any of us had seen. There was still a lot left when 'Van suggested it was time for bed for the children. There were mild protestations from Nigel who pointed out that there was still a large helping of the cream left. But mother knew best, and off to bed it had to be. To this day the accusation is levelled that 'Van's main reason for packing him off to bed was so she could finish the cream.

Suddenly, as we turned the bend, there it was, the Croix Blanche, standing out like a sore thumb. I wasn't going to pass by. We both agreed it was a stroke of fate and that we should, if possible, stop overnight. A brief word with the manager, and a reminder of what had happened a couple of years before, and we were welcomed to stay for a meal and park the caravan alongside overnight. The only thing missing was.... the raspberries and cream. We were a week too early for the fruit.

It happened that my brother Idris, his wife Bernadette, and the family, then living in Brussels where he was a member of the British Embassy staff, were caravanning at Finale Liguro at that time and we considered it worth a detour to surprise them en-route for Venice. According to the diary the drive through Finale was a nightmare... "it's a miracle we haven't bumped the car and caravan through these narrow streets, and we have driven six miles before finding the camp". Eventually we did, after a long climb up a mountain. It was situated in a forest of pine trees, and this, as we found out, ensured the complete absence of mosquitoes. Our appearance was met with delight and for two days we enjoyed the company of the family. Apparently the drill was to drive down to the beach in Finale each mid-morning and spend the whole day there. They had rented a bathing chalet for £12 for two weeks, allowing them a pretty full day on the beach before returning to camp about six o'clock for their main meal. It was an ideal situation, and our involvement, though for only two days, served again to emphasise the advantages of "go as you please and do as you please" caravanning. This was completely unplanned, and possibly for that all the more enjoyable.

July 28th. After a breakfast of bacon and eggs in the open, and with the scent of the pine trees enhancing the aroma, we said our goodbyes and began the next leg of the trip to Cavallino, Venice. Would we be able to make it in two days? Only if we used the Autostrada from Milan; so this is what we agreed to do. With the temperature soaring to 85 degrees even with the aid of the autostrada it seemed the one leg trip would be too much. And so it proved because we had covered 230 miles and still had some distance to go to the Verona exit when we noticed a very inviting lay-by, some 100 yards or so off the motorway and offering a reasonable amount of shade and facilities under trees. The temptation was too great, and the heat too oppressive to carry on, so at 4.30 pm we called it a day. There was plenty of room in the lay-by with only a few vehicles, including one other caravan, putting up for the night. A family of Greek campers followed us in and we had a regular entente-cordiale during the evening because the man spoke English and apart from the talking we shared our eats and drinks. It was a splendid evening, most enjoyable for the fantastic weather and the company.

An early start the following morning meant that we reached N.S.U. Camping by 8.30 am and received a warm welcome... no waiting and signing in, just a few handshakes and "you know where to go...". We found there had been many changes since last year, including horse riding and tennis courts in a new sporting complex. By the very nature of the existence of the camp which had began as a private camping and holiday centre for the workers of the German N.S.U. motor company it was only natural in those early days that there were more German caravanners and campers than other nationalities. When we found a place for our outfit it was in the middle of the German fraternity, and it was the best thing that could have happened to us. They all welcomed us heartily and with fulsome hospitality. In no time we had helping hands and had the outfit and awning in ship shape. These are friendships, which in many cases, have been sustained throughout the years until today, but for this particular occasion two names have to be mentioned. They were Wilma and Horst who, with their sons James and Rainier, were in a very large twin axle caravan which was at that time the very latest in sophistication. They invited us to breakfast while the boys put the finishing touches to the awning and expressed the wish to speak only in English. They wanted to improve their English, and especially they wanted James to converse with us as much as possible in English. He was a very bright lad and in a matter of days he had an excellent grasp of colloquial English.

It turned out that Horst had a contract with the largest German motor manufacturers for his factories' window cleaning operations and I learned a great deal in a short time about this side of the industry. No wonder he could afford such a caravan and a 25 foot motor launch which he had berthed in Jesolo, five miles away. Furthermore I gathered that the entire procession of two cars, caravan and launch, were transported by rail from Rheinhessen to Mestre, the railway junction for Venice, and thence by road in the case of the caravan and by sea with the launch, just like a military operation. But whilst Horst and the family were at N.S.U. they behaved and were treated like any other holidaymaker.

Our relations with the whole of our camping line in which we were the only Britishers improved daily, and with such a good sprinkling of English speaking professional men it was only natural I suppose that during those parts of the day when the heat made movement an unnecessary activity that we should indulge in comparisons between British and German modes in the various professions. There were doctors, lawyers, industrialists, a journalist, a chemist, and even a Trade Union official, and fortified with the German lagers and wines (supplied mainly by Horst I should add) these forums under different awnings became a feature of our stay.

Young James proved to be a gem for us. His English lessons in our caravans were rewarded by Horst's insistence that we should have our caravan wired for mains electric, as it seemed all the German caravans were. And he instructed James to undertake the work. Which he did with typical Teutonic efficiency, so much so that when we came away we were, electrically speaking, on a par with the Germans.

1st August: This is Swiss National Day. Our German friends do not need much of an excuse to organise a celebration, and early in the morning 'Van and I were told we had to attend a sole and wine function in Wilma's awning. It was 89 degrees, but this in no way slowed up the celebration which by this time had grown to a fireworks' display and a singsong on the beach. "How can I describe the wonderful evening adequately enough" 'Van writes. "First, the fireworks, it reminded me of Lake Balaton in Hungary and then we saw the Laplanders -just as they had been in Norrkoping - sitting around the table eating and drinking and making merry. It was at Horst's invitation, and a lovely touch to the evening".

One of the most picturesque scenes was the procession of lanterns along the beach and the camp lines and as a special concession the ten o'clock routine closedown on the day's open activities were suspended for a couple of hours. In fact it was near to midnight when the camp guards joined us for a celebratory and goodnight drink. On the morrow we would return to the normal rules and regulations of a wonderfully run and organised camp. Myfanwy signed off this day's entry as follows: "Very tired but went to bed feeling this had been one of the happiest evenings we have spent in years, thanks to Horst and Wilma and our other German friends. Language has not mattered for we have understood one another perfectly. What a lovely celebration!"

Monday 3rd August dawned with promise of another hot day. The weather during our stay so far has been absolutely splendid, with no hint of stormy showers which usually descend at this time of the year in this area. But it was to be also a day particularly special to us both. Before our departure from England we knew that our daughter was expecting her first child within a month and it was with this in mind that I telephoned our son Nigel for news. It was our intention to remain in N.S.U. until Saturday and then leave for Austria, Germany and on to Brussels where we should be spending a few days with Id. and Bernadette. Fate was to decree otherwise. It is recalled that on my return from that telephone call, and on settling down after the initial shock, Myfanwy writes "What joy! What wonderful news to hear about our lovely new baby, David John. Darling Mal is OK and baby alright and so good to know that John has given them both such happiness. My only regret is that I'm not home with them. I do so want to be home even though Heather - (our daughter in law) -has said we are not to come. Oh I wish I had been home when Mal had the baby. We came out early so we would be home when the baby came, but somehow I knew when Mal had the backache before we left that something was sure to happen."

News of the happy event spread through the lines like wildfire. First there was a crate of lager from Horst, then messages and flowers from others among the German fraternity. Myfanwy couldn't stop crying and there was only one thing to be done; start back for home. Tomorrow cannot be too soon. And so it happened that for the first time ever we cut a holiday short and hurried back to U.K.. There was no question that it was the right thing to do. We said our farewells with mixed feelings, had a celebratory dinner for the two of us at the Restaurant Principale, walked back to the caravan in a soft and welcomed shower of rain - first of our stay here.

As we prepared to leave the following morning who should arrive but our friends the Scotts. They understood, of course, and it was a case of hello and goodbye in the same voice!

The return journey was obviously uneventful because little was recorded. The greatest emphasis was on getting the first boat home by the shortest route... but there was one incident. On the way to Aachen we were stopped by the police for alleged speeding. A rather grim faced officer approached the nearside of the car, book in hand, and said we had been travelling at much more than 80 kilometres per hour whereas the speed should have been 48 k.p.h.. Sheep facedly we explained the reason if we had exceeded the limit... we had a new grandson awaiting us. He must have been a father himself because he relaxed, asked to see my licence then waved me on with a cautionary "don't forget now. No more 80k's... and good luck". There is one brief addendum: "It's lucky for us he did not flag us down when we started this morning. We were doing 60/65 miles an hour" Myfanwy observed.

Calais loomed out of a mist as we approached in the early hours of Saturday 8th August. It had been a breakneck journey but we were on the 3.30 am ferry for Dover and home at 8.15 am. Thereafter is given to the fulfilment of seeing and holding our daughter's first born, and our thanks for a never to be forgotten journey across Europe.

# Chapter 29

# Spain: When the Gremlins Took Over

The 1971 holiday had a strange air about it from the very beginning. We had arranged a resumption of our continental trip with the Davies's but whereas we thought of a holiday in Spain, and the attractions of virtually guaranteed good weather and an extremely favourable Peseta rate which would mean a cheaper holiday, our friends opted for a stay in the Midi area of France. Nonetheless we crossed over together on the Southampton to Le Havre route on the 11th August with a parting of the ways at the port. We made for Chartres, thence to Toulouse and Perpignon, and Len and Eileen set off for Rouen. There was a tentative agreement that we should meet in Annecy in about a fortnight's time at a camp where we had stayed ten years ago and then complete the journey back together. Reflecting now on that kind of arrangement it seems ridiculous that we could even think of coming together without considering what might befall the other. Yet, it had been done in the past; when we had lost each other at so many crossroads of Europe we had not once failed to link up again. So why should it be different this time? This was also one of the attractions of caravanning in those earlier days.

For the first time, however, we experienced some slight misgivings about the planned holiday. We had travelled 200 miles from Le Havre and pulled in at a lay-by when we met a British student hitchhiking - not a common thing in those days - from Spain back to Britain. He told us about the cholera which had struck Spain, and then tried to cheer us up by saying that it was all finished now, and in any case the weather there was glorious. We were a bit dubious. Should we go on or, without any commitments and free to change our destination, turn left as it were and head for the Midi. We agreed to carry on, but we did not encourage any further conversations with other travellers! As it happened it might have been better had we changed direction, but that is a story for further on.

Our first overnight was at Chateauroux after a day's travel of some 250 miles. It was an excellent site encompassed by fir trees and after a splendid dinner in the 'van, washed down with a first class local vintage, thoughts of what the kindly thinking student had told us were defused in an undisturbed night's sleep. Friday the 13th held no qualms for us as we sped towards Toulouse which we planned to reach by early evening. We have always tried to get in for the night before 4.30 pm on these long hops, and for this reason we by-passed the famous pottery town of Limoges and 215 miles further on had to acknowledge that Toulouse had to be out for this day. We had reached Cahors, the very attractive and Romanesque city, and it was just on 4.30 pm so we surrendered to the appeal of a beautiful and small camping site alongside the river and only a short step from the famous bridge.

After another splendid dinner of chicken breast and pomme frites in the 'van, and in the cool of the evening, we "dressed up" and walked through the town. It dripped of history, was extremely interesting and surprisingly without any visible tourist exhortations, but was very expensive. It was a lager and lemonade each at a small Bistro and back to the 'van where we went to sleep to the lulling sounds of a nearby weir.

The timetable had to be adjusted after only two days out. Instead of Toulouse we now had to make Andorra on the Pyrenees our next halt. The countryside developed into a Peachland. There were peach orchards and roadside stalls everywhere with signs inviting "Fruit to taste for the British". It seemed that only the British tourists ventured this far. Myfanwy's comments are "It may be a gimmick .. Vive le Common Market."

By 2 pm we had reached Ax-le-Thermes and climbing towards the fabulous tax free haven of Andorra through the Envalira Pass which took us some 7,800 ft to the peak. The mountains around us are surprisingly green and very lovely, it is recalled, and the journey was made all the more enjoyable because the car towed the caravan without any problems. If only the road surface had been as good we would have avoided the calamity which occurred when we struck a pothole and one of the cupboard doors flew open taking some toll of our glass dishes and spillages. Myfanwy was most philosophical about it. "If that's all that happens we won't worry" she writes.

The timing for our arrival at Andorra was perfect. Just on 4.30 pm we were turning into a site in Santa Coloma and our first reactions to this small and picturesque town where tourist shopping is a treat was that it had changed considerably since our first visit in 1961. It's become so commercialised. At the camp we met a couple from Ickenham, just a few miles from our own home, who were travelling the Continent in their retirement and living on their capital. Very nice too! Then there was a German couple who came on to us because they had spotted the Red Dragon on our 'van. "I've played football against your people in Wales" was his introduction, and it transpired that the game had been in Llanelli, our birthplace. It turned out to be a wonderful evening, made all the more so by the cheapness of some excellent vintages. Just another example of the advantages of caravanning and the camaraderie between those who have taken to this form of holidaying. It was also, for us, another instance where our Red Dragon symbol had singled us out!

Our destination on the Spanish side the following day was Montroig, even then a prominent name in camping and caravanning. By mid-afternoon on Sunday August 15th we had made it, and first impressions fully justified the 807 miles we had travelled to reach it. There was a surprise for us on the following day when who should arrive, unannounced as it were, but our friends Bob and Irene Scott and their two children. Two days later the Gremlins struck. Myfanwy twisted her ankle so badly that I had to take her to hospital in Tarragona where they diagnosed a suspected fracture of the ankle. There had to be some X-rays (which fortunately revealed no fracture but very severe bruising) and while this was taking place - and at the recommendation of the doctor I should add - I did a tour of the dockside adjacent to the hospital and which offered a plethora of what we called "sippers" in Spain. These were the establishments selling Tarragona wines according to your taste, and a sip from the various casks decided which one. Harmless enough, you would say. In my case, however, it proved anything but, as was to be revealed some months later.

I was not very impressed with what I was given to taste and, fortunately perhaps as it turned out, made no purchases but returned to collect Myfanwy from the hospital. We were back in camp by late afternoon, but she was in great pain and unable to do more than sit on a lounger outside the 'van. The weather was great, if anything too hot, which forced us to decide to shorten the stay. Regretfully we took our leave of Mont-roig and our friends on 22nd August, three days sooner than we had intended. For Myfanwy particularly, the journey through Spain and France so far as Annecy, which took us until the 25th was a painful one. Our arrangement to meet the Davies's had also been upended. Enquiries at the camp in Talloires, where we had spent several days ten years before, proved negative. The Davies's had not arrived. We stayed in an adjoining site for another day then set out for Basle with the intention of taking the autobahn through to Aachen and then Brussels where we were to stay a couple of days with my brother and family. It turned out quite differently. Those Gremlins had not finished with us.

The pain in Myfanwy's ankle was still troubling her and we were obliged to make an overnight halt in Freiburg where she received treatment at the local clinique. It was then that things started happening to me. I began having headaches and a temperature, and so bad were they that I had to hand over a share of the driving to Myfanwy. By this time we had progressed via Strasburg en-route for Luxembourg and reached a quaint mediaeval twin township of Traben-Trarbach. Not that either of us at that time were in a condition to appreciate the beauty of the place, which in years to come, would be almost a second home for us on our continental holidays. We could go no further and were extremely fortunate to find a most attractive site alongside the Moselle at Rissbach. It was spotlessly clean and the grass cut short; but if it had been no more than a ramshackle place we had no option. In retrospect this was one of the best things that happened to us in all the years of travelling.

A day's rest and both of us felt better. I was able to play games of boule with fellow campers and Myfanwy rested her leg in the lounger on the riverbank watching the barges pass by. It was an idyllic scene, and one we have enjoyed so many times since. But on the second day my headaches and high temperature returned. Myfanwy writes "Glan has not been well these last few days again. I think he is sickening for 'flu and have dosed him with Panadols and Beechams and he seems more himself."

But it was not to be. The condition obviously worsened and Herr Hack, the site owner, (Theo to us for the past twenty years, and Jenny his wife, have been our very close friends since this episode), obviously perturbed at the condition, suggested I should see a specialist immediately. He took me to Traben where the doctor did not speak English and neither did Herr Hack. I tried to explain how I felt, and it was getting most exasperating as they two tried to tell me what the doctor felt was wrong. Suddenly the doctor tried French and I was able to converse and discover what was wrong with me. The outcome: I was a suspected case of Jaundice, a notifiable disease requiring immediate hospitalisation under German law. That did it! Theo took me back to camp and within an hour with their help we were pulling out of camp en-route for Brussels. I was propped up in the front passenger seat dozing off periodically and poor Myfanwy had to drive. It was the most hazardous drive of her life and not only had she to take care of the driving but of me also.

At 6.30 pm we were only 22 miles from Brussels and a telephone call to Id and B. giving our location was swiftly followed by the appearance of Id. and his son Peter. Myfanwy followed them home and the entire drive had taken from ll.30 am. That night the Embassy doctor attended me and after some temporary stabilising tablets and a night's restless sleep Myfanwy and I were on the plane at 8 am 5th September for Heathrow. An effect of the tablets was to induce a condition which developed into pneumonia and which kept me in bed for a fortnight, but a sequel was that several months later, after a thorough inspection by a Specialist who had traced my movements back from Mont-roig to Uxbridge, it was established that the jaundice condition had been caused through unhygienic wines sampled in Tarragona. I counted my blessings then that I had not bought any of the wine. As for the caravan and car, they were kept in Brussels until brought back by my brother several weeks after our return. So ended the holiday 1971, but it in no way affected our liaison with caravanning and travels abroad. There were many more to come, and the trips became longer and more adventurous with the years. The Gremlins had had a field day on this occasion, but they found us Traben-Trarbach and that was more than adequate compensation.

# Chapter 30

# Lechbruck and the Floods!

Winter planning had decided us to attempt once again an International Rally. This time it was to be held in Germany and with the Davies's we had decided to make the venue with just our two caravans rather than join what promised to be a very large British contingent. So it happened that on the 2nd August 1972, after a wet and windy run down to Dover, we were boarding the 4.30 pm boat for passage to Zeebrugge. It wasn't one of the best crossings and we were forced to spend a couple of hours resting up on the other side before commencing the long trip into the heart of Germany. We followed the road through Antwerp and on the Breda and Eindhoven route ll. But misfortune struck on the approach to Rotterdam.

I reckoned it was the unceasing rain but whatever, pressing on doggedly in the lead and supposedly heading for Aachen, scheduled as our first overnight halt, I found I was on the wrong road. Fifty miles were added to the journey and, no matter about the weather, my name was MUD. Adding to the discomfort was the puncture which necessitated a change of wheel for Len in the unrelenting wet weather. A helpful garage some miles afterwards at Oirschot restored some good feeling - though it didn't please Len to have to fork out the equivalent of £13 for a new tyre; but from the outset it was obvious we were to be hard pressed to maintain the schedule we had set ourselves to reach the Rally on time.

"We don't know where we will be tonight nor when we shall get there" says the diary. Still, isn't it the case that caravanning, and especially when one is enjoying it, is a matter of unpredictability. If there is anything to contribute to the adage that even the best laid plans of mice and men go wrong it is caravanning. By the same token what does it matter because one has one's own house and entourage attached and there need be no pressures on time. Apart from a few tribulations time should be one's own.

And we did have a few of those tribulations ourselves before the end of this first day. "What a day" comments Myfanwy in the diary. "Everything is happening". This related to a brief stop for a light snack when she spilled a jug of milk over herself and Len, and in attempting to avoid the cascade Len jumped up and upset the whole table. We all had a fit of laughter. It was hilarious! "Hope that's the end of today's episodes" was the rueful comment as we pressed on during late afternoon in the hope of making Limburg before dark. "Nearly out of petrol" was the repeated warning as I desperately looked out for an autobahn Tankstelle. I reckon there was barely a cupful left when one came in sight and as I pulled up the look on Len's face was sufficient evidence that they too had been going through the same trauma. The only consoling factor in a very trying day were signs of an improvement in the weather, and the cheering comment by the petrol attendant which we took to mean that the weather would be better tomorrow.

Just on eight o'clock - or 20.00 hours continental wise which we were now familiar with - the sign Limburg came in sight and our fears that we might be too late to find some empty spaces were dispelled quickly. With 362 miles on the clock and hopefully the bad weather behind us a good meal of fried onions and tomatoes (soup first) followed by home made strawberry jam - according to the record the Davies's munched their way through two pork chops preceded by a bowl each of onion soup - put things in proper perspective. After a good night's sleep we would be off on an early start in the morning geared to make up any loss in schedule.

There is nothing more calculated to wreck a peaceful disposition in my experience than being marooned on a German autobahn surrounded by hooting cars and processions of stationary vehicles for as long as the eyes can see. And this is what greeted us less than half an hour after leaving Limburg. Ninety minutes and perhaps three miles later we discovered the reason... a very bad smash-up which had reduced the motorway to a diverted crawl and which seemed to have created a mass of ill feeling and bad tempered drivers and occupants of stopped then crawling vehicles. Bang goes our hopes of making up loss time! One consolation was the proverbial English cuppa and accompanying Welshcakes which we were able to consume in the caravan during one particularly patience-sapping halt.

On and on towards Augsburg it was a tale of congested autobahn and by teatime we still had seventy miles to go before reaching Lechbruck and the Rally. Despite the lateness our spirits were cheered immensely by the beautiful countryside which seemed to improve even as we finally got the Rally site in sight. But the final half mile brought a depressing anti-climax. In what must have been a vale of paradise now there were hundreds of caravans higgledy-piggledy, almost in each other's pockets, some wheel deep in mud and water. The rally pitch resembled a stagnant lake surrounded by countless outfits of many nationalities, but in reality, as we were soon to find out, was a flooded out area with the actual lake in the background. This unfortunate occurrence had forced the organisers to change the site and the situation which faced us, particularly after such a trying journey, made us think seriously of moving on. Some enterprising British rallyers had established their own "encampment" besides the real lake and it was towards these that Len and I drove after persuading him that we had to stay overnight because we were not in a fit state to face more driving that night.

Have you ever been in a state when enough is enough and been inclined to chuck it all? That's what happened to me a few minutes after the great disappointment and first reaction to first sight of the Rally mess. I drove on to what appeared to be no more than an exaggerated puddle when car and caravan got bogged down. Stranded in the car and isolated to the point of tears it seemed as though the caravan, too, was sinking slowly into the mire. Advices shouted in foreign tongues did not help any. For what seemed hours it appeared to be stalemate and then, in my mirror, I saw a huge Range Rover ploughing it's way towards me. The driver, a man of gargantuan proportions which made me fear for his safety in such a bog, got out and unhitched the 'van. His next move was to manoeuvre the Range Rover to the front of the car and hitch on a rope to the towing bar - it being a Saab and a front wheel drive there was a convenient hook at the front - and slowly the four wheel drive monster dragged me clear. The same was done to the 'van with the assistance of fellow caravanners and, half an hour after arriving at Lechbruck, we were again on terra firma.

Come the dawn, and what a dawn! Brilliant sunshine shimmered on the placid waters of the lake and reflected on the sides of caravans, each of which were being reorganised and washed down. It was an entirely new ball game. Only the rapidly drying mud and the much in evidence gumboots brought back to mind the chaos of the previous day, and with it vanished the thought of a quick turnaround and off to better climes beyond the Dolomites. What happened afterwards made full amends. The camaraderie and hospitalities under the vast beer tent during the remaining five days, and the excursions and sightseeing trips were more than adequate compensation for our earlier experiences.

Oberammergau, the setting of the world famous Passion Play, and the exquisite, almost unbelievable beauty of the Church at Weiss with the biblical paintings by the brothers Johanes and Dominic Zimmerman in the sixteenth century, lifted one above the petty problems of the week past. Myfanwy wrote with considerable feeling on our return to camp "I cannot describe the church to do it full justice. I have never in all my life, and in all the churches I have visited, seen such magnificent splendour... it gave me goose pimples!"

At that time we and the Davies's were members of the Middlesex Centre, an offshoot of the overgrown North London Centre, and it was a great pleasure before the end of the Rally to find so many of our Centre friends had been able to make the Rally, though widely dispersed. The Moscrop's, Bob and Jenny, and Ted and Mary Smith, discovered us tucked away amidst the multi-national lakeside campers and soon word spread. Although there were some misgivings on all sides, I suppose, that we all could not converse freely this was no barrier to the comradeship and enjoyment which made for a lovely holiday. Caravanners of whatever nationality are a special breed when it comes to gatherings of this kind!

And so it went on for another couple of days during which the weather relented and the warm sun dispelled the memories of earlier discomforts. This particular rally has remained vividly in our minds, and perhaps for another reason. It was the last time we and the Davies's caravanned together on the Continent. Two years later, in March 1974, Eileen was the cruel victim of the tragic Paris air crash when about four hundred passengers in a Turkish plane died when it ploughed into the forest of Ermenonville shortly after take off for London.

It was with a tinge of regret that we left Lechbruck and all our newly formed friends and set our sights for Venice and the sun. The run to N.S.U., again to be the venue of what was left of the holiday, was without incident, but it worth mentioning one item in the diary. An overnight halt at Bolzano prompted the entry "This site is very expensive. They are charging a £1 a night"! But at a restaurant across the way at which we had booked a table for dinner immediately on arrival at the campsite there was no ground for complaint. The meal was as follows: "First we, Glan and I, had soup with egg (this was really something!), then delicious river trout, grilled with pomme frites lettuce and tomatoes, followed by fresh peaches and cream - and cheese for me ; A bottle of Sylvaner to wash it down and Cappuccino to finish. Eileen and Len had noodle soup, same main course, Esmeraldo ice cream topped with neat whiskey, and fresh fruit. It was all very satisfying and it cost Glan, who was in the chair, £5 - including tip." Does this ring a bell among readers? Perhaps a smidgen of "those were the days"?

The remainder of the N.S.U. holiday, mainly on the bank of the Grand Lagoon, passed uneventfully because I cannot detect any occurrence worthy of special mention in the diary, except that on Wednesday the 16th August, the gas gave out and it had lasted us a fortnight. But the return trip provided several interesting highlights. For instance less than two hours after leaving N.S.U. we lost Len and Eileen. A snarl up on the autostrada was responsible. By evening, and still wondering what had befallen our friends, we decided to pull into a site in a charming little village of Calico, on the far end of the lake at Lecco. What the chances were of meeting up again with Len and Eileen must have been pretty slender but the following day just after pulling out of the camp and taking breakfast of bacon and eggs at a lay-by some fifty miles beyond we heard a car horn and there was Eileen frantically waving us to follow. I swore it was the smell of the frying bacon which had led Len back to us! Thereafter my third eye was pretty constant! Five minutes without sight of the second caravan in my mirror and I ground to a halt.

A deviation to visit again St. Moritz saw us climbing steeply into Silvaplana, and the Maloja and Julier Passes 5,922 feet. The day before we had been sweltering; now we were shivering in snow covered surroundings and not even the activities on the Olympic Games ski slopes and the skating, all a fantastic fairyland view, could arouse any enthusiasm. One night's stay was enough! The following morning we decided to press on especially after Eileen had said she had been too cold to sleep and, ironically and without realising the truth, declared "I'll never come to this place again".

The route back to Zeebrugge took us via the Mosel valley where we had the good fortune to coincide with the seasonal wine fests. At Cochem we visited the House of Schneider to sample their special vintages. They must have been very powerful for the ladies because on the arrival back on our campsite on the bank of the river they both rushed out of the car and straight into the men's toilets. I gather it was crowded too, but all Len and I heard was a scream and two bashful wives fleeing to the gleeful shouts of some disappointed young men!

Two days later, 28th August, we boarded the ferry and on arrival at Uxbridge found we had travelled 2,542 miles during a wonderful holiday.

# Chapter 31

# Asia in Our Sights!

No more ambitious project had been considered by us than that which emerged during the "close season" after the 1973 continental holiday. The caravanning fraternity was buzzing with the prospect of the F.I.C.C. rally in Turkey. Apart from it being the farthermost destination it was obvious that such a journey with a caravan would be bound to present some severe challenges both on the outfits and the personnel. It wasn't as though we would be travelling known routes, such as we had been doing for a great many years in our forays abroad, just the highways and byways of Western Europe through countries designated by the war as "this side of the Iron Curtain". It would mean going beyond the Curtain into countries and terrain known or thought to be hostile. And if we were decided to face these hazards a great deal of careful and minute planning would be necessary. Furthermore it was obvious that this was not something we could consider as a solo operation.

But the thought of visiting another Continent, and the attractions of a mysterious East, decided us to have a go. Who to accompany us though? I can say now that that decision to make the trip, taken one weekend in November 1973, was the beginning of an era and an itinerant friendship which lasted until July 1991 with the tragic death of our constant and beloved friend Margaret Rowlands. Until her passing there was not a single overseas caravanning holiday that we were not together as "twin couplets", for the Rowlands - Percy and Margaret - were the ideal companions. Now we have accepted that in her passing things will never be the same. Whilst Myfanwy and I are hoping to continue travelling in the manner which has become a way of life for us there must be an aching void which we shall never again seek to fill. A light has gone out and a fire which can never be rekindled.

When we approached our friends with the idea of a transcontinental trip the response was immediate and spontaneous. They lived 250 miles away in North Wales but despite this "handicap" the joint planning went on with hardly a hitch. The telephone lines between us were in use constantly and weekends in our respective homes with maps out and guidebooks at the ready sufficed to build up a state of mounting excitement as the day of departure approached. I would say here that this set the seal on a friendship which in complete honesty never experienced a single cross word or difference between us.

The Day and date was Thursday 26th July 1974, and as we set off for Dover the weather was sunny and warm, an excellent augury for our adventure. Not until we were more than halfway to Dover did we meet up with our friends. They were parked in a lay-by in Rochester Way and as we approached there was frantic waving by the three of them - their daughter Beryl has also decided to join the safari. But we had spotted them. The first chore was to affix a stencilled Welsh Dragon Rampant on the topsides of their caravan, a method of recognition we had agreed upon just in case we were separated. We had already fixed our "symbol", and it was from then on that we two became known as "The Dragons". And how well it worked, and has done in the years since! On occasions when we were "lost" to each other many have been the times when a roadside enquiry of fellow caravanners have elicited the reply "Oh yes, we spotted the other one..."

This was the first time we had used our brand new Swift Corvette caravan but we need have had no doubts. It was towing perfectly and on our way to the port I reminisced on the problems of the past few months and the difficulties of securing the necessary visas for the Iron Curtain countries we would have to traverse. As a journalist, and a political one at that based on the Houses of Parliament, it had been extremely difficult and very frustrating to secure the all important visas despite all the string-pulling. But now it seemed worth while (little did I realise then what lay ahead of us in this respect).

Arriving at Zeebrugge after a splendid crossing on the Enterprise V we were met with a sudden gale which cost us a lot of sleep, but by 4.30

pm the following day we had reached our second overnight halt at Limburg in Germany. "We have done something today we have never done at any time during previous visits here" it is recorded. "We toured the town and visited the medieval church on top of the hill. It was built in 1230."

After an uneventful journey through Austria our first hold-up was the Yugoslavia border with Italy where we had the first real evidence of the heavy caravan traffic heading for the International Rally. On to Bled, a fairyland vista and gathering place for ten Turkey bound outfits, where we decided to stay overnight, and during that time the sight of caravans from all countries west became common place, including an English contingent travelling in convoy. We decided not to join them but to proceed as a twosome and according to our calculations we still had more than a thousand miles to go to Kilyos, the Turkish resort on the Black Sea where the Rally was being held. A lasting memory of our stay in Bled was the camaraderie of the several nationalities, and the beautiful music of a German caravanner who lulled us to sleep with his piano accordion.

The Corvette was being towed by a Saab two litre which until then had behaved beautifully, but after leaving Bled we encountered our first spot of trouble. A red light appeared on the dashboard which worried me greatly because we were moving towards Bulgaria, a point of no return as far as car repairs were concerned. To my amazement, and relief, I saw the first SAAB garage since leaving Zeebrugge! It cost 137 Dinar (roughly £4) but within minutes the trouble had been put right and we were away again ahead of the other contingents, and heading for Belgrade and an overnight halt. But we hadn't calculated the experience of the Auto put-put, the so called motorway between Zagreb and the Bulgarian border. What a run! It was no more than a two lane road with a dilapidated surface and more pot-holes per mile than corn in a packet of cornflakes! Added to this was the don't care a damn attitude of heavy lorry drivers with whom for the most part we shared the route. It was the worst driving experience of my pretty extensive motoring career; my first and only trip along that fearsome Autoput.

We were still some sixty five miles away from Belgrade when Percy and I agreed to call it a day and we were lucky enough to find a glorious little camp site called Slavonija where the accommodation were chalets in the shape of huge half beer-barrels with thatched roofs. The only snag turned out to be the mosquitoes which appeared in their millions during the evening. We had covered 292 miles that day.

"Bulgaria tonight" is the terse comment in the diary as we by-passed Belgrade shortly before we came across the first real accident of our travel. Ahead was a French contingent, stationary because one of their number had crashed into a 12 ft ditch, a casualty of the confounded Put-Put. A team of horses from a nearby village was struggling to pull the caravan back on to the road. We offered to help but this we were told would only increase the congestion of a two lane road, so we went on our way with second thoughts about making the Bulgarian border on schedule. Mid-afternoon and we are enjoying another new autobahn toll road from Nis towards the border, some forty kilometres ahead. One of the more interesting sights was the town of Pirot dating back to the 2nd Century, but the road around it must have been put down around the same time! If only we had we but known then this was the least of our troubles for the day. Arriving at the frontier we encountered the first real example of how the Bulgarians lived under their Communist rule. It was bureaucracy at its worst. We had been promised safe and assisted transit through Bulgaria into Turkey but from the moment we pulled up at the custom post under the rigid scrutiny of armed guards we were treated worse than dirt. Cars and caravans were inspected in the most discourteous manner, passports were virtually snatched away and kept for more than an hour, and a coarse and dishevelled official demanded we purchased coupons for fuel and exchanged sterling into Bulgarian money before restoring our passports and visas. We gathered there was no possibility of purchasing petrol at any of the State run garages, and only a limited amount could be got in exchange for coupons. It transpired that motorcars were the prerogative only of higher ranking Party members and from what we saw during our brief visit there were very few of those. It took us nearly two hours to pass through the customs, by which time there was a build up of Rally going outfits behind for which we expressed great sorrow.

What seemed very strange was the wonderful four-lane roads from the border with hardly a car in sight, but plenty of armed soldiers and police. I felt very ill at ease, and so did the others. As we had been warned there was a dearth of garages and it was a relief as we entered a small town some thirty miles from the border to find a filling station, manned by a young man but with what could have been an escort of soldiers on the forecourt. This is where we first ran foul of "the system", and with no redress. I asked that the tank be filled up and was asked for my coupons. I observed that my three ten-litre coupons disappearing into a copious black bag around the young man's waist but only 27 litres registered on the meter. I asked for the change in money or coupons to be told by an onlooker (I was then informed by another bystander who spoke a little English that he was the Party boss) that the attendant had no authority to issue coupons, and he never handled money. Percy fell foul of the system in exactly the same way and lost two litres. My remonstrations and threat to raise the matter with a higher authority fell on deaf ears, and I wondered whether the presence of the soldiers had any real significance. Also that of the "boss". There had been no one there when we first arrived, but the sight of two British caravans had attracted a small crowd in no time. Some small satisfaction to me and Percy, however, was that an American tourist had approached us and said he had been stranded there several hours because his car had no petrol and he had been refused enough to reach the border. We insisted he should be given the 4 litres and saw him off before we left. I wonder whether he made it!

We had travelled 337 miles that day when we came across a recommended camping site called Pectopaht. There were already a sizeable vanguard of rally goers of all nationalities, and we joined in a meal of typical Bulgarian kebab and specialities we had never heard or dreamed of. The unease of the day's experiences was swallowed up by an evening's entertainment led by the German contingent. A band played local music and some boys and girls danced traditional dances. The diary recalls that we couldn't reconcile the hospitality at this camp, and the beautiful country through which we had passed, with the attitudes of the border guards and what had happened at the filling stations. To us it was the bad face of Communism and the privations of a regimented people suffering from the worst type of Privilege Order. On the morrow we would be glad to leave the country. But there was to be one more instance.

It took more than an hour to retrieve our passports from the site office before we could begin our final journey out of Bulgaria. Myfanwy wrote "It's 7.20 am and a warm day and we are glad to get shot of this place. We shall be glad to get out of Bulgaria. I wouldn't give a thank you for the country and the people who are glum and very rude, they couldn't care less". Further on, at Plovdiv where we stopped at midday for a snack and last minute shopping. The diary records "The shop assistants are all very dry, they cannot smile, it's a very peculiar country!"

On and on towards the border and suddenly we came around the bend in the road to see a caravan with GB and Scottish markings parked at the side of the road. It was surrounded by a band of people who turned out to be local gypsies. Inside car, alone, was a woman who was terrified by the threats she thought the gypsies represented. Her husband had gone off on foot to look for help after the car had stopped due to a faulty battery. Percy and I managed to get the car going just as he returned after a luckless trip looking for a garage. We followed them for about twenty miles until we were satisfied they were no longer in danger.

It was early evening before we reached the border with Turkey when the final incident occurred. I had gone into the frontier office to cash in a not insubstantial amount of petrol coupons I had been forced to take on entering the country. I was immediately accused of being in possession of more coupons than I had the right to. Furthermore they were not prepared to exchange (for Turkish money) the Bulgarian currency I had left, despite the assurances which had been given that any left-over would be exchanged. I was being cross examined and impugned by two men who reminded me of a couple of broken down actors. The interpreter, a young woman who was very sympathetic and even warned me about my interrogators, finally called out for somebody and the response was electric. A young officer, obviously from his red and gold epaulettes a high ranking one, approached and spoke to the two men very harshly in their own tongue. He had been told something by the interpreter which had greatly angered him and they reacted as though they had been whip lashed. Without any ado they took me to a small office and I was handed the money due to me, even though I had to explain that I did not have my passport with me when I was asked to produce it. It was with Myfanwy who had driven the outfit across the border. There I was, stranded in Bulgaria without a passport, and on the Turkish side Myfanwy and Percy shouting across to me to come on. I shouted back at them, pointed to them to the guard and rushed across. I half expected a round of fire, but I reached Turkey in one piece and very angry. Before I left the Bulgarians I asked the interpreter what she had told the Officer. "I told him, as you had told me, that you were a journalist attached to the House of Commons and would be calling attention to this treatment when you arrived back in London" she told me with a faint smile. "They (the two men) will be in great trouble" she added, and not without a tinge of pleasure I thought.

Those who took part in that unique Kilyos rally will no doubt remember the overnight camping site of Edrine which we reached by teatime after the frontier escapade. There we found a number of British caravans and the evening was spent in recounting experiences of the journey so far. A traditional dinner of lamb, shish kebab and red and green vegetables followed by the usual caravan type socialising meant we did not turn in until midnight... but no one cared. Tomorrow was our last day's travelling. We should be in Kilyos, and have a well deserved rest by late afternoon... or so we thought. News dribbled through that some English caravans had been turned back from Kilyos because the site was not quite ready, but we decided to press on. We got as far as Istanbul when another hitch occurred. We were advised by an official at a marshalling centre at the entrance of the City not to proceed singly or in pairs but to await a sufficient number of 'vans to form a convoy which would then be guided by a police motorcyclist through the City and its outskirts towards Kilyos.

We waited, and we waited. It seems that Eastern patience is much more restrained than that of Westerners. After a couple of hours with no sign of our promised guide we persuaded the official to give us a route map and Percy and I were joined by a couple of other 'vans and set off. We were impatient to see the Black Sea. Within minutes, however, we were witness to a terrible accident in which a young boy was hit and killed by a car. Only minutes earlier Myfanwy had commented on the "crazy" driving of local motorists. But then we also witnessed the seeming callousness also of the East, and how cheap life is held there. The body of the lad was rolled in a carpet, the boot of a car was opened and it was thrown in and driven off. Within minutes the scene was normal again with cars screeching through some of the heaviest traffic we had ever seen; and we were signalled on to complete our journey. The incident has forever been imprinted on our minds.

By mistake we took the more difficult route over the mountains and along roads through villages perched on terrifying bends, but we reached Kilyos safely and ahead of a cavalcade of caravans making up the rally. True, the site had not been completed but we got pride of place for our small convoy right on the edge of the Black Sea. It had been a journey forever to remember and to savour. As Myfanwy wrote "We shall always remember 2nd August, 1973 as the day we entered Turkey at the end of a 2,304 miles trek". We had not quite entered Asia, but at the conclusion of the Rally on the 9th August we got our Asia badge by crossing the Bosphorous on the old bridge. There was nothing dramatic about it. We had just taken a step further but it was into another Continent. The new bridge was about to be completed and a couple of days earlier we had sailed beneath it.

The return journey was to be made through Greece - no more Bulgaria for us though it would have been a shorter journey. One last memorable and nerve wracking experience which has to be recorded, however, was our exit from Kilyos. It was 4.35 in the morning (we were anxious to get through Istanbul before the rush period) as we nosed our way from the camp towards the hilly road. Without warning we were enveloped in a dense fog which brought me virtually to a stop. Percy was no more than a yard behind. Suddenly I heard the tinkle of bells and out of the ghostly mist emerged some donkeys ridden by what I took to be local goatherds off the beach. They were going the way we meant to go so I tucked myself behind the train, hoping, as he did, that Percy would be following. The winding road was treacherous, with steep drops on one side or other as we had discovered previously. The journey went on and on and I was almost a physical wreck, straining my eyes but relying more on the tinkling bells to keep on course, when suddenly we found ourselves out of the fog. It was then I found that we had been following about ten donkeys in file with only a couple of young lads who obviously, like me, were relying on the lead animals to take them safely out of the blind fog.

Our first experience of Greek camping and caravanning sites was at Alexandroupoli, 210 miles after leaving Kilyos. A highlight of our brief stay was the wine tasting festival being held in an adjoining park, and the experience we had during it. At the next table to us three locals were enjoying their wine and eating yellow melons. Overhearing us speaking English one of them came across and when told we came from London he proudly announced in limited English that he had been a seaman and had been several times to Liverpool. He invited Myfanwy and I (we were alone then) to join his friends. It was then we were introduced to Carlos, a delightful Greek who, hearing I was a journalist, fiercely declared himself opposed to the then government of the Colonels Junta. He cut a melon into five pieces soaked them in wine, and launched into a meticulous and angry description of how the Greeks were suffering from a dictatorial military rule. He admitted to be a leader of the local "resistance" and was on the Colonels' 'hit list'. "Tell the English people the true position here" he asked, and then made us promise to meet him again the next day in the same place.

We carried out the assignation, but there was no sign of Carlos, only a friend who asked us to call on a local wholesale fruit store - where Carlos worked - where there would be a message for me. I did so and was told that Carlos had fled, but I was handed a knife, the very one he had used to cut up the melon, with the message that Carlos wanted us to keep it "as a memory". We heard no more from him, except a hint that he had been taken; but that knife is still with us and constantly used in the kitchen and a reminder of that particular cloak and dagger incident. And if Carlos should perhaps read this and recognise the occasion we would dearly love to renew our acquaintance.

After our very pleasant stopover in Alexandroupoli, it was thence, alongside the Aegean to Thessaloniki, Yugoslavia, Trieste, to Venice, and our old stamping ground of Cavallino. The holiday ended on 1st September when on arriving home we made the usual check and found we had completed a round journey of 4,521 miles and consumed 242 gallons of petrol at a cost of £104.54. Now you can understand perhaps why this method of unfettered leisure and travel means so much to us.

# Chapter 32

# Tragic Moments

The experiences of our Bulgarian visit remained with us for several months and little thought was given over the mid-winter months to the forthcoming holiday. One thing seemed certain. Nineteen seventy four would not see us crossing the Iron Curtain again! But isn't it true that nothing in this life is certain? With the end of the bitter March winds of that year preparations in earnest got under way for the summer holiday. We had agreed with Margaret and Percy on our return from Turkey that we should again form a holiday partnership since we had found ourselves very compatible in all things. It was to be, of course, a relationship that was to last seventeen years. But what kind of a holiday this time?

It's surprising what a few months will do for the memory. Come April and the worst aspects of the previous year's holiday had faded into the background. Percy had read of the 1974 International Rally which was to take place in Czechoslovakia and in no time he had fired the imagination all round. The High Tatras mountains which was to be the venue suddenly became the focus of everyone's attention. What matter that we would again be disappearing behind the Iron Curtain! It was most unlikely to be a repetition of the Bulgarian escapade. And so, having ascertained, and late as it was, that there were still some vacancies we plumped for the High Tatras. It had such a romantic and mysterious ring to it, and the trek to Asia had awakened a new and keen desire to the more adventurous type of holiday.

And so the diaries relate that morning of July 27th dawned sunny and exciting at the prospect of foraging in another country which would be strange to us, and for me especially it might even mean the fulfilment of a long held ambition, namely the chance visit into Russia. As a political journalist it had not been possible for me to obtain a visa for that country and I had been led to believe that there was the possibility of a sneaky border crossing en route for the Tatras which overlooked Russia. In my mind this was sufficient inducement to cross the Iron Curtain once again; a reservation for the F.I.C.C. Rally could greatly ease the problem of an entry visa for Czechoslovakia.

We left home for the Dover-Zeebrugge crossing at 11.40 am in the company of our two friends who had arrived the previous evening. It is recalled that after an al fresco lunch of turkey and salad trouble struck. Percy's fridge wasn't functioning and my front tyre looked deflated. The tube valve was leaking badly. But fortune smiled because a friendly garage man on the outskirts of Dover was able to put both things right and by 6.15 pm we were aboard the Enterprise VI, and sailing out to a calm and sun drenched English Channel. It's all in the diaries, down to the smallest detail! Which is how I can recall the only event out of the ordinary which occurred on board was a shore to ship telephone call - a rare enough occurrence in those days - from Percy and Margaret's daughter, Robina, at home to say that his mother was unwell... but no need to worry. So we decided to press on.

After a night's rest on the Zeebrugge dock (a far different set up to that of today) we set off for the German border town of Aachen and thence Cologne en route for our overnight scheduled halt at Limburg. The only excitement, it seems, was that Margaret got locked in their lavatory and no one heard her shouts, poor thing. Talk about one of the three old ladies locked in the lavatory!

Nuremburg was our second overnight halt, during which our friends telephoned home to satisfy themselves about Percy's mother's condition and all seeming to be well we set off for the German-Czech border at Plzen, the agreed crossing for international rallyers. As we crossed Myfanwy noted that we had travelled 640 miles from home. First impressions of Czechoslovakia were of a beautiful and very fertile country, and it was lunchtime before we caught sight of another British caravan. But we did encounter quite a few tanks on the road to Prague.

"This reminds me of Hungary... I don't think it is a prosperous country" 'Van wrote.

The hedgerows were lined with cherry, apricot and apple trees. "It's a wonderful journey and I would not have missed it for anything. The few cars we have seen are small and the houses in the country not very posh". On the outskirts of Prague the milometer registered 740 miles from home, and it was a relief after a very hot day's travelling to arrive at the first F.I.C.C. stage camp "Stredisko, T.J. Slavia us Praha, Lyzarsky." This was where we tasted our first Slav meal. It consisted of a borsch soup with bread crumbed mushrooms and a tarter sauce, then a Shish kebab with freshly baked bread, all delicious.

Wednesday, 31st July, in Prague was a boiling hot day, but marred for me because I discovered the exhaust on our Saab had blown. Where would I find a Saab garage? But we did, and a large Saab-Scania repair shop it turned out to be.

Whilst they were attending to the repairs we four made a tour of the Capital, but I'm afraid we were somewhat disappointed by what we saw. The magnificent architectures were sadly in need of renovation, which was great shame but, I suppose, largely because of the war and the political upheavals which had resulted there were possibly more pressing matters to concern the authorities. One legacy of that wonderful visit is still with me, however. It is a mechanic's wrench still in my tool box. It had been left underneath the car and was found only when I stopped to examine the cause of a bad rattle some miles out of Prague. If the loser should happen to read this and is in need of the tool then contact me and I would return it willingly. The only problem during our continuing journey to Trencin, where the pre-rally was being held, was the great difficulty in telephoning home for news of Percy's mother. En route for Brno we experienced some awkward situations with the stone cobbled roads and also failure to get the promised petrol coupons. Petrol was costing £1 a gallon, making the journey very expensive. Another strange feature to strike us was the dearth of animals; not a cow, sheep nor horse to be seen in the countryside. Yet, 'Van notes that there seems to be plenty of meat on offer in the restaurants - at a price. Then we discovered why. Their cattle were housed in large barns and seldom allowed to graze. Perhaps there was too much rustling going on!

We couldn't get over the beauty of the countryside, and the superb views of the looming mountains reminded us of Switzerland. What were to find on arrival in these mountains? Excitement and wonder grew with each mile, and we became conscious of other foreign caravans converging on the venue, but we were still some forty miles away from Trencin when we had to call it a day, along with another English family we had met in Prague. Norman and Ella, and their son Paul, who were in a Bailey caravan, joined us to drink in the magnificence of the view over the valley. From our stopping place we could see the river below in which was reflected a flood lit castle, possibly lit for this special occasion, and with a glass of wine each we drank in the beauty of it all.

Trencin itself turned out to be a very old town, and given more time it would have been most enjoyable to study its characteristics. By this time at least one of our worries had been resolved. We had been handed some petrol coupons which slashed the travelling costs considerably. The old town was very pretty in every sense of the word, and its people charming and helpful so far as they could bearing in mind the language difficulties, but the going on foot was a bit tough. It was up and down hill each time we set out to explore. The day's towing had covered 234 miles and there were another 176 miles ahead of us before we would arrive at the actual Rally.

By 7.30 am on the 2nd August we were on the last lap, and according to the diaries it was a really lovely day, and as we progressed more rallyers collected to form a reasonably picturesque convey with the different national flags fluttering. Norman and the Bailey led the way with the two of us close behind, through the small towns of Banova and Martine the crowds cheered. We were all enjoying it immensely... and to think that exactly a week to the day was when we left home. The shimmering heat (it was ninety degrees Fahrenheit) only served to heighten the expectation of the end of a long but very interesting and enjoyable journey to the Tatry end. With the approach to Poprad almost in view, and by our assessment fewer than thirty miles to go afterwards we indulged in a foot cooling exercise.

The sight of a fast flowing stream alongside the road was too much of a temptation. We all pulled up and a dozen or more pairs of feet plunged into the refreshing waters. The sighs of relief were clearly audible to those who were bothered to listen. The sight of the usually sober minded caravanners cooling off in this way was something to behold, and augured well for the Rally... or so we thought!

Poprad itself and its surroundings presented a truly fairy book picture, and spirits were high as we pulled into an ideal setting within the woods which was to be our resting place for the next week. Within an hour and with Percy's aid our awning was up but before we could attend to his name was called over the tannoy. Two telegrams were awaiting him. The first said his mother was weaker, and the second was an urgent summons to return home at once... we guessed the worst had happened. Our first reaction was to pull down the awning and turn for home, but our friends would not hear of it. They hadn't even put down the steadies! With barely a few minutes elapsed they drove off the site to the condolences of those of the British contingent who had heard the news. A fortnight later on our return home we learned that they had driven night and day to return home in just over two days. It was a tragic occurrence and was greatly felt by us all who remained behind.

The Rally itself was officially opened on Sunday 4th August in brilliant sunshine, a change from the previous day which had threatened to drown the camp, and had caused the British section (including David Knight the British Club chairman) to move to higher ground. It was quite an experience to find a group from Japan present, including Yoko and Masa from Tokyo who had come on their honeymoon! They tried to teach us some Japanese songs, and offered us their traditional drink of Saki. It was the most "international" of any of the F.I.C.C. rallies we had attended, but the misfortune of our friends, and wondering where they had got to, was constantly in our and other people's thoughts.

One of the most exciting interludes of the rally was a visit to the famous Ice Caves of Dobinsca where, once again we found evidence of the camaraderie of the Caravanners' movement; there were no frontiers to cross and nationalities did not matter as friendships blossomed. And to this very day we still have and cherish the many friendships formed at this and other similar events. But of course our stay could not go on forever. Different as each day was time was irrevocably moving on and our permit would expire on the 8th August. We struck camp with the help of numerous friends on the 7th and set out for Bratislava and the Austrian border which we had to cross before the following midnight. It was a strange journey, being alone. Only a few hours out, at a place called Nita, we were stopped by three policemen and accused of exceeding the speed limit. But all ended well. Their demand for an on the spot fine of 70 Krone (about £3) was dropped after I had shown my passport. We had a good laugh - with almost nonexistent English - and because I had no cigarettes, which by sign language they hinted at, we handed them a bag of sweets which pleased them just as well and they waved us on our way.

An overnight halt at Camping B Sered which we had reached after 187 miles saw us well on our way to Bratislava which we reached before midday. There was ample time to do the necessary present and other shopping - including a beautifully sculptured Christopher Robin and Pooh, and a Rocking Horse for the grandchildren - before crossing into Austria. "Back in civilization" is the written comment, and I felt happier being able to go into a bank and cash a cheque!

Now that we were on the homeward run we decided to follow the better accustomed tracks which led us to the Grossglochner, Kitzbuhel and Innsbruck and thence to our much favoured camping platz at Traben-Traben on the Mosel. From then on it was virtually a repeat of earlier holidays with visits to places which have become known to us over the years and which, hopefully, we shall continue to visit in the years ahead. But there was one more thing which figured greatly in this year's commitments.

The 23rd August saw us approaching Paris, a deviation both of us had agreed to, for we had in mind to pay our respects at the gravesides of two dear friends lost to us in the great air disaster at Ermenonville, Eileen Davies, a partner over thousands of caravanning miles, and her cousin Marion. They had been the victims of the Jumbo Jet's plunge into the thick forest of Ermenonville only five months earlier, and this was our first opportunity of visiting what turned out to be the mass graveside in the Parisian Cemetery at Thiais. Eventually we found it, and paid our respects; and I can now reveal that what had been troubling Myfanwy every day and night since that sad affair suddenly lifted. She had been very close to Eileen over a score of years and from the moment of the crash she was aware of her presence, even to troubled sleep. But as soon as we walked away from the graveside she turned to me and said. "I feel a great weight has been lifted". That night, for the first time, she slept soundly as we stayed in a campsite not more than a mile from the scene of the accident. And although we still think much and often of our departed friend the "spirit" is more consoling.

That, en passant, was the second tragic moment of the holiday. Two days later we were back home having completed 3,280 miles and a holiday which will forever remain fresh in our minds.

Great friends and travelling companions enjoying an ice cream together. Percy, Margaret, Myfanwy and David.

## Chapter 33

## When Hari Krishna Came to Portugal

Portugal had been announced as the venue for the 1975 F.I.C.C. Rally and after the successes of previous international gatherings, plus the fact that we had yet to visit Portugal, there was no difficulty in deciding where our next holiday would be. It had to be the Largo Andre di Santos which the brochures assured us would be an ideal site, enhanced by warm summer evenings and general hospitality typical of that region.

Usually one has to make allowances for the poetic licence employed in the make-up of such attractive inducements, and with this in mind we all settled for a good and interesting trip there and back and be contented with what we would find. As it turned out not only did the journey prove to be all we hoped for but the sojourn on this beautiful lake and the surrounding countryside was an immense pleasure and an eye opener.

So Van and I agreed that with Percy and Margaret we would again take the long trek across the western part of the Continent, through France and Spain into - for us - the uncharted territory of Portugal. It was to be on 25th July and the day arrived with the promise of good weather for the crossing from Dover to Calais. With the Welsh Dragons on the two caravans fully rampant once more, and the prospect of another first time journey beyond the Spanish border we set out before midday in the highest spirits and arrived on French soil at 7 pm. So it was decided to put off the serious part of the journey ahead of us until the following day and spend the overnight halt in a pretty campsite we came across just outside Boulogne. It was called International Camping et Caravanning "L'Escale" and the rest put us in proper trim for the haul ahead. It was also the occasion when we decided on a format for daily journeys which we adhered to not only on this particular trip but on each and every one since. I think it is worth passing on to other caravanners who set themselves longish journeys to be covered in the quickest time.

Our method is, during journeys, to be up and about by not later that 6.30 am, just a cuppa and away for the first leg. This can be either 100 miles before breakfast or nine o'clock, whichever comes first. The stop for a satisfying breakfast at a lay-by means that by 10 to 10.15 am we are ready for the next leg. This, as with the start of the day, means usually a journey of not less than 100 miles or a stop at 1.00 pm, whichever comes first. The third daily leg goes on until 4.00 pm at which time, whatever distance has been covered, we lookout for the next or best campsite which comes into view. The golden rule, however, is to be on site and steadies down by not later than five o'clock. This allows one ample time for some sightseeing or to get in touch with local culture and the people, as well as the occasional local cuisine and drinks. It is a method that has been followed by us for the past fifteen years and I cannot recall any instance when it has not worked well; and I hope that for as long as we are able to continue caravanning we shall follow this pattern.

Our destination was to be on the western coast of Portugal, some eighty miles south of Lisbon, and within a half day of disembarking we were made aware of the large increase in the number of British caravans on the French roads. This, I believe, was the greatest invasion on French territory of this type of tourism, and it became noticeable that in subsequent years the perceptive French realised how much "le British caravanner" was contributing to local and national economy and set about improving the standards of their camping and caravanning sites. Never had we seen so many GB's traversing the Routes National, and with the increase came the demise of that once familiar and uplifting salutation of the toot on the horn and a friendly wave as we passed one another. To have sustained this up on this trip would have meant almost a perpetual toot!

"We have never seen such an invasion of British caravans as this year. Nearly every lay-by is full" wrote Myfanwy. In one lay-by into which we had pulled she noted "In front of us there are four British caravans, one of them a Swift Dannette, HMF 531 N. I'm sure they are all going to Portugal judging by the pennants, including one from Istanbul and another from the High Tatras. We have now done 105 miles and it is 9.10 am".

The second post-breakfast leg on this first day was over 104 miles and the third was yet another 124 miles which meant that by the time we had found our camping site we had travelled 329 miles. End of the first day was just outside Tours where a very helpful Gendarme suggested we should carry on to Camping L'Allouette. But we opted for the municipal campsite in Tours itself and a fine judgment it turned out to be. The weather was boiling hot and even if we had it in mind to go beyond our agreed 5.00 pm time the temperature ruled it out. That evening's meal was a treat out at a small cafe cum pub nearby where we became the "unofficial" guests of a local wedding party. The bride was still in her white wedding gown and, according to the diarist, "her veil was about six yards long and she looked really lovely". It turned out to be a very pleasant evening which we all enjoyed and reluctantly we left at 10.20 pm for "an early retirement" and an early start in the morning. See what I mean when I say "This is the life!"

We had set our sights for Biarritz as the overnight halt of our second day, but circumstances in the shape of a smartly dressed Gendarme, changed all that. It was an experience we had never met before, but as we entered the town and its promenade the arm of the law was resolutely uplifted. He approached us with a quizzical smile as if we were committing some form of crime in all innocence and informed us that we were not welcome in this place which from the time of the English Regina Victoria and MiLords had been kept very select. Caravans on the boulevard? Perish the thought! When I explained we were looking for a place to stop for the night since we were on our way to the Spanish border he firmly pointed us in the direction of the way out of town. And out of town we went... "Never to come back here" 'Van wrote, and we all concurred later. It was then 4.45 pm and at 5.35 pm we crossed into Spain, much later than scheduled. But we had to go as far as Alsasua, high in the mountains, before we came to a camp site and it was 9.30 pm before we pulled in, more than an hour having been spent on a narrow road where the police had held up the traffic due to a fatal accident some kilometres ahead. We had overlooked the fact that

Spanish time was an hour ahead of French time and that being so our day actually ended at 8.30 pm. However, we had arrived safely in Spain and were within our schedule.

It had been a tiresome end of day and this had resulted in a sleep-in until gone 7 am but by 7.50 am on Monday 28th we were on our way again with the object of making Madrid that evening. According to our calculations we had about 250 miles to go... and the weather was blisteringly hot! Negotiating Burgos was a nightmare; traffic came to us from all directions and controls were non-existent, but to reach this far we had come through some glorious mountain countryside which seemed worth all the travail we might encounter en-route. We had not been so far into Spain as this, and we were all really impressed with the lush and fertile expanse which, we were told, made up the floral part of Spain.

The tortuous journey into and beyond Burgos caused a change of routing plans. Instead of Madrid we were now making for Valladolid and thence Salamanca, but there was much more to contend with before that delightful City was to come into view! By 4.40 pm, and after three halts for rest and refreshments, we were within hailing distance of Salamanca when the Gremlins decided to make themselves felt. Until then our car, the SAAB, had performed well but it seemed that as soon as we had consulted our sites map for a likely overnight camping place things started happening. The clutch began slipping, and, on reflection, it was a feat to crawl into Camping Regio almost in the middle of the city. What a relief! The clutch gave up the ghost as were came to a halt at the entrance, but there were plenty of willing hands to push the van on to a vacant place. But what now? And still a third of our journey left.

The camping site was ideally placed, attached to a large park and alongside the Hotel Regio with its open bars and swimming pool. Local mechanics arrived very quickly to examine the breakdown and the verdict was "at least two or three days". But what better place to breakdown was the consolation we all felt. The evening and the following day were spent in the pool and meeting local people who politely commiserated with our misfortune. But, I asked myself, was it a misfortune. Whilst other outfits came in a left for the Rally and other parts we were enjoying our enforced sojourn. It was a holiday within a holiday.

The local garage felt they could only effect a temporary repair and returned the car with the advice that I should look out for a SAAB garage en-route, and so this became the first priority as we set off for Badajoz, and beyond, the Portuguese border, which we hoped to reach by early evening if all went well. Looking for a SAAB garage was like searching for a needle in a haystack, but careful nursing of the engine and faith in the Salamanca mechanics' repair job, kept us going. The journey was nothing like the first part. The country was barren with shimmering waves dancing on the roads and the earth, reflecting the scorching heat of the day, was not conducive to the most enjoyable of journeys.

By mid-afternoon we were approaching Cacares and conscious of the many ranches which, we gathered, bred the special and best fighting bulls for the Corrida bullrings. Misfortune struck again at Cacares for I took the wrong road for Portugal. Stopping at a wayside cafe for a drink and directions I discovered I had left my maps behind at an earlier stop. There was no alternative but to turn round and retrace our steps. Suddenly I spotted a lorry approaching and there, something clutched in his hand and waving to me, was the driver with my maps and papers. That augured well, and raised my spirits no end.

The N523 road to Badajoz seemed interminable but safely negotiated until we were actually on the frontier; and then the Gremlins struck again. The SAAB ground to a halt with the engine racing. The confounded clutch had given in. After a few minutes' stop I tried again and we were able to kangaroo a few yards to the frontier post where a very sympathetic Portuguese official waved us through. By this time we were barely moving under the constant motive power of the starter motor and I have no compunction in claiming this was the only time for a car and caravan to enter Portugal on a starter motor. Mind you, there was a slight decline which helped progress!

"How happy we are to have arrived in Portugal" is what is written in the diary, "Maybe we will now have something done to the car". Fortunately I was able to get the outfit going in second gear for the short distance to the old walled frontier town of Elvas and there we found a place outside the walls (not a camping site) where we stayed overnight. Fortune smiled for the first time in days when I fortuitously found in a local garage a mechanic who had worked on SAAB cars. Within a quarter of an hour he had discovered the fault and put it right, an adjustment of the clutch requiring no new parts. He was a good friend and would not take anything for his work. The only thing we could offer him was a miniature bottle of whiskey which he accepted with a smile and a handshake. He also directed us to a local site and by 7.15 pm local time we were ensconced in a most delightful site and joined very quickly by four other British caravans and two French, all going to the Rally. Now things were turning around for the better, and a jolly good time was had by all that evening. It was typical of the caravan camaraderie one finds everywhere. We had travelled 215 miles that day but due to the exasperations and heat of the day it had seemed twice as far.

But we were not finished with Elvas. There was to be more, and I will refer to this further on. Like Queen Mary and Calais it is ELVAS which is irrevocably imprinted across our hearts when it comes to the popular subject of foreign touring and caravanning.

Thursday morning, the 31st July, and with the milometer showing that already we had travelled 1,162 miles, we set off at the appointed time for Lisbon, capital of Portugal and the cross roads to the F.I.I.C. Rally. Shortly after 9 am we stopped for breakfast and to take stock. We were most impressed with the beautiful roads which were so vastly better than those of Spain, but a sobering thought was the price of petrol. Even then it was costing us the equivalent of £1.30p a gallon. The contour of the countryside with it's landscape of whitewashed cottages and more resplendent odd villas prompted the diarist to declare "What a wonderful trip this is through beautiful scenery which makes Portugal such a clean and attractive country."

By lunchtime we were at the vast wooded area in the approach to Santo di Andre which was about two miles from the seashore, and beaches of sand which resembled fine brown sugar. Experience had taught us that the first requirement on arriving at these rallies was to find a place adjacent to events and the core of activities but not too close. This time we were fortunate to secure an ideal place where the sea breezes fanned the two outfits which formed a 'V' with the two awnings facing each other. The trials and tribulations of the journey down were soon forgotten and what we had to look forward to now was a successful and enjoyable rally having covered 184 miles from Elvas. What a first evening it was. A stroll towards the sound of accordion music ended in our joining with a group of Bavarians in singing and dancing, and the Dutch contingent added their voices and colourful national costumes. Old friends from previous rallies came along and soon the whole scene was a throbbing and pulsating hive of activity. This, indeed, was the life! The accordionist, whom we remembered from the Lechbruck Rally, only had one leg. The other, he told us, had been left in Stalingrad during the horrifying period of Germany's world war two Russian Front.

There followed three perfect days of lazing on the beach, wining and dining in local cafes, and mixing with old and new friends. There is no quicker or better way of making friends and lasting friendships than by caravanning and camping. It is not them and us, or upper or lower classes. We are all one class - the best types. Thursday, 3rd August was the big day, the formal opening of the Rally and the arrival by helicopter of the President F.I.I.C.. The release of thousands of balloons and an evening of magnificent fireworks ending the official part was followed by the customary inter-nationalities get-togethers. What better way of settling problems of misunderstanding between the world's nations? And surprisingly enough the language barrier seemed at the end of the day to be no barrier at all! Our little group decided on a barbecue late meal and in no time we were joined by Charles and Peggy from Ealing, Walter and Inge from West Germany, "Bison", the friendly Pole we had met in the High Tatras, together with his wife, both then living in Blackpool, and a few others. If any of them read this I wish they could get in touch.

And so it went on until Van and I confessed to be absolutely pooped and retired to our bed... but not to sleep I fear, for the socialisation and fraternisation carried on well into the night. According to the diary there came complete oblivion at some time and it was 7.30 am before were returned to normality with what seemed a two gun salute, enough to waken the dead. Suddenly there was the clashing of cymbals and the tinkling of bells. Advancing on the site was a line of persons with shaven heads, and others with grotesque masks. They were bringing the message... and I instantly recognised them as the disciples of Hari Krishna. I had seen them often enough in London, but in much fewer numbers. But why they had advanced on this multi-national assembly I had, nor had others around us, no idea. For most of the rallyers I guess this was something quite new. As for the outcome of the intrusion, apart from waking everyone up and giving the children a fright, I did not hear of, or come across, a single convert. They seemed to have disappeared as mysteriously as they had arrived. And life went on.

It was the penultimate day of the rally and we four decided to visit two nearly villages of Grandola and Melides. It provided us with yet another conviction, if it were necessary, of what wonderful people the Portuguese are, and of their general awareness of their traditional close links with the British. As soon as it was known that we were from Great Britain - although, as always, we stressed that we were primarily Welsh - we were given the warmest of welcomes. The diaries recall among many other instances of kindness and goodwill the instances of our trip back from these two villages. We called at a farmhouse which displayed melons out front and tried to purchase some. Ever since our arrival in Santo di Andre we had developed a tremendous taste for the fruit. They were the best melons we had ever seen, and I'm afraid we made rather pigs of ourselves with perhaps an over indulgence. So we couldn't pass this particular display without purchasing. A gentle old lady was only too pleased to offer us the best on view. I couldn't understand the language but the arm waving said the lot. "Help yourselves, my friends" it said in response to our English question "How much please". She was adamant... no money. And I can see her now as we walked away with two beautifully rotund melons smiling and nodding her head as though she had been granted a fulsome satisfaction. It made us feel that we shouldn't attempt to make any more such "purchases": yet, a couple of miles further on we saw a donkey and cart approaching. It was piled with... no, not melons but marrows and pumpkins. I stopped to take a picture, and the driver insisted we helped ourselves to his load. Again we proffered the money, and again it was rejected. But he did accept very gratefully the Polaroid snap of himself and his donkey and cart. His chest ballooned out as he regarded the snap, and I doubt he had ever seen an instant picture before. I guess it found a place of honour on his mantelshelf or whatever, and may still be there today for he was younger than us.

The evening of Wednesday 6th August was our last at the rally and, as it had been throughout, the weather and the comradeship held. We strolled through the ranks of old and new friends, most of them preparing for the morning departure but still finding the time for a chat and farewell, and particularly so with the Finnish contingent who were having the longest trek back of anyone. They gave us a memorable national concert, reminiscent of that F.I.C.C. Rally in Norrkoping several years earlier. We still treasure the tasselled cap which 'Van was given then, the ones which indicate by the left or right hand hang of the tassel whether the wearer was single and eligible or married. As we strolled back to our respective caravans there was still one important decision to the taken. Which route were we to take for the return journey? It didn't take long to resolve. Unanimously the feeling was for Lisbon, and thence to Madrid. We felt we should take this opportunity to visit both capitals on this occasion, and so we would.

## Chapter 34

## Lisbon, The Ants and Madrid

We judged we had about four hours or so to travel before we made our first major destination on the return journey. Lisbon was new to us, and we were looking forward greatly to the visit. One thing struck us as we got under way shortly after 8.30 am, it being the 7th August, and that was the soft appeal of the countryside. Although during the day the heat was almost unbearable at times the fields never seemed to loose their verdant texture. The grass was a lush green everywhere and the water cool and refreshing. For miles on end we traversed good roads alongside fields of melons, marrows and pumpkins, stretching from Grandola to the dual carriageway beyond Setubal which we expected would lead us into the capital City.

It was 12.45 pm when we arrived in Lisbon and had no difficulty in finding the Municipal Camp site, but the temperature was in the sizzling 90's and spaces were few and far between. We managed, however, and safely bedded down after a light lunch it was time to look for that elusive SAAB garage, for I was much afraid that the outfit would not travel much further unless the clutch was properly attended to. We combed the city centre without success but thanks to a young doctor from the hospital we eventually discovered it.

The car had to be left overnight so the tour of the town had to be done by taxi, a wise precaution as it turned out for we ended up in "O Forcado" a restaurant famous for its Fado singing, the doleful music of the Portuguese people which has a kind of mystical appeal. Not everybody's cup of tea I suppose but for us Welsh it was something like our own Penillion. The night went on, and on, and on, and eventually we joined with a company of multi-nationality tourists in a coach back to camp. What an experience! Exciting? - no; stimulating? - partly; but certainly something quite new in all our travels through Europe up to that time.

There was one thing which upset our further tour of the city the following day before we collected the car. It was that section of the city where we came across the most abject poverty. It was hardly credible that amidst such beautiful and attractive buildings and parks, and crowded shopping streets frequented by well dressed and busy shoppers, one could find people living in extreme squalor. Perhaps our taxi driver had done it deliberately but he certainly gave us a view of the other side of Lisbon when he drove us through an area which housed the poor - not poorer - inhabitants. Their homes were no more than one roomed shacks with earth floors on which were dirty mattresses and few sticks of furniture, and the detour, if it was such, thoroughly upset us. "There are only two classes of people here" 'Van wrote. "The upper and the lowest, yet the amount of cars that are here are even greater than London, with the difference that the drivers here are the worst I've experienced... they're mad!"

At that time, out of a population of 10 million Portuguese, one million lived in the capital which twice in it's lifetime has been totally destroyed by earthquakes, the last in 1755 when the seven hills on which the present city is built were all affected by the tremors. Oh yes, rich or poor, the Lisbonites love their city and their pride is most obviously reflected in the magnificent statue of Christ, with arms outstretched and beckoning, which looks down on the city and its people from one of the hills. According to the diary it is said that as the sun goes down the statue lights up and stays lit until the sun disappears. Then there is the splendid bridge over the river Tagus, reputedly the second longest such bridge in the world after the Golden Gate of San Francisco. Named April 25th it commemorates the day of the revolution in 1974 and is a mile long.

Our two days in Lisbon were not long enough really, but we would not have missed it for the world. Having collected the car, and fully satisfied with the work done, we started our way to Madrid with the intention of a stop over in Elvas. And so we did. As I mentioned earlier it was here that we had one of the most disturbing experiences in the whole of our caravanning. Having found a nice shady spot for two 'vans outside the town's walls we made a casual tour of the town and on return found nothing untoward. It was a good night's sleep but come the dawn our friends the Rowlands were frantically fighting off an invasion of ants which had found their way through an open roof vent. The interior of their caravan seemed to be shimmering as dark lines of ants crossed the ceiling and made their way to the food stores and cupboards. They had found the sugar and other sweetmeats and in a second line the creatures were moving in parallel up the wall and back through the open vent on the roof.

At the best of times both Myfanwy and Margaret disliked crawling ants, but to see them in this state of frantic activity, and seemingly in their millions, put us all off. Strangely neither Percy nor Margaret had had any inkling of anything wrong until he had awakened before 5.00 am and got up to make a pot of tea for an early start. The ants had not ventured on to the two single beds on either side of the 'van but virtually covered that side wall above and at the foot of Percy's bed. It was all hands to the pump, and aerosols in full flow, in an effort to clear out the creatures by the pan full as they were swept on to the floor or dropped by the aerosols. It was then we discovered the cause. In our haste possibly to position the two outfits in a shady spot Percy had overlooked a straggling branch from the large tree which gave us both a measure of protection from the sun. The tip of it just touched the Rowlands' caravan roof and this was the way in for the creatures. They must have sensed the sweet things within the caravan, but when we looked more closely we discovered the tree was virtually alive with ants. The irony of it was that we had both taken the precaution on putting down the steadies of the 'vans to sprinkle quite liberally the steadies and the ground around with anti-ant and insect powder, which is a very necessary precaution when caravanning in hot climates.

As can be imagined this particular experience taught us a further lesson in the ways, whys and wherefores, of caravanning at home or abroad. Never again do we position our outfit beneath a tree, however inviting it might look. After several hours of cleaning up, and jettisoning of "contaminated" food (although I have been told many times since then that ants generally are clean creatures), we were ready to depart our beloved Elvas. It was a very long time, however, before our friends finally got rid of their unwelcome visitors. The odd ant or two would emerge for the rest of our holiday and our friends were not happy with their outfit. Before our next holiday together they had put their 'van in part exchange for another new one. But even now, as we are reminded of the episode, we cannot but cringe at the thought of those creepy-crawlies.

We made for the Portuguese-Spanish border just half an hour away only to find it was closed. It was seven-thirty but the guards apparently did not come on duty for another half an hour. The confusion was over the time change. Spain was an hour different and when we pulled up the other side of the frontier for petrol (cheaper than in Portugal) it was eight thirty. A brief stop for lunch found us with yet another 165 miles to go to Madrid which, after an uneventful journey, we reached at 7.00 pm and found room at Camping Osuna, but only just for it was very full.

The thing we discovered quickly about Madrid, apart from its splendour both architecturally and in its leisure planning, the parks and other open public places, was that life does not begin until after 9.00 pm, and even later. We were offered a City tour within an hour of arriving at the camp and thought it odd to be invited to do the rounds as it were at that time of night. But it turned out to be alright and we saw more of the sights and enjoyed the hospitality of Madrid during the three to four hours than we would had done in as many days alone. I am convinced we were lucky enough to have found an exceptional guide who was a cut above the usual tourist sightseeing type. Our first stop was at a famous Flamenco restaurant where we saw the dancing in all its vibrant glory and colours and sampled the wines of Moulin Rojo; followed by a stroll through the piazzas and then a call in at the "Yulia" night club where the champagne corks were flying around like mortar bombs with the accompanying plops. With a final walk around the square and paying our respects to the statue of Don Quixote's Cervantes we were whisked back to camp at 2.45 am... and it seemed that Madrid's ordinary lifestyle was still following its normal trends!

It was 10.00 am when we struck camp on the following day, 10th August, with the milometer registering 59,755 miles and our course was for Andorra which we hoped to reach sometime on the following day. Lerida seemed to be the ideal place for an overnight halt. We made good progress and filled up with eight gallons of petrol at Guadalefara for the equivalent of £6, about 75 pence the gallon compared with £1.30 in

Portugal. The diary records that we had now moved into very mountainous and rocky country. The roads were not of a high standard and contained many sharp bends. But for all that we found it most attractive to look at. Somewhere along the route we noticed that some people lived in little huts and in high caves in most primitive conditions. This was in the province of Zaragoza, and we were tempted to cry a halt at a small but attractive camp site called "Casablanca", but we still had a good distance to go to Lerida and the territory was not quite so inviting. It reminded us of the film Lawrence of Arabia, and of the face of the moon, with dry earth which resembled white sand and mile upon mile of craggy brown rocks.

Lerida was a disappointment, and not only because on arrival about five o'clock we had found the campsite on which we had planned to stay was full. It was the first time this had happened to us. There was nothing for it but to press on, though were all hot and tired. We had covered more than 300 miles that day and the prospect of another fifty miles with steep climbs to the Free State did not fill us with joy. Lo and behold, the small village of Villanuerva just a few miles along the road turned out to be heaven for us weary travellers. Welcome signs invited us into Raco d'en Pep which turned out to be the loveliest little campsite we had seen on this journey. Small, but with a modern swimming pool and a children's playground, it's status was enhanced by an attached hotel which served the best of food and drinks. It was an oasis in a desert, with peacocks and pigeons offering a welcome change from the barren terrain we had been driving through for the past two hours. These occasions are the bonuses of caravanning. We slept well and at 8.30 am on Monday 11th August we pulled out to resume the journey to Andorra.

Was it worth the effort to reach this mountain top duty-free resort? There was not a single disagreement when, having entered at 12.30 pm, the suggestion was made to press on. Andorra on this occasion was like Southend on an August Bank Holiday Monday, seething with holiday-makers and blaring with pop-music and funfair trappings. It had become so commercialised it wasn't true. By 1.45 pm we had escaped the hullabaloo and were on our way to Aix les Thermes where, 435 miles beyond the little camp of Raco d'en Pep, we found a resting place for the night, and mixed during the evening with the more sedate, even 'upper class'... holidaymakers for whom this resort, we learned, was an annual must.

There was still much to be seen and written for the remainder of the journey but repetition can become so tedious to the reader that I now take up the story on our arrival at Traben-Trarbach on the Mosel, a venue to 'Van and I as much as Aix les Thermes was to the people we met there. It had been five years previously that 'Van and I found Traben-T and it has, and I hope will continue to be for many years to come, our 'must' on future holidays. We were fortunate enough this time again to coincide with the festival of the pigs. This takes place each year during August in the quaint village of Wittlich, high above the River Moselle on the opposite bank to Bernkastel, and coincides with the Weinefest. For those in the vicinity at that time Wittlich is a "must". The whopping big pigs are spit roasted in public view and slices of the meat and the crackling are sold to the merrymakers who sample the dozens of different wines from the area. It is a really good occasion, and is always accompanied by one of the biggest funfairs in that part of Germany.

Another traditional gastronomic event during our Traben-T visits is the Haxen, a massive boar's trotter magnificently prepared by mine host of the Hotel Central, Ernst Ochs, and his good Frau, and guaranteed to satisfy the most pretentious gourmet. They await our coming each year, and long may that happy state of affairs continue. Needless to say the sojourn with our hosts Theo and Jenny Hack of the Rissbach camp site, Traben, was a happy one and it was with regret, as usual, that we left there for home on Tuesday 19th August, arriving back at Uxbridge on 22nd August. The holiday had been most enjoyable and educational, and had taken us over 3,617 miles. No thought at this stage of next year's foray, but no doubt it will be another, and possibly even more ambitious, continental trek.

## Chapter 35

## Holiday Blow Outs!

Nineteen seventy six promised to be a holiday to remember. In the first place, with Percy and Margaret in full agreement, we proposed a fast journey down to Spain and then a meandering and leisurely journey back through France and Germany along previously untraversed roads. It was to be pot luck, as it were, except that we had reserved through Percy's friend a week's stay at a site near Valencia. But we should have known better!

And so it was on Friday the 30th July, on a bright sunny morning, we left our Uxbridge home, "Four Winds", two caravans, and in high spirits, bound for the Costa Brava, Ole! First stop was the local weighbridge where we were shocked to find the combined weight of our car-caravan was two tons 48lbs, somewhat overweight... but what to unload and where to keep it? We had to press on. The crossing from Dover to Calais presented no problems and at 5.30 pm we were negotiating Boulogne and making for Abbeville, our intended first overnight halt. But we should have known better!

First indication we had that all was not as it should be was no trace of Percy's 'van. The rule is to stop and wait for your accompanist to turn up. After some thirty minutes, and with the first shades of evening descending, there was no sign of them. We stopped a passing motorcyclist and asked whether they had seen a British caravan further back the road. Was it the one with a Red Dragon on the side they asked? Yes it was. Oh, they've got the triangle out, we were told. Trouble! I had just unhitched the car to go back and see what was wrong when along they came. The trouble had been a blow out of the caravan tyre, and Percy had spent the best part of an hour searching for a new tyre (since in those days we did not carry a spare tyre for the caravan). It cost him 200 Francs (about £22). And now we were on the lookout for a place to spend our first night abroad. Abbeville was out of the question. But the portents were good for just before nine o'clock we came across "La Vallee Heureuse" - Happy Valley - a small but very picturesque site some four miles off the main road. Blow out number one had put the itinerary out in the first stage of our holiday and silly us, we did not think that it could strike again; but it did.

Leaving Happy Valley at 9.00 am in overcast skies and having travelled only 151 miles from home, we set sights for "anywhere south of Tours". Again the Gremlins struck! A brief stop for coffee around 11 o'clock had resulted in a malfunction of our new fangled 'fridge operated by gas, and an oversight in not disconnecting the car-caravan lead found us with a dead car battery. The former we could not correct but a pair of jump leads from Percy's car got us going again. Later that evening, when we found a site some ten miles before Tours, we found that the 'fridge had somehow righted itself, so it was all systems go again.

Limoges was our next scheduled stop and we spent four very happy days with the Pichaud family, friends of Margaret and Percy. It was here we sampled some of the best French bonhomie and cuisine, including the long to be remembered Rabbit Stew! Albert and Ghisselle were wonderful hosts and for the time we spent with them we virtually discarded the caravans. It was hospitality of every kind, but the evening we shall always remember was when Ghisselle's mother prepared a veritable feast the night before we left. According to the diary the long table was set for nine persons and "Mamma" served the first course of leek and noodle soup, followed by fresh melon, and then the piece de resistance, Rabbit Stew. Earlier we had been shown Albert's pet rabbits in an outside pen and mistakenly assumed what was served up was one of those. It wasn't, of course. What made it more difficult was that neither Percy nor Margaret liked stewed rabbit! But when the old lady, as 'Van affectionately dubbed her, offered a sizeable portion to Percy, including some bones, he gallantly put on a smiling face and graciously thanked her, declaring "I like bones". Her broad smile of "thank you", for she did not speak English, was the last straw! 'Van hurriedly left the table unable to contain her laughter. The rest of the meal was French at its best with all kinds of cheeses, sorbet with black currant jelly and champagne.

It was the 4th August at 7.30 am when we took our leave of Limoges aiming for the Dordogne, on to Montauban, then Toulouse and Carcassonne. It was a very hot day but we were satisfied with our progress and the ever changing scenery helped pass the time quickly. We had covered 236 miles and my watch registered 5.30 pm when we reached a small village of Pintaville near Castelnaudary. As we topped a small hill the glistening Mediterranean on the horizon was a welcome sight, just as was a small camp site set in an idyllic wood. It was very pretty and if there was need for any inducement to call it a day this was it. Pretty soon we were talking to other British caravanners returning to England from Tarragona where, they told us, the weather was glorious. Sixteen days there had turned their skins a chocolate brown. It only made us the more keen to get over the Pyrenees. Our interest was further fired by their report of a new Spanish motorway, but they warned it was a toll road; and we found it so, much to our cost!

Crossing the Pyrenees was no problem, nor entry into Spain at Perpignan, where the new motorway began. It was to take us to Valencia though it went actually as far as Alicante. Compared at that time with the English motorways system it was superb and well equipped with service areas which catered for restaurants and petrol stations, and these, we found eventually, did offset the tolls since we were allowed to "camp" there for rest periods and even overnight. The diary reminds us that this journey along the motorway was so different from previous visits to Spain. "The road is so smooth it is a joy to ride on it" Van wrote. "The scenery is beautiful, unlike the old journeys when the countryside seemed all burned up".

Every 12 kilometres were beautiful lay-bys and wooded areas which British motorway planners would do well to study and emulate; but the first pinch was felt at the peage before reaching Barcelona where we had to pay the equivalent of £2.80. It was here that we discovered Percy was no longer with us. And we could not retrace our journey on a motorway. An English couple arrived and informed us that they had passed a caravan some fifteen miles back with a Red Dragon symbol "and the driver inspecting the underneath of the caravan". More trouble! We had to move on for about a mile to the next peage (where we parted with the equivalent of 55 pence) and where we were joined half an hour later by our companions. Yes, there had been another blow out and a tyre change. This meant another deviation, this time into Barcelona, where the search went on after the lunch siesta for another tyre. "Let's hope this is the last one" the diary states. But it wasn't.

To get back on the motorway cost another £1.20 and we were aiming for Tarragona which brought to mind the 1970 visit and the misfortunes that involved. Suddenly the scene changed and we were travelling for miles alongside a raging inferno of forest fires. Peage number four cost another 70 pence quickly followed by another of 75 pence. These were blunting our appetite for motorway travel! Tortora saw the end of the motorway and another £2.10 before we could get off... but twelve miles further on we had the familiar image of another peage and a divvy-up of yet another £2.10, but at least it offered the consolation of a service area twelve miles further on and the offer of an overnight stay free of charge.

Up to this point we had travelled 418 miles, the longest pull so far, and it was just after 8.00 pm. Thankfully there was no need for the ladies to prepare a meal in the 'vans as the on-site restaurant offered good meals which cost about £1.60 per head. For this we had a pork cutlet, frankfurter, egg and chips, an aperitif of Cinzano and a long drink of lemonade. Not at all bad. Before we turned in I did a little calculation and found that so far our journey from home had taken us 1186 miles.

Our objective was Cullera on the outskirts of Valencia and we calculated on leaving the services that we could be installed in our proposed camp by 10.30 am. What a disappointment was in store. We found the site alright, but were told that no reservation had been made, and they were full up. More than 1,200 miles and no room at the Inn! We had the option of returning the way we had come without any idea of where at the height of the season we might find a campsite to spend a holiday, or press on down the coast. We did the latter and with great fortune and some perseverance a couple of hours later found "El Darada". It was a delightful orange grove, but there was a snag. It, too, was full. Exasperated almost beyond endurance in a temperature high in the nineties we pulled up outside the entrance for a snack and brief siesta before moving on. A short time later the camp manager came and offered us a site for two beyond the grove and on the beach. It wasn't much to look at but after a brief inspection and only an alternative of driving on we took the offer. It was the best thing that had happened to us so far. Both caravans carried wind breaks and by the time we had put these up, embracing both 'vans, we were in a little private encampment of our own. It turned out to be a wonderful six days. There was nothing between us and the sea 200 yards away. We lazed in the sun, swam in a warm and clean sea, wandered through the orange grove choosing a fruit when we felt like it and at night joining the locals in the village for a drink and meal. It was heavenly. Still vivid in the mind are the evening visits to Don Quixo with its special local ambience. And especially the standing order of one plate of chips and four forks! It was here also that we sampled traditional paella and, according to the diary "We walked back slowly in the cool of the evening with only the moon to guide us". What more romantic could one wish for?

But all good things come to an end and despite it being Friday the 13th we hitched on and began another long journey which would eventually take us to the beautiful Moselle in Germany. Was it too much to hope that this would be less eventful than the journey down? The portents did not seem too good to start with. Having passed through three tolls at a combined cost of £5.15 we suddenly found ourselves back on a non-motorway road which took us into Barcelona and the worst traffic jams we had ever encountered. Another 55 pence enabled us to rejoin the motorway to Gerona and a spellbinding climb through the mountains. By 8.30 pm and after 320 miles we reached the last of the service areas on the junction with Lloret de Mar where we stayed for the night. It was farewell to Spain when at 8.30 am the following morning we made for the border and set sights for Nimes in France. But it was at Bagnols les Bains, 230 miles on, that we spent the night at a delightful and small campsite, "Sante Margaret", run by an English speaking Frenchman who gushingly welcomed our arrival and explained his daughter was at an English school.

It was here during the night that we experienced our first heavy storm, thunder, lightening and drenching rain, and it being a Sunday we decided to carry on the next stage, hopefully to Besancon, by motorway from Veinne. Our first peage was 28 Francs (about £3.50), but at least we hoped the extra cost would give us a faster journey. It was at a quaint village of Cousance - where the trip meter showed we had already travelled 2,000 miles from home - that we felt the outfit lurch. Catastrophe! The off-side caravan tyre had punctured. In some twenty years of caravanning this was the first time it had happened to us - and on a Sunday on a French motorway! But lady luck had not deserted us altogether. Percy still had a spare tyre for his caravan and very fortunately it turned out this fitted our 'van too.

Besancon was out of the question now, and the rain kept falling. Out of the blurred windscreen we suddenly picked out a Camping sign, which is how we discovered "Camping Marjorie" at Lons le Saunier. It also happened to be Margaret's birthday which we celebrated with a lovely dinner of bacon, eggs and mashed potatoes followed by apple and peach desert. And with the patter of rain drops on the roof we brought the day to a close with a hotly contested game of scrabble... but it is not recorded who won.

Our ultimate goal was Traben-Trarbach on the Moselle and this was reached without further incident, except that at Saarbrucken we had to purchase for the equivalent of £19 a spare tyre for our caravan. End of the trail at Camping Rissbach saw 2,396 miles clocked for the entire journey. Eight days of bliss in excellent weather included one outstanding experience, the Feast of the Pigs at Wittlich, about ten miles away. This is a mediaeval tradition of spit-roasting whole pigs, served with the tasting of dozens of new wines from the vineyards of the region. Anyone who has the opportunity to attend the Pigs Fest of Wittlich, and to indulge in the vast pleasure fair which accompanies it, should not miss it. Usually it takes place around the end of August.

Having said our goodbyes to Theo and Jenny, our hosts, and Marion and Michael, Ruth and Thomas, two other old friends from Denmark, we set out for home on 28th August. The crossing on Enterprise 5 from Zeebrugge was uneventful, as was the rest of the homeward trek. When we reached "Four Winds" the trip meter showed we had travelled 2,900 miles; quite an achievement by present day standards. But from start to finish it proved an enjoyable, satisfying, holiday with, as always, some new experiences to be stored for the future. This is where Caravanning has the edge every time on hotel and set holidays. We now had to prepare for next year.

## Chapter 36

## The Jubilee Holiday

Preparation for the 1977 holiday had included our fifth venture for a new caravan. At the November Caravan Show we had been greatly impressed by the improvements displayed by every manufacturer, but our choice was a Swift Dannette. The attraction here was a see-through vision which the deep rear window afforded. Now, we thought, it would be easier to keep our companions in sight. And so it proved. Our preparations over the winter months had concentrated on a then highly publicised "Soak in the sun" campaign for the Yugoslavian islands within easy reach of the Trieste border. It was to be special, for this was the 25th anniversary of the saga of our camping and caravanning life.

Friday 29th August saw our two caravans (with Margaret and Percy again) crossing from Dover to Zeebrugge where we parked overnight. By 7.30 am the following morning in brilliant weather we were making for Aachen. It was our first experience of the new Belgium motorway and we were greatly impressed. The journey was the quickest we had done on this particular route and the link up with the German autobahn enabled us to reach Limburg, south of Frankfurt, by 3.30 pm, with 285 miles on the clock. This was a familiar camp for us and although pretty full we found ourselves two places near the river.

It was on this holiday that we resumed a practice we had initiated a few years earlier, namely that on breaking camp we would travel for 100 miles, or until 9 am, whichever was first, before stopping for breakfast. In this way we usually encountered less traffic and made better time. It being a Sunday we were thankful for the ban on heavy lorries which made our journey easier and quicker so that by 4.30 pm we had reached Munich and were pressing on for the Austrian border and Kufstein which we reached before seven o'clock and after 345 miles that day.

Never had we seen such rain as during our overnight stop in this most charming of Austrian villages. It was a case of should we press on or stay put until the weather improved. We had to bear in mind that the next part of the journey would be over most difficult terrain, several steep climbs to contend with on the way to the new Felbertauern Tunnel. We decided to go on, the thought of all that sun and warmth we had read about during the winter being the driving force. Within a couple of hours out of Kufstein we were having second thoughts already, and the journey became one of nightmarish proportions as we continually were compelled to take deviations because of floods and landslips. A major road subsidence beyond St. Johann almost convinced us that discretion was the better part of valour, but that sun and warm sea prospect was an irresistible magnet.

We made the tunnel through mist and continual heavy rain. But what would be at the end of the three mile traverse? This was a truly tremendous feat of engineering, the most impressive we have yet encountered. For a toll of 270 Schillings - about £10 - we drove through a well lit bore-hole in the mountain and out to... rain first and then snow! Was it worth the effort we wondered? The vagaries of the weather in this part of Austria were not unknown to us, so we battled on in hope. After another two and a half hours driving we reached a delightful village of Matrei, but it had taken us five hours to do the 100 miles. A major consolation was that the rain had not reached these parts.

Sun at last! Now it was all systems go for Villach where we had planned an overnight halt. However, we were unfortunate in receiving some bad advice during a brief lay-by halt outside the town which altered the whole course of our holiday. A casual chat with another motorist elicited the information that we should make for a small but little known camp site at Cres, and not Pula which had been our original objective. "Paradise" was how it was described to us. The fellow must have had shares in the place. The route was changed and, urged on by the promise of paradise we reached Udine after 287 miles of the worst conditions we had ever known. There were heartbreaking scenes. Demolished buildings and scarred earth, subsidence and hurried prefabricated shelters which served as homes for the population, were all evidences of the drastic earthquake which had decimated the area. It had a most disquieting effect on our spirits. The sun and sea and paradise did not seem to matter at that time.

From here on to Trieste it was motorway and we made good progress to the Yugoslav border where we picked up the sign for Brestovna. This is where we had been told we could get the ferry to Cres, and excitement mounted. It was 10.45 am when we reached the steep slope leading to the quayside which serviced three ferryboats. Ahead of us were at least a hundred cars and two caravans... and this is where the doubt started to creep in! It cost about £7 for a one-way ticket and the crossing took twenty minutes. On disembarking the one feature which struck us was the bad state of the roads. As Van remarks "This place reminds me of Madeira with its undulating roads and curves. One moment you are at the bottom and the next you are at the top of a mountain". But there was worse to come.

Except for a slight accident when boarding the ferry the crossing to Cres was beautiful and our spirits were high. We disembarked after less than thirty minutes' journey, then by bridge on Mali Losinj, a small island, which was the promised paradise. Within thirty minutes our expectations had been dashed. "Paradise" was nothing more than a desolate volcanic left-over, abounding with basalt rocks, and fir tree outcrops. There were only two small towns but the ill-made roads made driving difficult, even dangerous on the narrowest strips. Where was the camping site we had been advised about? Our searches led us along the waters edge and beaches which were almost totally rock and stones with a few tents set up higgledy - piggledy and obviously these holiday makers were mainly boating enthusiasts. We pressed on and eventually saw the sign "El paradiso". The site itself was in a large pinewood forest and had none of the camping facilities which we had become accustomed to. We had travelled fifty miles over the most demanding conditions and being confronted with this was the last straw. This was not Paradise, but more Paradise Lost. There was only one thing to do. Swallow our disappointment and head back for Pula, our original objective.

We were told it was possible to go direct from Mali Losinj, but on the quayside found it would cost at least £27. A hurried council of war and we were back on the road to the ferry, some fifty miles away. I let the diary now relate what happened. "It is already six o'clock and we are on our way to the ferry... It is 7 o'clock and we have still another 34 miles to do.... We are five miles from the ferry and hoping to make it before dark and catch the last ferry which leaves at 7.45 pm... We are here. It's 7.45 pm and we can see the ferry ready to leave... It's dark but we have just made it after a trying journey for Glan and Percy over mountains with sheer drops and no protection. It's been most hazardous and exhausting".

This most memorable and disappointing day ended with our having to stay overnight on the quayside at Pula. Up at 4.30 am, awakened by the noise of vehicles arriving for the Cres ferry, we were en route for Pula and arrived at the campsite at 7.10 am. The site was not listed in the Caravan Club's foreign guide and turned out to be very full. It was on the seaside but again obviously more suitable for boating than caravanning. "So disappointing" is the diary comment. "We have decided not to stay but to make our way to N. S.U. (now Camping Lido at Cavallino, Jesolo)." It had been a wasted four days, but we had learned another lesson. Do not put too much credence on lay-by tittle-tattle. Thursday, 4th August, saw us off to N.S.U. when, after an uneventful journey we arrived at 3.30 pm. It was with relief that we settled down in what seemed to us to a much improved site offering more room for individual outfits and electricity and water ready to hand. It was much the same routine as previously during the twelve days we spent here; clean beaches, warm and clean water, sunny days and cool evenings, a delightful background to our type of holiday. It was here, too, that we made many friends and enduring friendships, among them John (then a lecturer at the Swansea University) and Mavis Williams, Peter and Audrey Jackson, a delightful couple from Swansea, and many German and Continental friends.

A few days before we were to leave N.S.U. a suggestion by John and endorsed by us all led to one of the most memorable events of our lives. Why not an overnight stay in Verona on our homeward journey and spend a night at the opera? So it happened that on Tuesday, August 16th four outfits pulled into reserved place in Camping Romeo and Juliet, Verona, keyed up for that night's visit to the vast Roman amphitheatre where the performance was of Il Pagliacci and Cavalleria Rusticana. It also happened to be Margaret's birthday, so this would be a special celebration.

We had been warned to arrive at the centuries old, and possibly the best preserved, Roman structure of its kind in the world, before dusk though the performances did not commence until 9 pm. It was a warning well heeded because when we got there we found a milling throng of thousands waiting for the stone pillared doors to open to admit them. There were elegant men in full evening dress and bejewelled ladies in their evening gowns milling with the more mundane of us. But the excitement had obviously seized everyone. There were the ticket less patrons flashing notes to attract the touts who were demanding and getting ten times the price. We had purchased ours days before for 7,000 Lire, about £5 for a couple!

Each one was handed a candle on admission and the reason became apparent soon enough. As the crowds filed in to take their places along the many tiered stone benches, polished to a smoothness by centuries of cushioned usage, and with dusk giving way to a typical Italian blackness, the hubbub was at a crescendo. From on high the stage and auditorium seemed a long distance away but such was the effectiveness of the acoustics in this vast arena which seated 25,000 people that one became aware of activity on it by a clarity of movement as props and players were got ready long before the footlights came on. Suddenly, a gong sounded. It was the signal to light the candles. A momentary eerie silence gave way to terrific applause as the amphitheatre glowed in a myriad of candle lights. It was the perfect setting to an evening of superb opera, and one which will never fade from my memory. Each Act and every aria was applauded with such sharpness that it could have been happening in an enclosed premise and not an edifice erected more than two thousand years ago.

The performance went on until well after midnight and the walk back to our caravans was punctuated by the comments and emphases of us all on a night always to remember.

The following day we were homeward bound via Austria's Resia and Arlberg passes, a brief stay on Lake Constance and thence, just M. and P.'s and our outfit, to the Mosel. The only incident en route was our stalling on the Arlberg and being towed to the summit by an Army truck. As in the previous six years, we had planned the last few days of the holiday at Rissbach in Traben Trarbach. Our friends, Jenny and Theo Hack, had kept two places for us on the river side and it was a surprise when a couple of days later we were unexpectedly joined by

Beryl, Margaret and Percy's daughter, and her young man, Chris. The reason, as Van and I were taken into their confidence, was that they wanted to become engaged but only with her parents' consent. What a romantic interlude to the holiday, and what more romantic place than on the banks of the beautiful Mosel! Permission was granted, and we celebrated that evening with dinner at Hotel Central where Mine Host Ernst Ochs did us proud. The event was recollected and revealed two years later by me at their wedding in Caernarfon. Today they are the happily married parents of five children and living in Australia.

It was Tuesday, 30th August, when we arrived home, having parted company with our companions who were travelling direct to North Wales, and it was a tired but satisfied and fulfilled pair that trundled in to "Four Winds" with the milometer showing we had travelled 2,574 miles, and again garnered a wealth of experiences and memories which would last a lifetime.

# Chapter 37

# The Swedish F.I.C.C.

It had been some years since we had attended an International Rally, so when En Route published the details of the 1978 Rally in Sweden we, that is, the Rossers and the Rowlands, decided this would be our objective for the coming year. It meant extra-special planning because we intended taking the land route rather than cross the North Sea by ferry and then, from Gothenburg, by road to the site at Jonkoping. It would entail a route through Holland, north Germany, Denmark and then some 230 kilometres through southern Sweden.

We calculated a journey of just over a thousand miles, and most of it over new ground for us. And so it was that on Friday, 28th July, 1978, we set off with growing excitement at the prospect of seeing new places and people in Scandinavia. It was ten years since Van and I had been in Sweden. For the Rowlands it would be their first.

Our crossing to Zeebrugge was on the Townsend-Thoresen "Enterprise 7", and so heavy was the demand by cars and caravans that caravans had to be unhitched and man-handled into the smallest space to make room. A far cry from the present day roll-on and drive through system! It was a lovely crossing and the journey to the Dutch-German border at Venlo was without incident. Weather good and the outfits performing splendidly, but that first stage turned out to be very demanding. We couldn't find a camping site in nearly ten hours driving and eventually, after 328 miles, we were compelled to pull on to an open space outside the stadium in Dortmund for the night. Thereafter, the route took us to Hamburg via Bremen and the splendid bridge over the Weser, and Kiel, names still vivid in the memory from the war years.

A new autobahn from Kiel to the German-Danish border at Flensburg was the best we had experienced until then, and according the diary the scenery approaching the border was a fascinating recurrence of lakes crammed with small sailing craft and miles of luscious grazing land. We had provisionally arranged with our Swedish friends from Rissbach, Traben, on the Moselle in Germany, Ruth and Thomas, to meet them on 29th July at a camping site near the border. This was the Jarplunder, on the German side of the frontier. We found it alright and as we drove in they were rushing to meet us. What a reunion! And we had driven 310 miles that day. Apparently the cost of buying and maintaining a caravan in Denmark and Sweden was virtually prohibitive so many Danish caravanners left their caravans in sites on the German side of Flensburg and used them at weekends and for holidays.

After a sun scorching and lazy weekend we were on the move again. It meant we had to return to Kiel, and the ferry at Puttgarten, about 150 kilometres back, to get into Denmark and the direct route to Jonkoping. It was at Puttgarden that we joined a crowd of caravans from many countries all heading for the rally. Our return tickets cost us £30 and the "Deutschland" took one hour to make the crossing. By 5.30 pm we had reached Copenhagen and were safely installed in Camping Sundbyuester near to the city centre, a beautiful site with every facility. But we were too tired to do the sights which would have included the Mermaid and the Tivoli. These would have to await the return journey.

In an effort to spearhead the "convoy" of 'vans to the Danish-Swedish ferry at Helsingor, 28 miles away, we had left camp at 7 am. Half an hour later we were flagged down by a broken down caravan. I wonder, if they read this, the family involved will remember the incident? They were a Basque family, mother and father and five small children, from Bilbao, and they had suffered two punctures. Already, on their way to the rally, it transpired they had survived two car crashes and a big-end! We took both tyres off, one car and the other the caravan, and carried them to a garage some distance off the motorway. There we arranged for them to be repaired and taken back to the stranded Lopez family. The diary confesses that all the way to the rally we were troubled whether the garage man had kept his word and returned the tyres.

It was the "Karnan" which ferried us across the 20 minutes crossing

(£23 return) and we still had about 130 miles to go to Jonkoping with a road which reminded us very much of the Yugoslav "Put-Put". The one redeeming feature was that it meandered through about 100 kilometres of forest, a very picturesque drive. It was a most enjoyable ride in the end and we were surprised that most of the houses and bungalows were made of wood. We shouldn't have been, of course, with all the timber that was available!

The end of the journey was anything but a rainbow's end however. We found the rally site without trouble, but our first impressions were terribly disappointing. We expected many hundreds of caravans, but not the thousand plus which stretched the facilities and space to breaking point. Every odd spot and corner was commandeered... and we had two of the worst because we were "late-comers". We had travelled 1,056 miles for this?

The second day was not so bad. Disappointments abated when we made the rounds and met fellow caravanners from almost every country in Europe. Our near neighbours were the Finns and Norwegians, jolly people and justly proud of their nationalities which they flouted in their national costumes and hats. The Finns, for instance, told us that by wearing a bauble cap on one side or the other a young woman would indicate whether or not she was eligible for marriage. Their aisle parties were tremendous with tables stretching 30 yards and laden with food and drinks. We half promised we would see them again in 1981 when the International Rally would be in Finland. Alas, it was not possible.

We were still worried about the Basque family, but the following day all was well. They descended upon us with whoops of delight. They introduced us to some of their friends as "our good Samaritans" and we joined in a splendid party... more special since they had learned we were Welsh, and the Basques and the Welsh have a strong cultural and Celtic affinity. There was Jamie Lopez and wife Begonia, Alex, Suzanne, Xavier, Willie, and Inigo. The party was one of the most colourful we can recall. Dressed in their national costumes, the men with their saucy Barralina hats and ladies in their colourful dresses, they danced their folk dances, and the sippers drank from those quaint long stemmed globes raised to arm's length. The then Caravan Club President, David Knight, and his wife Hilda, joined the party and all cares appeared to be forgotten. It was a wonderful night, and only something which could be staged in this type of get-together. It was caravanning at its best. But reality the next day, and the problems of over-crowding, and the heavy rain which threatened to continue, decided us that the morrow would see us depart.

The day of our return was wet and stormy but with very little traffic about we made the journey to Helsingborg, the ferry terminus to Helsingor, without incidents worth reporting. Not until we reached the outskirts of Copenhagen did we encounter any problem. So convoluted was the route and so heavy the traffic that it took us nearly three hours to find our Sundbywester Camp. By 4 pm, and after 165 miles on the clock, we arrived. The odd thing was that we had not discussed and decided where would go after Denmark. We were just pressing on. And why not, indeed! We had our "homes" attached, and no worries about hotel or any other reservations. We were fancy free and able to roam at will. That was, and to a large extent still is, the beauty of caravanning.

It was the weather which was the deciding factor about our movement from here. After an evening's sightseeing tour of the city, and the expected viewing of Langeline (The Mermaid) who, incidentally, came as a surprise and disappointment to us because she was very small compared with the pictures we had seen of her, and a hilarious couple of hours at the Tivoli, the gloomy weather forecast prompted a very late council of war and the decision was to move on and look for the sun. We had almost three weeks left of the holiday. It seemed natural somehow that Italy and the sun should project themselves into the discussion. So Italy it was to be, and an early start in the morning. That we were facing a journey of more than a thousand miles did not matter. No one mentioned N.S.U. at that juncture, but that's where we ended up.

Sunday 6th August, at 7.30 am we left a wet and windy Copenhagen for Rodbyhaven and the ferry to Puttgarten and north Germany. The Konig FREDERIK was a beautiful ship and the biggest attraction for us was the smorgasbord which offered those famous Danish open sandwiches, including a bounteous smoked salmon. We were adequately sustained for the next leg of the journey which was Hanover. Travelling by autobahn practically all the way resulted in our reaching Hildesheim around 4.40 pm. A slight detour of 15 kilometres into Dernaburg presented us with a lovely site, "Seecamp", and we were settled down by 5.15 pm. We had done 314 miles since Copenhagen. Just as important, though, the weather had greatly improved and we felt fully justified in our decision to make for sunnier climes than remain in Copenhagen, as attractive and interesting it undoubtedly would have been.

It was a day of beautiful if sometimes sad memories the following day as we drove on through the Harz mountains. It recalled our last visit with the Davies'. For those who have not visited this gloriously beautiful region there can be only one recommendation. Repair the omission quickly! We were loathe to depart, but Fulda and beyond beckoned. The mediaeval walled town of Rothenburg was to be our next scheduled stop and with a turn in the weather again to heavy rain it wasn't until nearly three o'clock that we reached it. We were immediately struck by the changes that had taken place since we last visited Rothenburg in 1968, not least that part of the ancient wall that had been converted into a car park. Advancing with the times perhaps, but to returning visitors this was sacrilege! The day's journey was 250 miles. Our overnight stay was at the "Tauber Idyll" campsite.

Still we had not mentioned where journey's end might be, but subconsciously, and on reflection, there was only one place we could have been aiming for... N.S.U. It was still raining heavily when we pulled up the steadies at 6.45 am the following morning and the portents were not good. Within a short while we discovered we were on the wrong road, and we covered 74 miles before we could get back on track for Augsburg and the Austrian border. Stopping for breakfast at 9.00 am near Aalen Van discovered to our dismay that the 'fridge door had opened and a litre of milk and a jug of ice-water had spilled on to the carpet. And you know what spilled milk will do to a carpet if not mopped up and washed immediately! Another enforced stop cost us more than an hour but by 10.15 am we were on our way again. Still the rain persisted!

Approaching Ulm the river Kocher had overflowed its banks. It was Umleitung after Umleitung and we doubted whether we could reach Innsbruck for our projected overnight halt. Again the ever increasing network of new autobahn brought us relief and we made Vils the Austro-German border and then the Fern Pass and down into Innsbruck without further untoward incident. What a relief to pull into our old site in Innsbruck at 5.30 pm after a journey of 284 miles in the worst possible conditions. By this time there was no question in anyone's mind that beyond the Brenner and Tyrolean Alps would be the welcome harbour of Cavallino and N.S.U. What had started off as a Scandinavian holiday was to end more than a thousand miles and more away. Already we had travelled 2,084 miles since we left home and we still had nearly 400 miles to go.

That didn't matter so much now. We were on familiar ground and the rest of the journey to Cavallino was so repetitive that I knew almost every undulation on the Italian autostrada from Verona to Mestre and beyond to Jesolo. By today, however, the whole of the approach roads system to the Aegean Sea is changed as it continues to be the magnet and the Mecca for campers and caravanners from all parts of Europe. Our journey's end came just after the siesta hour (1 pm to 3 pm) at N.S.U. We had covered 2,450 miles from home, and we were here to stay for two weeks.

The pattern for the rest of the holiday was as it always had been, leisurely and in consolidating old friendships and forming new ones. The journey home was punctuated with a week's stay at Traben on the Mosel again and by the time we arrived back in Uxbridge on 30th August we had travelled 3,760 miles.

## Chapter 38

## The New Outfit Arrives

The idea of a new outfit had been very much in our minds during the winter months after the Swedish-Italian trip. This had been fired mainly by the new caravans and fresh ideas we had seen during that enormous journey. Early spring, after a thorough scouring of the new lists, and having acquired some ideas from the numerous caravans centres we had visited, found us in Mildenhall vetting the Cranbrook, a new model. We were impressed. Somehow the "sales talk" was much more convincing and persuasive in those days than present day, an opinion much strengthened by our personal experience in the purchase of our latest - and twelfth - caravan in 1993.

This sturdily built two berth 'van with its many "extras" or embellishments gave added zest to preparations for the forthcoming continental holiday which, again, we were to share with Percy and Margaret. But where to go? Our first step had been an early reservation for crossing the channel to Calais. After that it was to be an unscheduled roaming holiday for four weeks; first to Normandy perhaps, thence across to Belgium en route to Germany and possibly a fleeting visit to Austria... but no thought was given to crossing the Tyrolean Alps and making a beeline to the Aegean Sea.

That was how the early planning went, but, as usual, how oft the plans of mice and men gang algae!

We didn't cross from Calais at all. We changed it at the last minute to a crossing to Zeebrugge and August 12th 1979 at 2.00 am saw us on deck in bright moonlight watching the lighthouse on the famous Zeebrugge Mole flashing a welcome. Embarkation at 2.45 am enabled us to find a quiet corner berth for two on the quayside where we managed to squeeze in four hours sleep before setting off for the German autobahn and Cologne, a first leg of our holiday which carried on for 295 miles. It seemed that we were being dragged by a supreme gravitational pull towards those lovely sun drenched days the other side of the Alps because, although none of us voiced our minds, everyone's thoughts were in that direction it transpired later. Of course, the main reason for this and the change in the original ideas was the inevitable rain. It had dogged us all the way from Zeebrugge. And to cap it all when we arrived at Cologne at around six o'clock and were fortunate to find a small camp site (overcrowded but good enough for an overnight halt) our brand new caravan had its first tantrum.

Not yet having reached the sophistication of mains electric - and even if we had there was no such amenity in the camp anyway - we found we could not use the water taps because the 12 volt battery, which was the only power source, was flat. It would have been even more miserable had we not had our friends' supply to fall back on. It was an awful stormy night, and each crash of thunder only served to harden our resolve (unspoken as yet) to get away from these conditions as quickly as possible. After an early morning cuppa, thanks again to the benevolence of our friends and their water, we set off "South". This holiday at this point actually marks a milestone in our continental meanderings for it was here that the suggestion was made that whilst en route we should cover at least one hundred miles, or drive until nine o'clock, before breakfast. We managed it, that Monday 13th August 1979, despite the continuing rain, and we have done so every continental holiday since! On this occasion it enabled us to break the back of the journey to our next overnight halt before lunchtime when we voiced our opinions on the ultimate destination, and agreed it should be Italy via Austria.

Innsbruck was to be the overnight stop, and the decision having been reached we were all in better fettle. But the Gremlins were not long before putting their oar into our affairs. There were two roads which led to Innsbruck from our lunchtime halt. Until now we had kept in close touch with each other, but a motorway jam and Umleitung resulted in our friends taking the Karlsruhe road whilst we went on the Ulm road.

Fortunately we had agreed our overnight halt would be Innsbruck which we reached at 5.45 pm having travelled 330 miles. No sign of P and M!

We were just about to start our meal at around 6.45 pm - I had been to the camp chip shop for "pomme frites" as the notice declared, when who should be coming on site but the Rowlands'. Together once more, and all set to tomorrow's journey over the Brenner and into sun swept Italy, the holiday spirit was brimming up again. Despite the rain and the trials and tribulations of the water problem and the break in contact we were all set to enjoy ourselves as only caravanners can! It had to be an augury for fine weather ahead when, the following morning at a few minutes after seven o'clock, we broke camp in brilliant sunshine and set out for the climb over the Brenner. "Margaret and Percy are close behind us and not likely to lose contact again" Van records in the diary. "After the ordeal of yesterday the panorama stretching out before us takes a lot of beating. It's like turning over the pages of a picture book".

Within two hours we were well into Italy, with hearts beating faster at the prospect of sunny days and fine weather. This was what we had come for, and the holiday was well into its way.

The Dolomites have a special fascination for those who have been fortunate enough to have traversed its peaks and picturesque villages and we savoured it to the full as we descended from 1,518 metres down to Cortina which, several years before, had hosted the Olympic winter games. It was lunch time and an alfresco meal in such surroundings was very enjoyable.

Our ultimate destination was to be Cavallino and our favourite Union Lido Camp, and it was just half a day's journey away by autostrada but the magnetism of the mountains made it easy for us to change our minds and stay overnight, which would leave a comparatively simple journey on the morrow, a mere 219 miles which was accomplished without further problems.

As we entered Union Lido it was just like returning home. It had been our holiday venue for so many years and this time it seemed little had changed. The first of the British contingent to make contact with us were our Welsh friends Mavis and John Williams, and our near neighbour was Andrew Gardner and his family. The TV newscaster and presenter was an old friend and in no time we had settled down to the usual routine of mornings on the beach and afternoon teas 'neath the awnings. There was, however, one major difference; we were joined after a few days by our eldest son David who spent most of the remainder of our stay with us and enhanced the holiday.

As ever one of the features of a Cavalino holiday was Market Day and it is recorded that this time we found the market very much larger than hitherto. But gone are the days when the British holidaymakers were money wise popular with the stallholders. This time that mantle had fallen on the Germans who appeared to be more wealth wise than us. It was the first real indication for us that British was best in everything no longer applied... at least in Cavallino!

August 28th, a Tuesday and fourteen days since we arrived, broke in torrential rain. It also was the day we left, and the record shows that we got as far as Lake Garda on the homeward journey before pulling into an Agip service area for the night. The next day saw an improvement in weather conditions and the trip between Trento and Bolzano was delightful with its mosaic patterns of vineyards and fruit orchards waiting to be harvested. Will we ever tire of these caravan journeys when one can please oneself when to stop and indulge in fantastic views and be carefree in beautiful surroundings? We hope that will be very many years ahead!

One memory which is awakened by the diary is the "anguish" caused by the Italian autostrada tolls. "It's a beautiful day (August 29th) and we are going to have bacon and eggs for breakfast when we reach the mountains" Van wrote... then "We have just come off the motorway and had to pay a toll of 13,650 lire - nearly £8 - it's scandalous!" The Italians are no doubt one of the best motor-road builders in the world but to us, as to most caravanners from U.K. at that time, the privilege of driving along those wonderful roads was blunted by the high toll charges (especially after the no-pay German autobahns), and the added factor that we had to pay virtually double charges for towing drove many back to the lesser but quite adequate secondary roads.

Fortunately the incident of the toll charge did not prevent the bacon and egg breakfast which was thoroughly enjoyed on the lower slope of the Resia Pass. This is one of our favourite journeys to and from Venice and it is to be recommended to fellow caravanners for its ease of climb and also the breathtaking canvass of changing sceneries.

It was 1.30 pm Italian time / 12.30 pm Austrian time when we crossed the border, and making for the Fern Pass. Three hours later we came across one of the prettiest, if small, camp sites along the route tucked away behind a Gasthof-cum-petrol station. It was simply crying out to be patronised, and we relished the thought of once again eating a Tyrolean meal that evening with the Gasthof at hand. The Rossers and Rowlands did themselves proud with a dinner which consisted of first course soup-mit-ei (traditional soup with egg), blue trout from the local lake with frites and salads, followed by cheese, ice cream and coffee..., wines and afters of one's choice. It was the first time we had come across Lermoos, but for very many years thereafter Lermoos, with the hosts Willy and Maria Schonger, was a "must" on our journeys to and from Italy. It was here, also that we formed the friendship with our German friends Albert and Gerda Harter of Tubingen which has been sustained for fifteen years.

No holiday since 1970 on the continent has been complete without a few days on the lovely banks of the Moselle and Traben-Trarbach was our next and natural port of call. September 1st saw the two caravans pull into Camping Rissbach in Traben where we were welcomed by Jenny and Theo Hack and their daughter Marian. This sojourn, as in Union Lido, was as always the same pattern, but we cannot ever say we are tired of our rest by the Moselle with its constantly changing pattern of river traffic, including the working barges and the pleasure steamers.

Five wonderful days! On September 6th we pulled out, but only as far as Trier, the furthest bastion of the Roman Empire in Germany, and a place which has been an enormous attraction to the ladies for many years. We stayed for only one day and a night, but have since made this a welcome stop on most occasions. It is also, of course, the birthplace of Karl Marx.

It had not been our intention to dawdle on this last lap of our homeward journey but attracted by a notice of a famous Grotto of Han near Marche we were tempted to make an overnight halt. This is just another example of the attractions of caravanning that unscheduled stops such as this was are just part of the holiday. The visit to the Grotto turned out to be one of the highlights of the holiday. Van makes the point in the diary... " This is even better than the ones we have seen in Wookey Hole, Salzburg and Czechoslovakia. Our guides have taken us on foot up and down fantastic caves and caverns in which there are the most beautiful stalactites and stalagmites we have ever seen. Some caverns are massive, making the most wonderful shapes. All had names, like Mont St Michael, Budes, and of animals. In the centre of the mountain was a lake and above it a huge cavern where an organ played its eerie music; tables and chairs all around the lake where refreshments were served. For three kilometres we had to cross bridges and water. The highlight was the trip through an underground river, where our heads sometimes almost touched the ceiling, until we came to the opening and as we emerged into daylight there was a terrific bang. Someone had fired a shot which scared everyone. I do not think we would have missed this for anything."

Our last night's camping was spent in the delightful border town of Sluis in Holland from where in less than thirty minutes we were at Zeebrugge port ready to embark for Dover. One further memory of this holiday was that Van and I celebrated our 41st wedding anniversary on 10th September at Sluis before returning to Four Winds on 11th September, exactly one month after leaving. We had travelled 2,563 miles.

## Chapter 39

## The Herald of Free Enterprise

In retrospect this holiday of 1980 was to be memorable for at least two things. First we made our crossing from Dover to Calais on the new ferry vessel, the Herald of Free Enterprise, then hailed by the operators as the flagship of the fleet, and some ten years later the victim of circumstances which caused its end and the deaths of so many passengers in the ill-fated sinking outside Zeebrugge harbour. It took us on the fastest yet crossing, one hour, and the memories of that exciting trip still hold fresh in our minds.

Secondly this was to turn out the most ambitious of our holiday journeys to date covering more than 3,400 miles in less than five weeks.

Again we were two caravans and with the Rowlands' concurrence it was intended to be a free roaming journey through Western Europe with no set itinerary... except one. That was Cavallino, supposedly the farthest point. But once again things did not turn out as anticipated (not planned).

It was a beautiful summer's evening when we left Four Winds for Dover on 23rd July and as we drove past the House of Commons there was a tinge of something! It was the first time in 34 years that I had been able to begin a holiday whilst the House was in session. It was my retirement, and no longer was I tied to Westminster, but with all the rooms lit up and my colleagues still hard at it to meet the deadlines it was unavoidable I suppose that there should be a touch of sadness in my heart. But it was momentarily; the channel and Europe beckoned and we were all excited at the prospect of what lay ahead.

Our crossing was for 7.30 pm but with the aid of a helpful attendant we were able to board the 6.30 pm ferry, the magnificent Herald of Free Enterprise. Little did one realise then the fate of such an outstanding and luxurious vessel!

The diary came into play at once and records that we had reached Aachen some 230 miles from Calais before we made our first overnight halt. The temperature had been in the eighties. The second day, again in very high temperatures, we had reached Karlsruhe, another 254 miles before putting down the steadies for the night at Camping Turmbergblick. The third day saw us at Lermoos (190 miles in sizzling heat) and this is where we remained for an extra day savouring the delightful walks on the lower slopes of the mountains and enjoying typical Tyrolean repasts whenever possible. This was a real treasure which we had found by accident the previous year. Again we renewed friendship with the Harters and found that Albert had been a prisoner of war in West Wales and was delighted to meet some Welsh people again. He had spent a couple of years on a farm outside Tenby.

It was here we decided to make the next stage of the journey for Cavallino, but by the following day, July 29th, the whole pattern had changed. Having negotiated the Brenner Pass on the new toll road (120 Schillings (£4)...) and again on familiar ground in Italy we decided to change the route and head for Rome and points east! Partly responsible for this were reports from locals of the heaviest rainfall for years, and changeable weather. Rivers were in flood, and we had come for the sun, not a wetting. So off we went on the autostrada with Florence ringed on the maps as our destination.

The journey over the Apennines may not have been exciting as that of Hannibal and his elephants but for us it was packed with interest and the expectation of what was awaiting us. The first dampener was our failure to make Florence that day. We had travelled 390 miles in torrid conditions but traffic into the city from the motorway was an insurmountable obstacle. As the sun dropped behind the mountain luck came our way. Alongside the motorway we spotted Platz Laterina, a wooded lay-by... and were we relieved!

We enjoyed one of the best night's rest and come the dawn - actually it was 5.30 am - we set off again, only this time with another change of plan. The traffic into Florence had caused us think again. We decided to "do" this haven of the Arts on our return, and so we set off for the tiny seaside resort of Pozzuoli, a little place Van and I had last visited 13 years previously, and some 290 miles further on. Looking down on Rome from one of its seven hills as we journeyed southwards we promised ourselves we would make this our rendezvous on our return leg. We did say Pozzuoli was to be the next resting place, but again it was not to be. A little place called Solfatara, also known to Van and me from the last visit, was in our path as it were and this is where we turned in, only fifteen miles from Pozzuoli.

Solfatara is known locally as the safety valve of Vesuvius. So long as it continues to bubble and emit its powerful sulphurous smells so shall Vesuvius, some twenty miles away, remain quiet. It was here we found our camping site, and where we remained for four days recovering from the pressurised journeys of the previous three days. What can one say about this place? Its whereabouts is strongly obvious long before it is seen. The powerful odours of sulphurous gasses greets one a kilometre away, but it is fascinating to watch the ground around you tremble and plop-plop as gases are powered up from underground boiling lava.

These were days of exciting sightseeing and discoveries. A trip to Vesuvius's crater recalled a previous visit and we were saddened to learn from a guide that Frederico (Barbarossi) Rossini had died a few years earlier. We noticed many environmental changes, but by and large the routine for tourists was unchanged. A trip to Ischia was our second day's excitement. We drove to Pozzuoli from where the Ferryboat Michelangelo took us the 90 minutes crossing to the island. From past experience we recalled the best way of seeing Ischia on a brief visit was by the quaint three wheel car. Our driver was Peppino who turned out to be a replica of the famous racing driver, Fangio. "He drove like the clappers" wrote Van. "…but it was great fun for the four of us squeezed up".

In no time we were whisked 15 miles to a lovely cove called San Angelo where a treat of ice cream and coffee for four cost £5 - "terribly expensive" it is noted. Peppino brought us back to Cassamicciola Terme in time to see a funeral procession, complete with priests and choirboys who had just disembarked from the mainland for a burial at a little church adjacent to the pier. The whole trip from Pozzuoli to Ischia return (including Peppino, but not the ice cream) cost Percy and me £12 each! But the only really exciting event of the day happened back at camp where, lighting a barbeque for the evening meal I mistakenly threw some methylated spirits - thinking it was water - over some lighted grass. There was a loud bang and I and the tinder dry grass was enveloped in flames. Percy rushed to my aid and fortunately did not make the same mistake when he doused me and the flaming grass with water.

One experience in Solfatara which is still vivid was the "Sauna" which Percy and Van took. This apparently is as much a must here as taking the waters is in British spas. One goes into a cave on the hillside which is another outlet for the hot sulphur gases and remains as long as one can bear the terrific heat. For them two it was nearly fifteen minutes; for me it was just a couple of minutes. But the experience was worth it even though it made very little if any impact on my rotund ness.

Pompei, the fossilised city buried in 79 AD during an eruption of Vesuvius and which is still being excavated and rediscovered, was to be our third sightseeing expedition (for Van and I our second visit). Unfortunately it happened that the City was closed due to a local strike, but our visit had its compensation for Van and me. On our previous visit thirteen years before we had met Tony, the beach boy we had befriended in San Remo. His entrepreneurial achievements since then had enabled him to "corner" the trade in tourist souvenirs in this area. His cousin Armand recognised us as we sat sipping coffee and after introductions took us around the sellers and shops with a warning that "these are Tony's friends". The outcome was a reasonable percentage off all purchases... but more important, we were not pestered thereafter. For the rest of the time it was visits to Sorrento, Naples and Positano, all places famous in Italian lyrics, and always the lovely caravans to return to at night. The Solfatara sojourn was in all senses a holiday within a holiday.

Rome and Florence were the first leg destinations on the return journey which we commenced on August 4th with just over a hundred miles to go. Finding an acceptable campsite in CAMPUA however was anything but easy, but eventually we got into Camping Flamina. The heat was just bearable, and a typical evening meal, according to the diary, consisted of boiled egg, rice, ham and melon, with lashings of tea or coffee. I suppose our wanderings through Rome and its myriad sights and interests were just normal, and it all had to be done by public transport which was most sensible. One exception was the taxi ride with a driver who turned out to be a very good investment! He took us to the Sistine chapel, again to see the works of Michael Angelo, Victor Emmanuel's Wedding Cake, the Spanish Steps, and then Trevi di Fortana (of three coins in a fountain fame) where he whimsically advised the ladies "One coin you wish, two coins you marry, three coins is divorce". Needless to say they did not stop at three coins but threw in a handful (of small coinage!) to the driver's delight.

After three whole days in Rome we left for Florence, only this time and because of the heat we left it until early evening before starting. It was just as well for we could only make 80 miles on the autostrada in one and three quarter hours due to heavy traffic. It was at Fabro that we toyed with the idea of going again to Pisa, but this would take us another 100 miles off route so another change of plan! It would be Florence in the morning.

Come morning it was another second thought! We would skirt the City of Arts and plough on to... yes, Cavallino. And in this circuitous and roundabout programme of change and change again it eventually happened that we reached Union Lido Camp and stability late on 6th August, having covered 275 miles. What a journey, and what relief to reach the end of the road for now.

From now until 22nd August, sixteen glorious days, it was a repetition of previous visits. Sunshine and lazy days on the beautiful beach, meeting old friends and making new ones. John and Mavis, Andrew Gardiner and the family, Peter and Audrey Jackson, Grant and Stella Baxter, were among the first. Restaurateur Fernando and "Anytink else plis" who served in the delicatessen, were pleased to see us. It is worth noting that in the diary there is the one and only entry by me. On 11th August I wrote "We have just enjoyed a superb meal cooked by my wife "par excellence". Veal done in a wine and cream sauce accompanied by green peas and mashed potato, with a delicious blackcurrant jelly and cream to follow; the meal topped with white wine. Excellent! Could not have been bettered."

Among new German friends made on this visit were Herman and Maria Klenert from Ohringen, and as with so many others they remain friends of along standing as do Ian and Gwyneth Butler, of Treorchy. These friendships are the hall mark of camping and caravanning abroad and I have no doubt do more for international relationships and better understanding than governmental bodies.

As had been the case over so many years of our partnership Margaret's birthday on 16th. August was celebrated in style, and it is worth recording that this celebratory dinner in Fernando's, with the best of everything including a complimentary bottle of the best wine, cost Percy as host only £15. But all good things must come to an end and it was for the Dolomites and then the Brenner that we set out on 22nd August. According to the diary this return trip was practically uneventful, and included a lovely two day stop-over in Nuremburg where we camped at the Stadium, famous as the venue of Hitler's mass rallies. We stood on the very spot where the Fuhrer made his most dramatic speeches.

Bingen, at an ideal campsite on the banks of the Rhine, was another enjoyable stay before pressing on for Traben-Trarbach and the now traditional few days with Jenny and Theo Hack at Rissbach, at the equally traditional Haxen dinner at Hotel Central with mine host Ernest Hochs.

For the rest it was a leisurely homeward bound journey with arriving back at Four Winds on 4th September and 3,000 plus miles behind us.

# Chapter 40

# Before the Wall Came Down

Three features dominated our 1981 holiday. It had to be a later start than previous holidays because of a commitment which the other three willingly accepted, namely to attend the National Eisteddfod at Machynlleth in the first week of August when I was to be made a Bard. This is a great honour for any Welshman and I was very proud to have been one of the year's chosen few. My Bardic title had already been accepted... Dafydd ap Elli - David a son of Llanelli, my birthplace. It was a title I shared in that year with the Lord Chancellor, Lord Elwyn Jones (Elwyn ap Elli). Van and M. and P. had no hesitation in changing our dates to meet this auspicious occasion.

The second matter featured in this year was the arrival in time for the holiday of our new car, the Silvery Saab. Together with the Cranbrook caravan it made a very attractive outfit, and we were excited at the prospect of such a dazzling combination.

As for the third, this was to be an adventurous intrusion into the then Iron Curtain of East Germany - if we were able to secure the necessary visas.

And so it was that not until August 8th did we began our travels after a placid crossing to Calais and en route for Traben and the Moselle which was to be our first leg of the holiday. The diary reveals that by the time we reached Valenciennes before midday I was so overcome with tiredness that Van had to take over. We had covered only 135 miles and were due in Traben before nightfall. "I carried on until we reached

Namur when Glan (that's me) took over again. He feels a lot fresher now" wrote Van.

We battled on through the Ardennes almost to the outskirts of Luxembourg before we were compelled to stop for the first petrol refill. I wonder now what was the matter with such an experienced campaigner that I had not judged the fuel position better because when we came to pay for seven gallons (equivalent) of Belgium petrol it proved terribly expensive at almost £2 a gallon. A short drive away across the frontier and petrol was less than half that price.

There they were, to the left of us, to the right of us and predictably ahead of us for kilometre after kilometre, the typical Belgian "Fritures", but as Van states "we haven't succumbed to temptation yet - but there's plenty of time!"

It was exactly six o'clock when we pulled into Rissbach to be greeted by Jenny and Theo, having travelled 317 miles. It was a quite uneventful journey except for the shock of the price of petrol. Those were the days of the rising prices, and they certainly made a big hole, and quickly, in the holiday fund! One gets used to the upwardly creeping imposts I suppose, but looking back over the years presents an alarming picture of how it used to be.

After four days at Traben we took a short step back to Trier where we stopped over for two days and then headed down the new autobahn towards Karlsruhe which was to have been our next halt; but our progress had been such that we were able to reach Bad Urach, a small town near Stuttgart, by late afternoon. "This is quite a lovely site" the diary reminds us "but it's more a weekend place for posh Germans because it's expensive, costing us £3.80 each caravan!" The weather was perfect and a barbeque meal of chops, sausages, potatoes in their jackets and onions filled the inner man to complete satisfaction, and topped up with a lovely bottle of Traben wine. We also spit roasted a chicken for travelling. By this time, of course, there's no prize for guessing where we were heading... Yes, it was Cavallino which we made by the evening of the 16th and found the Campsite offering ample spaces. I reminded myself that for some future occasions this was the time to arrive at N.S.U (Camping Union Lido today). For the remainder of our twelve days sojourn at the camp it was the routine as usual, renewing old friendships and cementing new ones. "Will we ever get tired of this?"

Van asked in the diary as we were preparing to leave for our next destination. The answer was "Never".

The date was 28th August, and a beautiful evening as we left Union Lido around 6 pm. It had been planned thus because we had arranged to spend that night in the village of Cavallino, not far from the Horse Statue from which the village takes its name. We had been offered two places in the village restaurant car park alongside the lagoon after partaking our dinner. It turned out to be a perfect arrangement. The meal of soup, spaghetti, fresh fish with side salad, followed by ices and coffee could not be faulted... and we felt we were already on our next journey even though we had travelled less than ten miles from camp. Came the dawn, again a glorious day, and by 6.30 am, an hour and a half before we could have departed from Union Lido, we were on our way. It seems from the diary that we were a little vague about the next stage, but the decision to make Berlin before turning for home had already been taken. We had no idea how long it would take.

The journey through Austria included the Tauern Tunnel (toll was 120 schillings, about £5.50) then another new tunnel called the Malm which was free. It was here that we met in the lay-by a helicopter pilot who graciously directed us to the night's camping. It was at Radstadt which turned out to be an ideal and delightful site in a valley with an attractive little town of old buildings and a mediaeval tower whose clock chimed every quarter of an hour.

It is difficult to count the number of times we have travelled through such Alpine scenery but this trip, somehow, seemed to be so different. The scenery reflected the changing seasons with trees bedecked in their gold and multicoloured foliage, and as we approached a bend in a steep mountain road we were all fascinated to watch an eagle swoop down to pick up its prey from the road side before gliding down the valley and then soar above us towards a snow capped mountain. At a height of 2,400 metres we negotiated another tunnel, one and a quarter miles long, then found ourselves in Hallein where some years previously we had experienced the tour down the salt mines. But this time we seemed to be noticing so much more. There must be some connection though I cannot say what it is but Hallein is pronounced as it is in Welsh, Halen, and they both mean salt.

At Bad Reichenall, on the border with Germany, we were still 450 miles from Berlin, and it was 9.15 am. Here we took another decision -

to forsake the autobahn for the national, or lesser international, route which was a more picturesque road to Regensburg. This reveals the really beautiful wooded Germany countryside, and it did not matter that we would lose a couple of hours on the journey. The sights more than compensated for lost time!

It was 3.45 pm when we pulled into Stadion Camping in Nuremburg. Once again we were on familiar ground, and we decided to stay the next day and enjoy the fine, if somewhat colder, weather. The Volk Fest in Nuremburg is something one has to experience... as with the Munich Beer Fest. We were lucky to have arrived at the right time and the funfair in which we spent part of the evening was really something out of this world. But Berlin was calling, and shortly after 7.00 am the following morning -September 1st - we were on our way again, heading for the Harz Mountains and our pre-arranged campsite at Northeim which was to be, we hoped, our last stop before Berlin. Up to this time no one had a visa, and we had to rely on the frontier guards of D.D.R. permitting us to cross at Helmstadt. From there it would be a mere 125 miles to Berlin.

From Braunschweig to the border we noticed something unusual. We hadn't seen a single caravan! Was this an omen? My concern that my passport bearing my profession as a journalist would be a stumbling block turned out to be needless. At 10.40 am we were accepted almost without formality. All they required from us was 10 D.M. per person, and we were in East Germany!

Our instructions were simple but rigid. Only one autobahn led to Berlin and that was the road we had to take without any deviation. Furthermore, we were given a time for the journey and it was made clear to us that had we not reached Berlin within that time they would come looking for us. It was the first time I had felt any apprehension. The journey, however, was completed without problem. That was to come after we had been passed through the Checkpoint into West Berlin. It is worth quoting Van's observations on this journey. She wrote "We're off through East Germany, but we have to remain on this autobahn until we get to East Berlin. This autobahn is so different to any of the others... it badly needs repairs. The fields are full of vegetation, in fact, although it's flat at the moment, it's quite pleasant. It's hard to believe we are in a Communist country. There's not a great deal of traffic and we haven't seen another G.B. since leaving camp. We can see the city of Magdeburg in the distance with what looks to be a cathedral with twin steeples, and buildings which look like blocks of flats. It's strange to see women customs officers and women workers."

Risking a brief halt to drink a cup of coffee (and try to see something more of the country from the lay-by) we nonetheless reached Brandenburg at 12.45 pm, within our time, then to the outskirts of Potsdam with 60 miles to go to Berlin. More noticeable here were road signs in Russian. Somewhat timorously I must admit, we were passed through Checkpoint Bravo at Wannsee into the more prosperous and pulsating West Berlin. It had been an experience which none of us would have missed; but now was to come another worrying circumstance. We had chanced on Berlin during a week of television promotions and conferences... I suppose it was THE THING then to choose West Berlin as a venue. Wherever we tried there was no room at any camps. The R.A.F. tried hard to find us a place on their airfield, but to no avail. It was suggested I contacted the British Military Headquarters, and was given a telephone number.

A rather imperious voice answered, Major General somebody. I forget the name. Not that it mattered who it was as long as somebody could help us out of our dilemma. In equally "imperious" tone I explained that we had the problem of nowhere to go with two British caravans and that as a Lobby Correspondent from Westminster I would appreciate some help. The voice the other end modulated with an unexpected "of course. I'm sure we can. Hang on I'll get sergeant major on to it."

In a thrice Sgt. Major was instructing me, "sir", how to reach headquarters where I would find "Sgt. Brown" at the barrier who would lead us to our places. It went just like that! On reflection I believe that when I mentioned Westminster I was mistakenly taken to be a Member of Parliament. But when eventually we arrived at the barrier there was Sgt. Brown, with a salute and a smile (I forget in which order) inviting us to follow his jeep. We ended up at the edge of the playing field-cum-parade ground with water and electricity facilities ready to hand, and an invitation to "stay as long as you like, sir". It was the best site in Berlin, easily accessible to the public bus services and, what's more, we had no need to fear any intrusions because the site was guarded constantly.

How was that for luck? Our stay was fantastic, and lasted five days. One of the most memorable events of any holiday.

I had been to Berlin twice before on assignment for my newspaper, but this was quite different. And we made the most of it as "guests" of the Army. To try and compare in detail East and West Berlin at that time would be futile. Whereas on the east side of the wall all was drabness the west was like a wheel of constantly changing flashing lights with bulging stores – "KA. De. We." was then one of the biggest multiple stores in West Germany - which made it a panacea of shoppers' delight; the product of a seemingly endless fund of American dollars and other allied support, and intended as the political showpiece of the West.

But for us one of the more memorable events within West Berlin was our visit to the Royal Air Force cemetery. Beautifully kept - no, immaculately maintained - it has the youngest age average of any other war cemetery I have seen, aircrews shot down over Berlin during the mass strikes in the last eighteen months of World War Two. It was a very moving two hours. We could not have chosen a more appropriate day for this. Here we were, on 3rd September, the thirty second anniversary of the outbreak of the war paying our tributes to fallen comrades.

Another was our packaged tour of East Berlin. That was the only way we could do it. The first difference from the west we noticed was the hold-up at Checkpoint Charlie. It took more than half an hour for the Russian guards to satisfy themselves that we had no contraband or "foreign bodies" on the coach which then took on board a Communist guide to point out "the more interesting" points and to emphasise that we were now in the democratic part of Germany.

I recalled the first time I had entered East Germany via a "courier route" from West Berlin in 1951. I had been an illegal political entrant for twenty four hours, and left alone to find my way about the Verboten sector before my "pick-up" returned me to my Hotel, the Am Zoo. I had stood on the burned out, but still recognisable, Hitler's Bunker, and walked down the facade of large shop frontages known as Stalinalle, which had very few goods on view but none for sale! This time much of those had been excluded from the itinerary, but the drabness and lacklustre general appearances brought so easily to mind that previous visit.

This time we were shown the University of East Berlin built by the brothers Humboldt, the Opera House, the Reichstag where Hitler seized power in 1933, and the historic museums. Progress was signified by a new large building which housed the D.D.R. Parliament (it stood out like a sore thumb) and Leipzigstrasse, a modern street with high rise flats and shops. The Telefuncken Tower, completed in 1969, and Karl Marx Avenue built in 1960, was shown to us with pride. Outstanding during this tour was the visit to the Russian War Memorial situated in a beautiful park. Van has summed up the tour commentary "it's been very political up to now".

The crowning stroke, however, was on our return through Checkpoint Charlie. Apparently one of the passengers, a Tongan, had been suspect and was taken off the coach for questioning. Then a severe search was carried out on the coach and off it. "We've been here four hours" the diary notes. "It will be nice to get back to the West".

Our five days stay in the Berlins had been packed with interest and very regretfully we began our return on 6th September, again on the one way route to Helmstadt, back into West Germany and on to Holland with overnight stops in Utrecht, Rotterdam and our favourite Sluis. It is recorded that we arrived home on 12th September at 1.30 am only to find that Four Winds had been burgled three weeks previously. It was a great shock which momentarily dulled the feeling of a happy homecoming, and for several hours it was little satisfaction to be told that one of the two culprits had been caught.

The entire holiday had lasted just on five weeks and our total mileage was 2,856 miles.

# Chapter 41

# We Join the Circus!

There is no reason given in the diary, and therefore I have no clue why it was, but our 1982 holiday started earlier than hitherto. We were en-route for Dover on the 18th June with a schedule which was to take both our caravans, yes it was the same contingent of M. and P. and Van and I... through France, Germany, Switzerland and Italy, back to the Gulf of Venice and Union Lido. This time we had decided to cross France by a different route and enter Germany by way of Strasbourg, crossing the Rhine at Kell, and on to Basle and Switzerland.

Our first surprise was the ease with which we were able to make the first leg of our long journey, that across the Channel, considering it was high season. But within half an hour of our arrival in Dover at 6.30 pm we were aboard an earlier boat than we had booked for and set sail. The diary notes "How lucky can one be? We are the first caravan on board what is the latest of the Townsend ferry boats "Spirit of Free Enterprise"". One could not have given the slightest thought then to the ill-fate of this splendid vessel in less than a decade ahead.

It is recorded that the first leg of the journey was not without mishap. We were traversing the Flanders' fields around Ypres in wet and windy weather and took the wrong turning for Roubiax which was on our route. Fortunately a passing Frenchman realising we were in some diffi-culties stopped and graciously offered to take us across country and put us back on the AutoRoute for Mons where we partook of a much needed bacon and egg breakfast. There's a lot to be said for the British breakfast in such situation as we can readily vouch.

The rest of this part of the journey as far as Luxembourg via the Ardennes went without trouble, and it was a nostalgic experience when, for the first time since the war, I went through St. Hubert. A night halt in the Duchy had been planned but the camp site was so unappealing that we drove on to Thionville where we were lucky enough to find a lovely Municipal site which cost us only the equivalent of £1 a night inclusive of electrics.

This site was alongside the river and the diary reminds us:

"It is so lovely and the river is alive with small craft and work barges just like the Mosel at Traben Trarbach. We will have to remember this site, so quiet and restful and so near the town and the AutoRoute". This was our last overnight stay in France and 125 miles further on the next day we were crossing the Rhine into Germany , but not before a slight accident when the 'van was damaged by striking a "deviation" sign when entering Strasbourg.

The change in motoring, and especially caravanning, conditions from here on was tremendous for we had before us the German autobahn network which enabled us to swallow the miles at an amazingly consistent rate. Our route took us straight to Basle and then into Switzerland. My mid-afternoon we were camped in Camping Lido alongside the majestic Lake Lucerne, the date, 20th June. We had travelled 476 miles already.

Up to now the trip had been most invigorating. The weather perfect and the run most picturesque were promising ingredients for another enjoyable holiday. Attractive as Lake Lucerne and its environs were however necessity required that we left early the next morning in order to reach the St. Gotthard Pass early in the day. In those days a good maxim when one had to negotiate Alpine passes was to get over the top before early afternoon thereby escaping the mists and clouds which usually came down even on the finest days. And so at seven o'clock we were trundling out of the camp heading for the pass; but even though it was mid-June it wasn't long before we were negotiating snow covered roads and some hair-raising bends. This required a reappraisal of our intention to drive over the pass. It seemed the more sensible thing to go through rather than over the Gotthard. Within two hours we were being loaded on to the flat bottomed carriages and hurtling through the twelve miles long tunnel to the Airolo terminal and the gateway to Italy. This, the reader may remember, was our second journey through this marvellous tunnel, a construction at that time which may have been thought to be almost equal to the Channel Tunnel of twelve years later.

Another two hours travelling through the province of Ticino saw us at the frontier crossing of Chiasso with Milan, and possibly Parma, our objective that night. But, as very often, plans were changed again. Because of our rapid progress - we had covered 256 miles and it was still only 4.30 pm - the urge to carry on saw us an hour later pulling into a motorway lay-by for a free overnight halt. According to the diary it was a very pleasant site... "We are sitting out overlooking a delightful valley, with a flowing river below and the most beautiful scenery. Who could wish for anything better?" Van wrote.

But we were soon having company. A travelling circus pulled in and before long we were being subjected to all sorts of animal and human noises. A police car pulled in also, and to ensure we would be alright for the night we asked their permission. "Si si" beamed the fatter of the two. Whether they thought we would be a restraining influence on the circus or vice-versa we didn't know, but it is recorded that we had a very disturbed sleep that night, and not only because of our companions. It turned out to be the hottest night we had ever experienced in the caravan! But it was worth it. How many caravanners can claim to have bunked down in the middle of a travelling circus?

By nine o'clock the following morning we were parking the outfits in the square in Pisa. The leaning tower seemed to be leaning more than the last time we had seen it and the challenge to Van and Percy was too great to withstand. They each paid 2,000 Lire to climb 274 steps and eight floors to the top. It was a wonderful experience Margaret and I (the wise ones!) kept being informed, and in retrospect so it was, since no longer are visitors permitted to do the climb.

Florence was our next objective where we had planned to stay at the camp site on Viale Michaelangelo. It turned out to be a superbly organised camp situated on the summit of an imposing hill with a full view of the City. That evening was memorable for the visit to the beautiful piazza which gave us a stupendous panorama of the City of Arts, the Basilica and the River Arno and its many bridges all illuminated, whilst we sipped our cappuccino.

One does not leave an attraction like Florence without paying one's respects to what it has to offer and so early the next morning we caught the No13 bus and then joined an organised tour (cost £7 each) during which we saw a 24 years old Michael Angelo's "David", famous paintings, and the Cathedral which, we were told by a guard, had a magnificent outside facade but inside was the authentic old-aged building.

By four o'clock we were up steadies and away, making for Venice which we calculated would be two days' journey away. Without any recorded problems we made such good time however that after only one overnight halt on the motorway we reached NSU Camping in Cavallino by mid-afternoon on the following day, there to stay for the typical Lido holiday for the next fortnight.

We had planned a different route for the return journey and set out on 7th July heading for the Tyrol and then the Fern pass. Lermoos was the natural objective which we planned to reach within two days, but the overnight halt en-route gave us another enjoyable experience reminiscent of the earlier caravanning days. We came across an old time Gasthof, the Fremden Zimmer at Fernblick not far from Telfs, where we were invited by the landlord to rest our caravans for the night whilst he prepared a dinner for four. It was an ideal set up and worthwhile recording our menus that evening. First there was the traditional soup mit ei - the clear soup with egg poached - then a typical Hungarian Goulash with rice, a green salad and noodles, and a choice of pancake. For a sweet there were assorted ices and a piece de résistance... a cherry or banana flambé. The wine was a particularly good German Hock, and the whole meal was topped with coffee a la crème. Even today the thought of that special meal makes one's mouth water!

Van records that our host that night was a young man named Conrad who had just taken over the business. He spoke perfect English and took great pains to see we were satisfied with the quality, quantity and service of the food. If ever we have the opportunity to pass that way again this will certainly be a port of call. This sort of occasion is what enhances the pleasures of continental caravanning, and certainly for us was a night to remember.

Our journey to Lermoos the next day was uneventful but during our two days stay we squeezed in as much sightseeing, a lot of it covering old ground, as could be managed. High on the list was a return visit to the

Weiss Church, mention of which has already been made, then came Oberammergau, scene of the great Passion Play which attracts visitors from all over the world, and a quick trip to Garmisch-Partenkirchen, this time without the snow which makes it one of the world's most famous winter sports resorts. This part of the Austrian Tyrol in either season is nothing short of a fairyland for visitors. The Plansee Lake with its myriad coloured waters and background of wooded slopes is a sight to behold and enjoy, and at this time it is particularly lovely. We were not surprised on enquiry to find there was not a single pitch available on the lakeside camping platz which seemed to have hundreds of outfits.

Another must on this circular tour was the visit to the Schloss Linderhof, the castle home of former King Ludwig. It was a spectacular sight with ornamental rooms in gold, silver, and porcelain from all over the world, and paintings worth a King's ransom. Outside was the Grotto and flower gardens which are breathtaking.

For the remainder of the holiday the pattern was roughly similar to that of our previous continental holidays. From Lermoos it was a two days run to Traben Trarbach where we were received warmly by Jenny and Theo Hack in Camping Rissbach and settled down to a five days rest in the familiar surroundings of the Mosel, something which had become almost an essential since those harrowing first few days in 1970 when we chanced across this pleasant site on the river bank and met the Hack family for the first time.

Allowing one overnight halt on the journey from Traben Trarbach we made Sluis on the Dutch-Belgium border by late morning on 16th July and had no problem in finding a good site at Camping Meidoorn still being managed by our old friend Honnie Ultee and his wife Mariane. This, as we have found in the past, is an excellent spot as the ultimate site for those travelling on the Zeebrugge ferry crossing - regrettably nowadays only operating between Felixstowe not, as in those days, also between Dover - since it takes less than half an hour from the camp to the port of Zeebrugge.

The holiday had already entered the fifth week so we determined to make for home on the following day, even though our booking was not until the 19th July. Thus, on the late afternoon we found ourselves trying to persuade the ferry operators at Zeebrugge to take us on the next ship to Dover. Alas, it was not to be so. Our entreaties fell on deaf ears, even though we were maximum stockholders. It wasn't until the 4.00 am crossing the following day that we were able to get aboard. What to do with the 36 hours seemed to present a problem, but it turned out alright in the end.

We spent the remaining daylight hours of the first day along the Zeebrugge promenade, and most enjoyable they were too. Never having been on this particular prom we were surprised with the people frequenting it, mainly Belgians on holiday. The weather was fine and sunny and we did what the locals did, munching and drinking from the various Belge fare of which there was a great deal all along the promenade. That night we spent in the caravans parked on the harbour car park and after a splendid night's sleep strolled around until lunchtime when on further enquiry we were told we could catch the 4.00 am boat on the following day rather than the later one on which we were booked. This did not actually spoil the holiday end but had we known or realised it would have been better to have remained in Sluis for another day at least. Still we had had one new experience, that of a day on the promenade doing what the "locals" do.

Without further disappointments we came to the end of our long and again very happy holiday, arriving in "Four Winds" before eleven o'clock with no fewer than 2,553 miles under the belt. It was a great holiday and for so long as we can physically manage it long may these caravanning holidays continue. It is being proven with each one that no two are alike. There is always something new to see, different experiences to recall, and, perhaps above all, new friends to be made and friendships sustained.

Relaxing together in the clean warm waters of the Adriatic at the N.S.U. camp site.

## Chapter 42

## Our Farewell to Switzerland

We, that is our friends the Rowlands' and ourselves, had been particularly painstaking over the winter and autumn months in preparing a schedule for our 1983 holiday which was again to be spread over familiar terrain on the Continent, but switching routes. These preparations were always a welcome build up to the holidays, in fact just like a mini-holiday in creating a sort of jig-saw of where to go, for how long, and most important the logistics for at least a month.

Looking back now to that year it seems that everything that could go wrong did go wrong, from the first half hour of leaving home to the closing stages on return. First of all we had gone no more than five miles from Four Winds down the Western Avenue near White City when we were struck by a fast moving overtaking army lorry. The impact shattered the offside front side window of the 'van and tore the trim off the front window making it impossible to open. The car likewise was gouged almost its full offside length. What had only a few minutes earlier been a shining outfit now looked a dismal sight, but we were grateful no injuries had been caused. The lorry had disappeared at speed up the Avenue, but by good fortune a police officer arriving on the scene a few minutes later was able to alert a squad car which intercepted the lorry at the Marylebone end of the Avenue and it was brought back to the scene of the accident half an hour later.

A subsequent court case settled the legal claims for damage but for an hour or more it was touch and go whether we could go on with the holiday. A helpful police officer persuaded us to carry on by covering the damaged windows with some cellophane, but it was a frightening beginning to our holiday.

Still shaken by the traumatic event of the previous evening, but having safely arrived in Calais where we stayed overnight, the following day, though rainy and overcast, saw us heading for Luxembourg which was to be our first scheduled overnight halt. Belgium's infrastructure was not what it is today, with its multiplicity of AutoRoute's by courtesy of the European Union, and stopping places were at a premium along the route. Nonetheless we covered more than 200 miles before the first brief halt and made Bastogne by 3.30 pm.

Normally, I suppose, we would have pressed on to Luxembourg but the affects of the accident compelled us to make an early day of it. Consequently when we came across Camping Los Angeles on the Luxembourg road we decided to call it a day. Before four o'clock we were settled in and had a good night's rest.

Martelange on the Luxembourg-Belgium border was the first stop the next day. This is worth knowing for its cheap petrol prices and the pumps at the many garages here are seldom unoccupied night or day as travellers pull in to fill up. Our next step, the trip to Saarbrucken via the Metz motorway, was not without incident again. We were flashed down by a following car and discovered that the car boot could not have been properly shut down because some cushions had been ejected and strewn across the road. The diary records this was the third happening of the holiday, and we were only on our second day out! Earlier I had driven out of our Camping Los Angeles without raising the jockey wheel of the 'van and only by a stroke of luck had avoided smashing it on the road! Percy retrieved the cushions - minus one - and we set off again for Zweibrucken, Pirmassens, Landau and Karlsruhe. Lunch at Annweiler at 2.30 pm meant we were on good time and only some 35 miles from the autobahn which would take us to Karlsruhe.

It turned out to be a beautiful and hot day and gradually the incident was fading from our minds. After a short day previously we had decided to carry on as far as we could reasonably go; and that was until 8.30 pm on the road from Ulm to Kempton. By this time it must be evident to the reader that we were heading for Italy and the hardly annual Lido Union in Cavallino. At Illertissen we were fortunate to find the ideal stop over site (listed in the Caravan Club's Foreign Touring handbook).

It was a very pretty site, and fortunately with electric hook up because the first thing we found on unhitching was that the battery in the 'van was as dead as the proverbial Dodo. Number four set-back in three days. The milometer showed we had already travelled 653 miles from home.

A welcomed rest saw us fresh and eager to continue on the morning of Tuesday 9th August with Lermoos our next objective. We were now conscious of the change in the countryside and, leaving the motorways, a reduction in our average speed. The Tyrolean aspect as I like to regard it has always increased in appeal since the first time we set eyes on its mountains and wooded slopes and abundant lakes, and this particular run is of special attraction. The small village of Nesselwang, gateway from the north to the Fern Pass, is one of the prettiest of its kind... we shall never get tired of the sights. Lermoos appeared as we topped the last hill and it was so inviting. Although only just on lunch time there was question among us that this would be our stop for at least a day and a half. That evening, in the company of old friends in the Camp, we had a jolly barbecue and all tribulations had disappeared!

Early morning on the 11th we bid farewell and thereafter, until our arrival in Cavallino late that night, the journey was uneventful. We had to remain outside N.S.U. until the following morning but we were soon surrounded. First our daughter and son-in-law, Mally and John, appeared followed by John and Mavis Williams, then Peter and Audrey Jackson and our grandchildren David and Bonnie. We had a jolly get-together, and were thankful that we had completed the mishap strewn journey unscathed. By 8.30 am on Friday 12th. August we were on our sites and with the help of willing hands had the awnings up and settled down for eleven days of sun, sand, sea and social functions. This is what we had travelled over a thousand miles for, and we were not disappointed. There is no point in noting the day to day affairs at Union Lido as they were as they always are... lazy, restful and enjoyable.

Tuesday, 23rd August: This was the morning we left Union Lido (to us it is still N.S.U.) intent on making the return journey through Switzerland. A few days earlier when discussing the return with my old friend Duncan Gardner, the well known TV news presenter who had been a familiar figure at the Camp for several years, he suggested a "must" was a camp site at Interlaken. So, after bidding farewell to our children and Welsh friends, we set out. It was a hot sultry day and by 6.00 pm we had come through Verona and found a small parking place to spend the night. The intention was to make Interlaken by the following evening.

Avoiding the autostrada we made Verona by early evening and stayed overnight. This put us within our schedule but we found the following day is was necessary to return to the motorway to Como and the Swiss border where we were astonished to face an autostrada payment of 20,150 lire. "This is very expensive" comments Van, but we had to pay. It was, however, the forerunner of a pretty expensive sojourn through the rest of our stay in Switzerland, not least being the "entry tax".

Little did we realise it then but this was to be our last visit to Switzerland, much as we loved the country and its beautiful and appealing environment. The reason for this was the strange and some ways crass decision of the Swiss government or Cantons to impose what the majority of caravanners I believe hold to be both a foolish and unfair tax on cars and caravans using or intending to use their motorways. It did not matter whether it was the intention to use the motorways or not but the tax was payable as one entered the country, and those who may have strayed unwittingly on the fast roads were liable to a heavy fine if they had not paid the frontier tax.

We were not happy having to meet this condition of entry and I am convinced, with thousands of others of like mind, that this lovely country has lost a great deal of tourist revenue over the years. Indeed, many believe as I do that the Swiss have lost much more than has been gathered in by the tax both financially and in international camaraderie. If, and when, the condition is removed we may again pay our respects to this wonderful land of lakes and mountains, and it is a shame that so many have been prevented from enjoying the superb natural attractions and the social and cultural contributions that are Switzerland's.

But to revert to our journey to Interlaken. Faced with some stiff climbs we were somewhat apprehensive but the going was eased by the fantastic tunnels which had been completed since our last visit to this area. And a new autobahn was being built which would within a year or so make things so much easier again. However, as we approached the San Gothard tunnel at Airolo we encountered the snow line and from here on the going was more difficult at times. The long but least difficult of the passes, the Susten, 2224 metres high, was a chore and as we arrived at the summit the cars reached boiling point. It was almost three o'clock but a half hour's rest and a bite to eat set us up for the almost fifty miles journey "downhill" to Meiringen, then Brienz, a charming town on the lake Brienzer Sea, and on to Interlaken. As we reached the lower levels we were very conscious of the descending mist, and were glad that we had not left it later to start the journey, remembering the adage that these passes should not be attempted after 3.00 pm.

Arriving at Interlaken at 5.45 pm we found the Lazy Rancher Camp just as Duncan had explained it, selective, attractive, and very full, but at the equivalent of £6.50 a night it was by far the dearest camp we had stayed at. Perhaps it was some consolation that this had housed some of the actors of the James Bond film -so we were informed - "On Her Majesty's Secret Service" which had been filmed at the nearby Jung Frau and the Schilthorn Glacier!

More interesting for us the following day was the Rally of 25 caravans from West Wales, many of whom we met. Interlaken at this time of the year is all that the terms beautiful, lovely, exhilarating, exciting can convey, and we began our exploration with enthusiasm. The visit to the Schilthorn Glacier and its environs is still very real today, ten years later. It is worth quoting from the diary: "We have stopped for lunch is a lovely village full of enchanting houses covered with Alpine flowers of every shade and description; water cascading down the mountain into a fast flowing river is throwing up spume like a very fine mist with rainbow colours reflected in the sun; it is breathtakingly beautiful and gives a feeling of tranquillity. I felt and thought how good it is to be alive in this little village of Lauterbrunnen".

There was one other experience on the following day. It was the visit to Murren the mountain village reached by cable car and a terrifying experience it was too. We were promised that the car was the self same cable car featured in the James Bond film. It was the crowning event of our two days' stay in Interlaken and within a couple of hours we had set out for Basle, some 95 miles away through Bern and the expectation of finding a camping site in Germany that night. As it happened we crossed the border at 6.20 pm. and 27 miles further on the gremlins struck again with the offside caravan tyre blow out. Try as we might it was not possible to switch our spare tyre. It just would not go on, but fortunately Percy's spare fitted and an hour later than anticipated we were on the move again in search of a garage. We had done only 129 miles. Not until we reached the little village of Bad Krozingen in south Freiburg were we able to get the proper replacement tyre, by which time we discovered the other tyre was faulty. The two new tyres cost us £50, quite a bit in those days!

Our plan was to spend, as usual, a few days in Traben Trarbach but there was one more overnight halt which happened to be at Bingen, the picturesque Rhine and wine-growing area. We were so taken with the place that we decided to stop over another day. It was Monday the 29th when we left for Traben by way of Simmern and the high road which gives one a majestic sight for many miles of the winding Mosel below. By coffee-time we were safely ensconced in Rissbach Camp having received the usual warm welcome, and three days later were off again for Sluis and Zeebrugge. The final misfortune was yet to come for when we arrived at the port we learned the weather was so bad in the channel that all sailings had been cancelled. It was not until the following day that we were able to sail after a night of stormy winds and rain spent on the quayside. The round trip had covered 2,276 miles in one month. How many more would we be able to enjoy? The diary notes that before M. and P. left for home the following day we had already agreed on a February 1984 meeting to discuss next year's programme.

## Chapter 43

## A Tragedy Averted

We were well equipped for the 1984 holiday so we thought for apart from having done our winter home work on the route and all the preparations we had also purchased a new - our tenth - caravan at the November caravan show. It was a Compass with a separated dressing room and toilet at the rear, and we were eager to try it out. This was to be it's first run as we set out for Italy on Wednesday 25th July. But it wasn't long before the first disquiet was aroused. Before we got to Dover to embark for Zeebrugge the car, a Saab only 18 months old, showed signs of boiling over. Then, at Dover, there was further frustration. A dock strike had caused a tremendous build up of lorry traffic and the boat we were booked on could not take us or several other outfits. It wasn't until nine hours later, at 5.30 am, that we were able to board.

There was a little compensation however. The diary notes: "This boat is virtually empty and the Purser whom Glan and I met on a trip to Holland in June spotted us. We had a lot of fun talking to him and at 8.15 am we went for breakfast. Percy and I had kippers and Glan and Margaret had egg, bacon, and sausage. The kippers were the best I have ever tasted, but I could only eat one. For fun I asked could I have a doggy bag and lo and behold the waiter had packed up my kipper which he gave me to a lot of laughter. We'll have it tonight". Our Purser friend came to wish us Bon voyage as we were first off at 10.15 am local time and setting off for Aachen.

But it was not to be. The car started misbehaving again and 10 pints of water later we were stuck in a restplatz on the motorway with Aachen out of the question. It was not until the following day that we made Aachen and was able to find a Saab garage. However, before the Thursday was out the garage had found and rectified the fault at a cost to us of £74! Nonetheless the day had been spent in holiday spirit with visits to some of the big stores in the town and tea and cakes in Hortons.

Spirits were high the following morning and in fine weather we set off for Nurnberg where we knew there was a delightful camp site in the historic Stadion, scene of Hitler-day rallies. With the car behaving "like a dream" and according to 'Van's observations the roads having improved greatly in the past few years it was 4.00 pm when we arrived at the camp site, having done 308 miles. It poured with rain all night, but it didn't dampen our spirits. That night we telephoned Marilyn and were told they were setting off the next day for Italy and Union Lido, as we are.

An early start on Sunday 29th July, meant we could make Munich as the next overnight halt and we did, having covered 110 miles. The camp site Thalkirchan was one of the largest we had seen, and was very crowded, but a couple of hours going around Munich, sightseeing places we hadn't seen for years, gave us a great deal of pleasure. And for those who may have thought that I am somewhat tight fisted on these outings let it be noted that the diary recalls "Glan bought me a lovely white and yellow handbag for 30 D. Marks, reduced from 50 D. Marks. Well, one could not resist a bargain like that could one?"

It was early afternoon before we left Camp for what was to be the penultimate leg of the journey. Within four hours, in excellent driving conditions, we had reached Innsbruck where we found our regular campsite alongside the River Inn almost empty. This in itself was a bit of a surprise, but there was another. The prices had rocketed since the previous two years and the £8 a night we paid was double the last charge. We spent the evening browsing through the old town, still very much unchanged, and at first light on Tuesday 31st July we were negotiating the Brenner and set for Cavallino in a pleasurable anticipation of once again traversing the Dolomites. This is a wonderful area of the country and possibly the most enjoyable part of our almost annual trip.

Through verdant countryside with snow capped mountains as the backdrop we passed through Brunico to Dobbiaco, then right for

Cortina d'Ampezzo and on to Ospitale and Ponte nelle Alpi. It was very hot by this time and the many lakes looked so tempting. No wonder we can never get too much of this yearly trek! From previous experiences we knew there was one place en-route we had to reach for a brief rest. This was Vittorio Veneto. We arrived at 3.30 pm and lounged blissfully in the tropical garden cafe enjoying ice cream and coffees until almost 5.00 pm. The diary shows that I had a lovely spaghetti ice, Van had a coffee ice, Margaret an ice cream drink and Percy an ice cream soda (after a great deal of gesticulation to explain what it was) - we guessed the waitress had never before been asked for one! But if only we had known what was happening about that very time!

From here to Cavallino was a fast run by autostrada and we arrived at 6.40 pm with some 235 miles done that day. It was policy in those days not to enter the Camp in early evening because there are no admissions after 8.00 pm. So we stayed outside along with our other newly arrived friends, John and Mavis Williams, until the following morning, and by mid-day on Wednesday 1st August we were well settled in.

All was not really well, however. Van records she suffered a terrible bout of depression, wondering whether Marilyn, John and the children were alright on their journey. Capping this I noticed there was dripping water from the side of the caravan and instantly realised that we were having more trouble with the hot water tank. We had had the same fault with the new 'van before leaving home and the Morco man from Hull had seen to it. Obviously not well enough because it was happening all again. Rescue was at hand however in Dave Bashford, an R.A.F. Warrant Officer in Germany, whom we had met with his wife Pam the previous year. Adept with tools he soon had the fault repaired, here again an example of the camaraderie of the caravanning set; but it was the gnawing feel about the family en-route that persisted. They should have arrived already.

It was at that very juncture that Marilyn and John appeared and we learned they had had a terrible accident. "Mal and I just broke down" 'Van writes. "We couldn't help it". Then we were told how their outfit had suffered a terrible snake on the hill approaching the bridge over Limburg. Both car and 'van had turned over. It was a terrible experience because those who know Limburg will be aware that there is a terrific drop from the bridge on the town below. Had the outfit gone over none could have been saved. It was a tragedy which by the grace of God had been narrowly averted. The accident had occurred about the time we had arrived at Union Lido which probably explained the sudden bout of depression. The 'van was smashed to a matchstick, and the car caved in along the offside, but was patched up sufficiently by a local garage to enable the family to proceed to Cavallino, but still suffering from the effects of shock. The police said that theirs was the 30th accident on that spot that day.

Needless to say we were glad they were not physically affected by the accident but it was heartrending to hear how they and the grandchildren, David and Bonnie, had climbed out of the car and how they then tried to pick up as many pieces and belongings as they could from the wreckage - including David's birthday cards. Would he ever tow a caravan again? John was certain he would; and he did three years of further caravanning before turning to motor caravanning which he still does because, like us, the attraction of caravanning is still like a magnet.

We have to thank the Union Lido management for the way in which they responded to the situation. News of the accident had spread through the Camp and friends and others came in droves to enquire and offer what help they could. The family were offered a reserve executive suite for a few nights and were afterwards accommodated in a static caravan for the duration of their holiday. Thereafter things settled down - and a good time was had by all! Including John and Mal, both of whom entered for the N.S.U. 10km race which John won with a six minutes lead, with Mally second in the ladies' section. They took home a bronze and Onyx trophy which today serves as a reminder of that harrowing accident.

Compared with this occasion the rest of the holiday proceeded with little discomfort. We left Cavallino on the 17th August to make the return journey along the same route as on the way out. Nevertheless it is always a changing pattern with the mountains and snow capped peaks giving one a tremendous enjoyment. The possibility of making Austria over the Brenner that day was very much in Percy's and my thoughts, and we would have made it but for a Gasthof we spotted outside Vipiteno, only some 15 miles from the Pass. We were offered some delicious Goulash and a Tyrolean sweet, and were able to stay that night without charge in their car park. Just like old times! The Gasthof was the Burgfrieden.

We had planned to spend a little time in Lermoos which we made without difficulties arriving before lunchtime to be greeted by Willy and Maria who readily agreed to find accommodation for Marilyn, John and the two children as soon as they arrived, which they did later that day. They had left N.S.U. the day after us hoping their car would not give trouble. A highlight of the three days we spent at Lermoos was the dinner for the eight of us which Van hosted, and when a few tears were shed in a thanksgiving.

There was one other duty to be undertaken on the return journey. This was to return to Limburg to pick up those possessions which the family had not been able to carry away after the accident... and also to view the scene. Limburg was not new to us. We had made this a fairly regular stopover during all the years we have been travelling the Continent, but this time it had, and still has, a special significance for us.

For the remainder of the holiday it was almost as per usual; from Limburg to Traben Trarbach where the good weather finally gave out. Nonetheless we spent three enjoyable days resting alongside the Mosel before leaving for Sluis in Holland and then Zeebrugge where we left for Dover on Wednesday 29th August. This was at least a week earlier than had been planned but in the circumstances it was nice to get home, safe and sound, having travelled no fewer that 2,298 miles.

# Chapter 44

# A Wonderful Holiday

That is how the diary sums up the 1985 holiday. After reading it, and refreshing our minds on the many happenings, the feeling I got was that it provided more than adequate compensation for the dreadful event of the previous year. As if to make up for that we had decided to extend this holiday to at least five weeks and that is just how long it lasted.

As a change from earlier times we had agreed this time to make a beeline for Union Lido in Cavallino and not to meander, seeking out fresh fields. But in fact we did go off course for a couple of days at the beginning to fulfil something I had always wanted to do, namely to see in greater detail the Flanders fields and scenes of some of the epic events of the Great War. When we left from Dover on Thursday, July 25th the weather promised well. The following day, after a night spent at a roadside halt only 29 miles from Calais, we made for Arras where we found a large number of British caravans. It was some sort of rally. As the diary reminds us it was a long time since we had really motored through this part of France and it was in a leisurely way that we passed through Lens, Amiens and Bethune, names famous in World War One history, and along Vimy Ridge. "I am surprised how flat and very fertile this part of France is. The hedgerows are full of poppies and colourful shrubs" Van wrote. At that time we promised ourselves we would be back... and we did a couple of years later.

I think it will be a change on this holiday to dwell more on detail and give the reader a clearer impressions of how we saw the journeys. And so from Arras we took the D roads to St. Quentin where we stopped for coffee in the vans. These stops are so pleasant. They give us the opportunity to take in more of the locales and slow down the journey. After all what's the use of having your "house" attached and not make use of it? The next stop, for lunch, was at Reims where I stopped at a roadside bakery for a freshly baked baguette which we thought was super and provided a wholesome lunch with a little pate. It was here we decided to make for Chalons sur Marne, a place we had never visited, and which turned out to be the best thing we had done over many years.

The Municipal site at Chalons sur Marne was one of the best we had experienced in our many years of continental travelling... and still is, for we have used it many times since and are now well known to "the management". Each outfit has its own hedged space which gives excellent privacy but still does not cut one off from one's neighbours. As a base for the Champagne country it has none better and during the two days we spent here a tour of the vineyards and the vintners was a natural. We also visited the original Fort Pompelle, untouched since 1918 and still smacking of the 1914-1918 conflict. The village of Ambonny on the Champagne route was where we lunched at the Auberge St. Vincent. It is indeed remarkable how memories, and even tastes of the meats, salads and cheeses, come so vividly to mind!

It was a quiet Sunday morning, July 28th when we left for Basle which was to be our stepping off place for the Austrian Tirol and thence Italy. Nothing has ever tasted better than the bacon and eggs breakfast at Joinville, some 60 miles from Camp. The aroma from both caravans must have permeated the whole restplatz judging from the sniffing from other parked vehicles! Basle was reached at 5.30 pm and we were fortunate in finding a site at Lorrach without any difficulty because Margaret suffered from sickness brought on, we thought, by the sudden increase in the temperature. It had been touching on the eighties during the afternoon. We decided to stay another day which was very welcome for all of us.

Lake Constance and then the Arlberg were our next objectives and we crossed into Austria at Bregenz at 2.25 pm after a very slow journey around the lake. We could have taken the road over the Pass but for about £5 each outfit it was quicker and less demanding to go through the eleven miles tunnel which came out at St. Anton, favourite winter resort for skiers. Only this time the weather was scorching! The tunnel took us twenty minutes, and it enabled us to reach Prutz, at the foot of the Resia Pass before driving into a little site alongside a very fast flowing river. It was here that the weather changed suddenly and a persistent and torrential rain kept us in our own caravans until the morning... except, that is, for a brief foray by the two wives in search of fresh milk. It is still a matter of fun to us because the farmwoman offered them something from "the coo" - but it turned out to be milk alright.

Along the Resia summit early the following morning the scenery again was something to marvel and breathtaking, even though we had done this journey before. A brief stop at the "drowned village" which is now a reservoir with the old village clock poking its spire through the water and we were set for the Italian foothills, wending through a myriad small Tyrolean villages down to Merano, then Bolzano, Trento, Bassano del Grappa and Traviso. By any standard this particular run was outstanding for its timetable and trouble free because by 7.45 pm that evening we had reached the square at Cavallino. All that was left now was a change of clothing, dinner at the local restaurant, and a wait until 8.00 am the following day, Thursday 1st August, to be welcomed by Martin, the receptionist at N.S.U. or Union Lido to give it its present title.

We found many changes in the year since our last visit, not least a new shopping precinct which has helped considerably to make the site a self contained one. No wonder it is classed with the best in Europe. Old friends who, like us, have made N.S.U. their holiday site over many years were soon dropping in for a chat, or socialising over the traditional Cappuccino, among them Fred and Barbara - doyen of the Senior Citizens - who had just celebrated their Golden Wedding at the camp. The British community at this site has been prominent over the years but for some reason we were pretty thin on the ground this year. Nonetheless the days passed happily enough in lazy fashion, with plenty of sun and hours spent on the tidy beaches and clean sea. Typical "wish you were here" conditions.

At the end of the first week there was a short break in the weather with a day's storm of tropical intensity which threatened heavy flooding. Although mid-summer we heard on 7th August that the Brenner Pass was blocked with falling rock and a landslide due to torrential rain. This caused us some worry because we had been told the family were on their way to Union Lido on this route and we hoped there would be no repetition of the previous year.

The occasional dinner out was always much enjoyed and the search for a good, or particularly good, restaurant had become an essential ingredient to a holiday. "Fernando's" whom we had patronised from the very first visit to Cavallino, and when it was little more than a tin roof hut but providing first class meals, had expanded to a very imposing building with still attractive menus, and Fernando continuing giving personal service. But Martin had suggested we might try another nearby place where the locals ate. It was "Al Angelo" and the diary notes that we had our meal outside and that it was delicious with a choice of veal cutlet, mountain trout and a variety of seafood, giant scampi, with a selection of salads and chips. Between the four of us it cost £22, and we felt we had had our money's worth.

Thursday, August 8th: All anxieties about the family were put to rest early on for who should appear just after breakfast but Marilyn and John quickly followed by David and Bonnie. Theirs had been an incident free and enjoyable trip in their replacement caravan and with their appearance we all felt we could now settle down to really enjoy ourselves. There was, however, one strange occurrence this day. For the first time since we had been coming to N.S.U. bathing was interrupted. Storms which had lashed the Adriatic the previous day, and the Gulf of Venice that night, had washed up on to the beach a mass of seaweed. It was thick on the water and prevented swimming for all but the bravest. It was the first time we had seen anything like this but within a couple of days the beach was returned to normality with the tides taking out the floating seaweed and the camp staff having restored the beaches to pristine condition.

It was a special occasion for the four of us, that is, M. and P. and us two, on the 16th. Margaret was celebrating her 70th birthday and we had decided to spend it in Venice. We motored to Punta Sabbioni from where we took the Rapido ferry through the Lagoon to St. Marks Square. The trip took forty minutes at a cost of 8,000 lire return for two. On disembarking the first call was the San Marco Church, already jammed with tourists from all over the world. It had been some years since we had visited Venice but nothing had changed. The same pressure of tourists, the same jostling and problem to find an eating place which did not charge extortionate prices, and the almost total absence of any public toilets which meant that one was forced into a cafe or restaurant for the facility which was not available unless one was a customer.

We had a meal at a small place we knew from our previous visits, not far from the Rialto Bridge and afterwards sauntered through the romantic narrow winding lanes which make up this Queen of the Adriatic. The one thing we avoided was the Gondola! Van writes "It is so strange walking through these narrow streets with their quaint buildings all steeped in history. It gives you the feeling of living in bygone days. One can imagine the aristocratic people who once lived here, and indulge with those who still live here".

Memories of some twenty years earlier when we first visited Venice came rushing back as we meandered through that bay in the City which offers the visitor some of the most exquisite glassware from the factories at Murano and Burano. We saw the identical chandelier we had purchased then for about £75 but which now was priced at £625, and a lovely mirror which we bought then for around £90 was now on offer at £450. As Van commented then, we shall have to take great care of our then acquisitions with inflation at such an unheard of rate!

The days passed without care, and our circle of international friends grew from meetings on the beach and in the many cafes and restaurants with which this large leisure complex is now blessed. In the few days preceding our departure large gaps appeared in the ranks of caravans as the multi-nationals said their goodbyes "until next year" and set out for their homes. Our turn came on Monday 19th August when we set off at 8 am being seen off by the family who were staying on for a few more days and some friends. It was a beautiful day as the diary records, not too warm but sunny, ideal for the first leg of what was to be a very long journey and we had reached the Bessano region two hours later before we pulled in for breakfast in the village square of San Senione. The locals were very friendly, passing the time of day and pointing us in the direction of the bakery where we purchased freshly baked bread. The one thing about Italian bread we had found was that it had to be eaten soon after baking otherwise it staled quickly and became tasteless.

After three weeks lounging in the sun and sea and sand it was wonderful finding oneself once again in the cool fresh air of the Tirol mountains as we followed our incoming route to the Resia pass. After Trento we encountered the largest area of apple orchards we had ever seen - it must have been there of course when we passed this way before but we had not noticed. Larrgeti was the place and the fruit bearing area went on for miles and miles. The Italian - Austrian border at the top of the Pass was reached at 5.00 pm and the time had come to look for a suitable night halt. Prutz was out of the question, but Landeck and Imst were within our reach and less than an hour later we were safely lodged in the Imst West Camp site. The day's journey had been 271 miles, but we were still fresh enough to dress and go out for an Austrian dinner. At that time there had been a scare that exported Austrian wines were suspect after an accusation that some had been laced with anti-freeze. So when we reached the hotel to which we had been recommended for a meal and were seated the waiter asked which wine we preferred. When we hesitated, and no doubt looked embarrassed, we were quickly assured "The wine here hasn't got anti-freeze in it". Which, taken literally I suppose, could have meant that the wine elsewhere in Austria did have. After all, until the waiter mentioned it, nothing had been said about anti-freeze. We had a good laugh and decided to order wine. It was alright.

It might be correctly guessed, and without the aid of a map, that the next stop would be Lermoos which turned out to be just 29 miles over the Fern Pass from Impst. So the following day, August 20th saw us entering by 11.00 am to be greeted like long lost relatives by our friends Albert and Gerda Harter, of Tubingen, who have for many years been spending the whole month of August at this campsite. They were four happy days we spent in Lermoos on Saturday 24th August we were on the road again heading for Traben Trarbach. One might be forgiven if thinking that this repetitive trail year upon year could be boring or uninteresting; but not a bit of it. No two holidays from the beginning have ever been exactly the same. Places change, surroundings and scenery are different year by year, and most importantly we have always met and made friends with those of our own ilk whether from Britain or the Continent. Friendships have been made and sealed, and new horizons open up with each year. This is and will continue to be the attraction of continental caravanning and were we given the opportunity again we have no hesitation in saying that this is the life we would choose.

Zeebrugge 3rd September. After two days' rest in Sluis we are boarding the Enterprise 7 for Dover at 4.00 am. This ship has happy memories for Van and I. It was the vessel first captained by Capt. Dawson, then Commodore of the Townsend Thoresen Line, on which we sailed. Capt. Dawson had befriended us on a much earlier voyage out of Dover and we had maintained the friendship to include his wife and son who had been our guests to dinner at the House of Commons. This time, however, it was a different skipper, but the voyage was delightful and we pulled into Dover at 10.40 am. Home in Uxbridge at 1.30 pm in brilliant sunshine was a fitting end to a holiday during which we had travelled 2,632 miles. The last entry in the diary, before we had even got of the car, is "A wonderful holiday".

# Chapter 45

# From Mud Bath to Garda

The 1986 holiday was to start differently. First priority was to be given to attending our National Eisteddfod at Fishguard in Pembrokeshire. I had been inducted a Bard two years earlier but this time it was Percy who was to receive the honour. Therefore it had been decided to spend the first week of our holiday on the Eisteddfod field and then travel to Dover to cross channel to Calais, a crossing we had not made for several years.

The experience of Fishguard however was anything but an augury for a good holiday. It had started raining before we left home on Sunday August 3rd for the traditional Monday opening of the event, and it got wetter and wetter as we got nearer Fishguard where we had already arranged to meet the Rowlands'. It was with great difficulty we negotiated the entrance to the caravan field which was already a sea of mud, and we were apprehensive about getting out again unless the weather improved. Improve? We had never seen it so bad. On the Monday it poured almost non stop. On the Tuesday it was getting extremely difficult to walk from one 'van to the other. After Tuesday's Crowning of the Bard ceremony and continual rain conditions were so desperate we wondered whether we would be able to bring the caravans out in time to catch our booked ferry on Saturday 9th. Wednesday saw no improvement, more rain and deeper mud. Come Thursday and the options were running out. We discussed possibilities with our friends from Caernarvon, Meurig and Marion Williams, keen caravanners as well as Eisteddfodwyr, and discovered there was a farm tractor nearby which might be the answer to our prayers. This was Percy's day and that morning he was inducted a Bard with the title "Pyrs Gwaungynfi".

Before evening, still raining and against a gale force wind, we had negotiated our "rescue" from the mud bath that was the Eisteddfod caravan field and had the two vans hitched hoisted and towed to a more stable place alongside the main road. But what a sight! Mud from front to rear, questionable brakes, and to cap it all, batteries which had been run down due to extreme use in awful conditions. As we said goodbye the next morning and set out for Dover we could not but pity those we had left behind, and at the same time feel somewhat crestfallen at the state of our own outfits. When we reached Pont Abram on the new M4 our first chore was a thorough wash and clean of the outfits. Thereafter, and fortunately with the rain ceasing, we were able to reach Puesdown, the old coaching Inn on the Chepstow-Gloucester road, for an overnight halt in the most peaceful night conditions for almost a week. We sailed from Dover on August 9th with the set objective being Chalons sur Marne via Rheims where we discovered that petrol in France had gone up to the equivalent of £2.25 a gallon. This would undoubtedly put our financial calculations out, but we reached Chalons s/m that evening and determined to stay at least two days. The weather had changed completely and we were now basking in sunshine with the temperature broaching the eighties. This did much to dispel the Fishguard experience. It would also give us the opportunity we did not have last year of seeing the old town of Chalons and its environs. As for the site it seemed to be overflowing with British outfits. Someone must have let it be known!

Italy and Union Lido was again to be the end of our journey, but we were in no great hurry. It would be a more casual trip as we left Chalons on August 11th, and we were enjoying the sun. We skirted Nancy enroute for Luneville and Sarrebourg and then Strasbourg, with stops every couple of hours. "We are really enjoying this run" Van wrote. It was so noticeable as we approached the German border on the AutoRoute on the French side that the rest places were more plentiful, prettier and quieter. By the time we had reached the bridge over the Rhine it was approaching teatime and also time to look out for an overnight camp. Kell had little to offer so we took the lesser road in the direction of Offenburg with the thought of a Gasthof with a meal and overnight parking in mind. And it came to pass...

It was a small and pretty village called Zell Unterentersbach at Offenburg. There was a Gasthof, and I leave it now to the diary to describe what happened. "We stopped to ask if there was a parking place if we ate in the Gasthof. The farmer (it was part of a farm) was so thrilled to see us he couldn't put us in the farm yard quickly enough. We've got two places outside the cow sheds, under the fruit trees, pears and Marabella plums. We were ushered into the Gasthof where we joined the Familie Schmeider and the locals in drinking our health in local wine."

Apparently they saw very few touring caravans on this secondary road so it had developed into an occasion, and we enjoyed it as much as the locals who flooded into the premises when word went around that the British were there. By this time it was gone seven o'clock. We were hungry and I think could have done justice to the old horse in the stable; but when the food came it was well worth the wait. There was roast pork, freshly done, mushrooms with mixed salad and noodles and the proverbial chips, and a magnificent local brew of soup and bread as a starter. This was washed down with the local wine and the whole lot (including our overnight stay) cost 47.D.marks per couple. We thought that the food was a trifle expensive, but the experience was worth more than that and it was a happy four some that turned in that night. It transpired that we were in the cuckoo clock area and we had done 202 miles.

It rained heavily during the night which accounted for the fact that we were up and ready to leave by 6.30 am, but the Schmeider's were already up and insisted we helped ourselves to pears and plums before leaving. "For the journey," or words to that effect the farmer insisted. Whilst the rain persisted we kept going, even around Lake Constance, for by this time we were heading for the Arlberg Tunnel again. It seemed hardly a year since we were last here but on payment of 140 Schillings we were soon on the Austrian side and back into sunshine. This time we made for a nice little camping site called Sonnencamping at Pfunds, but for some reason there was no one there who could admit us and so we carried on over the Resia and at Merano got on to the Bolzano-Trento autostrada with the intention of finding an overnight stop at one of the Parveses. It was 8.30 pm before we found the Agip station, and after travelling 320 miles we were thankful to put our heads down. Sounds like we were gluttons for punishment, but we knew we were now within a day's distance from Cavallino and our ultimate destination. In fact we had only 190 miles to do the following day and this was accomplished by midday, with the speedometer showing us to have travelled 1,074 miles from home. And the date was August 15th.

The family, Marilyn, John and Bonnie (David had opted for another trip to Norway with the scouts) had arrived before us and with their help and that of Theo and Marrian, and Herman and Maria Klennert, we soon had the awnings up and everything ship shape. We were there to stay for nine days, each one it seems just as all the others in the past had been, lazy and enjoyable. We had given much thought to the return journey and decided a break at Lake Garda would be a nice change. Van and I had not been there for many years. And so, on Saturday 23rd. August, we left Cavallino, taking the autostrada to Desenzano, then up the eastern side of the Lake to a camping site, Toscolana, which we had been recommended. Throughout the journey the weather had become heavy and oppressive. There was no doubt a storm was gathering. We had heard about these Garda storms but never experienced one. Suddenly, down came the rain, such rain as we had never seen before. It put Fishguard in the shade. It was like a dam bursting its banks, and made worse by the wind. But we made the camp and in these inclement conditions were glad to accept any places on offer. Our intention of spending a few days on Garda had been totally dispelled over night not only because of the conditions but also the fact that the camp was full almost to overflowing, and if there is one thing we cannot abide it is being pushed into one another's pockets. So the programme was changed again. After a belated breakfast we moved off, around the lake through the many Galleries or small tunnels, to the tip at Riva. We did ourselves the pleasure here of a coffee stop and took in the full expanse of Lake Garda. The wind having dropped we were surprised at the activity on the water. It was a most colourful scene with dozens of sailboards skimming the water which was itself multicoloured from the shade of the surrounding hills. No wonder it attracts so many campers and tourists each year and we were reminded of our last visit many years before with Cedric and Cynthia Barradell. From here it was on to Trento and we were back again now in familiar territory.

Free of incident the journey saw us coming through the Italian - Austrian frontier on the Brenner by mid-afternoon but on the way down we were unfortunate enough to take the wrong road. There was a new autobahn for Telfs which we took believing it to be via Innsbruck. It cost us 120 schillings before we could get off to take the dual carriage road back to Innsbruck where we stayed overnight at the riverside campsite.

The journey thereafter took in two days in Lermoos, then, with the weather showing signs of improving we made for Traben Trarbach along a different route staying a night at the Murgtal camp in Radstatte, following the French frontier for a little way and then back into Germany at Zweibrucken where we joined the new Trier autobahn and arrived in Traben Trarbach late afternoon of August 28th. The ritual of Haxen supper at The Central where mine host Ernst Horst had everything ready for us as usual, and meeting with new friends Jean and Derek Weston from Cheshire, and the Welsh couple Myfanwy and Elwyn Jones who ran the pub at Penmaenmawr, were the highlights of this sojourn.

It was 8.00 am on September 2nd when we left Traben for what was to become a helter-skelter ride through Luxembourg, the Ardennes in Belgium, where we narrowly escaped a nasty accident when a passing lorry travelling very fast caused the unlocked caravan door to open and smash into the side of the van causing a marked dent, and over the frontier towards Lille and eventually arriving in Calais at 7.00 pm. We had originally intended to cross back through Zeebrugge on September 12th but the weather generally, except for the stay in Italy, had been so disappointing that we curtailed the holiday by ten days. So Fishguard had been a bad omen after all! The rush to Calais meant we had covered 350 miles on this last leg, and I vowed never again.

Arriving home at 11.45 pm Percy and I checked our mileage and agreed we had done between 2,660 and 2,689 miles. The difference I reckoned was because his tyres were slightly larger than mine.

# Chapter 46

# When We Got Submerged!

Events that followed soon after our return from the previous holiday had required a complete rethink on our part of what was to happen during 1987. Was this to be the end of our careering across the continent? Indeed, was it to be the premature end to our great love, caravanning? In the first place we had moved away from Hillingdon and had settled in the Royal Borough of Caernarfon, some 250 miles up north. Now we were living adjacent to our fellow caravanners the Rowlands' so if there was to be another foray across the Channel at least we would be setting out together from the start. But the great upset in our lives at our then ages of seventy plus had imposed some very serious questions; could we carry on? Should we carry on? Our outfit was still intact but confusion was a very detracting force.

After a great deal of thought, firstly between Van and myself, and then as a foursome, the decision was reached... Yes, we would set off again, but I must confess a great deal of the heart seemed to have gone out of the venture. Without the usual preparation as to the routes and the requirements we decided it would be another Continental safari, to go as the spirit and one or two other considerations directed. From the start we had accepted that this might well be our last adventure, but come the big day, 6th August, we were in better fettle as, for the first time in almost twenty years, the Rossers and the Rowlands were setting off together. We had moved to Caernarfon on 13th March of that year, and it seemed strange as we headed together for the Llanberis Pass over

Snowdon for the A5 road and on to Dover. The first leg to embarkation at the port would be close on to 320 miles. Hitherto that distance had meant we were well through France or Belgium en route for the Mediterranean or the Adriatic coasts.

The one thing that had not changed was Van's passion for keeping her diaries, and so we have on record almost every detail of the journey. It was strange, for instance, that we considered the first leg to Dover would be too much without an overnight stay, and this turned out to be the Hilton Park Services Station on the A6, but not without incident. We found the caravan 'fridge door had burst open and all the contents strewn over a lovely new carpet, including eggs and milk (and caravanners will know the problem when a carpet is saturated with milk!). A temporary repair was called for in the shape of some curtain wire and hooks stretched around the 'fridge, and it proved effective for the whole of the holiday.

Our next new experience was the Dartford Tunnel (cost per outfit £1.20) thence to Dover by dual carriageway which meant a fairly fast run. But again we were travelling under a changed condition. We had replaced our car from the Saab to a Peugeot 309 shortly before leaving and found a drop plate was necessary for the hitch-on. This had been done prior to our departure, but I was not happy with the effect on towing and consequently had to have the plate changed on our arrival at Dover. Thereafter the outfit towed like a dream. Although this had taken some time we had no doubts that we would have an early boat. This was the first time we had not made advance reservations for the crossing, but early doubts were soon dispelled. We crossed on the Pride of Dover, then the newest of the Townsend Thoresen fleet, at 7.30 pm and at 10.00 pm French time we were pulling in for a night halt at Nordausques just before the AutoRoute payage. And still we had not determined which route we were to take, except that at the end we would be arriving at Cavallino and Union Lido, all things being equal.

Perhaps it was inevitable, bearing in mind our experiences of the previous years, that we should eventually find ourselves in Chalons sur Marne, again at the Municipal site. I find that on arriving at Rheims en route and filling up with diesel we had spent £20 in fuel. It was perfect weather during the journey, hot and only a fair wind (which perhaps was the reason for what followed during the night). The first mishap was that the bed collapsed - due we thought from the heat affecting the glued joints - and second, when we went to drive to the supermarket in the morning we discovered the car's inside was under several inches of water... it was virtually submerged. There had been a heavy downpour during the night and I had forgotten to close the sun roof. The front seats also were soaking. That meant only one thing. We would have to stay at the camp until we had dried out the car. Several things were tried during the day, and the most effective was Van's hairdryer and the small electric heater... but why we had brought that on a summer holiday I shall never know, unless it was some premonition!

By this time we were wondering whether it had been a good decision to take this holiday. Two days in Chalons in beautiful weather put paid to that dreary supposition and when we set out on Monday 10th August to resume our journey we were all in a much happier frame of mind. In fact it is recorded that when we reached Vitry Van wrote "This would be a good place to stop next year instead of Chalons. The camp site is in the town and it looks so pretty. It's only half an hour from Chalons". This presupposed that we would be on our travels again next year.

Varying the route from previous occasions we made for the German border via Colmar - where we noted a lovely camp alongside the river and a huge Lion Supermarket - but it was too early to stop and we made our meandering way via secondary roads marked Donaueschingen until we came across a small village Geisengen. It was time to halt, and the old practice of searching for a suitable Gasthof with room for two caravans and an overnight stay was soon in motion. The Gasthof Zum Hecht proved ideal and a friendly landlord assured us we would be welcome to a meal and parking platz. This was one of our joys of roaming the highways and byways of Europe, giving us the chance to receive and give hospitality, and to know how the other parts live. The Gasthof turned out to be all that we could have wished for. The food, veal and pork cutlets cooked in the manner of the region, with frites and salad, was superb and the friendly atmosphere and relations of the locals only reinforced our determination for the future to carry on as long as we could! The overnight stay did us a lot of good.

The next day we set off for the Arlberg Tunnel, again as our way to the Resia Pass and Italy. At Bregenz before climbing for the tunnel I found a Peugeot Agent where, to my great relief, I was able to have a 1,000 miles service for the new car. So far the car and caravan had behaved well, and we were able to make Bolzano by late afternoon. We would have stayed at the designated camp here but the problem of getting the outfits up a steep entrance on to a crowded place was too forbidding so we moved on. Two hours later we pulled in to an Agip service station on the Trento autostrada and by taking the Castelfranco route we arrived at Cavallino, without further incident and in good shape, by midday on 12th August, there to be welcomed by a host of the usual faces and good friends, Herman and Maria, W/O David Bashford and his wife Pam, Theo and Marianne, the Barrett family from Yorkshire and, of course, our own Marilyn, John and Bonnie. We knew for the rest of the duration here that we would be enjoying the holiday. And so it proved until our departure date 24th August. Unlike the outward journey we knew exactly which way we would be returning and the schedule was spot on when we pulled in at Pfunds on the Resia that night at Sonnencamping in heavy rain and with a mind to get down to the lower reaches and possibly better weather early the next morning.

It was still raining heavily when we surfaced the next day, so there was no argument. It was off to Lermoos, and as speedily as possible in these conditions. We had less than sixty miles to do and by midday we had arrived. With an improvement in the weather the next two days gave us the opportunity of again exploring the surrounding areas. For those who are unaware of Lermoos it should be noted for a worth while sojourn. Not twenty miles away over the border into Germany lies Garmish-Partenkirchen the famous winter resort, and the circular tour of the country there and back is an experience thoroughly recommended. This time we spent a couple of hours in the town where we were whisked back to the pre-war days atmosphere of the tea dance fashion. At the local hotel restaurant we were served Kaiser cake and tea, and the diary reminds us that we were entertained "by a man playing old time songs the piano. It was a joy to sit and listen to him". We are also further reminded that before leaving Lermoos for Garmish Van had dropped her jacket during a walk into town. We retraced our steps but could not find it, which brought the retort from her "I hope it's been found by someone who needs it!"

Approaching the end of the summer season we were very interested in local preparations for the winter season and ventured a walk over the mountains, a popular local practice as well as checking the potential ski runs. These are the kind of activities we could not find at home and which make our annual continental visits so appealing and anticipated.

The eve of departure saw us at the Schonenburg Hotel for a typical Tyrolean dinner, and next to us was an elderly American lady with her 14 years old grand daughter. As had been the custom in her youth, she explained, she was taking her grand daughter on "the grand tour of Europe" so that she could enhance her education. These are the type of moments to be savoured as one recalls such encounters in one's travels.

From Lermoos, which we left on 28th August, we took a familiar route to Traben-Trarbach and the Mosel and since the diaries record no particular incident, except for an overnight stop in Bingen, there would be no point in repeating much of what has been written before about this journey. After four days in Traben it was off again on 2nd September, this time through Luxembourg to Lille in record time, thanks to the continuing improvement of the Belgium motorways, and finding ourselves in Calais at 6.00 pm. What a journey! No fewer than 381 miles in ten hours and only three brief stoppages. As I have already explained we had not pre-booked this holiday but within fifteen minutes of arriving in the port of Calais we were boarding the Pride of Dover again and ninety minutes later were back in England, but still faced with a 300 miles plus journey to North Wales. Good old Farthing Corner, the services station on the Dover road. This gave us the breathing space we needed before tackling the final sprint. After a good sleep we were off early the following morning and arrived home intact on 3rd September at the end of a 2,335 miles journey. Was it to be the last of its kind? That would have to wait until further consultations, but at least these were easier now that we were near neighbours.

## Chapter 47

## Limburg and Verona Revisited

The joint decision in February of the 1988 holiday was that we should make for the sun again this year. The problems of yesteryear had been cast aside and cross channel reservations made immediately we had agreed our departure date should be 23rd July. As it happened it was as well that we did book early because this was the year it seemed that everyone with a caravan had decided to go abroad. On our way to Dover it is recalled in the diary that we had never seen so many caravans on the road. Could this have been the industry's bumper year; were more people becoming aware of the attractions of life along the open road to destinations new and also far away?

Going for the sun meant, for us, only one thing - Golfo di Venezia and some more "parliamo Italiano". Inevitably it would be traversing old paths and routes but, as in the many years past, we expected to see new things, meet new people and renew old friends and acquaintances, and revive memories of times before. And the expectations still roused the excitements which we had always experienced as we set off on holiday.

As on the previous year we had agreed that the trek to Dover non-stop would be too much so we aimed for an overnight stay within the first 200 miles. It happened to be the Caravan Club site at Welwyn Gardens. As in the past our membership of the Club proved invaluable because, having telephoned ahead and made a double reservation, we found two lovely adjacent places awaiting us and with the very acceptable help of the warden we were soon settled in, and electric hook ups functioning. It was a great start to the holiday; so much so that after the first night we decided to stay on for another day. The Rowlands' took advantage of the extended stay to visit their daughter Beryl, and son in law Chris, in Royston and we did likewise to see Marilyn and John and the grandchildren in Uxbridge and also to see Paul and Pauline Pang, our Chinese friends, and have a meal at their Pang's Cottage restaurant. We returned that night to the caravans and the following morning made our way to Dover. It is recalled that we were stopped on the Dover road by the police and had to undergo an eye test, something to do with the driving regulations and which we have never since experienced, and were allowed to proceed with an OK.

The crossing again was to Calais, but for some reason we deviated after Calais and took the coast road via Dunkirk, Ostende, Knokke-Heist to Sluis for our first continental overnight halt. The gateway to Germany was now before us, en route through Antwerp and on to Aachen, which we reached at 11.15 am. Again it is recorded that the number of caravans on the roads, that is British caravans, was greater than we had seen before, but by using the autobahn we calculated we would be able to reach Limburg by tea time. And we did.

Approaching the old town down the very steep hill which three years previously had been the place where Marilyn and the children had encountered their near tragic accident was a moving experience for Van and me. Spirits were quickly restored however as we entered the now familiar campsite where we found two places on the riverside. And the weather was so glorious that we immediately decided to stay on for two days after travelling 261 miles. That was one of the great advantages of our caravanning holidays, the ability to change one's mind and not be tied to a strict schedule.

It had been a long while since we had been in Limburg with time to explore and the following day saw us strolling through the new part of the town. We had already visited the Old Church and browsed through its medieval history and this time it was the recent transformation of the new town which held our interest and attention. Limburg has grown out of all proportion to the place we first knew in our camping days nearly forty years ago, and well merits a sustained visit. And as one relaxes in the campsite a notable attraction - apart from the river - is the famous high bridge which carries the autobahn around and over the town. We felt that we had renewed links with a forty years span, and it made us feel good!

We knew what we could expect when we left Limburg early on 29th July, and the expectation was amply fulfilled. The drive on to Austria and the Dolomites was enhanced by the stupendous scenery (but again we encountered a seemingly increasing number of 'vans daily), and after an overnight stay at the Kempton service station by kind sanction of the owner we arrived at our next agreed stay over, Verona, at 6.15 pm on 30th July, exactly one week after leaving home and with 1,490 miles under the belt. The Romeo and Juliet campsite in Verona was not new to us, and we were looking forward to another couple of days' rest and a ramble through the quaint streets which typify this part of Italy. The delights of the Roman amphitheatre and the season of open air operas were already ours, but there was one world famous offering which we still had to see. The Balcony from which Juliet was wooed by Romeo is a must according to the local brochures. Shakespeare had already created the scene which the whole world has long been familiar with. But was there really such a place? We wanted to make sure. Unless it is the fabrication of the authorities of Verona to cash in on William Shakespeare's work in the interest of their tourist economy we can vouch there is A Balcony. I must confess I was somewhat disappointed with what I saw, or rather what was visible above the heads of a massive crowd of international sightseers. I suppose it could have been anybody's balcony - there were several of them around in Verona and elsewhere - but there are the inscriptions which claim it to be the real thing. At any rate we were glad we had stood where untold thousands had stood before us, and undoubtedly will after us, to gaze upon the scene of the world's greatest love scene. For those who can I say go for it. Keep up with the world and enjoy the spectacle. Who cares about reality!

It might be thought that after this and the next day's activities in the town arriving in N.S.U., or Union Lido in Cavallino, would be an anticlimax. It was nothing of the sort. We were warmly received on 2nd August and from that moment settled into the same routine as hitherto, a social round, sun, sea, beaches and the usual fraternisation, no matter what the nationalities. Union Lido to us is the same magnet today as it was when we entered the camp, the first British caravanners permitted to do so, way back in the early fifties. It has grown tremendously since those days to become a dream leisure place but the management under

Mr. Balerin, and his aides, carries on the hallmark set by his predecessor, Captain Neuman, who had become a familiar figure to thousands of caravanners of all nationalities in the post war period.

One event which was different from previous stays at N.S.U. was the day we spent in Vicenza - no, not Venezia - some eighty miles away. An old friend Giro Rossi, head of a papermaking company, had invited us to the old city and it took us less than an hour and a half, and 5,600 lire on the autostrada, to reach our destination, but the journey was well worth it. The old Romanesque atmosphere and the leisurely, almost casual, way of the city's people, was a delight to indulge in as we went on our sightseeing tour with Giro. Then a most exquisite lunch with him and his wife Maria at the Cinza and Valerio restaurant consisting of scallops and prawn and herb starters followed by a salmon mousse and a rich salmon bass with lemon sorbet. All this was accompanied by the appropriate local wines which were superb, and as desert there was an enormous plate of assorted fruits, followed by cappuccino and a very distinctive "after eight" type chocolate.

The mouth still waters as I write this. It really did make our day. It was the 7th August when we were joined at the camp by Marilyn, John, Bonnie and her friend Pippa. They had decided on a different holiday this year and had travelled by coach to N.S.U. for a holiday under canvass which the camp offered as a change from caravanning. Our ten days stay in N.S.U. saw us depart on the 12th August, saddened to leave behind the family and so many friends, but the long road back beckoned and shortly after eight o'clock we were on our way to the Brenner. After one or two slight incidents, for instance Percy running out of petrol within a couple of hundred yards from the summit and I having to go ahead and return with a half gallon of petrol to enable him to reach the summit petrol station to fill up, one example of the advantages of travelling accompanied rather than solo - we were coasting down the Innsbruck motorway at five o'clock. With the weather holding fine it was agreed we could reach Lermoos within a couple of hours, and we did. At 6.30 pm we were pulling into the camp site, tired after a 279 miles trip but elated at the prospect of at least three or four days rest in this beautiful Tyrolean surrounding.

One of our more enjoyable exploits on this visit was a trip on the train to Reutte - the first time we had taken a train ride in Austria. Little did we realise then the part this particular town would have in our near future travels as a pair. However, the day was a great success. And there was one other event which is amply referred to in the diaries. Tuesday, 16th August was Margaret's birthday. As part of the celebrations we took a long walk around the mountain, taking periodic rests on the wooden benches provided. Van's written comments are "I don't think there is a prettier spot in the whole of Austria. The chalet type houses with all the window boxes and gardens aflame with colour from all kinds of flowers and shrubs, and the mink coloured cows grazing with their bells clanging as they move around the lush emerald green grass makes one feel like being in a picture book of Heidi's stories, only this isn't make believe, its real". That evening we were taken out to dinner by Percy in the beautiful Edelweiss Hotel and sampled a typical Tyrolean meal which proved a fitting climax to Margaret's 73rd birthday and to this stay in Lermoos. The following morning we were off again.

It was a very hot day, the occasional temperature gauges en route were registering between 84 and 90 degrees, but the journey across Germany was steady and by lunchtime we had reached Pirmassens, well on our way to our next objective, Traben Trarbach. Search as we would we still had not seen a suitable Gasthof for the usual meal and overnight halt; that is until we found the Hotel Waldfried which, as the name implies, was in the middle of a forest and on a road we had never before come across. It was like a light beacon to a ship lost at sea! Could they allow us to stay alongside overnight now that it was getting late evening? Of course they could, and they offered a splendid meal too. The cost was equivalent to £12 a head, wine included, and well worth it for we had done 308 miles that day. The following morning we were passing through Birkenfeld and on our way to Traben which we reached by 10.30 am, only to find that the camp was full to capacity. However, within an hour several outfits had left and we were found two adjacent places alongside the Mosel where one of our idle pleasures is watching the barges and pleasure craft ply up and down the river. It's quite a busy waterway from Koblenz through Luxembourg to Thionville in France.

Another is barbequing and especially the evening feasts which are prepared by Jenny and son in law Michael and daughter Marian. There were twelve of us on this particular barbeque which ended in typical Moseler style with a sing-song of river tunes led by Marian and fired by a champagne, pear and plum punch.

The following day was shared between a trip to Wittlich for the roasting pig fest, a throwback to the medieval history of the town, and not our first visit to it. For this annual event there is gathered one of the biggest and most exciting and fantastic fairs in Europe which goes on for at least a week. On our return we paid a visit to our old friend Peter Griess and his fabulous Wein Keller in Traben where we sampled and then purchased some of his wonderful wine to bring back with us. The Mosel wine is particularly appealing to us, much preferred to that of the Rhine vintages. In this respect we were lucky that on the following day Traben was celebrating the anniversary of Dr. Ernst W. Spiess of Brunnen who developed T.T. as a wine centre. What an occasion! In marquees behind the Hotel Mosel Schlossen, at the edge of the river, the wine flowed freely, no less than a thousand litres of it, without charge... and the bands played the traditional German Oompa-Oompa and everyone joined in with gusto; and no one fell into the river!

There was one more custom (at least it had developed into that over the seventeen years Van and I have been coming to Traben Trarbach) to be fulfilled. This was the Haxen meal at the Central Hotel, and bid farewell for another year to our host Ernst Hoch. All went well and on 23rd August we set out on a short run to Trier and Camping Monnaise where we had planned to spend one evening. The attraction, of course, was Trier itself, the most western city of the Roman Empire, and, we were told, "floating" on a wine lake. Shopping here is simply great.

The holiday was fast running out and the following morning we began our last leg of the journey to Calais. A new autobahn to the north of the City gave us a flying start and by midday we had reached the Luxembourg-Belgium border at Martelange where we filled up with the cheapest fuel of our journey. Hitherto the weather had been perfect but as we approached Namur the heavens simply opened up. "It's Donner und Blitz" Van writes. "We cannot go on. We'll have some tea until it stops because we have plenty of time. The boat does not leave Calais until a quarter past midnight".

It was almost 7.00 pm when we reached Dunkirk and it seemed incredible that we had travelled through four countries, Germany, Luxembourg, Belgium and France since leaving our campsite in Trier that morning. As we entered Calais port the clock showed ten minutes to eight and the trip meter 304 miles. The Pride of Dover with Captain Rutherford at the helm took us across the channel and after an overnight stay at the Caravan Club site at Welwyn Garden we finally reached home on 26th August, five weeks and three days from the start of the holiday. And the reading showed that on this holiday we had travelled 3,176 miles. Fantastic.

# Chapter 48

# Italy Forsaken

According to the records we had decided early in the new year that the two outfits would be off together again in 1989, and furthermore that for the first time in what seemed ages we would not be heading for Union Lido (N.S.U.) Why this was I cannot say. We had decided instead it would be a roaming holiday of Western Europe and ferry reservations from Dover had been made for a late crossing on 12th August.

We left Caernarfon on 11th August and travelled as far as Chipping Norton where we stayed the night after a rather slow and tedious journey of 197 miles due to heavy holiday traffic. The only untoward incident was at Corwen on the A5 where, after filling up with diesel and driving some ten miles for lunch at a lay-by, I discovered I had left my petrol cap behind. Although I unhitched and raced back to the petrol station no petrol cap had been found. We had to continue with a makeshift "cap" until the following day.

Things went smoothly and according to plan afterwards and at 11.30 pm we arrived at Calais and put up on the port's adequate parking reservation. Sunday 13th August saw the beginning of the Europe travels and our first objective was Challon sur Marne. Our journey on French soil had been perfect; weather sunny and warm, no hitches, a snack lunch at Aire de Cauroy, some sixty kilometres from Rheims, and arrival at Challon s/M Municipal Camp at 2.45 pm. Although we always carried our awning Van had made a sun flysheet this time to avoid the more tedious job of erecting the awning for short stops, and it was here we tried it for the first time. It worked beautifully and we were much relieved. Our first surprise on arrival, however, was the increased cost of camp charges. These had gone up since last year from £11 per day to £13.

As I have repeatedly emphasised one of the attractions of our travels has been the friendships made. It was here on our first evening that we met Brian Fox and his wife. They came from Poole in Dorset and within minutes we found we had a number of mutual caravanning friends. They were returning home from Union Lido where they had spent some time with John and Mavis Williams and Fred and Barbara and others and they eulogised the wonderful time and weather they had had. There was a tinge of regret then that we had not included Union Lido again in our holiday schedule... and even a momentary suggestion we might still make it! But this time we resisted the temptation and decided after one more day in Challon to move on to the Black Forest area of Germany, and in particular to the mountain areas south of Freiburg where, we had been told, we would find some marvellous camp sites and enjoy a new type of holiday.

Except for one small hitch when we drifted apart for a short while after I had taken a wrong turn in Vitry, but soon got together again, the drive over familiar terrain to Strasbourg, where we crossed the Rhine into Germany at 3.45 pm, was uneventful to Freiburg. Then we had a little spot of bother. We were making for Todtnau-Muggenbrunn over entirely new ground to us, and it seemed we were negotiating one steep climb after another. One climb had gone of for nearly half an hour when suddenly a cloud of steam from under the bonnet and a frantic warning light on the dashboard indicated an immediate halt. We were boiling. But more serious was the fact that we had stopped on a bend which barely allowed a second car to pass. I couldn't restart the engine whilst the warning light was on. We were in a predicament. Van and Percy (whose outfit was behind us) had to get out and direct traffic. A massive hold up both ways was threatened, and I was helpless. Suddenly a car stopped and the driver, a Polish gentleman, offered to help. "I also am a caravanner" he said in broken English. "My car will tow you and your caravan to a wider place up the road and then you should be alright". Bless him. We were towed to a safer place and half an hour later we were again on our way to a campsite at Todtnau. It was a case of international camaraderie among caravan folk, and one for which I shall be eternally grateful. Should he, by chance, read this episode I proffer him my thanks again.

After refilling with water we carried on in search of what seemed a most elusive camp site. The diary informs me: "We have reached the camp site, but not very impressed at the moment. I don't know if there is any room here for us. The scenery is beautiful and cable cars are crossing above our heads, crossing the road. It's so high up here, but the tall fir trees and beautiful chalets help to ease the frustration we have felt. It is now 6.30 pm" We had covered 277 miles. The camp apparently was proving just right for us, and it helped that the kindly Patron found us two places alongside but outside the crowded site which had a marvellous view clear to distant Freiburg. We were certain we had done the right thing when, later that evening, we went to the small camp restaurant for a meal. The pork schnitzels and salads were perfect, and an adequate combination with the local wine. I can easily wax romantic on this occasion because we had seen nothing more beautiful than the scene that evening with the full moon rising over the mountain tops and shedding a silvery light on the valleys below. This is the stuff that our caravanning is made of!

It had been many years since Van and I had "done" the Black Forest and this time we were determined to explore as much as possible. Our three full days at the camp were packed with a variety of picnicking forays. Wednesday, 16th August saw us sightseeing in the charming old town of Todtnau with its beautiful church then undergoing renovation. From here it was only a short drive to St. Blasien in the heart of the forest where the centre of interest was the already renovated (1983) church with its white marble interior and benches painted white. The ceiling was magnificent. As for the town itself it was a blaze of colour. The people here are obviously very fond of their multicoloured flowers which could be found in almost every nook and cranny. It was most impressive.

Our next shift was up the highest mountain in the Schwartzwald where from the summit we looked down into the valley in Prag. This was the spot for our picnic, and suddenly, through the towering firs trees below us, we saw the most unusual sight, a family swimming in a pool of clear mountain water and all in the nude. Their pleasures were soon disturbed however. A forest ranger emerged and obviously warned them off for they quickly dressed and disappeared. Upon investigation we found the pool was fed by a beautiful waterfall. But how the family could have endured the ice-cold water baffled us.

That evening after a superb dinner at the Adler Hotel, some couple of kilometres from the camp, we were entertained by a wandering gipsy band and the whole camp joined in the singing. It was a fitting climax to a wonderful day, and one which had set the seal on the "different" holiday on which we had embarked.

Titisee was our next exploration, and it proved to be just as exciting and enjoyable. Van reminded me that it was twenty years ago that we last visited this great tourist attraction in the company of Len and Eileen and our young children. It was not possible to recall what changes had taken place but sufficient to say that it was still a very beautiful place. We toured around the lake and were astonished at the number of people doing just what we were doing. The woodcraft and clock making, much a local industry here, was greatly in evidence and very tempting. But for us this time it was just sightseeing and after our picnic on the grassy slope of the lake we were off to Freiburg. The dual visits had taken the best part of the day because Van records that we were back in camp by 9.30 pm, physically tired out but mentally refreshed.

Our last day in the Muggenbrunn was largely a pied. We walked well traversed mountain paths, took the cable car from Shauinsland to the summit and back to the Talstation from where a bus took us into Freiburg. It may not be a man's idea of Kaufhalle shopping as part of a holiday, but the women loved it and a tired team made its way back, this time by tram, to the cable station from where we were whisked up to our campsite half an hour's ride away. Oh yes, this was proving a really splendid holiday and break from sea and sand. But tomorrow we were to be off again.

It was with more than a tinge of regret that we departed from Todtnau on Saturday 19th August with a loose itinerary, but aiming for Lermoos again. Traffic wise there was no problem and we arrived in Lermoos by teatime, and prepared to stay on for a few days. After all there was still a lot of the Fern Pass and its neighbourhood that we were strangers to. For those who are partial to historic buildings, and especially the castles of Germany and Austria, a visit to the two castle-palaces of King Ludwig Von Bayern is highly recommended. High up the mountain in Fussen the Konigsschlosser Neuschwanstein (The

Royal Castle) and the Hohenschwangau were built in 1869 when the King was only twenty four years old. He died in 1886 at the age of forty one but the two castles, edifices which attract many thousands of tourists every year, are a striking monument to his spendthrift ideas which earned him the title of Mad King Ludwig. The views from these castles are truly wonderful and ample recompense for the efforts to reach them. All around the vast estates are lakes and in the distance what seem to be dolls' houses or chalets, and farmlands on which at this time the farmers were reaping the harvests.

We did a lot of walking, zigzagging up mountain walks and through forests which link the two buildings, before joining the coach which took us back to Fussen and our car. This and similar outings was how we spent our six quiet days at Lermoos using the camp site as a touring base. One surprise was the arrival on our penultimate day of Marilyn and John in their newly acquired motorised caravan "Johmar III" en route from Union Lido where we learned they had both won their respective half-marathon runs and had their trophies, two lovely silver cups, on display.

The rest at Lermoos had done us all much good and when we departed on Friday 25th August we had set our sights on Heilbronn, or possibly Bad Durkheim where we had agreed to spend a few days with our friends Karl Heinz and Jenny. It was at Heilbronn that our N.S.U. friends Herman and Maria Klennert lived and we had a standing invitation whenever to call upon them. So when we arrived at Heilbron just after 4.00 pm and spotted Camping am Breitenauer there was no desire to press on further. The camp was, in Van's parlance, "Posh" and beautifully turned out and the charge 23 D. Marks (£8) a night. We were received enthusiastically by Herman and Maria and the six of us sat down to a splendid meal and spent the time afterwards recounting our individual experiences of the holiday, with promises to meet again next year at Union Lido.

From Heilbron to Bad Durkheim the following day was only a four hours journey, and we had obviously timed our arrival to perfection because Saturday 26th August coincided with the start of the annual wine fest. We were met by Karl on the motorway - having telephoned him - and taken to their home on the Saltzbrunnen Weg where provision had already been made to house both outfits alongside the house. Here we were to stay for three days, and what days they were!

Ultra hospitality perhaps would be a suitable description of the manner in which we were treated during our stay, and the experience of the Wine Fest in the heart of the Pfalz wine country was, to us, something out of this world. They take their wine and winemaking very seriously here, as they have to for it is their life and their living. I learned more about wine in this weekend than I had ever throughout my forty two years as a political correspondent at Westminster.

Not only were we wined and dined almost to excess by our friends and their friends but were taken around some fifty miles of vineyards and shown off as British caravanning friends there for the fest. Would that we could have stayed longer - but perhaps it was as well that we did not! This was without question one of the real highlights of the holiday and when we left late on Monday 28th there was but one other venue left to us - Traben Trarbach.

Our six days at Traben were much in the pattern of previous years and on 4th September when we left it was very much, according to the diary, a case of pointing the noses towards the coast and see where we end up. We ended up in Ypres that evening and decided to do a short tour of the 1914-18 battlefields. Our stay was at Camping Ypres, described by Van as "one of the prettiest and well kept sites we have been on in this holiday". A must for me whilst we were here was the Menin Gate ceremony and at 8.00 pm the following evening we all attended what was the most moving experience of our lives. For seventy one years the bugles have been sounded within the Gate which was designed by Sir Reginald Blomfield and which is the most sombre reminder of the slaughter of the Great War and on whose walls are recorded the names of those who made the Great Sacrifice.

For the rest of the holiday after three days touring the Flanders fields from Ypres we crossed from Calais on 8th September and arrived back on Caernarfon the next day just three days short of a complete month away on what we had to admit had been a wonderful explorative holiday; but with one notable omission... we had forgotten to record the final mileage.

# Chapter 49

# The Foreboding That Was

A great deal of thought had been given to whether this holiday of 1990 would again be a continental one or a grand tour of Britain. After all we could have done most of the U.K. in the mileage we averaged annually on the Continent. What taxed us most, however, was what appeared to be Margaret's failing health; not that she had in any way indicated doubts about another cross-channel trip. But, on studying the diaries now, there had been signs in the two previous years which might well have aroused queries in our minds. However, it was agreed that we should go again and so it was that on 10th July the two outfits set out from Caernarfon to Felixstowe. The cross channel ferry from Dover to Zeebrugge had been suspended and therefore we made for the east coast port from which we were to depart and found that it was almost exactly the same distance as to Dover, in fact 293 miles. This necessitated again an overnight halt, this time at an attractive campsite, the Priory Park beyond Ipswich. It proved an ideal stop over for Felixstowe which was just twenty minutes drive away and by 10.30 am we were boarding for the 11.00 am departure. Surprisingly enough only nine outfits were on board, the least we had ever experienced since the first time we had begun our continental caravanning.

It was a glorious day and when we arrived at the dock at 9.20 am and had had our reservations confirmed the diary ventures the observation "It's such an improvement on Dover with the reception much better. We are all sold on this way to the Continent. The route for us is better and the traffic generally much lighter. This is the route for the future". The crossing itself was like a dream, sunny, warm and hardly any breeze - just like a cruise, and the five hours voyage went very quickly. By 6.00 pm we were well on our way to Brugge where we had decided we should stop at least overnight.

That place turned out to be the very pleasant Camp Saint Michael and the cost was £7.00 a night. With the weather continuing and the camp offering us all that we might require it seemed ridiculous to press on, so we spent the day sightseeing Brugge. Although we had been there before this was the only opportunity so far to have a really good look around. Much has been written about this placid "olde worlde" Flemish town, noted for its lace and Begonias and canals, and a really good way of seeing its sights, as we discovered, was by the small pleasure craft. We learned that Brugge has 35 churches, and that in 1958 it was the location for a Hollywood film starring Audrey Hepburn and Peter Finch... oh yes, the people of Brugge are very proud of that! That evening we indulged in our first barbeque, and right royally we dined on chicken, salad and boiled potatoes, washed down with a pleasant Liebfraumilch from the camp shop. The holiday it seemed was well under way. And still the sun shone the following day and persuaded us to still awhile. We spent this day with the trip into Holland and, on the return journey, stopped at Damme, a small village on the outskirts of Zeebrugge, for a restaurant dinner. They had been two lovely days.

But the journey had to proceed and before 7.00 am Saturday, 14th July, we were moving off. Then a strange thing happened. Less than a mile from camp I noticed the Rowlands' outfit was nowhere to be seen. I retraced our steps and discovered Percy's van had careered into a ditch as he was leaving camp. The hitch on the tow ball had not been secured properly but fortunately no damage had been done, only a short delay. What I had omitted to mention earlier was that the Rowlands' had purchased a new Abbey caravan for this holiday and naturally there was concern on their part that the 'van had not been damaged.

They were four blithe spirits as we continued in tandem towards Aachen and thence to Limburg which we reached in very good time - by 3.30 pm, having travelled 272 miles. That evening we pored over the maps, not certain which route to take from here but having agreed that this was not to be the year for Italy, come what may. We decided to go east and to make for Nuremburg where, if the weather persisted, we might stay a few days because we liked this part of Germany. The overnight halt in Limburg had been uneventful. It was like home ground to us after all the years we had stayed there, and at 7 o'clock, as soon as the camp opened, we were on our way again in expectation of reaching Nuremburg by mid-afternoon. Again in lyrical mood Van noted in her diary "Everything is so fresh in the early morning with verdant scenery all around and the massive forests of Germany, and the little villages we are passing through, make the journey a real joy. This is, indeed, a beautiful country."

Having set a mid-afternoon schedule for Nuremburg we seemed to be doing extremely well, and after an hour's stop for lunch in a forest lay-by it seemed we were well on time. It being a Sunday we were not surprised that the autobahn traffic was heavy, and then it dawned upon me as the leading vehicle that we seemed to be going away from our destination. I was quite disorientated and wished I had not left my car-compass at home as an oversight. Suddenly, and quite by chance, I found we were travelling on a road which seemed to be leading into the City, but which part I did not know. We were absolutely lost! In desperation I flagged down an overtaking car and enquired which way to our camp site at the Stadion. Very generously he signalled us to follow him and within a quarter of an hour we found ourselves at the entrance to the camp site. Without this aid I doubt we would have found the site even though we had been there several times before. This was a lesson I did not forget in the future. An essential item in the car for our journeys since has been that little compass of mine. Should our benefactor by some chance read this we offer him our most grateful thanks. He drove a BMW whose registration number was N.NL 580.

During the winter we had purchased a new awning and this was the occasion to try it out. It fitted a treat and we were snug as a bug in a rug before teatime, which meal was taken in the awning whilst outside the temperature was upwards of 80 degrees. This was a splendid augury for the holiday, and especially as the weather forecast promised continuing hot and fine weather.

Monday, 16th July, saw us walking into the town and enjoying a casual look-around. We walked through the woods to the Bahnhof, crossing the Nuremburg Stadium where those remarkable torchlight Nazi party rallies of pre-war days took place and Hitler addressed his troops. It did not take much imagination for us in the comparative silence of this particular walk to be aware of those now historic occasions. We had, of course, as of our particular generation, seen many of those rallies, and heard the ranting of der Fuhrer, on news reels of the late thirties and early forties. A comment in the diaries is worth repeating: "We have reached an underground station where we have had to purchase special tickets to board the train and travelled eight stations before reaching the Centrum. My goodness", Van writes, "London could learn a few things on cleanliness and orderliness here - no graffiti on the walls nor the trains, and it's a pleasure to ride on them." Among the local purchases that day are recorded a blanket for under £6 and a coffee maker for about £10, but there is a comment that the pastries of Nuremburg are among the dearest we have ever encountered! We paid more than a £1 for a small cream cake... and that was a lot at that time. Still the stop over had been most enjoyable and it was in the expectation of another good day tomorrow that we turned in after planning the next day's route which was to take us to Salzburg.

Two casualties, one physical and the other material, were responsible for a delayed start from Nuremburg on the following day. Van had suffered badly from a blistered heel for a couple of days and had to have it bandaged up, and Percy was experiencing problems with the caravan rear lighting which required adjusting before we could take to the road again. But the delay was less than an hour and we were again en-route for Munich, only this time the autobahn traffic was pretty heavy. To add to this unforeseen complication there were indications of a break in the weather. The clouds thickened and looked heavy with rain and our hope was that we might clear the traffic before a typical German rainstorm lashed the roads. We had experienced several of these heavy downpours, and at least they are uncomfortable and at worst a distinct hazard to moving traffic, and especially caravans on the move.

As it happened it was a slight accident, not the weather, which had caused a build up of traffic and as we entered Munich, past the scene of the accident, the sun shone again and spirits were raised when a sign indicated Salzburg as being only 80 kilometres away. The change in types of houses and appearance of high mountains testified our entry into Austria, but according to the diary there was also a sudden and pretty drastic change in the weather. It was well into lunchtime when we arrived at our campsite, Camping Salzburg Schloss Aigen, and it coincided with a terrific downpour. Because of the traffic conditions during the journey from Nurnberg we had not been able to make a single stop for refreshments and the downpour gave us the excuse, if one was necessary, to provide for the inner man before bedding down the two outfits.

There was a nice little restaurant on site and we enjoyed a wholesome meal of fish and chips and a dessert of fresh peaches and cream while the rain hammered the roof to the accompaniment of thunder reverberating from the mountains and ferocious flashes of lightning. It rained for hours and the outfits remained unattended until the weather improved, but I must admit we enjoyed the respite from driving with cat naps and a nip or two! By seven o'clock however, the weather improved and it was noticeable that the little restaurant was attracting a considerable clientele. If it was that good then why not give the ladies a rest from caravan cooking? So we did and the four of us enjoyed a typical Austrian schnitzel meal for less than £8 a head, including wine - German Rhinessen not Austrian!

Since our arrival on the continent one thing had been troubling the Rowlands, and consequently us too. Their younger daughter Beryl who lives in Australia had been expecting her child since the 7th May. Each day, wherever we were, there had been 'phone calls to find out if the happy event had taken place. Now it was 17th and still no news. Naturally Margaret was becoming increasingly worried and was showing the signs of anxiety, but unknown to us then there were far greater complications.

Wednesday, 18th May: "After a very wet night the morning looks much brighter, and let's hope it will be nicer today, and also bring us all good news from Australia." Thus the diary opens on this eleventh day of our holiday. Plans had been made to take a trip to Berchtesgaden. It was exactly thirty years since Van and I had last been to this attractive and famous resort, and we looked forward to seeing what changes the years had wrought, and especially to Kehlsteinhaus, Hitler's "Eagle's Nest". Our stop for ham, cheese and salad, and a turkey roll with coffee, American style, was at an American Hotel called "General Walker". This had been used as a U.S. forces retreat after the war and the meal was cheap and more than adequate, quite enjoyable. A kilometre or two further on to a car park saw us take a coach up to the "Eagle's Nest" at a height of 1,836 metres, a nerve racking journey with precipitous drops which sent the heart pounding. Kehlsteinhaus itself had been well preserved almost as a national monument and to get to the lift, embossed with highly polished brass and lit with beautiful crystal glass, which was the only entrance to the building one had to traverse a long tunnel which accentuated the one time security measures during Hitler's days. Van recalls "This is a magnificent place but today we are high in the clouds and missing a lot of the panoramic views".

With hindsight, however, it was here that we saw the first real signs of Margaret's dormant illness which was to have a devastating effect upon us all in the near future. We did not stay long because she complained of not feeling well, cold and shivering, and we returned directly to our campsite. Obviously the lack of news from Australia had affected Margaret more than we had thought for she had a bad night. The decision had to be taken: Percy felt, as we too did, that to go further than Salzburg was out of the question in the circumstances. But then the good news was received. The 'phone call the following morning, the 19th. revealed that Beryl had given birth to a baby boy and both were well. We saw a change in Margaret immediately, but not enough to warrant further travel. It was her desire to return home, but leisurely. Although they urged us to carry on it was unthinkable that we should do so, and so we turned for home via Lermoos and Traben Trarbach, both places well known to all of us over more than twenty years caravanning together.

The trek back from Salzburg began early on 20th and by 2.30 pm we had reached Lermoos where Margaret's continuing illness decided Percy to take her to the hospital at Reutte immediately for consultation and tests. Here it was revealed that her condition was serious and necessitated her immediate return to U.K. Yet, on her return to the caravan she appeared a lot brighter and all the talk was about the new baby. But the warning had to be heeded and the following day we were again homeward bound. Insisting that we should stay a while at Traben while she said she was feeling better we made for the Mosel, staying overnight at Landau and again at Annweiler en route. But Traben was not to be. We were told there was no room at the site so we pressed on to Trier, a site well known to us both. The opinion was expressed that we should stay a few days because Margaret wanted to. It seemed strange but she showed little signs of her illness then and we all enjoyed a quiet respite from travelling. Indeed, it was not until 9.15 am Thursday, 26th July, that we pulled out for the final run for home and at 4.30 pm we had reached Calais and ninety minutes later were crossing the channel. Little did we realise it then but this was to be the end of our long and eventful saga of the Welsh Dragons, the two outfits which had crossed and re-crossed the Continent, and into Asia even, together, and recognised wherever we went by the symbols of the Red Dragons rampant which graced the front of both 'vans. We reached home on Friday 27th July having covered 2,300 miles. Van's closing testimony in her diary "Home again after the shortest holiday we've had since being the four of us. We are hoping now for good news of Margaret."

But it was not to be. Margaret died on 22nd July, 1991.

# Chapter 50

# We Carry On

It had been a dreadful winter and spring for all of us. Holiday planning had been out of the question as Margaret showed progressive signs of the illness which eventually compelled her to take to her bed. Yet, whilst she was reasonably comprehending, she continued to show an interest in caravanning. After all it had been much of their lives for more than quarter of a century as we had forayed the Continental scenes. Our own preparations, whilst refusing to accept the inevitable, had included purchasing a new Abbey caravan so that we would have identical outfits.

When finally Margaret passed away a great void opened up. We had made provisional reservations in January for a channel crossing for the two outfits, from Felixstowe again, for 27th July 1991. Despite all the worsening indications, or perhaps because of them, we had not cancelled the bookings. And so, on 22nd July when Margaret died, Van and I agreed we would have to cancel. It was Percy who persuaded us to change our minds. Margaret would not have wanted it, he insisted. And fate decreed that our final act before leaving for Felixstowe on 25th July was attending the funeral and, in our own way, bidding farewell to a dear and greatly mourned friend of more than twenty five years' caravanning saga... and accepting that things would never be the same!

It was in anything but holiday spirit that we made that first leg of the journey, arriving in Felixstowe shortly before midnight for the following morning's ferry. Van's diary records almost hourly our depressions and the temptation to call off the whole thing. "We are missing Margaret and Percy so much" she noted. And the last straw was when we opened the curtains after a fitful night to find a caravan alongside us. "It's brought a lump to my throat; how wonderful it would be to have our two dearest friends with us" the diary states.

Our neighbours turned out to be a family from Durham and they, too, were in trouble. Their car battery had run down overnight and they were worried about being able to board the ferry. If Lynn and Peter Luke from Durham, and their two girls and a boy, chance to read this they will recall how I managed with the aid of my jump leads to get them started, and we shared their friendship on the crossing which helped Van and I greatly.

Without a prepared schedule we just let our thoughts take us and we found ourselves entering Brussels where we sought out my wartime friends, the Van Lanckers. Again we found some solace in friendship for it turned out to be Albert and Jenny Van Lancker's Golden Wedding and we were made more than welcome at the family party. They, too, had known the Rowlands. We spent three days "lodging" with Martine and her husband Philip; by this I mean that the caravan was parked outside their home in Anderlecht, a suburb of the city, and we ate and slept in their home, at least that part of the time we were not with Albert and Jenny. They did their best to take us out of our sadness and for this we were very grateful, but still, when we left the Van Lanckers the aching hearts were still much in evidence.

We set out for Rijswijk on the outskirts of Den Hague in Holland on the 30th July and were fortunate to find a most pleasant campsite en route at Delft. The object of the trip this time again was to look up old friends, John and Louisa Halim, formerly of Jakarta, Indonesia, whose relationship with us over more than twenty years had developed into more of a family connection. They were delighted to receive us at their home in Rijswijk on the following day, and it was then, really, that our holiday for 1991 began.

The campsite, a Municipal site in a delightful beauty and sports ground area outside the town, is ideal for short or long stays and our brief stopover was most enjoyable and gave us time to settle down to our new situation as did the friendliness of the British couple. Rob, an engineer who worked in Rotterdam, and his wife who stays on the site for some weeks at a time, were good companions. But then, this is one of the assets of international caravanning as we had experienced over so many years.

Thursday, 1st August, dawned bright and prospects were of a warm day as we struck camp and set out for our next objective which was to be Limburg. We enjoyed a typical British breakfast of bacon and eggs, the first caravan breakfast since we had started out, and spirits were lighter in anticipation of making the Limburg camp which was one of our first camping experiences way back. Van records the journey as most enjoyable because traffic was comparatively light and progress from Arnhem to Koln was uneventful. By midday we had covered 186 miles and after forty five minutes stop in a restplatz we were again well on our way.

Arriving at the camp just on three o'clock we found it pretty full, but at reception the duty man recognised us from previous visits and we were allocated a super site near the river and the welcome breezes. "Now for a well deserved cup of coffee" Van entered in her diary, and that pretty well sums up the day except for the few leisurely hours we enjoyed before turning in. It was really beautiful sitting close to the river watching the pleasure boats pass by and scullers practising their skills in the open racers; then there were the myriad of ducks waiting patiently at the river's edge for the crumbs which campers threw at them to the annoyance sometimes of the anglers who, I must confess, never landed a fish in my sight. Two sounds filled the air, that of trains passing on the opposite bank and the town clock striking the quarters and the hour from its tower high above the river. And another reminder was of Marilyn's and John's and the children's accident as we looked up at the motorway bridge which high up crosses the river... but more recent and very much with us in our minds were the more acute memories when we were two caravans together, so many times before.

This entry in the diary takes the mind flooding back to the times previously when we walked along these beautiful banks, and we wondered whether, and how many times ahead, will we be able to enjoy a repetition of this enjoyment.

Our itinerary meant a next day's run to Bad Durkheim on the Weinstrasse where we were to spend some time with our German friends Karl and Jenny Walter, and the prospects were good. After a good night's rest the day began with bright sunshine and a light breeze. The diary records "It is so very pleasant driving through forests and country roads and hilltop villages with their church spires pointing to cloudless skies as we make for Weisbaden on route 54".

When we rejoined the autobahn we were at Rudesheim and crossing the Rhine to Mainz and Bingen, another place of memories. From there we travelled to Alzey where we turned off for Bad Durkheim. Arriving shortly after lunchtime we noted we had done ninety miles since leaving Limburg, and every one of them had been delightful.

It was a grand reunion on the Walter's patio and that evening we were joined by two other friends, Inge and Walter Chelius. This was yet another example of the friendships and international relationships which caravanning and camping abroad fosters. In our case these friendships have endured over many years and we are grateful for them, and the understanding they bring. That evening we were entertained to a "fabulous dinner", as the diary reminds us, at the Gasthof Marktschunte. "It was too much for me" Van notes "and Inge and I were given a doggy bag. This is turning out to be a wonderful holiday".

Sightseeing with Karl Walter is an amazing experience. Born and reared in the famous Weinstrasse which stretches from the French border for 75 kilometres into the Pfalz country it seems that there is nothing about the area and the people that he knows not of. Although he speaks little English and we similarly with Deutsch we have formed a perfect understanding, helped more than a little by Jenny's Englische speaking as she calls it. We were shown the incredible vineyards which are virtually unbroken along the Weinstrasse, visited the Hambacher Schloss near Neustadt, taken to a Gasthause for a superb open lunch of Haxen and sauerkraut under the umbrellas, tasted the best of Pfalz wines and were introduced to a young man who spoke excellent English and who, with his parents, was buying masses of wine for his wedding which was to take place the following weekend. We were even invited to the wedding!

Early that evening we were taken up the mountain overlooking Bad Durkheim to the cloisters of a church ruin from which we heard music and singing the like of which we were experiencing for the first time. It was awesome and inspiring. The end of a perfect day!

We had planned a three day visit and so we had one day left when Karl and Jenny told us on Sunday that we would be out for the day - and what a day it turned out to be. "It's a glorious day and we do not know yet what Karl and Jenny have planned for us" the diary notes. The starting point was a wholesome breakfast of grapefruit, a two yolk egg with brown bread toast, cheese and assorted meats and lashings of coffee. Thus set up for the day, as we imagined, we lingered for an hour meeting again Gerd, the Walters' younger son whom we had not seen since our first meeting with the family in N.S.U. some twenty years ago, and his young family, and then set out for a wine fest in the woods. "Pfalzerwald Verein c.v." was a fabulous setting for the fest - a wine tasting celebration after harvesting the first crop. Following immaculately kept tracks through the forest we suddenly found ourselves in a clearing with several long trestle tables clothed and almost groaning with typical German food and wine galore. There were hundreds of people in high spirits, all enjoying this most amazing (to us) occasion. There was folklore dancing to a five man band and old and young alike were dressed in traditional Pfalz costumes. It was the first time for us to witness such an event and we acknowledged then, and still do, that the German people know how to enjoy themselves and how to choose the occasion.

In addition to the inevitable Bratwurst and mixed meats and salads there was a large cauldron of meat and vegetable soup which we sampled and enjoyed along with other dishes. We stayed on for a couple of hours and then were ceremoniously bid aufwedersein as Karl and Jenny and we took our leave. We walked back slowly through the forest, fully replete... but that was not the end of it.

A couple of hours rest at their home and we were off again, through another "Waldweg" where, after a half hour's stroll through the most picturesque wooded scenery, we came into another clearing wherein stood a timbered hotel, just like in fairyland! And who should be waiting there for us? Why Inge and Walter. They had been there for a meeting of the Ski Club of which Walter was President. After the business it was everyone to the barbecue. Here again we found how the Germans in this part really do enjoy themselves. We were introduced to everyone then took our places at the trestle table, gorged ourselves on all sorts of cooked meat, indulged in the customary wine gurgling, and joined in the robust singing of jaunty German tunes to the accompaniment of one of the most enthusiastic accordion players we have ever seen. It being early August and long days there seemed no urgency on the part of anyone to bring the festivities to an end and it was 10.45 pm before we arrived back at our caravan which was parked in the spacious foreground of the Walters' house. Where she got the energy from to record all this when we arrived back I do not know, but record it Van did with the closing line "What a marvellously fantastic day!"

Monday 5th August 1991 saw us take our leave of our perfect hosts. It would have been nice to respond to their pressures and stay on but the open road was beckoning, with Union Lido and the golden beaches at the end of the road. We said our farewells and according to our itinerary Lermoos in the Austrian Tyrol was our next destination. So good were the weather and road conditions that by lunch time we had done 146 miles. It was 4.10 pm when we arrived at our Lermoos Camp site to be greeted by Willie and Maria Shongau, the owners, and a full sign. They found us a space, however, and soon we were meeting Albert and Gerda Harter, from Tubingen, another couple of caravanning friends over many years. They were shocked to hear of Margaret's death as we were to hear from them of the death of another friend, Clara Van Steen, of Belgium.

With old friendships rekindled we rested at Lermoos for two days and on 7th August were crossing the Fern Pass to the Rescia Pass and the Austrian-Italy frontier which we reached at 10.30 am after an uneventful and enjoyable journey. We saw our first snow on the mountain tops in the distance, but we were not concerned because we knew that once we were into Merano we would be almost certain of continuing hot weather. And so it proved. We chose to use the autostrada from Belzano and headed south in excellent conditions. Throughout our caravanning it has been a rule - not entirely inflexible I must admit - to get in for the night not later than 4.30 pm, but this time I felt once we had covered 250 miles, and with the opportunity of staying overnight at one of the AutoRoute Service Areas, we should call it a day. It was 6.30 pm when we reached the Venice autostrada and there we pulled in for the night with the speedometer showing we had travelled 264 miles from Lermoos, and including two mountain passes. Tomorrow it would be an easy run to Union Lido.

And so it proved. A 6.30 am start from the Padova Service Area saw us pulling in at Union Lido on 8th August, shortly before 8.00 am, when newcomers were permitted to enter. There was a message from our Welsh friends John and Mavis Williams bidding us welcome, and in no time we had found a place alongside two new friends Derrick and Barbara Milner. Within an hour and with all hands to the pumps the awning had been erected and everything was ship-shape. It remained now only for us to relax and enjoy our stay. As usual word had got around and within a day or two we were renewing many friendships, among them the Barrett's from Yorkshire, and Ron and Marjorie from Pontypridd.

A highlight of this particular stay was the surprise arrival five days later of Marilyn and John in their caravan on Tuesday 13th August, and the news that they would be joined by David and Michelle on Thursday. With the weather continuing to be very hot it was no surprise that on Wednesday night we experienced the grandfather and grandmother of electrical storms, but fortunately not much wind. A new attraction at Union Lido this year is the new aqua complex with a built in "white water" jet propelled "river". It was a change from the beach, and very enjoyable. David and Michelle arrived as expected and now the family was complete. And so the days passed in the manner we had long become accustomed to, relaxation and laziness... but after all that is what a holiday is all about.

# Chapter 51

# Lost in the Schwartzwald

We had allotted twelve days to Union Lido, and so on Tuesday 20th August, farewells having been said and with Marilyn and John and the others waving us out of sight, we set off for Lermoos which was to be our first overnight halt. For those who intend to make the trip to Lido de Jesselo wherein Union Lido and scores of other campsites are now ensconced the route via the Rescia Pass is recommended. We never tire of it and so it was this time at the summit which is 1,455 metres - and 220 miles from Union Lido - we revelled in the beauty of the village of St. Valentino and its lake and another Lago di Rescia in which the tip of a drowned clock tower can be seen above the turquoise water of Curon. It is a relatively easy pass. We reached Lermoos just after six o'clock having journeyed 288 miles.

Of all he times if one can choose for a holiday in this part we reckon the month of August to be the best from the point of view of scenery and colour. The main obstacle though must be the heavy traffic. Reliving this particular journey by the diary we recall the splash of vivid colours in village after village throughout the Tyrol. Window boxes in every timber chalet drooled with multi-coloured geraniums and local flora. "The country is glorious at this time" it is written. "And adding to the pleasure is to see the farmers and their families reaping the harvests to a background of coffee and cream coloured cows, many of them with the traditional cowbells which one can hear in the distance".

We had deviated from our planned journey and were headed for the

Black Forest, a route we had not done for many years. How it happened is still a mystery but we suddenly found ourselves in Baden Baden and got completely lost. With time marching on and the watches showing 6.30 pm we were once again in open country and no idea where we might find a camp site. We decided to do what we had done many years before, namely to look for a Gasthof which offered the possibility of an overnight halt and room for the caravan. And find one we did in a cute village, Bietingheim, where the people were most friendly and helpful. We were led to Gasthaus zur Goldener Krone and offered a place in the spacious forecourt with the promise of a good dinner. And so it turned out. Their pork Schnitzel Mit Kartofle and mixed salad was out of this world and as an added bonus we met the Greenwoods of Kettering who were staying there with their Swiss aunt. What earlier had been a disquieting period without hope of finding a camping place turned out to be a lovely evening. We chatted and mixed with the locals for several hours before turning in, tired but contented. After all we had done 258 miles that day.

The following day, still with the weather holding, we set off later than usual heading for Trier. We knew that the autobahn that was under construction the last time we travelled this way would now be completed or nearly so and the trip to Trier passed uneventfully. It was nice seeing old places along the 140 miles and we decided to stop over in this last outpost of the old Roman Empire for a couple of days. These passed quickly with a few visits to the town and a few purchases. We like Trier and it is useful that the camp site on the river Moselle at Schweich is only five kilometres away. This is a place where you can while away the time without too many distractions, if that can be applied to watching the traffic on the river and the pleasure boats which abound. Our ultimate objective, however, was Traben Trarbach which we had first encountered in 1970, and the Rissbach Camping, and our friends the Hack family.

And so on 20th August we left Trier and ninety minutes later, and forty three miles registered on the clock, we were pulling into Rissbach. For reasons which are not material here, and with no connection with Jenny and Theo Hack, this was to be our last stay at the Camp. But for as long as we can caravan on the Continent Traben and Rissbach and the Hacks will continue on our schedule.

That first evening we enjoyed a family gathering with the Hacks and their son in law and daughter, Michael and Marion. It was a marvellous barbecue evening and Michael, who is a very useful chap, having built a new arbour on the lawn overlooking the river was now cooking a stupendous meal of huge pork steaks ("meat from the neck of the pig and special" he told us) and veal bratwurst with seasoned potatoes, all cooked on a particular wood which he had gathered that day. Scrumptious cannot be too exaggerated a word to describe the feast which was washed down first with champagne (Sekt) and then with lovely local Moselle wines. It was a pleasant ten minute stroll back to camp.

One of the features of our visits to Traben Trarbach from the very beginning has been dinner at the Central. This consists of specially prepared Haxen supplied by Mine Host Ernest Hochs, and served by Anna Maria. We look forward to this all the year and, as ever, we were not disappointed this time... except we sadly missed Margaret and Percy. An unexpected visit to the site by our friends Karl and Jenny Walter from Bad Durkheim, and a trip down river to Bernkastel Kues, were among the events which made our stay here so enjoyable - as always.

Thursday 29th August was our departure day and the diary records that "this has been one of the nicest stays we have had here". What lay ahead of us was the journey through Luxembourg and then the Ardennes as far as the E42 and the motorway to Mons. We have always been fascinated by this historic town but never been able to see much of it. So this time we decided to repair that omission. After 218 miles from Rissbach we arrived at the most delightful camp site in Mons and immediately decided to stay for at least two days. Very near to the Grand Place the site was both pleasant and cheap (at £3.15 a night the cheapest we had encountered on the holiday). The only minor discomfort we had was walking the cobbled streets to the market and the shops. They must have been the original cobbles which the troops trod during the first war!

It was a delight, however, to shop and take some sustenance at the many lovely restaurants. "I had some hot chocolate and Glan (that's me) bought me some smoked salmon slices for which the shopkeeper gave me a lemon" it is recorded. For dinner that night, cooked in the 'van of course, we had two grilled lamb chops with sauté potatoes and green beans bought in the market, with tinned pears and ice cream to follow. We opened a bottle of Moselle wine which I had bought in Traben and wound up the meal with a delicious percolated coffee. We certainly live the life of gourmets in our caravan!

They were two very happy days and on Friday, 30th August, we bid Mons au revoir and set off for Brussels where we were to spend a day with our wartime friends, Jenny and Albert Van Lancker. There was yet one more link in this holiday chain and that was Sluis, the Dutch-Belgium frontier town from where, as we did on this occasion, we set out on the last lap for the ferry at Zeebrugge, less than half an hour away. It was the 2nd September at 11.00 am when we boarded the Baltic Ferry which landed us in Dover at 4.20 pm. It was strange because this was the first time in more than twenty years that we had made that trip without Margaret and Percy, and the journey back to Caernarfon was strained. Van wrote "It's been a strange but wonderful holiday. But we have missed Margaret and Percy such a lot. In future it will be just us two."

Midnight had just chimed when we arrived home in Caernarfon where is remained for me just to check on the total mileage. It showed we had travelled 3,140 miles of perfect towing, and glittering sunshine for almost six weeks. Before we turned in, tired but happy, we posed to ourselves the question: What and where will it be next year?

# Chapter 52

# The New Outfit Does Well

During the late autumn and then early spring of 1992 we had splashed out on a new outfit. We had been impressed with the new Abbey 13/2 van at the Caravan Show and had made the purchase. This was followed by a new car, a Peugeot 405 Turbo diesel which we were assured was the best towing vehicle, and so it proved. I cannot speak too highly of the performance of the new car, then and since. A thirty miles trial run a few days before we had made up our minds where the 1992 holiday would be spent, and how, proved the outfit to be ideal to our needs and decided us that again this year it had to be a continental one. But this being only the second holiday without our two companions we elected to give Italy and Union Lido a miss.

Which was just as well because in March we heard from our old friends, David Chaplin and Gerald Brookes, by now well established in their farmstead in the Loire Valley, and whom we had visited a couple of years earlier. Strangely, it was at the old N.S.U. that we had first met "the boys" as we affectionately called them, then school teachers in Devon, and from that first meeting we had kept in touch. Today they are retired ex-teachers who share a wonderful life for most of the year on their own quaint French farm as to the manner born. They are never short of visitors, naturally, and their invitation to us to spend some time with them, with the caravan sited alongside their lake, was manna from heaven!

And so it happened that on July 20th we set out for Dover with nothing more than a roaming commission in mind after spending a few days with "the boys" at Noyant in the Loire. We were lucky enough to have a place on the newly commissioned P. and O. "Pride of Dover" ferry, by that time one of the finest ferry vessels we had encountered. It had been stormy when we left Dover at 2.30 am and was still raining when we left Calais at 6.30 am. Our route took us via Abbeville (of wartime memories) and Rouen and before midday there was a complete change in weather. The sun shone strongly and the temperature soared. The journey to Noyant is relatively short and simple, but when we reached Bernay we decided to call it a day. It was the sight of Bernay's municipal campsite which prompted the stop as much as anything. It was pretty, and very appealing, and it was just on lunchtime. For the equivalent of £7 we spent the day and night there with electric included. Things were beginning well for us! A late afternoon 'phone call to David and Gerald fixed a meeting place at Le Lude the next day, and we were left to enjoy the typical caravanning companionship of several English caravanners on the site. This is where we met Ken and Sheila from Leeds. But we were also mindful that evening that exactly a year ago the morrow we had lost Margaret.

The Loire is a wonderful place to spend a holiday, and better still if you have a farmstead to go to. Within three hours of leaving Bernay on 22nd July we were met and guided to "Tellue" where our site alongside the lake had been well prepared. The following morning a clear blue sky and a light breeze which made for a comfortable 70 degrees plus augured well for the start of the holiday which, thanks to the boundless hospitality of our friends, we were to enjoy to the maximum. Not a day went by that we were not taken here, or there, wined and dined in true French style, and introduced to so many of their "friends of the earth". But as much as anything we enjoyed the chats about old times and old friends, seated in the open barn or between alfresco munchies in the open. They were idyllic days which, in reliving them now through the diary, we dearly hope we shall savour again.

With the temperature soaring into the 90's occasional visits to small towns like Genetals and Saumer and many villages whose names are not mentioned were most enjoyable for the traditional cafe and bistro sippers - the wines, cafe, beers and ices, all served in the open. One lunch we sampled at a quaint restaurant in Denzies run by their friends was typical of the truly Normandy fare of these parts, and it went on, and on, and on... The next day we were in a small village of Vouille Loretz. There we had the Langoustine, oysters, pike and perch dishes served with exquisite sauces, roast duck with all the trimmings - much of which we had never heard of before - with appropriate salad, with a selection of mousse and gateau and a variety of cheeses to follow.

Of course it could not go on! We had to call a halt for fear of being shackled to a life of Riley which we might find hard to surrender. And it came on July 27th. We literally tore ourselves away to the protestations of both David and Gerald; obviously they had enjoyed the period as much as we had. We bade our farewells and set course for Chalons sur Marne which would be our jumping off place for the next, as yet undecided, part of the holiday.

Our route, kindly mapped out by Gerald, took us via Orleans, just 100 miles away, and it was here at 1 o'clock that we pulled into a typical French Service station for a quick lunch. The Dragon symbols on the 'van were soon noticed and, as usual, we were approached by some Welsh people from Swansea who were also keen caravanners. Regrettably we omitted to note their names, but it was nice talking to some fellow Welsh especially as they came from so near to Llanelli. The stop took longer than we anticipated and by the time we had got under way again it was obvious we would not make Chalons that day. However, from previous journeys through this area we knew there was a site somewhere near Marie De Courtenay and it was not difficult to find. Rather a nice homely site we thought and it was here that we met Bill and Robin and their three children and enjoyed a friendly drink outside their caravan before retiring at 11.30 pm. It had been such a casual day, and we had covered only 172 miles.

The diary records that the weather was continuing to hold good, warm and with only a light breeze, we were amazed at the proliferation of truly large sunflowers which seemed to be the main harvest in this part of the country at that time. Past Sens and through Troyes, and on to the motorway, the journey had been idyllic. There was no sense of urgency. This was caravanning at its best and most enjoyable! During a brief lunchtime break at a Service station 'Van was approached by a German caravanning family who professed their considerable interest in the British built 'vans. As is customary on such occasions they were "shown around", expressed their admiration of the Abbey and said they hoped to purchase their first "English made" caravan when they would be visiting for the first time the Caravan Exhibition in London in the autumn. "Hope we've helped someone to make a sale" are the wife's comment in the diary!

With the aid of the new motorway we were able to drive into our usual site in Challon sur Marne by mid-afternoon, found our pitch shipshape and then to our consternation discovered that somehow the jockey wheel was smashed and virtually unusable. How it happened and where between lunchtime and Chalons we were at a loss, but we decided it would have to remain such until we reached our German friends, the Walters in Bad Durkheim, in a few days before any reparation. We had done only 121 miles that day and despite the accident it had been a very enjoyable one.

If any reason or excuse was required to stay over for another day the jockey wheel provided it, not that there was any need mark you! The following day was yet another gorgeously warm and necessarily lazy one. A wander around the old town of Chalons where the compelling sight of local produce in the open market resulted in a beautiful melon, a freshly baked baguette and "some of the nicest jam doughnuts I have ever tasted" finding their way into Van's basket" - yes, it was an old fashioned wicket shopping basket - was followed by a visit to the Hypermarket where we purchased what had become a necessity, namely an oversize sun umbrella. We were relaxing under the selfsame umbrella when an Eldis caravan pulled into the next pitch to us. As is usual with our fraternity we offered a helping hand and that was how we met Geoffrey (now I gather a retired teacher from the Manchester Polytechnic) and Kate Rhodes. We enjoyed a grand evening and have since continued our friendship with the occasional letter and 'phone call.

Much as we would have loved to stay on the call of the road, and by this time a sort of itinerary for the remainder of the holiday having taken shape, we bade our farewell to the Rhodes' on 30th July and set out for the N3 and Verdun (where we replenished our supplies and diesel at LeClerc's) and made for Trier. There was an unusual occurrence at a layby where we had pulled in for a snack lunch. We were joined here by what we thought was a stray Collie dog. There was no sign of habitation within miles of open country but as soon as we had pulled in the dog emerged from a thicket and began the most mournful howling, almost non-stop. It had a tattered red scarf tied to a collar around its neck. The situation bordered on the eerie for after each bout of howling the animal retreated to the thicket. Van opened a tin of corned beef and fed it to him. He would only take it when we retreated. Then, back it would go into the thicket howling all the time. I ventured as near to the thicket as I could to see if he was calling to help someone, but found nothing. We left after an hour with the sound of the howling still ringing in our ears.

There was nothing more out of the ordinary as we made our way through Luxembourg to Trier where we had stopped on previous holidays at the campsite in Schweich alongside the Mosel. With the weather still sweltering we reached the campsite at 4.20 pm and were lucky in a packed camp to find one pitch. We had driven for 153 miles and were thankful for the rest; cold drinks under the umbrella, a light supper and the luxury of the electric fan to cool our perspiring bodies. We slept well until just after 2.00 am when an almighty roar of thunder and flashes of lightning awoke us. Within minutes the camp was almost under water with the heaviest rain we could recollect. So ended our first eleven days of holiday!

Sunday, 2nd August saw us leaving Trier for Bad Durkheim which we calculated we could reach by late afternoon. We had decided to leave the autobahn and cut across country through wonderful wooded scenery and mountainous terrain. And it was this decision which brought us to Wachenheim on the outskirts of Bad Durkheim where one will find Camping Im Bergtal. What a beautiful place to stop! But easily missed because it nestles off the road through the woods and the Camping sign at that time was partly covered by greenery. However, though we had overdriven by a few yards we managed to recover and reversed into the entrance.

Because the camp is closed between midday and 3.00 pm we were the third caravan in a queue waiting to be directed to our places which happened to be next to some Dutch caravanners. Again, it was not long before we were exchanging information. As with most Dutch people they spoke excellent English, but we couldn't pronounce their names. He settled for Bob and she for Katherine which she then changed to Tiny. In no time we knew one another well enough to exchange professional and family information. Bob, it transpired, was a restorer of old buildings and churches. Their family name was Braun - or Brown - and they came from a small town near Amsterdam. In the cool of the evening, to the cooing of wood doves and the singing of other birds all around us, we chatted and drank coffee and marked up yet another delightful and successful day. We had done only 96 miles, and were only a couple of miles away from Bad Durkheim itself.

And so it went on for a second day. The Browns and ourselves had hit it off well. We exchanged titbits, including Tiny's Dutch cheeses and Chinese noodles for Van's Welsh cakes and Bara Brith, and it was sad when, after two days of pure enjoyment, we said our goodbyes and went our different ways. We went to Karl and Jenny where we were soon found adequate space alongside their house for the remainder of our stay. The date now the 4th August, and we were with them for what turned out to be another tremendous episode in the holiday with a difference. The Walters are so kind and undemanding, friends in every sense of the word. Karl was always taking us to different places along his beloved Weinstrasse, explaining the ways and wherefores of winemaking which is the biggest industry in this part of the Pfalz, introducing us the Durkheimers and their wines and pointing out the highlights of the traditional wine fest which is accredited the largest in the world and takes place during the first two weekends every September.

Remember the smashed jockey wheel? As I expected Karl did not take long to rectify matters. Within a couple of days I was taken to a place where I was able to procure an almost exact jockey wheel, and all was well once again. And it seemed that from our arrival to the 10th August when we departed we ceased to be caravanners. Every meal was at the Walters' or out. The 'van was just for sleeping in. It was a wonderful ten days which kept the diarist extremely busy. There are descriptions of the meals, of the places where we ate out, of the many special German recipes, and almost every activity in which we were all involved; of the walks through woods and areas of indescribable charm, of the companionship in which two other friends, Walter Chelsius and Inge, took part... Walter tragically died of a heart attack while returning from a caravan rally in Berlin in the following year.

One of the highlights of our grand tour of the area was a visit to Oggersheim where we were taken to number eleven Marbacher Strasse. There we saw in this wide and exclusive street a lovely white house whose letter box bore the name H.Kohl. It was the home of the German Chancellor, unobtrusive but "protected" by a small police station next door. We didn't suppose it had the attraction to the public as that other No 11 (Downing Street) in London.

We believe the Walter's and the Chelius' had kept the best to the last for us when on Sunday, the day before we were due o leave they took us first on a forest run through some of the most magnificent woods whose villages were bedecked with flowers of all colours and where the public spirited local communities had set out special picnic areas with wooden tables and benches. "Wouldn't it be nice if our people showed the same initiative to do something like this" the diary offers. This part of our tour ended in Neu Lienggenbourg whose castle high on the mountain can be seen for many miles.

The second part was, if anything, even more beautiful and memorable. The six of us walked for the best part of an hour through forestland where walks followed babbling streams with occasional stone crossings which took one on to another circuit. This was Stilles Tal (The Silent Valley), and the walks end in a clearing where stands the most beautiful timbered restaurant. It was here we sat down to a sumptuous five course meal, the end of a perfect day and one for which we shall forever be grateful to our German friends. They made this holiday what it turned out to be... unforgettable. And when we left on the morrow, 10th August, it was with a mixture of sadness at having to leave so much behind, and pleasure that we had over the years, and mainly through our pursuit of caravanning, been able to form such friendships.

Our schedule from here was to Traben Trarbach. A holiday without Traben Trarbach would be like peaches without cream, and 245 miles on we pulled in at Jenny and Theo's Mosel home. We were not the only visitors. We met Ruth and Bent Aadal, a lovely couple from Odensee in Denmark, and since then we have nurtured a friendship which has already seen them visit us in North Wales with the promise of a return match soon.

A barbecue under the arbour always was a feature of our Traben visits and so it happened this time. Michael and Marion provided the best cut in pork and deer (venison) together with bratwurst and brat kartoffle with gemuse salad, and the beautiful local weingut wines added up to a superb feast (whilst I am writing this now my mouth is watering with the memory!). I wonder what we will do when circumstances may compel us to bring these wonderful days to an end? But enough of that now. There are, we hope, some years ahead of us still!

We stayed in Traben four perfect days, enjoying the additional company of Ruth and Bent, and on 15th August we began our homeward journey. This took us via Rijswijk in Holland where we spent two days with the Halims and thence to Sluis (one day). Unlike previous arrangements this time we decided to cross the channel from Calais instead of from Zeebrugge a journey of 208 miles. When we arrived home in Caernarfon late afternoon on 20th August we had covered 530 miles from Holland and no less than 2,183 miles for the complete holiday. Now we are preparing for 1993... what does that hold for us?

# Chapter 53

# Another Outfit - and Not So Well!

The holiday this year, 1993, was presaged by the most unusual event. As had been customary we arranged to take the caravan for its pre-holiday service a month before our scheduled departure in mid-August. It was not more than eighteen months old it will be recalled, but for some reason instead of having the check done locally we decided to take it to an Abbey dealer in Derby. That, we were told, was the nearest approved agent. The fact that we had to travel 130 miles to the agent did not enter our minds as being foolish. After all it would be a day out. But this innocent decision had, what some may think, its just outcome in the short time ahead.

What I am trying to say is that when we set out for Derby the only thing in mind was a full service and the assurance that we would be well prepared for another Continental holiday. The outcome was quite the opposite. We found ourselves in a situation where the dealer company was about to be wound up and in the process was offering new unsold caravans at knock-down prices. The temptation was too great.

We returned home later that day with our Abbey, the Swift Corniche which we had purchased having to be left for the after sale inspection. So far, so good. A week later, and fortunately having disposed of the Abbey to a delighted first time caravanner, we returned for the latest acquisition and again, a week later, in high holiday spirits, we began the holiday. The date was 20th August and the final objective was to be again the Union Lido Camping in Cavallino, Venezia.

The omens were not right from the beginning... with hindsight that is! Fine rain and fog to start with and after just over two hours the first mishap. The wardrobe door did not latch properly and the movement in motion caused it to swing open resulting in the attached mirror crashing to the floor. What's this about seven years bad luck? We weren't thinking of that as we proceeded to London which was to be our overnight stop en route Dover. At Uxbridge, however, a traffic hold-up gave us the first inclination that all was not well. The car battery seemed flat when attempting to restart. Popped into the first garage to be told the fault was with the caravan. The fridge, with a faulty fuse, had drained it and the caravan battery was dead.

We decided it was best not to proceed to Dover and the ferry until both mishaps had been corrected and Saturday, the worst day to try and make contacts, was spent first in having a new mirror fitted and then abortive telephone calls to those responsible for the 'van's electrical wiring to find the fault. This was possibly the worst beginning to any holiday. There was no prospect of catching our reserved ferry crossing and we were faced with having to wait until Monday before having the fault identified and put right... and all this with a brand new caravan which supposedly had been inspected and passed okay after sale!

There is hardly a need to refer to the diary because this episode is still very fresh in the mind. We left Uxbridge on Sunday morning having been told there was a Swift agent in Orpington. There was, and helpful they were too. Within an hour the fault had been identified and corrected. A new fuse box was necessary and a replacement battery installed in the 'van as a precaution. We cannot speak too highly of this assistance and it was in better spirits that we boarded the first available ferry for Calais 378 miles after leaving home. Ah, but if only we had known what was to come!

Our first overnight halt on 23rd August was the Pijnacker Campsite at Delft, Holland, and two days later we were on our way to a rendezvous on autobahn 61 with our friends Karl and Jenny Walter. It had been arranged early in the year that we would spend part of the holiday together in Union Lido. That night was spent in Bad Durkheim after a journey of 340 miles, and early the next morning, 26th August, we were on our way with two caravans making for Lermoos in the Austrian Tyrol, a recognised staging post for us on this route to Italy.

Progress was so good in this first stage that we decided to press on beyond Lermoos whilst there was ample daylight and good weather. Karl and Jenny knew of another camping platz at Naturn, some eighty miles further on and this we made before 6.30 pm, having travelled 370 miles. It may seem a hefty whack to some but whilst the going is good, that is weather and travelling conditions generally, we have not found this distance too demanding. And to make matters easier Karl had arranged an intercom which meant we were in constant touch even when out of sight of each other and this was helpful and a new experience for us. Naturn turned out to be a delightful camp situated among tall fir trees with the most attractive scenery, but we were there for only one night and the beauty of it all was a bonus.

According to the diary it is only 179 miles from Naturn to Cavallino and we arrived there at 4.05 pm despite the most awful weather. From Bolzano to Cavallino it rained unceasingly and to add to the discomfort we discovered at a lay-by in Trento, where we had to pull in because it was raining so heavily, that the lock of the toilet door had jammed and had to be forced open. We found the door had warped and this had caused it to jam. This was getting to be a bit too much... but there was to be more!

Our first day in Union Lido saw a change for the better in the weather and something else which pleased us more was to find our granddaughter, Bonnie, and her companion Andy, had arrived for a camping holiday. They were with us to help erect the awning and all seemed to be going well. Holidays in Union Lido, as explained already, almost always follow the same pattern: sun, blue sea, social gatherings, old friendships revived and new ones made, and generally a lazy existence in ideal surroundings. Which assumes I suppose that there was little or nothing to worry about. But in this instance there was something. We had noticed since arriving that there was dampness under the offside single bed, the side on which the built in water container and the hot water cascade equipment is located. It seemed to be getting progressively worse and then the hot water pipe burst causing a mini-flood in the compartment. We had to call in professional assistance and temporary repairs were made. But by this time we had had enough. The holiday had been ruined... and we still had more than a thousand miles to go before reaching home base!

Had it not been for the help of friends and the cheerfulness of Bonnie and Andy I think we would have packed up and left after this last mishap, but we stayed on. At that stage I think we felt it safer to remain static than to attempt the return journey alone. Then there was the trouble with the double bed. Because of a miscalculation in measurements the laths which were drawn out to make the double bed kept falling through and several times the whole structure collapsed leaving us on the floor.

And so it went on until 7th September when Karl and I hitched up and (with crossed fingers I presume) left Union Lido, and Bonnie and Andy, for the journey to Bad Durkheim. We were very touched, and our misfortunes seemed not to count, when Van opened an envelope which Bonnie had thrust into her pocket just before we set off. Inside was a note thanking us for being with them and a £5 note..."for a coffee each for you both and Karl and Jenny". It was typical of them and we greatly appreciated the action.

It wasn't until we reached Bolzano, some 150 miles from Cavallino, that we made our first stop, and then an al fresco lunch of bratwurst and roll from a Schnell Imbis in Schlanders about 25 miles from the Resia Pass, fortified by some doughnuts which Bonnie had thoughtfully slipped into the 'van. Although the weather had greatly improved and the journey was interesting and without incident the diary confirms that there was a foreboding in both our minds: when will the gremlins strike again?

There were 285 miles on the clock when we drove into our camp in Lermos just on 5.00 pm. That evening the four of us decided that no matter what the cost we would have dinner out. We plumped for local trout and on advice chose a hotel in nearby Ehrwald. "It was super - the biggest trout we've ever eaten". Those are not my words. They are what Van wrote in the diary. What she did not add was our reaction when the bill came. Karl and I were speechless - and almost broke after the bill had been paid. It was such a shock that I had to pay with credit card and Karl has used the occasion since as a good after dinner story. At any rate for the time being it put the miseries of the caravan happenings out of our minds! Gerda and Albert Harter of Tubingen, regulars at the camp and already old friends, enjoyed the story and what passed between him and Karl I don't know since it was wholly in Pflaz German.

The following morning, the 8th September, we set off for Bad Durkheim which we reached without incident just after 6pm., a journey of 257 miles. We had decided to remain with the Walters' for a few days and on 10th September, our 55th wedding anniversary what greeted us at the breakfast table was unbelievable. It was a proper wedding table, strewn with roses and leaves, lighted candles in a candelabra and champagne on ice. The centrepiece was a beautiful wedding cake. Who could ask for more, and what a way to express friendship? It relegated any worries we felt and was the start of a superb day for it coincided with the annual Weinefest. For the best part of the day we toured the magnificent fair and ended with a Haxen dinner in which we were joined by Walter and Inge.

It was much the same the next day, with Inge and Walter acting hosts during the morning and taking us on a visit to friends who grew luscious grapes used in the local weingut for the making of a special wine. We sampled the wine, a kind of rose which seemed to have all the qualities of a champagne or sekt, on a patio overlooking the vineyard and with a superb panorama. Having thanked our host Guntar and his wife, Ursula, we were returned to the charge of Karl and Jenny who, with a dozen or more friends, carried us off to the Weinefest. These are jolly occasions and, as I have mentioned before, these people know how to enjoy themselves and the various special occasions which are many. There is nothing I know of better than good wine, good companions, and the occasion to enjoy both. This is what the Bad Durkheim Weinefest does and we employed it to the full. But all good things must come to an end sometime, and for us on this occasion it was Monday 13th September when we set out for Traben Trarbach, by now the customary last link in all our holiday chains since 1970.

Again it was virtually a repetition of the standard stay over with Theo and Jenny in Rissbach. The hospitality was faultless and unfettered. I cannot recall any visit to Rissbach which was not enjoyable and, again as happened last year, we had the pleasurable company of Ruth and Bent, our Danish friends. One of the highlights of this visit was an afternoon with Ruth and Bent visiting the 600 year old castle of Krovburg high in the mountains above the Mosel and from which you can see the longest and widest expanse of the river. It was delightful and a visitation highly recommended.

When, on 17th September, we eventually set off for what was to be the final leg of our homeward journey it seemed the summer was over because there had been two days of rain and it had turned cold. We set out for Brussels to call on our wartime friends, Albert and Jenny Van

Lancker, and the next day off to Sluis ready for the ferry for Felixstowe on 21st September. Here again it was the pattern as before over more than thirty years, two nights at Camping Meidoorn which included visits to our friends the Ultee's and copious cups of coffee and pancakes, and then a twenty minutes run to the quayside and the ferry. Another strange occurrence as we were boarding the vessel. We were approached by a couple from Nottingham who were the owners of a new Swift Corniche caravan, identical to ours. Expecting to hear praise for their outfit we were flabbergasted to be given a catalogue of complaints including some which were similar to ours. What had gone wrong? It fortified my decision to make known in no uncertain terms to Swift what we had experienced, and what I expected as recompense. In bringing this chapter to an end I must admit that our complaints were dealt with to our satisfaction in the end, but nothing they did could compensate us for the incidents which spoiled an otherwise fulfilling holiday. The 'van was returned to Swift's appointed agent and kept for several weeks before being restored to us with another full twelve months' guarantee. But the nagging question remained... what would it be like next year? And could we depend on it being trouble free if we repeated a continental holiday? This one, when we arrived home, had covered 3,210 miles.

# Chapter 54

# Maastricht Revisited

The problems with the caravan in the previous year, although now satisfactorily dealt with by Swifts, thanks to the personal intervention of Managing Director Tony Hayley, to whom we gladly acknowledge our appreciation, had decided us not to venture so far for the 1994 holiday. Italy was out. It was not a difficult decision, however, because with their usual Xmas card David and Gerald had extended an invitation to spend part of the holiday again at Tellue in the lovely Loire Valley.

A few weekend sorties having satisfied us that the 'van was in trim condition we planned a start to the holiday in mid-July with a crossing from Dover to Calais on the 16th. The only problem encountered on the way to the coast was with the stabilizer and this had to be taken off so that for the first time in many years we were towing without a corrector. It is not to be recommended in these days but we managed and after a smooth crossing we travelled as far as Bernay where we found a splendid municipal site "Brionne" for the first night's halt. This is where we met Sandra and Colin from Cardiff. She was a nurse and our joint connection with Cardiff resulted in a long chat, not least about people we knew. But this is caravanning generally.

The diary records that the weather became very warm and that evening all windows were kept open. I am also reminded that it was at this camping site that I saw the final of the World Cup when the manager kindly installed a television set in the lounge for the occasion and Brazil beat Italy. The following morning we set out for Le Fleche and by 3 o'clock we were safely ensconced at the most attractive campsite "de la Route Do'r" which is an asset to this beautiful old town on the banks of the river Loire. It was to be only for one night because the following morning we made our way without problem to Tellue where we were expected, and where we found another old friend, Irene, widow of my old colleague in the Lobby, Robert Scott. With the five of us together, but only for two days as Irene was returning to England then, the talking hardly ceased, even during mealtimes for one of which David had cooked a superb meal of duck with all the trimmings of pineapple and fresh French fruits crowned with a crisp white wine, and port and coffee following the customary cheese and biscuits. Bravo David, whose culinary prowess provides every visitor with a first class and distinctive meal... and they live like this even when there are only the two of them!

The four days' stay here was featured by visits to neighbouring towns and villages, each one offering a variety of experiences. The return to Le Fleche with the others gave us a greater knowledge of this town through which the Loire along its 800 kilometres flows. The word pretty does not do it full justice. The inhabitants are fiercely proud of their historic town, and justly so. Flowers bedecking private as well as civic buildings give it a glorious splash of colour, and it has become one of our favourite French places in this area. Another is Samur where a Saturday morning visit to the open market is a must. In the nearby village of Genneteill we enjoyed a lunchtime meal of local recipes which included a steak and vegetables, a pate (with a difference), cheeses and a bowl of cream caramel with fresh fruit. Now we know why David and Gerald spend so much time sampling the local cuisines. But the piece de résistance for us was the "supper" we had on our last day in Tellue. David had been shopping at La Fleche fish market. He brought back Van's favourite smoked salmon, and an abundance of Langoustine, coupled with a variety of local vegetables and herbs and in the cold box a Viennetta as a sweet. But it was the presentation of the dishes that complimented the meal and made it unforgettable. "Let's call it 'The last supper in Tellue'" David suggested. So we did.

As if sorrowful that we had decided it was time to go the weather turned overcast and showery as we took our leave of David and Gerald on Sunday morning 24th July. We were heading for Chalons sur Marne again. Conditions were not conducive to a long drive and by mid-afternoon, and 127 miles from Tellue, we spotted a camping sign at De Chateauneuf-sur-Loire et Sigloy. This turned out to be a large and lovely site on the banks of the Loire with its own sandy beach. With the weather changeable, and the time at our disposal, the beach did not matter, but it is something we have noted for the future. Came the dawn and better weather made us anxious to be on our way again. Our calculations were that Chalons could be reached within five hours and so it proved. It was well into the eighties before lunchtime at Troyes. "We are not complaining" Van wrote. By early afternoon we were in the Chalons municipal campsite having received a hearty welcome from reception where we were instantly recognised. We found the site had been altered and for the better, and it was proving extremely popular with the Brits. I think we made up the largest national contingent. Alongside us in the next bay were Pat and David Branscombe from Doncaster and in no time we were passing a pleasant couple of hours demolishing a bottle of wine. That helped us to decide we would stay for three or four days although Pat and David were leaving the next day.

It seemed during our stay here that the thermometer was going up steadily by the hour because this was the hottest we could recollect in many years. It was too hot to walk, too hot to drink, and even too hot to sleep, but we did manage an evening barbecue on our last night. This was possible only because during the afternoon a fierce mistral blew up and thunder accompanied the terrific downpour which lasted for about an hour. Thereafter the coolness was heavenly.

Friday 28th July, saw us preparing for an early start with the intention of making Traben Trarbach the following day. The start was delayed, however, because the car refused to start. Foolishly I had left the engine on during the heavy downpour and the battery was completely flat. And for the first time in years I had forgotten to pack my jump leads. Help came from another British caravanner in the shape of an electric charger. He delayed his departure for an hour whilst the charger was fitted to our car. Finally the engine co-operated, but only due to the help we received at the expense of an hour's delay on the part of the other outfit. My regrets at not giving the name but in the circumstances I forgot to ask. My thanks are given now, and, as Van notes in the diary, "That's what caravanning is all about; we all help each other".

Our route took us through Verdun where for the first time we saw the massive "They shall not pass" memorial of the First World War when

Marshal Petain held up the German advance. From there we made for Luxembourg, and now on familiar territory we linked up to the Koblenz-Trier motorway. Turning off at a signpost for Berncastle Kues I'm afraid I got lost! Eventually we came across Camping platz Keuser Werth on the Mosel where a night's halt was greatly appreciated by us both, and the following day we arrived at Rissbach, Traben Trarbach.

It was about an hour afterwards that we were joined surprisingly by our Danish friends Ruth and Bent and it being a Saturday we all pitched in that evening for the customary Mosel-side barbecue, this time an international one with Ruth and Bent, Denmark, and Shell and Elsa from Norway and Van and I from Wales making up the foreign contingent.

This stay has been especially wonderful with so much companionship and it seems we were more than a little loathe to leave, but leave we did on 3rd August after fulfilling the previous evening our traditional date with Ernst Hochs and the Haxen dinner at The Central Hotel. We were reminded that Rissbach is something very special to us on these continental holidays, and that we have not missed a year since we first discovered it in dire circumstances in 1970. We both hope that the association will continue for many years to come. And it was the evening before that Van and I decided to detour our return journey to another place which held memories for us of thirty years ago. We wanted to see Maastricht again.

Which is how, on 4th August, we pulled into the outskirts of this Dutch town which has become the conference centre for European nations. It wasn't, however, the Maastricht we had known, and we both wondered whether we had been right in coming back and not maintaining our minds' picture of so many years ago. En route from Rissbach the previous day we had traversed the Ardennes, through Bastoigne and Liege almost to the Dutch-Belgium border, and at 1.20 pm we had called it a day and pulled into Camping de Bosrand. The speedometer showed we had covered 206 miles, and the thermometer showed a temperature of 95 degrees. The heat and the distance had taken their toll. A visit to Maastricht itself would have to wait until the next day.

The campsite was quite pleasant and afforded some shade from a burning sun. We also met some more Dutch caravanners who were interested in the British style of caravan. They were Dick and Rykje van den Berg who came from Brandweg, 't-Harde in Holland, and who had experienced the Arnhem airborne invasion and were fiercely pro-British. Taking stock of our holiday so far Van came to the conclusion that the weather this holiday had been fantastic and also that we had had some of the best camps. Even though there were still a couple of days to go the opinion was "We have enjoyed this so much". It was in this frame of mind that we set off for that last leg to Sluis and thence Zeebrugge shortly before 10.00 am on 5th August, but there was one thing more to do before we shook the dust of Maastricht off our shoes. A young Dutch caravanning family in the camp had had trouble with their vehicle and had taken the car to a garage in Maastricht. In observance of the code we offered to take the Family van der Bech of Bleusden to their car, an offer gratefully accepted. After dropping them and ensuring their car was ready we began our journey. A few miles further on Van looked back and on the back seat were a couple of boxes of Swiss chocolates. It was the Bech's thank you.

Not until we were within a short distance of Sluis was there any change in the glorious weather, but suddenly the North Sea ushered in the first heavy rain since Chalons and our arrival at de Meirdoorn was very wet underfoot. Although very crowded we were fortunate to find a good spot and soon settled in. To us over the years Sluis and the Ultee family have become like second home. And so it was that we spent the last two days of the holiday visiting our old friends and generally winding down.

It was the 8th August but Zeebrugge had never been so crowded in our experience over the years. It seemed everyone was going home early. Although we were first in the embarkation line when loading started we were the last vehicle to be taken on board, but at least we were homeward bound. From Felixstowe where we landed at 5.45 pm it took us another five hours to reach Oswestry. Any thoughts of getting home that night had to be abandoned. It was too much of an effort so our last overnight halt of this holiday was in the Little Chef compound from which at 6.30 pm on the 9th we began the last leg, arriving home at 10.10 am. And the diary ends "After a really lovely holiday it is nice to get home". The round trip had taken 24 days and the mileage 2,031 miles.

## Chapter 55

## The Best Yet!

We are into our forty second year of camping-caravanning and the question uppermost in our minds as the January days of l995 lengthen is: How much longer can we maintain our main and favourite leisure pursuit?

I remember in our earliest days of rallying being astonished that one of our North London Centre members, known to us affectionately as Mr. Davies the Radio - he was a businessman was a regular attendee at our rallies and he was approaching eighty. Now we have to face the fact that I shall go into my 8lst year before we take a decision to call it a day or carry on, something we have thought about obviously but left unresolved. And if we decide to carry on what is to be the factor which determines how much longer! After all we still have our health, and we have in our newest caravan and car the means whereby to continue; but if we do are we to be limited to home and not our much beloved continental sojourns?

There was a great deal of heart and mind searching but Van and I decided that we would press on with our established way, indeed we became so enthusiastic about it that by my June birthday we were talking about being even more venturesome. It is the way of it. Once the bug gets you there is no shaking it off! Which is how we agreed that this would be a holiday without much pre-planning. We would do as most free spirits do, go where we liked and when we liked, and not be tied to a ritual planning. Routes and dates were out - except for two special events to which we felt we were committed. We did not even consider advance bookings for ferry crossings.

By early July we had formulated a loose plan which included acceptance of a proposal by Karl and Jenny Walter that once again we should go as a twosome to Union Lido. When, would be up to us. That was enough to dispel any further doubts we might have. It was as if a great weight had been taken off us both. But still no attempt had been made to formulate a schedule, or even a starting date.

The first week of August saw us attending the Welsh National Eisteddfod in Abergele where I had to fulfil my obligations as a member of the Gorsedd of Bards. It was a great week and we enjoyed the stay at a very pleasant campsite, Manorafon Farm, Gwrych Park, owned by the Arrowsmiths. This is where the final decision to go ahead with the 1995 holiday was taken, and it is something we shall never regret.

Monday 28th August saw us leaving Caernarfon for Felixstowe and, hopefully, that night's crossing to Zeebrugge - no reservation but in high hopes. We were lucky. There was room, and we enjoyed the comfort of a double cabin which we had not done before. So it was a new start and augured well. Although we had done this first leg of 332 miles several times in the past this time it seemed different. We couldn't get on the vessel quickly enough and it seemed that we were as excited as if doing this for the first time. In retrospect, however, how ridiculous it now seems.

The crossing was not so smooth, but it did not matter. When we disembarked it was a case of heads this way, tails that way, which resulted in our making for Brussels. A telephone call en route established that Jenny van Lancker would be pleased to welcome us and her daughter Martine was there to greet us. Later that evening, having booked in at our campsite in Beersel, we spent our first holiday night the guests of the van Lanckers at a dinner in the outskirts of the City.

Our journey the next day was to Rijswijk in Holland. This was one of the commitments mentioned earlier. Our very old friends, John and Louisa Halim, were celebrating their 55th wedding anniversary on 2nd September and the entire family, from Indonesia and Australia, were gathering for it. We had promised on our last visit that we would be there, and now we were in the process of fulfilling that promise.

In the three days preparatory to the celebration, and whilst we were encamped at our Delftse Hout site, we retraced old visits. Den Hague was where we browsed through the flower market before enjoying a snack lunch adjacent to the European Courts of Justice. We had not done this for more than twenty years and the changes were astonishing. The next day it was Amsterdam and the diary recalls that it was twenty eight years since we had gone there with our friends Len and Eileen. How memories rolled the years back! And already we were glad that we had decided to do this kind of thing. For instance the trip by launch around the city's canals, and a stroll through the back streets munching a custard doughnut and a coconut cake bought in a canal side patisserie. It was a lovely visit and we enjoyed every minute of it. Back at camp early evening we spent a little time with our neighbours, Mr and Mrs Brewster from Peterborough and their two small sons, before retiring after a very satisfying day.

September 2nd, the Halims' big day, began with the promise of a fine sunny day but there was one small hitch with the caravan. Being without running water in modern caravans these days is like being without a candle in the dark. When Van turned on the taps and found nothing emerging it was a real crisis. It transpired the water tank was empty, and when I tried to refill the pump did not work. Calamity! Our plight had been noticed however by John Partilla from Derby, who, with his family, were in another Swift Corniche caravan opposite us. It turned out to be a bad electrical contact which John quickly located and corrected, but without him we did not know what we would have done. Thank you John if you see this attribution.

The celebration turned out to be a fantastic affair. The Rose Garden on the outskirts of Den Hague had been reserved for the night, with some 100 guests. It was the same venue as five years earlier when we had attended their Golden Wedding and the festivities, recorded on tape and video, went on until nearly midnight. Here again was the occasion for making new friends, especially Elli and Stephen Langendam whose friendship we now greatly value. We returned to the campsite tired but very happy. Our commitment fulfilled and old friendships consolidated with new friendships made it had been a great day. But what was to follow?

The roads out from Delft point mainly towards the eastern frontier with Germany, and this is the way our outfit was pointing when we left camp on Sunday 3rd September, bound for... we did not know yet. It must have been the party - well I have to look for an alibi somehow -

but after more than an hour on the motorway we thought would take us to the German frontier via Utrecht we suddenly found ourselves on the outskirts of Rotterdam. We were on the ring road and going the wrong way! Fortunately we spotted a British lorry in a lay-by and this was our salvation. After a bit of a laugh at the expense of a very experienced continental traveller, and I deserved all the ribaldry, Derrick from Minehead, and his mate Adrian, also from Minehead, who turned out to be a farmer enjoying a part-time job, invited us to follow the lorry to Eindhoven and thence to Venlo. We had a pleasant coffee break in the caravan and took the opportunity to catch up on our map reading! We were grateful to them for their help.

The journey thereafter went well enough except for two things; I suffered an attack of gout (but I don't blame the party for this) and shortly after entering Germany the heavens opened, as it always does for us it seems. Using the autobahn mainly we managed to cover 377 miles before finding a campsite. It was 6.45 pm. The site was Camping am Muhlenteich, on the Ludwigshaven route, and although it was pricey (£11.80 with electric) it was a delightful camp and worth another, and longer, stay. After a lovely night's sleep, and with the gout responding to the tablets, we were off shortly after ten o'clock, with the weather greatly improved. Again there was no set objective and when we found ourselves at a sign marked Bingen there was no alternative but to turn in and look for an old camping platz of ours, the Hindenburghbrucke. We found it without trouble, and it brought back many happy memories. We had done only 32 miles - but what the heck, this was to be a holiday with the difference and it was turning out that way.

Within a few minutes of settling in we had made more friends in Nienkke, and her husband Klaas Koopmen, who come from Voorburg in Holland, He was a former Air Commodore in the post war Dutch Air Force, and therefore he and I had at least two things in common - the air forces and caravanning. Van and Nienkke also found common interests and before we parted the next morning we had bonded the new friendship with a few drinks and snacks in our caravan which they found very attractive and became potential buyers. Again Van and I wondered how many British caravans are likely to find a home on the continent next year as a result of the general interest shown during this holiday.

It was six years since we had last stayed in Bingen and the two days we remained this time was as enjoyable as any. But on Tuesday, 5th

September, we set off for Bad Durkheim which turned out to be only 67 miles away. We were happy go lucky on our way because the sun had come out again and it was very warm. There was also the Weinefest in prospect - and my gout had practically disappeared!

# Chapter 56

# The Union Lido Recognition

Karl and Jenny Walter are first class hosts. Within a few hours we were really "at home" and looking forward to the five days we were told we would be at Bad Durkheim. One of the features of the early part was the drive we were taken by Karl along the Weinestrasse through the vineyards of Landau and Neustadt right to the French border where this fantastic 72 kilometre route begins. It was a lovely sunny day and for the record Van and I crossed into France without any evident sign that we had. Highlight of the return journey was the visit to a brand new restaurant, the Bachenheim Haus der Deutsche Weinstrasse, the construction of which we had seen started two years previously. For those who have the opportunity of visiting this place it will be an experience to taste the superb wines they have on offer.

During our visit we expressed our preferences for the Spa'tsburgunder Weibherbst Spatlase, the Halbrochst and the Doornfelder Rotwein.

There was one other memorable occasion when we visited the Capel St. Michael, a tiny church on the hill overlooking Durkheim. In the old days this was the place where the workers in the vineyards gathered for the harvest thanksgiving, and they still have a special respect for the Capel.

Whilst there Van noticed the abundance of sloes on the blackthorns and we harvested quite a few for ourselves. These have now been used for Van's 1996 vintage Sloe Gin which I am sure in the drinking will bring back happy memories of this particular visit. The Weinefest opened on Friday 8th September for two weeks and this is when everything else is relegated to the importance of this occasion. This time we found it even bigger and more attractive than previously, and it certainly lived up to its reputation of the biggest wine festival in the world. During this time we paid a visit to Herr Hoffman whose weingut has a particular significance for us. It will be remembered that on our last visit Herr Hoffman and his wife gave us a studied run-down on the making of wine and we now class them among our good friends. Isn't it surprising how caravanning opens the many doors?

Sunday 9th September, was the day that we left Bad Durkheim for Cavallino, Venezia, and in one particular respect a happy day it proved. Breakfast had been prepared for us by Heidi and Karl Heinz and what a surprise it turned out. The table had been strewn with roses and a decorated candle's solitary flame enhanced the magnificent Black Forest gateau. It was their celebration of our 57th wedding anniversary and Van and I were quite choked. Then Van was presented with a magnificent framed picture of Capel St. Michael depicting a winter scene which now has a special place in our lounge.

It was as a caravan twosome again that we departed with Karl in the lead and set for the first overnight stop in Lermoos, but the best laid plans are often upset, as they were on this occasion. By lunchtime after an incident free journey of 153 miles we had reached Kempton and heading for the Austrian border. With the weather and general conditions in our favour we arrived at Lermoos at 3.45 pm, much too early to pull in; and Karl had the idea of making for another site they knew. This was a mistake because when we arrived the "Full" notice had gone up. Where now? We could only press on towards Merano and hope for the best. And it came in the providential shape of Camping Latsch. By this time we had travelled 349 miles, and at 7.15 pm we were noticeably tired. Again we were confronted with a full-up notice but were offered two places in the forecourt of the Gasthof Latsch which we accepted with alacrity. In no time Van and I had arranged an anniversary dinner for four which proved very successful, especially when the English speaking proprietor gave us a complimentary drink ... "to your good health and good fortune". Not a bad ending to a very demanding day... "...and the holiday is continuing to be different" Van wrote in the diary before retiring for the night. What we had done had been contrary to our prescribed rule which was always to get into camp not later than 4.30 pm but this time we got away with it.

With the weather continuing fine we lost no time in getting under away the following morning. We had decided to take the motorway from Bolzano, an hour's journey, and remain on the motorway to Venice. Another mental aberration and a right turn instead of a left saw me pulling away from Karl, he on his way to Venice and us heading back for Merano. Was it a bad sign that for the second time on this holiday I had committed this massive clanger! Fortunately, after twenty miles in the wrong direction, we were able to cross over and take the road back. An hour later we spotted the Walters waving frantically from an area servicio and once again we were together. From then on it was plain sailing and after a 245 miles stint, and the poorer by 30,000 Lire toll, we arrived at Union Lido, and were fortunate to be allocated two places next to each other. The travelling had ended. Now it was to be a time for leisure and pleasure. It has to be confessed that the beginning of our Union Lido stay was the most disappointing in the long saga of our holidays there. We were not enamoured of the limited choice we faced over where to park the 'vans.

Since our last visit the camp had been largely upgraded to accommodate outfits with the new pattern of direct water supply and waste facility which resulted in the number of "traditional" places such as we have been used to being greatly reduced. Of course we realise that these changes are inevitable with the modernisation of caravans, but for us this time it meant we had to be accommodated in a different part of the camp to that to which we had been used. Then there was the unusually bad weather which kept us indoors more, so much so that we did not once enter the water or sit on the beach. But there was one event which overshadowed everything else, and one of which we are extremely proud.

A couple of days after arrival we were visited by Mr. Ballerin, the Union Lido director, who invited us to dinner a few days later at the Union Hotel. Not only we two, but also our friends Jenny and Karl. We had no idea what was happening. That evening, which happened to be a celebration of the Camp's fortieth anniversary, we found ourselves in exalted company enjoying the most superb reception and dinner. Suddenly we heard the name Rossers mentioned from the top table and were escorted by Mr. Ballerin to "the presentation". This turned out to be a magnificent silver plated plaque to us both as the first British campers to register when the old N.S.U. was established forty years ago. It is inscribed "Mr and Mrs David Rosser, with gratitude for your loyalty. Cavallino, Venezia, September 1995". This turned out to be one of the highlights of this holiday and we shall forever treasure it.

Tuesday, 19th September, saw us take our farewell of Jenny and Karl. They had decided to stay on another week, but we had to leave. There was one other commitment which had to be fulfilled by us two. Within an hour of leaving Cavallino we were subjected to the most horrendous storm. The rain was the heaviest we could recollect, and it forced the speed on the motorway to a veritable crawl. But we managed to carry on despite an accident to the nearside windscreen wiper which meant most of the time that Van was travelling blind. Our objective on this first leg was Lermoos. It took us eight hours and 343 miles to reach Lermoos but there was ample compensation for the effort. We found our friends Albert and Gerda Harter were there, preparing to leave for home in Tubengin the following day.

After a good night's sleep and with the sun out again it was not difficult to decide to remain at least another day. This we spent touring the nearby countryside and enjoying a pleasant tea and gateau at the "Simon" in Ehrwald. The rain had returned when we left Lermoos the next day with our sights set for Traben Trarbach, and that commitment to which I have referred. According to the diary this was an uneventful journey and after 358 miles, and with the clock showing 5.30 pm, we pulled into Theo and Jenny Hack's place in Rissbach. They had been expecting us and the reason why was clearly evident. Alongside the place which had been reserved for our outfit they were erecting a marquee where, the following day, we would be joining in their Golden Wedding anniversary. We had promised them the year before we would be there, and we were fulfilling that promise. It was a wonderful family party with some fifty guests, and it went on until the early hours. We were so glad to have been involved because we had known the Hack family since 1970, and the dramatic incident which led us to Rissbach. Now we were coming to the end of the holiday, the one about which at the start of the year we had expressed some concern but which had turned out to be one of our most memorable and enjoyable. We had more than managed; we had carried on as if we were in our prime, and it was a lovely feeling.

When we set out from Traben on Sunday, 24th September, for the final leg to Calais, it was with a tinge of sadness. Yet, we had told our friends we hoped to see them again next year. How long was this to go on? It had been a 3,300 mile trip to Calais, and the magnificent ferry Pride of Calais which brought us to Dover, and thence to Caernarfon where the milometer registered a final reading of 3,486 miles. And the final entry in the diary sums it all up: "We arrived home after a wonderful holiday. Both of us said it was one of the best we have ever had... but it is nice to be home again!" And after this, what? On reflection we have no doubts that the forty years plus span of camping and caravanning which has taken us over the numerous frontiers on the continent, and even into Asia,( a seemingly too adventurous, even impossible journey in the conditions as they applied at that time), has given us a fulsome life for which we are deeply thankful. It has also brought to us friendships and situations which otherwise would have passed us by. Dare we carry on?

## Chapter 57

## End of a Saga - Farewell to Towing

The diary gives us the date 5th July for the 1996 holiday which, in our hearts, we felt would be the last of the kind we have done and enjoyed for more than forty years - towing our beloved caravans, thirteen in total. Strangely enough we had not indulged during the winter and spring months in the normal practice of preparing our routes, and for the simple reason that we had nothing planned except that once again it was to be the Continental open roads.

We had agreed to attend Nigel and Anne's joint birthday party in Oldham on 5th July which proved a brilliant sending-off gathering for our holiday since, with the unavoidable exception of David, our eldest son, and Elizabeth, all the families were there. What gave us a special satisfaction was the presence of our two great-grand children, Charlie and Fraser. The joint celebration went on well into the night and with "Bon Voyage" wishes ringing in our ears Van and I set off for our crossing from Dover, being escorted part of the way by daughter and son-in-law, Marilyn and John, in their motorised caravan. They were leaving for Bilbao about the same time we were crossing to Calais on the Pride of Burgundy, P and O's newest addition to the fleet.

Our journey to Dover, however, had been anything but enjoyable. We discovered on stopping for a "cuppa" that the entire 12 volt electrical system had blown and we had no power and no 'fridge or tap water. What a start to a holiday, and we were still in England! We spent hours going from one centre to another to try and get the problem sorted, but without success and eventually decided to go on and trust we could have things corrected on the other side.

"It's a glorious evening, clear blue sky and warm sunshine" the diary reminds us as we made for Arras where we stayed overnight in the lay-by at the beginning of the AutoRoute to Rheims, a 90 miles journey, and thence to Chalons sur Marne again. By this time we had decided that Italy was once again to be our main holiday, but with a difference. This time we would go through Switzerland, forsaking the threat we had made many years earlier never again to caravan through this wonderful country of mountains, lakes, and expensive byways. And in truth we now say we were glad we did!

After a two nights' stay at Chalons we followed a familiar to us route on the A44 to Nancy, thence to Colmar by way of the seven and a half kilometre St Marie tunnel - a £5 or 38 francs 'investment' well spent - and arrived at the Swiss border to pay out an 80 Swiss franc toll for the privilege of crossing the frontier and on to the road for Basle. Our objective was Lucerne, reminiscent of a visit twenty years earlier. This time, however, we found a very big difference, and especially at the Lido International Camping which was the only site with an available overnight halt. We had travelled 304 miles in one day just to get a couple of hours sightseeing of the town - and the only thing familiar to us was the wooden bridge at the far end of the lake.

It rained all night and by 7.30 am on 10th July we were en-route for the Gothard Tunnel and gateway to what we hoped would be a sun drenched Italy. Van wrote "All the Swiss names on the signposts bring back happy memories. Changes in buildings and roads are good things the Swiss have done since we last came here, but Glan (that's me) and I prefer it the old way... as he says 'perhaps we shouldn't go back'".

Altdorf, of William Tell fame, was just the same as we recalled it and ten miles further on we were entering the 10 miles long Gothard Tunnel which must be among the greatest feats of tunnelling and engineering in Europe. We had one disconcerting experience, however. Less than half way into the tunnel traffic came to a sudden stop. No indication why, but after ten minutes standstill we began to feel uneasy. Then, when movement began it was start and stop. The journey through lasted three quarters of an hour longer than it should have and the reason we found was a truck which had offloaded its load of hay bales near the exit. "This is an experience I do not like" 'Van wrote as we waited helplessly.

On the Swiss side of the tunnel it was pouring as we entered but on the Italian side the sun shone brightly and once again we congratulated ourselves on seemingly having done the right thing in pressing on. Our target most definitely now was Cavallino which we estimated would be reached within a day of crossing into Italy at Chiasso. It was then we encountered the mother and father of all traffic jams and it took several hours before we reached the A4 at Bergamo. This is the Autostrada which takes one to Venice and beyond, to Jesolo and Cavallino. We did make Union Lido that evening, but too late to enter the camp. Still, we were happy to have made the journey safely and in such good time. After a good night's rest in the Camp overnight lay-by we began our static holiday on 11th July. I must confess I had enjoyed every minute (almost) of this tow and often wondered whether this would be our final caravan sortie, a thought which gave me, as I know it did 'Van, a miserable feeling. It's not so easy to lay aside a practice and mode of more than four decades without any feeling at all.

Our welcome, as always, by Martin, the chef de bureau, and his staff signalled the fact that we were back on "home" territory and within a very short time we had settled in and were receiving calls from old friends across the Continent and Britain. The tom-tom of new arrivals was actively proclaiming that "the Rossers are here" and capping all was to find that John and Mavis Williams were already there with their friends - and now added to our long list of friends - Graham Trenholme, of Yarm, Cleveland, and wife Jan.

Thanks to Graham our problems with the van - it turned out to be an elusive fuse which had blown - were soon rectified and we were back to normal. Our grateful thanks to Graham who, we learned later, suffered an injury to his back in a fall and they had to curtail their holiday and fly back to U.K.

Our stay at Union Lido was typical of life at the camp over the years - lolling in the sun, taking things easy, meeting new people and renewing friendships, and a social round for which the camp is well suited. We recall one occasion at the hotel restaurant where we met a lovely Dutch family at the next table. They were the Geurts from Stoffardery, Malden. Frans was an upholstery renovator, Lily, his wife, and the two children Lieke, aged nine and Niek aged six. Now we know a lot more about the upholstery business and the Geurts know about

Wales, and especially Snowdon; in fact they have earmarked Snowdonia for a future holiday.

This type of international camaraderie is a valuable by-product of caravanning. Not only does it widen the horizons on both sides but it brings better understanding and relationships which are conducive to peace and prosperity. The Williams' and two travelling friends, Cicely and David Penny, left on 18th July to return via Verona where they spent an evening at the Opera, but there were many friends still with us. There were the Danish family of Hans Martin Jepson, the school inspector from Kolding with his wife Jytte and daughter Lotte, the Swiss family Rudi Muller, and not least our next door neighbour Herr Nortmann of Loningen whose hobby was collecting small sea shells and converting them into miniature Mickey and Minnie Mouse figures. From East Germany this Christmas came a card signed "your friend the mousie shell man..." We shan't forget either the other Germany family of five from Altbecken, the Jurgen Weisers, whose two young sons were models of courteous, considerate and responsible behaviour.

We took our leave of Union Lido on Sunday 21st July and headed for Lermoos, again a normal routine, and we were pleased on arrival to find Albert and Gerda Harter there. It wouldn't be the same after all these years if they were not "in residence" when we turned up like the proverbial migrating swallows. We spent a day in Garmish with them and enjoyed a cream bun tea, did some shopping, and shared a bottle of wine in the evening before we departed on 23rd July.

One thing in particular had struck us so far during this holiday and that was the scarcity of British cars and caravans. "If we've seen a dozen on our journey from Cavallino that's about the lot" wrote 'Van. It cannot be that the attractions have waned. It must be that rising costs in general along our routes had been a strong dissuader. I know we noticed a difference.

Our sights had been set for Bad Durkheim and our friends Karl and Jenny Walter. We knew we could not make the journey in one day but had no idea where to stop overnight. At Pforzheim we drew a blank, so on to Karlsrhue and Durlach where our guidebook told us we would find Camping Azur. We did, and we were extremely happy with it. It was a pretty and appealing site and the weather was very hot. The evening meal had scarcely been completed however when the most terrific thunderstorm broke; but who cared! We were snug and very contented communing with nature in this way.

What a welcome greeted us when we arrived at Bad Durkheim shortly after 10.30 am. The Walters were on their balcony waving a greeting as we turned into their Imsalz Brunnen strasse. It was like returning home! One thing to which we always look forward in Bad Durkheim, besides the Weinefest that is, and this visit was two months too early, is a call on the various Weingut friends of Karl and Jenny, and especially Herr and Frau Hoffman. This time the wine tasting was superb as always but we were particularly interested in a special Spatlesse which was offered to us for a special occasion; and that was to be 'Van's birthday. Instead we shall keep it for our Diamond Wedding which will be in September 1998.

An evening out at dinner is another "Bad" occasion for us and this time we took the Walters' and Inge, widow of our dear friend Walter Chelius who died two years ago, to a charming restaurant "Echter" high up in the vineyards overlooking the town. It was most enjoyable; but all things, good and bad, must come to an end and two days later, Sunday 28th July, we said our goodbyes and set off for what has always been our last port of call on holidays, Traben-Trarbach on the Moselle. The only difference this time was in the route.

Taking the autobahn for Saarbrucken and Trier we branched off for Nohfelden and were delighted with the camping site at Birkenfeld situated in the middle of a wooded area. This is where we met Roger and Kara Thomas from Newport. They were on their way to Impst in their Compass Caravan which we had spotted because of the "CYM" badge similar to our own. Birkenfeld is a small town but quite attractive and our only claim of recognition would be that this is where we bought a gazebo, a kind of open tent which seemed to be very popular along our travels. Two days later, July 30th, we began the last leg of our journey to Traben-Trarbach. It was at Longkamp in the mountains overlooking the Mosel that we noticed a Welsh flag flying from the Hotel Longkamper Hof. Obviously we could not pass without finding out why. This was where we met David Lloyd from the Rhondda, and the proprietor Nora Weischede who surprised us by responding to us in Welsh. They had been friends for a long time and she had learned a little of the language. "David was interested to talk to Glan about politics and it was nice to hear the Welsh accent even though he spoke perfect German" the diary notes.

We stayed for lunch - a specially prepared mountain lake trout and left for Traben where we knew the Hacks, Jenny and Theo, were expecting us. Here again it felt as though we had never left. The welcome was terrific and it added to our pleasure that other old friends from Norway, Kjell "Shell" and Else, were there too. It was an occasion to celebrate and that evening, in typical Mosseler style we joined in a massive barbecue cooked by Shell and preceded by a delightful but potent punch. It was all the more enjoyable and lively with the arrival of two other Norwegian friends of Jenny, Oddbjorn and his wife Kari. It was a truly grand evening!

The diary reminds us of one notable omission during our stay. We did not go to the Central Hotel this time for our Haxen, which has been specially prepared for us by Frau and Ernst Hoch over many years. Instead, Jenny made a lovely dinner of Haxen, Mosel style, which we thoroughly enjoyed. But we wondered whether we should ever again savour the Central meal which had been an annual event over so many years.

Saturday 3rd August was our departure date and as a farewell Marion and Michele, the Hacks' daughter and son in law from Bonn, and "Shell", prepared another gargantuan barbecue the previous evening in which we were joined by Margot and Wilfred two old continental friends. Our farewells having been made with promises of meeting again next year 'Van and I set off for Calais and the ferry home. By 6.30 pm we were in Dover and with an uneventful last stage arrived in Uxbridge, some 434 miles from our starting point, by 9.30 pm, and what did we find when we arrived at John and Marilyn's house? We were invited to participate in a "welcome home" barbecue!

And now we reach the end - not only of our never-to-be-forgotten holiday during which we covered 2,720 miles, but also the saga of four decades' caravanning. It is something we shall always treasure, but there is continuing hope that our forages near and far will carry on though in a different style. Under pressure from our caravanning children we have been persuaded to carry on roaming, but by motorised caravan. Many hours were spent between Van and Nigel as to how this could be accomplished. Here again we were back to a beginning, planning the type of motor home best suited to our needs and advancing years. I must admit to a resurgent excitement as ideas took shape and now the vehicle has been converted by a small private company, Nu Venture of Wigan Pier, to Nigel and 'Van's own design. We take possession in the Spring. Our appreciation goes to Kevin Prescott and Ian Robins by whose labours we shall now have a 'van which we hope will see us happily through the years to come. So look out fellow caravanners you will be seeing more of us yet. Watch for "VANDA" and the Welsh Dragon Rampant along those Continental routes as symbols of the die-hards!

The author relaxing with a cuppa!